T0001597

Praise for Lesley Crewe:

Her Mother's Daughter
"Crewe…manages to speak truths about the enduring nature of family and the value of friendship."
—Atlantic Books Today

Hit and Mrs.
"Crewe's writing has the breathless tenor of a kitchen-table yarn…a cinematic pace and crackling dialogue keep readers hooked."
—Quill and Quire

Shoot Me
"Possesses an intelligence and emotional depth that reverberates long after you've stopped laughing."
—The Halifax Chronicle-Herald

LESLEY CREWE

Ava Comes Home

Vagrant
PRESS

Copyright © 2008, 2011, 2021 Lesley Crewe

All rights reserved. No part of this book may be reproduced, stored in a retrieval system
or transmitted in any form or by any means without the prior written permission from
the publisher, or, in the case of photocopying or other reprographic copying, permission
from Access Copyright, 1 Yonge Street, Suite 1900, Toronto, Ontario M5E 1E5.

Vagrant Press is an imprint of
Nimbus Publishing Limited
PO Box 9166
Halifax, NS   B3K 5M8
(902) 455-4286

Printed and bound in Canada
NB1587

Interior Design: Kate Westphal, Graphic Detail Inc., Charlottetown, PE
Cover design: Heather Bryan
Author photo: Nicola Davison

*This novel is a work of fiction. Names, characters, places, and incidents are either the
product of the author's imagination or are used fictitiously. Any resemblance to actual
persons, living or dead, events or locales is entirely coincidental.*

Library and Archives Canada Cataloguing in Publication

Title: Ava comes home / Lesley Crewe.
Names: Crewe, Lesley, 1955- author.
Description: Originally published: Halifax, N.S. : Vagrant Press/Nimbus Pub., ©2008.
Identifiers: Canadiana 20210117540 | ISBN 9781771089647 (softcover)
Classification: LCC PS8605.R48 A93 2021 | DDC C813/.6 — dc23

Nimbus Publishing acknowledges the financial support for its publishing activities from
the Government of Canada, the Canada Council for the Arts, and from the Province of
Nova Scotia. We are pleased to work in partnership with the Province of Nova Scotia to
develop and promote our creative industries for the benefit of all Nova Scotians.

For Mom.

"I've got a good mother, and her voice is what keeps me here..." Jann Arden

CHAPTER ONE

"CUT! That's a wrap, everybody. Thank you."

Ava slumped into the chair she was standing in front of and let her arms hang down awkwardly by her sides. The skirt of her period costume created a huge bubble of material around her.

"Help! I'm being eaten alive by swathes of silk and taffeta."

No one came to her rescue. Her co-star walked away without a backward glance and the crew was busy wrapping up on this final day of shooting—dismantling the set with unseemly haste, removing miles of cables and lights. All of them wanted to get back to the hotel and celebrate the fact that they were finally leaving the most boring small town west of the Mississippi.

The director approached, wearing a big grin. "Are you under there?"

"I think so, but I need rescuing."

He reached for her hands and pulled her out of the chair and into his arms. "Thank you for being a real sweetheart on this shoot, Miss Harris. You certainly made up for your leading man and for that I'm forever grateful."

Ava patted his shoulder. "Why do you insist on calling me Miss Harris? We've been together now for three months."

He let her go but his hands stayed on her shoulders. "To give you the respect you deserve and because you're such a lady. It's been a pleasure working with you. I'd do it again in a heartbeat."

She smiled at him. "Me too."

"Are you coming to the wrap party at the hotel?"

"Maybe later." She looked down at her dress. "I want to get out of this monstrosity first and put my feet up. I'm in the middle of a good book and I have to see what happens next."

"I know you. You'll be asleep by nine."

"No, I'll be there. I do want to say goodbye to everyone." Ava picked up her voluminous skirt and walked towards her trailer, scooting around the cameras and empty directors' chairs. She spotted Lola, her assistant, stuffing her face at the craft service table. Lola happened to glance over at her and started to shake a pepperoni stick in her direction. "Do you need help getting outta that dress?"

"No. The buttons are in the front."

"Okay, because I've got to go to the drugstore and pick up some Gravol."

"Stop eating. That might help."

"Oh, ha ha. It's for the plane tomorrow. I'll be back in fifteen minutes. Do you need anything?"

Ava shook her head. She opened the trailer door and with difficulty managed to get up the narrow stairs in the dress. A cameraman walking by saw her dilemma and closed the door behind her.

She loved coming "home" at the end of the day. All the noise and confusion outside was replaced by the classical music playing on the stereo. While it was a luxurious space, it was filled with normal things too, like books and jigsaw puzzles and balls of knitting yarn. Ava found the long hours of waiting on a movie set perfect for making sweaters, scarves, and mitts for the crew, but she usually knit when she was alone in her trailer. It was easier than enduring the inevitable comments about how boring and domestic she was.

Ava proceeded to unhook the tiny silk-covered buttons of her bodice in the living room, where there was space to move around. There have to be at least fifty of the damn things, she thought. Her fingers were sore by the time she finished. Down came the dress. She stepped out of it and tossed it on the sofa, though yards of it still puddled on the floor. She'd let Lola deal with that.

Still wearing the petticoat, Ava went down the hall, stopping to look in the bathroom mirror. She couldn't wait to wash her face, but decided to undress first. The costume designer on the film was something of a tyrant, and Ava was a little afraid of her. The last thing she needed was to get a spot of makeup on the antique linen.

She was about to leave the bathroom when she saw something move behind her in the mirror. She gasped and spun around.

"Who's there?"

Only the music played. Her heart pounded as she crept forward. "Hello?" There was no one in the hall. Lola was at the store. Telling herself not to be so silly, she walked into her bedroom and shut the door. There stood her leading man.

Ava took a step back and cried out.

He came forward and grabbed her at the waist. "Stop it. It's only me."

She struggled against him. "Let me go, Scott. You frightened me."

"Stop with the dramatics," Scott laughed. "The movie's over."

"Leave me alone."

He held her closer. "I don't want to leave you alone. You've driven me crazy for weeks and you know it. All those love scenes. You're not that good an actress. I know you want me."

She pushed against his chest but he didn't move. Instead he reached down and put his mouth against her ear. "I've had all my leading ladies. No one's ever refused me, except you. What makes you so special?"

"Lola will be here any minute."

Scott pushed her away and she stumbled backward. "Great. The guard dog."

"Get out."

He pointed at her. "All it takes is one phone call and you're back filming infomercials. I'm one of the biggest movie stars in the U.S. of A. People like to keep me happy. I'd remember that if I were you."

"Well, I'm not one of them. Now get out of my trailer this instant or I'll call the police."

"It's your word against mine, babe."

"And I wonder who the police will believe after they've talked to the cast and crew?"

Scott gave her a filthy look. "You're a second-rate, stuck-up bitch. You stay out of my way on the junket, have you got that? And don't even think about showing your face at tonight's party or you'll regret it."

Storming out of the bedroom, he nearly took the door off the hinges when he slammed it leaving the trailer. Ava put her hand on her throat to quiet her breathing. After a few minutes she went to the kitchen and took a bottle of water out of the fridge. Standing there with the door ajar, she drank half of the water. Then she carried the bottle to an armchair and dropped into it, letting her head rest against the back cushion.

Lola appeared five minutes later and emptied her shopping bag out on the kitchen counter. "They had a sale on Pringles. Do you want some?" She took the top off the long canister and shook it at Ava.

"No, thanks."

"Good. More for me." Lola reached in and popped a few chips in her mouth. She looked at Ava. "You okay?"

Ava nodded.

"You look tired. Why don't you skip the party tonight? We'll stay in and play Parcheesi."

"I'd like that," Ava whispered.

❀

Scott and his brutish behaviour were nothing but a distant memory two months later. Ava's mind was preoccupied with something infinitely more nerve-wracking. So nerve-wracking, she peeked out from under the luxurious goose-down duvet covering her bed and tried not to scream. She'd hidden under it all night in an effort not to look at the clock every hour on the hour. They said if she got a call before 6:00 a.m., it was great news. If not, better luck next time. It was 5:50 a.m. So far, the phone was deafeningly silent.

"This is stupid." She threw off the covers, jumped out of bed, reached for her woolly robe and slippers, and padded across the thick cream-coloured rug to the balcony doors. She opened them and stepped out into a chilly Malibu morning.

Crossing over to the far edge of the balcony, she rubbed her arms to keep warm as the sun rose. That morning the waves rolled towards the beach in uniform lines, crashing against the shoreline with a thunderous roar before disappearing back to the deep.

As she leaned over the steel railing she remembered as a little girl her father telling her that you could predict the coming weather by looking at the way a wave came to shore. But that was years ago and she couldn't remember what this particular kind of wave meant. If only she could ask one of her brothers— but she never called about something as silly as that.

Out of the corner of her eye she saw her neighbour, a studio producer, out for an early morning walk with his dog Muffin. She waved at them.

"Any news?" he shouted at her.

"No."

"Well, if it makes you feel any better, Muffin and I voted for you."

"You're both very sweet. And just for that I'll..."

The phone rang.

"Oh my god, the phone!" She tripped over a large planter in her haste to get back inside and nearly fell headlong over the threshold. By the time she scrambled upright, the phone had rung three times. She made a dive for it, landing on the bed.

"Yes, hello?!"

It was her agent, Trent Osgood. "You did it, babe! It's official. Ava Harris is nominated for Best Supporting Actress at this year's Academy Awards!"

Ava's mouth dropped open.

"Are you there?"

She nodded.

"Ava?"

"Sorry, yes I'm here," she whispered.

"This is it, Ava. Your life is about to become a whirlwind of promotions, television interviews, and photo sessions, not to mention having to decide who to wear on the red carpet! I was thinking Olivier..."

Trent continued to talk a mile a minute and Ava tried to comment a couple of times, but it was no use, so after a while she tuned him out, content to stare at the ceiling and let it sink in. She eventually realized the strange noise coming from the phone was Trent whistling into it, trying to get her attention.

"Sorry, you were saying?"

"Ava, this goddamn habit of zoning out drives me up the wall. It's imperative that you cooperate with me. For the next month we are on a runaway publicity train. You have no idea what you're in for. I need you to be prepared."

She sighed. "Can you give me five minutes to enjoy this before I hop on?"

"Fine, all right. I'll call you in a couple of hours. I have some people to track down anyway."

"You're calling people at six in the morning?"

"Do you honestly think anyone who's anyone in Hollywood is still asleep? Which reminds me, I better put in a call to Variety. I want your photo front and centre in that magazine. I should also give the major studios a call and see if we can't book you on the talk show circuit."

He hung up without so much as a goodbye.

She looked around her beautifully decorated bedroom, everything in shades of white, off-white, and cream. Only the month before, Fashion Out Front Magazine did a spread featuring her beach house entitled, "Fit for a Hollywood Princess."

And her bedroom was perfect. It was just too bad there was no one in it to share her good news.

The phone rang, which made her jump. She picked it up. "Hello?"

It was Lola. "Have you heard anything? I've been up all night. You'd think they'd put us out of our misery by announcing the blasted nominees at a half-decent hour, or why not in the evening? Then everyone could get drunk and go to bed. Now don't be upset if they didn't call. You have a long career ahead of you. This is only the beginning."

"Nah, I think I'll pack it in. If they don't recognize talent when they see it, that's their tough luck. I'm bored with all this nonsense."

There was silence for a good five seconds on the other end of the phone. "You know, the scary part is that I think you're serious. You say it often enough to really mean it."

"No, I don't."

"Yes, you do."

"Well, I'm not aware of it. Now I wish you'd pipe down and help me decide something. Should I wear Olivier or Lee Kim?"

Lola screamed, nearly blowing out Ava's eardrum.

Once the morning news shows broadcast the Oscar picks, the phone never stopped ringing. Her favourite people in the world besides Lola were the next to call. Maurice, her hair and makeup man, a genius in both departments, and Harold, her stylist. They were a couple who insisted on talking over each other every time they phoned. Ava was used to the rapid repartee. It always made her smile.

"Honey child," Maurice burbled, "with Harold at the helm, the Best Dressed list will have your name at the very top or my name isn't Morris Ginsberg."

"Your name is Morris?" Ava laughed.

"Not anymore."

"Harold, Lola thinks I should wear Lee Kim but Trent thinks Olivier. What do you think?"

"You're going to take fashion advice from a spiky-haired wing nut and a guy who wears blue socks with a brown suit?" Harold ended on a high note.

"Maybe."

"Kill me now!"

"Oh, do hush, sweetheart," Maurice soothed. "She's joking."

"It's not funny."

"Sorry," Ava laughed. "Do you still love me?"

"Endlessly," Harold declared.

"There's only one fly in the ointment," Maurice said.

"What's that?" Ava asked.

"It's just your luck that Scott was nominated for Best Supporting Actor this year as well. Talk about ruining a great evening."

"I'm not going to let the likes of him spoil my night."

"That's our girl," Harold cried.

Ava walked around the house that morning, the phone to her ear as she poured a glass of orange juice and scooped spoonfuls of plain fat-free yogurt out of a container and into a small bowl. The minute someone hung up, someone else called. At first it was exciting but after a couple of hours of it, she had a sore ear and a stiff neck.

She let the answering machine take the rest of the calls so she had some peace. She decided to shower. When she emerged from the bathroom, forty messages awaited. Did she know that many people? She played the messages back as she towel-dried her beautifully highlighted blonde hair.

She remembered as a young girl watching the Academy Awards with her sisters, but she was always sent to bed before the Best Actress or Best Actor was announced. Her mother insisted it was too late for her to stay up.

It still rankled that she was never allowed this one treat.

The phone rang yet again and she looked at the number display. It was long distance, area code 902. Her family. With her heart beating a little faster, Ava hesitated before picking up the receiver. "Hello?"

"Is it true?!" her sister Rose shouted in her ear. "Best Supporting Actress?"

"It's true," Ava smiled. "Can you believe it?"

"Of course I can believe it! I went to see that movie seven

times and cried my eyes out every time, and so did everyone else in the theatre."

"Thanks, Rose…"

"Everyone here is so excited. The phone hasn't stopped ringing!"

"That's nice. Listen, while I have you on the phone, how's Ma? She never calls me."

"You know she hates the phone. God knows why. Anyway, the sad truth is she's getting older, as are the rest of us. I find her slowing down lately, but I guess that's to be expected. Is there any chance you can come home soon for a visit?"

That question. Always that question.

"Rose, I can't come home right now…"

"You've been saying that for years. Ma misses you. We all do."

"Don't. Please don't. The next four weeks will be nuts. My life is scheduled every hour on the hour."

"You're a big movie star. Are you telling me that you can't take one or two days off to come and visit?"

"That's what I'm telling you, so please drop it."

"All right, all right, I'm sorry. Look, we just wanted you to know we're proud of you."

"I know that."

"Everyone sends their love."

"I was going to call you."

Rose ignored her. "So who are you going to take on the red carpet? Someone famous?"

"I'm not sure."

"What are you going to wear?"

"I have no idea, Rose. I just found out a couple of hours ago."

"Okay, okay, I better go. This is costing me. Love you."

"And you. Tell everyone I love them too. And tell Ma..." Ava couldn't continue.

"I will. Take care, baby sister."

Ava put down the receiver and sat on her bed staring at nothing. She didn't answer the phone after that and when it continued to ring, she reached over and pulled the cord right out of the wall. Then she crawled under the duvet and hid from the world for the rest of the morning.

❄

Traffic was a nightmare.

"Why are we driving around in this tin can?" Ava's publicist Camilla Dove griped. Camilla always griped, which was a rather odd habit for a Hollywood publicist to have. But Ava liked her because she looked like the Sunday school teacher she had growing up in Cape Breton. Not that Camilla wore floral ankle-length dresses that tied at the back or hoot-owl glasses. Still, Camilla was the spitting image of Hughena MacIntyre and that always cheered Ava enormously.

"At least you're in the front seat," Lola moaned from the back, her knees up around her chin. "What did I do to deserve this kind of treatment?"

They were stopped at a red light on San Vicente Boulevard in West Hollywood. Even with her sunglasses and ball cap on, the teenage boys in the next car recognized Ava. She ignored their increasingly ardent facial gestures by turning to her passengers. "Stop belly-aching, the both of you. I'm being environmentally friendly. Did you know that this hybrid Citroen C2 Hatchback has a 1.4 stop and start sensodrive?"

Camilla rifled through her appointment book. "Speak English."

"I'm doing my bit to save the planet, but I still wish I could ride a bike."

Camilla looked at her in horror. "And have the damn pa-parazzi sell Gossip News a picture of your butt hanging off the seat? I think not."

"Gee, thanks. Is my bottom that large?"

"I keep telling you," Camilla sighed. "Wizard computer geeks can make your bum look as big as a house if they want to. You can avoid all that by not giving them the opportunity to see you in a compromising position."

Lola snorted. "I thought that was reserved for late-night trysts in a hot tub with the pool boy." She looked out the window. "Or maybe one of those idiot guys in the car beside us."

"These days eating an ice cream cone in public is forbidden tutti frutti," Camilla said.

"Good one," Lola laughed.

"Look what those miserable photo hogs did to Julia Edwards," Camilla continued.

"She beat them at their own game, didn't she?" Lola reminded her. "She's lost weight and looks fantastic. But then I always thought she looked fantastic, weight or no weight."

The light changed and Ava crept forward. Luckily the car full of obnoxious boys was in the turning lane. As it disappeared from sight, she leaned over the steering wheel. "Speaking of food, I'm starving. Isn't The Lounge around here somewhere?"

"You're a genius. It's on Melrose," Lola said. "Just a few blocks away."

Camilla threw up her hands. "How am I supposed to work under these conditions? I could be riding in a limo with a television, a laptop, and a fax machine, but instead I'm being held hostage in a bird cage with a hungry client and a no-good hungry assistant. Have you two any idea what walking the red carpet means? Today alone, I've set up appointments with two stylists, not to mention a scheduled pit stop at Giorgio Armani. Harold's meeting us there. Then we head to Harry Winston's."

"How can I pick out jewelry if I don't know what I'm wearing?" Ava spotted a parking space and quickly pulled over, maneuvering the small lime-green car between a Hummer and a Cadillac Escalade. She jumped out of the vehicle and held the seat back for Lola, who had a difficult time unfolding her long legs. Ava grabbed her arm and helped heave her out. Camilla had no choice but to bring up the rear.

"I suppose I can schmooze while we're here," Camilla muttered.

Ava turned around and looked at her. "Schmooze away, but don't you dare bring anyone over to the table."

Camilla feigned horror. "Now would I do that on your personal time?"

"Yes."

"If you happen to run into George Clooney send him our way pronto," Lola laughed. "I don't care what Ava says."

The Lounge was definitely the place to be for lunch, with its sleek, expensive décor and serious waiters who moved effortlessly around tables filled with Hollywood movie moguls, artistic types, and young socialites. Most were there to be seen; they spent their time looking over at other tables, gossiping about who was with whom. But it was also a perfect venue for business negotiations among studio executives and a great spot to run into the ordinarily inaccessible.

Ava soon realized coming to the restaurant was a bad idea. All she wanted was a salmon sandwich. By the looks of it, it would take her ten minutes to get to the nearest unoccupied table. Several hands went up to greet her and diners whispered to each other as she walked by. A fat guy with a goatee stood and shook her hand. "Congratulations, Miss Harris."

"Thank you," she murmured and kept going.

Lola whispered behind her, "Who's that?"

"Someone who didn't give me the time of day two weeks ago," Ava said over her shoulder.

Camilla whispered too. "Oh my god, why didn't you stop? I'm pretty sure that was Gavin Peters. He's very influential…"

"He's two-faced," Ava insisted.

Camilla rolled her eyes. "You're in Hollywood. Being two-faced is how one survives."

With the help of the maitre d', they made it to a far table in the corner. Ava sat with her back to the crowd—a necessary tactic she used on occasion. Some days it worked, but today wasn't one of them. A man approached with two giggling teenagers on his heels.

"May I have your autograph, Miss Harris? My daughters are your biggest fans."

"Certainly. And your names?"

"Heather," said Heather.

"Bonnie," said Bonnie.

She took the proffered napkin and scribbled, "To Heather and Bonnie, All the best, Ava Harris." The girls examined the napkin closely. She thought that was the end of it, but no such luck. He wanted pictures, so she turned around and pretended to smile into his cell phone while his daughters squealed on either side of her. "We love you Miss Harris. We never miss your movies."

"Thank you."

Surely that was it—but no. He passed her the phone. "If I ring my wife, will you talk to her for a minute? She'll die."

Camilla stepped in then.

"Do excuse us, but Miss Harris has a busy schedule. We're here for a quick lunch."

"Of course. Well, thank you. Come along, girls."

"Bye!" said the girls several times.

"Goodbye." Ava turned around and sighed. "I think we better go to a drive-thru."

"Nonsense," Camilla said. "Every fan you meet translates into mucho money."

"I already have mucho money. I want a sandwich."

The waiter came to their table and Ava placed her order. Camilla ordered decaf coffee, black, and Lola asked for a triple chocolate milkshake. Thankfully, their lunch arrived quickly.

"It's ridiculous that you can drink that garbage and still look like a railway tie," Camilla said, eyeing Lola's shake.

Lola held out her glass. "Do you want some?"

"Of course I want some. Now leave me alone!" Camilla took a sip of her coffee and made a face.

"Oh, oh," Lola said. "Here comes trouble."

Ava swiveled her head. Trent barreled towards them with a look of utter triumph. When he reached the table he grabbed the empty chair. "Mind if I sit down?" He sat without waiting for a reply.

"How did you know I was here?" Ava asked him.

"I have spies everywhere." He pulled several sheets of paper out of his leather briefcase.

"You do?"

"Of course not." He tossed his head to the right. "I was finishing up a lunch meeting with Forrest Kavanaugh when I saw you walk in. He's a World-Wide Pictures executive and you're not going to believe what he's proposing."

Ava took a bite of her sandwich and waited.

Trent looked up at her. "Aren't you going to ask me what it is?"

She nodded and continued to chew.

"You are the most exasperating woman, did you know that?" he sighed. "Most clients can't wait to hear what I have to say."

"We're waiting with bated breath." Lola stirred her shake before making a big slurping noise with her straw.

Trent gave her a dirty look. "Who asked you?"

"No one."

"There's a reason why," Trent informed her. "No one's interested in what you have to say."

"Be nice," Ava warned. The animosity between agent and assistant was well known. Camilla had asked Ava several times in private why she put up with Lola's sauciness. The only reason Ava could think of was that Lola always said out loud the very things she was thinking.

Trent made a point of turning his back to Lola. "Now that your name is on the lips of everyone in town, World-Wide Pictures wants to enter into negotiations that could mean a three- or four-picture deal. It's a once-in-a-lifetime offer. You'd be crazy not to do it."

Ava's stomach did a sudden flip. She put the sandwich down and took a sip of iced tea before folding her arms on the table. She leaned towards Trent. "You promised me that once this September's shoot in New York was out of the way, I'd be able to take some time off."

Trent looked at her with incredulity. "That was before you were nominated for an Academy Award! Now all bets are off. If we don't capitalize on your celebrity in the coming days, we'll lose out on potentially millions of dollars. You're hot, Ava, and everyone knows you have to strike while the iron's hot."

"And it doesn't matter in the least what I think?"

"Of course it matters what you think," Trent frowned, "but

you're obviously not thinking clearly. Who would be crazy enough to turn down World-Wide Pictures?"

The question hung heavy in the air. Trent kept blinking with his mouth open, as if not quite understanding what was happening. Even Camilla had the look of a woman whose child was misbehaving.

Ava turned to Lola. "Am I crazy for wanting some time off?"

Lola reached out to touch Ava's hand. "Of course you're not crazy. What you are is exhausted. You've been going flat-out for eight years." Lola turned to Trent. "I was there when you swore up and down that Ava would get some time off after that September shoot. If she's this hot, can't she simmer for a couple of months? Surely people won't forget her name that quickly."

If the tips of his blood-red ears were anything to go by, Trent's blood pressure was escalating at an alarming rate. "I am a highly successful, highly sought-after film agent. You are a baggage handler. I believe I know the best course of action for my client's career."

Lola nodded her head. "And there's the rub. You're concerned about the career. I'm concerned about the woman."

Trent gave Ava an exasperated look. "Tell your lap dog to go bite someone else's ankles."

"Lola is a friend of mine. Being rude to her isn't going to help your case."

"Ava..."

"I'm sorry, Trent, but I can't discuss this now. We have a slew of appointments this afternoon and we're already late. Aren't we, Camilla?"

Camilla took the hint. "Yes, we're in an awful rush." All three women rose from their chairs.

Trent had a face on him like thunder. "You haven't finished your sandwich."

Ava ignored him. "Would you mind picking up the tab, Trent? I'll pay you back later." She walked away before he could answer.

When they got back in the car, Ava turned to them. "I don't want to talk about this, all right?"

The afternoon was spent looking at glorious gowns in designer showrooms. Ava could have asked for the samples to be sent to the house, but she liked to gather her own impressions of the establishments and their work ethic. How they treated their employees was something she always factored in. She had once refused a magnificent gown that she'd been planning to wear to an AIDS fundraiser. When the designer screamed at the young man in charge of bringing them coffee, Ava walked right out the door without a backward glance.

Harold, her personal stylist extraordinaire, knew all about this quirk and took pains to forewarn the designers ahead of time. They were kindness itself when Ava was in the room.

Harold took a stunning dress of aqua-blue chiffon off the rack. "This would set off your eyes beautifully." He held it up to her. "Why don't you try it on?"

Ava wrinkled her nose. "There's no front. I'd be spilling out everywhere. I don't want a 'wardrobe malfunction.'"

"As you well know, I'm a master with double-sided tape."

Ava's eyes went to the rack. "For this occasion, I want classic. Simple."

Taking another gown off the rack, Harold draped it over his forearm. "What about this? It's got a floor-sweeping train. It's in the most delicious shade of cloud, with just the tiniest hit of blue."

"Cloud?" Lola repeated. "Is that what we're calling grey these days?"

"It's got a ridiculously huge bow in the front." Ava touched the offending item. "I'd be fiddling with it all night."

"Ridiculously huge bows are very hot right now," Harold said.

"There's that word again," Ava muttered. "Hot." She rubbed her head and tried to ignore the fuss going on around her. The people in the room were at her disposal and so spent most of their time staring at her. This aspect of fame wore Ava down. If only they knew who she really was, they wouldn't bother to look at her.

The designer wanted to take her measurements again but Harold held up his hand. "There's no need. She's a perfect size two. I should know. I've been dressing her for years."

Ava reached into her cream Chloe Betty Bag and searched for some Tylenol. Lola tapped her on the shoulder and produced two pills in the palm of her hand.

"How do you always know when I have a headache?"

"You get that look," Lola smiled. "The one that says 'Beam me up, Scottie.'"

Ava threw back her head and swallowed the pills dry, but she knew headache tablets weren't going to help her mood. She had to let Harold down gently.

She went over to him and laid her head on his shoulder. "Would you be awfully cross if I went home? I don't feel up to this today."

"We don't have much time. The Oscars are only a week away and you haven't decided on a thing."

She straightened up. "All right, I'll make an exception. You gather up as many gowns as you can find around town and bring them over to the house. It will be easier there."

"Haven't I told you that all along?" Harold sniffed. "Why on earth do you pay me if you don't listen to a thing I say?"

"I'll be good. I promise."

Two days later, after hours of trying on gowns, she reached a decision and chose a black Anise Godfrey jacquard bustle-back gown. The exquisite dress fit her small frame perfectly before falling away from her hips in a full skirt of intricately patterned fabric. With the neckline straight across her bodice and simple straps over her milky shoulders, she and Harold agreed she'd need only a pair of diamond drop earrings set in platinum to show off her ensemble.

Ava's entourage breathed a sigh of relief that at least something was decided. It was Lola who was chosen to broach the subject of an escort, since Ava hadn't mentioned it one way or the other. She got her opportunity the next night as the two of them were being driven to the club du jour, Leo's in West Hollywood.

"Why did I say I'd meet Hayden at Leo's?" Ava sighed. "I hate these places."

"Because Hayden practically lives there, that's why. Speaking of Hayden, have you thought of who you're taking to the Oscars? I suppose he's your logical choice, since you've been dating him off and on for a couple of months."

Ava looked down at her hands. "I know that's why he asked me out tonight. He's dying for an invite."

"Hayden Judd is the perfect date, if you ask me. He's the hottest star on television at the moment. You'll make a gorgeous couple."

Looking out the car window, Ava leaned against the palm of her hand and watched the buildings go by. "I don't want people to know I'm dating him. Besides, he's a show-off."

"Well, that's true enough," Lola agreed. "He'd grab the

first microphone he could find and interview himself on the red carpet. So if you don't want Hayden, then who?"

She turned around. "You wouldn't like to go, would you?"

Lola's mouth dropped open. "Are you joking?"

"Well, why not?"

"Can you imagine what Trent will say?" Lola laughed. "Or Camilla for that matter. I can hear her now. 'The tabloids will say you're a lesbian!'"

"I don't give a monkey's uncle what they say. Will you come?"

"Of course I'll come! But you better break it to Hayden gently."

"I know. I know."

The driver let them out at the front of the club where there was a line-up of beautiful people waiting to get in. Some of them, including a few paparazzi, shouted Ava's name. She smiled and kept going as the doorman unclipped the velvet rope allowing her and Lola to slip inside.

The music was pounding and the dance floor crowded with bodies, thanks to two DJs who worked their magic by spinning records at a furious pace. The Mod-inspired interior was surprisingly bright. Cocktail waitresses decked out in mini-dresses and white patent-leather boots moved surely across the floor.

Ava looked around and spied Hayden on a low leather Barcelona chair against a retractable glass wall. He had a drink in his hand and two young blond women sitting on either side of him, trying to get as close as possible. Hayden was typically handsome, well-toned with the piercing blue eyes and square jaw demanded of most leading men. All that and dimples too.

And while he was clearly delighted with his situation, the minute he spied Ava he excused himself and hurried towards her, leaving the two disappointed Barbie dolls in his wake.

"Hey you, you look fantastic!" He grabbed her around her leaf-green silk pleated dress and pulled her in tight; trying to give her a kiss, but Ava stopped him. "Not here."

Lola tapped him on the shoulder. "Remember the rule, Hayden. No groping in public."

Hayden pulled his head up and turned towards Lola. "Do you go everywhere Ava goes, or is it just my recurring nightmare?"

"I go everywhere," Lola smirked. "Don't I, Ava?"

Ava made a face. "Would you get me a champagne cocktail, Lola? We'll be over there." She indicated an empty couch to her left. "I have to talk to Hayden."

"Sure," Lola said. "Would you like anything, Hayden?"

"Some privacy." He pulled Ava over to the couch before Lola could say another word. They sat down and he reached over to trace her jawline with his finger. "How are you, Buttercup? I haven't seen you for awhile."

"I've been busy."

"I watched you on Celebrity Hour and The Steve Harris Show. Have you had your interview with Georgia Barker yet?"

"I did that today. It'll be broadcast the night of the Oscars."

"Did she manage to make you cry?" Hayden laughed.

Ava didn't think it was a laughing matter. The veteran interviewer had come very close to making her weep when she asked about Ava's family. It required all her skill for Ava to stay composed. "No, she didn't make me cry."

"Georgia is losing her touch then," Hayden laughed again. It seemed that's all he ever did. But he wasn't laughing for long.

Ava cleared her throat. "Hayden, before you say anything, I want you to know that I've asked Lola to come with me to the Oscars. I know you're disappointed, but I've given it a lot of thought. We've managed to keep the public in the dark about the fact that we're dating and I'd like to keep it that way. If you go with me, the media would have a field day."

Hayden gave her a shocked look. "What's wrong with people knowing we're going out together? Sure, I understood it in the beginning, but it's been a couple of months now. It's serious. As serious as I get."

"I know."

"You don't want to share the limelight, is that it?" He looked and sounded pissed off, just as Ava knew he would be.

"Don't be ridiculous."

Hayden looked away for a moment before turning back. "This would be a golden opportunity for me to be seen around the globe. I'm not as big a star as you are, and you know that. I could use the publicity."

"Of course the Oscars are all about you."

"I didn't say that."

"Were you nominated for an award, or was it me? I forget."

Just then Ava noticed Lola making her way towards them. It was clear that Hayden was hurt, and Ava hated hurting people. The trouble was she was good at it. She grabbed the drink from Lola, downed it and asked for another.

Lola gave her a funny look. "Are you sure? Isn't one your limit?"

Ava glanced at Hayden's brooding face. "Not tonight." She reached for his hand. "Come dance with me."

He resisted at first, but she knew the offer was too tempting. Hayden wanted every man in the room to know that he was with the famous Ava Harris. To rub their noses in it would suit Hayden just fine.

And she was right. He put his drink down on the glass table and followed her into the crowd of swaying bodies. Famous young men and women grooved to the music. Ava smiled at him and put her arms in the air as she moved her body, turning around so that her back was to him. He came up behind her and placed his hands on her hips, pulling her closer. They gyrated against each other, her arms slipping behind her head to caress the nape of his neck as his hands roamed her fabulous curves.

Hayden soon forgot all about the Oscars.

※

Ava slipped out of bed the morning of the big day with dark circles under her eyes. She showered and went downstairs to find that her housekeeper had arrived at the crack of dawn and had a full breakfast waiting for her in the sunroom.

Pouring a large mug of coffee, Ava smiled at Mercedes. "I don't think I'll be able to eat all this. It looks delicious, though."

Mercedes hovered over the serving dishes filled with scrambled eggs, bacon, and ham. "You have to have something. You won't be eating again until the Governor's Ball tonight."

They heard the side door open and close. "It's only me!"

Lola skipped into the room. "I should've stayed here last night because I didn't sleep a wink at home. Oh, Mercedes, you didn't make your famous blueberry pancakes by some miracle of miracles?"

Mercedes whipped off the cover of a chrome platter to expose a thick stack of them. "Do you think I'd forget you?"

Lola gave her a big kiss. "I love you." She sat at the table and helped herself to three of them. "Are you having any, Ava?"

"No. Harold would kill me. I have to fit in that dress tonight." She reached for a small helping of eggs and took a half a piece of whole wheat toast. "This is as much as I dare eat."

"I'll put a granola bar in your purse," Lola said with her mouth full. "You can shovel it in when you go to the loo."

"Don't forget a pack…"

"…of Juicy Fruit gum. I know. I know."

The rest of the day was all about pampering. A Swedish masseuse arrived after breakfast to give the two friends a relaxing massage, followed by a visit to Ava's favourite manicurist at a chic downtown spa. After their French manicure, pedicure, and facial, Harold and Maurice arrived and they got down to serious business.

"With that neckline we need to pull your hair back," Maurice suggested. "That way we can see your pretty little neck and collarbones. Did you ever see such collarbones?" he asked Harold.

Harold nodded vigorously and put his hands on Ava's shoulders. "Why do you think I picked this dress?"

"I picked the dress," Ava laughed.

"I seconded the motion."

Lola sat on a divan in Ava's dressing room and watched the proceedings. "What are you going to do with my hair?" she asked Maurice.

Maurice turned to look at her. "I can't do a thing with that spiky mess except make it even spikier."

Lola clapped her hands. "Oh, goody."

When Ava finally got out of Maurice's chair, her makeup was perfectly applied to her alabaster complexion and her hair was divine, a smooth chignon at the nape of her neck, perfect for photographs from any angle. Even Ava couldn't stop looking at herself. "Wow. You outdid yourself, Maurice."

Maurice collapsed dramatically into an overstuffed love seat. "My job is done!"

"Hey, you haven't done me yet!" Lola said.

"Oh, you'll only take a minute."

"Gee, thanks."

"You're lucky I'm doing anything at all, so zip it."

Harold had his head cocked to the side. "I think we need one more thing. He picked up a thin velvet headband and placed it behind Ava's ears. It was the perfect finishing touch.

Once they helped Ava into the magnificent dress, the last accessories were her shoes, a pair of silk-organza platform sandals with Swarovski diamante details. Ava put them on and went to the full-length oval mirror in the corner of her dressing room. She stood there for a good minute, taking it all in.

Her three good friends were delighted for her.

"You look like a china doll," Maurice sighed.

"You look like a princess," Harold chimed in.

"Forget princess. She's a hot tamale!" Lola shouted.

They were laughing when Mercedes knocked softly on the door. She had a long rectangular box in her hands. "This came for you," she said to Ava.

Ava flicked her wrist. "You can put them with the other flowers, if you don't mind, Mercedes." She had been inundated that day with flowers from friends and admirers alike.

Mercedes hesitated. "I thought you might want to see these."

Ava took the box from Mercedes' hands and placed it on her dressing table. She slid the small card out of its envelope and read the message.

"We wish we could be with you. We'll all be together at Aunt Vi's tonight, cheering you on. Good luck. We love you. Xoxo."

The box was filled with white daisies, her favourite flower. She could so easily picture the fields and meadows back home.

Ava immediately grabbed the back of her makeup chair and sat down heavily. Tears welled up and she couldn't stop them from rolling down her cheeks.

"My god, are you all right? Don't cry, honey. You'll ruin your makeup." Maurice held a tissue to the corner of her eye.

"I'm sorry," she whispered. "I'll be all right."

"Who are the flowers from?" Harold asked.

"My family."

They knew that talking about Ava's family was forbidden. Maurice knew more than the other two, but being the loyal friend he was, he never talked about it with anyone, including Harold.

"I'm sure they're very proud of you," Lola ventured.

Ava nodded and continued to dab at her eyes. "They're going to be at Aunt Vi's tonight. I wish I was there too." She got up and turned away from them. "I'm always alone."

Her friends looked at each other and collectively felt a faint dread, knowing the excitement of this big day was overshadowed by something none of them could understand.

"Excuse me a moment." Ava walked out of the room.

Maurice took the opportunity to give Lola a quick hairdo that was true glam rock, straight out of The Rocky Horror Picture Show. She loved it.

Once she got into her white fitted gown there was nothing else to do, so they went downstairs where they were joined by Camilla and Trent, who planned on traveling with Ava and Lola in the stretch limousine. They opened a bottle of Moet's and sipped from crystal champagne glasses while they waited.

Ava eventually came downstairs, subdued but smiling. They poured her a glass of champagne and toasted her success. She thanked them just as Mercedes poked her head in to tell them the car had arrived.

Assuring Ava they'd be fine, that they'd invited sixty of their closest friends over to their place for a fabulous Oscar night party, Maurice and Harold waved them off. Ava promised she'd call them as soon as she was able.

Traffic was awful. They waited in an endless line-up of limousines converging at the intersection of Hollywood Boulevard and Highland Avenue in front of the Kodak Theatre. As the minutes passed, excitement was replaced with anxiety. Lola grabbed Ava's hand and tried to reassure her that it would be a walk in the park, but when the door was finally opened and Ava was ushered out in the limelight, it was as if everything intensified. A kaleidoscope of images swam before her eyes but she was all alone. Lola, Camilla, and Trent had to follow a few steps behind her, out of the way of the cameras. Ava looked around several times to make sure her friends were still nearby.

The screaming fans sitting in the bleachers along the red carpet started calling her name and flashbulbs popped crazily as she slowly made her way through the throng. Whenever Camilla touched her lightly on the back, she knew she had to stop for photos. Immediately, she'd turn sideways with her right foot forward slightly and give a peek-a-boo look over her shoulder.

Then it was on to the riser for the television show Movies Now! She climbed the stairs and was momentarily stunned to see Scott Fredericks standing there, with his wife on his arm. Ava and Scott hadn't laid eyes on each other since that day in her trailer. She wanted to turn around and run but the hostess Jan Munroe grabbed her arm and with her dazzling smile drew Ava close to Scott before turning to the camera. "Look who we have here tonight: Scott Fredericks and Ava Harris. Both nominated for an Academy Award for different movies, but isn't your new film together slated for release this summer?"

"That's right, Jan," Scott said. "It's great to see you again, Ava." He reached over and gave Ava a kiss on the cheek. She smiled at him.

"Ava, did you enjoy working with Scott?" Jan asked.

"Very much. He's a great actor."

"Now before I let you go, Ava, who are you wearing?"

Ava rhymed off the dress designer, the shoemaker, and the jeweler, which she considered an accomplishment considering she could barely remember her own name. Jan Munroe asked the same question of Scott and then sent them on their way with a "Good luck to you both."

As they turned to go back down the stairs, Scott paused and whispered, "Hope you lose."

Ava ignored him.

Then on with the continuous smiling and chatting into microphones as she made her way to the grand spiral staircase that connected the four lobby levels. Trent and Camilla said goodbye there and went off to their balcony seats while Ava and Lola continued on. The theatre, which seated over three thousand, had three balcony levels and twenty-four theatre boxes set off by a highlighted "tiara," a striking oval coated in silver leaf and intertwined with smaller ovals high above their heads within the vaulted ceiling.

It was overwhelming and Ava wanted to take it all in, but there were so many people trying to maneuver down the aisle that she didn't dare stop. Eventually they made it to their seats. She was two rows back from the stage, right on the aisle, along with most of the nominees; for those who won, the walk to the microphone would be as smooth as could be.

Lola counted down how many awards were to be presented before they got to her category. "Only seven before you."

"Stop talking. You're making me nervous." Ava reached

into her jeweled clutch and pulled out a hankie. She dabbed at her upper lip. "It's warm in here."

Lola leaned over and whispered, "This place is crawling with Hollywood royalty. These people are so hot it's a wonder this entire building doesn't spontaneously combust."

Ava nudged her with her elbow. "Don't make me laugh."

"Sorry."

Ava smiled at some of the biggest names in Hollywood taking their seats in front of her. Most of them didn't acknowledge her, too preoccupied with their own big night, but a few gave her a brief nod or a quick smile. She refused to look at Scott, who as luck would have it was seated in the same row across the aisle. Her first award of the evening turned out to be the look on Scott Fredericks' face when he lost the Oscar to a relative newcomer.

Ava held Lola's hand and tried to look relaxed if she noticed a camera trained her way, but inside she was shaking. She honestly didn't know if she wanted to win. The thought of climbing those steps up to the stage was daunting. She'd rather stay in her seat and clap for someone else.

In the end, when it was announced that the Best Performance by an Actress in a Supporting Role was Ava Harris, she didn't hear the words. It was Lola's reaction that clued her in. She grabbed Ava around the neck and gave her a kiss. "You did it! You did it!"

Everything was in slow motion after that. She heard a roaring in her ears. She saw that people were clapping and expecting her to do something, so she slowly rose from her chair and walked towards the actor who was waiting with an Oscar statuette in his hands. She couldn't for the life of her remember his name. But at the last minute she did recall Harold's instructions to pick up her skirt before she climbed the stairs. Luckily she made it to the top without incident and crossed the stage towards her presenter, who kissed her on both cheeks and whispered, "Congratulations" before he handed her the Oscar.

It was heavy. It was too heavy. She looked out towards the sea of people, unable to remember a thing she was supposed to say. At the Nominees Luncheon held at the Beverly Hilton Hotel, the ceremony's producer told them they had an obligation to make their moment memorable. If they pulled out a list, they were done.

Ava had no list. She practiced some kind of speech in the bathroom mirror a few times, but never thought she'd have the chance to say it. All that ran through her mind was that millions of people around the world were watching her at this very moment.

Her family among them.

She opened her mouth but no sound came. She started again. "Thank you so much. I...I'd like to thank the Academy for this wonderful award. Isabella was a dream role for me. To become an actress working in Hollywood has been a privilege I'd not thought possible growing up in a small town in Nova Scotia."

She paused then and fought to keep her composure. "I'd like to thank my friends, who know who they are, but most of all I'd like to thank my family...the people I left behind. They mean everything to me."

Unable to continue, she panicked a little and looked for the presenter, who quickly came towards her and ushered her off the stage with the help of the hostess as the audience clapped once more and the movie's theme music swelled from the orchestra pit.

The rest of the night was a blur. She was hustled from the back stage to the Press Gallery, through a throng of people who congratulated her as she maneuvered down the corridors. Eventually she stood like a scared rabbit in front of the world's press reporters as they bombarded her with question after question. It still hadn't sunk in that she won. It was only after the ceremony was over and she was reunited with Lola, Camilla, and Trent that she allowed herself to believe it was real.

Then it was off to the Governor's Ball held in the ballroom at the top level of the Hollywood & Highland Complex. Champagne flowed as the Hollywood A-list mingled with the Oscar winners and nominees. Ava had a quick sip of champagne, but was too busy being congratulated to enjoy even the smallest morsel of food. Then it was off to the Vanity Fair party where another round of celebrities danced and laughed the night away.

Music and conversation mingled with the clink of glasses and the sound of cameras whirring. The network reporters given clearance to attend the party all insisted Ava pose with the Oscar. It was a dizzying round of flashing lights and fixed smiles, made suddenly better when Hayden came through the crowd. He held out his arms and she ran into them.

"How's my girl? Too famous to associate with a struggling actor?"

"Never," she laughed. "How did you get in here? I thought it was invitation only."

"I worked very hard for my invitation," he smirked. "She's called Dagmar."

"You're terrible, did you know that?"

He kissed her neck. "Why don't we get out of here and have our own little party? Just you and me and Oscar."

Ava looked over Hayden's shoulder at her agent, who was walking proudly in and around the Hollywood big wigs, no doubt passing out his business card. "Trent wants me to show my face at a few more parties. How about I call you when I'm finished?"

"How about I go over to your house and let myself in? I'll be the naked man under the covers."

She laughed and reached in her clutch for the house key. As she did, her cell phone rang. She picked it up and looked to see if she recognized the number. Area code 902. "Excuse me Hayden. I've been waiting for this. It's a call from home."

She turned her back on him and put the phone to her ear. She covered her other ear with the palm of her hand, trying to hear over the din of revelers.

"Hello?"

It was her sister Rose.

"Did you see me?" Ava shouted with excitement.

"You were wonderful."

"What did Ma and Aunt Vi think? Did you like my dress? I can't remember what I said. Did I make a fool of myself?"

"Stop," Rose pleaded. "Please. I have to tell you something and I can't believe I have to do it now, but it's Ma."

Ava's heart started to thud. "What about Ma?"

"I'm sorry honey, but she's sick. She was diagnosed with cancer three weeks ago."

"What? What do you mean three weeks ago? Why didn't you tell me?!"

"She wouldn't let us. She didn't want to ruin anything for you, but I put my foot down tonight, because she had a bad spell today. The doctors don't think it's going to be too long."

"Before what?"

"Before she dies. I'm very sorry love, but I think it's time you came home."

Ava slipped to the floor in a dead faint.

CHAPTER TWO

The jet was cleared for landing. The pilot's voice came over the intercom.

"We'll be landing in Sydney in a few minutes, Miss Harris."

Ava pressed her forehead against the cold window and tried to see something, but there was nothing but swirling grey clouds and small raindrops hitting the glass.

"I wish it had been a nice day out," she sighed. "The scenery is beautiful on a clear day. You can see nothing but green trees and blue water. Of course in the winter only the fir trees are green."

"That's nice." Lola obviously wasn't paying attention. She sat in the leather seat opposite Ava with her nose in Vogue. "Look at this. Your dress is being touted as one of the best at the Oscars."

"I don't want to talk about the Oscars."

Lola put down the magazine. "Sorry, kiddo. You have more important things to worry about."

Ava reached over and gave Lola's knee a pat. "I can't tell you what it means to me to have you here. I don't think I could have come alone."

"Why is that?"

Ava shrugged and looked back out the window.

The grinding sound of the wheels being released signaled that it wasn't going to be long now. Ava's stomach was in knots. She gripped the arms of her chair and closed her eyes.

The touchdown was surprisingly smooth, and as the engines roared to a crescendo, the private jet slowed considerably. They approached the airport terminal, but Ava was too nervous to look out the window. She busied herself gathering up her possessions. Lola did the same. Ava had told Rose that they had a car to take them to the hotel in Sydney, but Rose had a bad habit of not listening to a thing anyone said.

And Ava was right. When she walked down the stairs of the plane in the frigid air, there was a mob of relatives waving in the terminal window.

"Oh, God."

Ava walked towards them, stifling the urge to turn and run. It was this sort of display that embarrassed her horribly. She knew there was no need for them all to be there. They just wanted a look at the girl who ran away from home and became a famous actress.

"Who are they?" Lola whispered in her ear, as she hurried along with the tote bags. "Rabid fans?"

"This is my family. Don't say I didn't warn you." Ava took a deep cleansing breath, walked through the two sets of doors and suddenly there was no escape. She was swarmed from all sides. Lola was pushed back against the wall by a wave of humanity.

"Oh, Jesus, Mary, and Joseph!" Aunt Viola screamed. "It's herself, in the flesh." She grabbed Ava in a death grip. "Oh girl, we can't believe it. Your Ma will be so happy to see you." Auntie Viola weighed a good two hundred pounds, with hands like hams and a helmet of stiff hair lacquered into place with Aqua Net. Her several chins quivered with excitement.

"Hello, Aunt Vi." Ava couldn't expand her lungs, so tight was the hug she was locked in. Her arms hung limp by her sides.

"For jeezly sake, let her go," Uncle Angus ordered, as everyone hopped up and down around them. "Come here, Libby." Now it was his turn to grab her in a clinch. He looked exactly like Aunt Viola, except for the hair and the moustache. He didn't have either.

"I prefer Ava, Uncle Angus."

He held her at arm's length. "You'll always be Libby to me, my darlin'. Vi, look at this girl. She's a beanpole! Don't you worry, my love. We'll fatten you up in no time."

"I'm afraid my trainer would have your head."

For the next ten minutes she was grabbed, kissed, hugged, pinched, and squeezed by her eight siblings and their families. Her teenaged nieces squealed like pigs at feeding time, while her nephews stared bug-eyed at her. Not that Ava saw them. She was blind from the camera flashes. Dots danced in front of her eyes and she couldn't find Lola in the crowd.

"Lola?"

An arm rose and waved from inside the moving mob. "I'm here. Over here." Lola propelled herself through the crowd with a flying elbow or two. She finally reached Ava's side. "This is worse than a mosh pit!"

Ava grimaced. "It gets worse."

"That's not possible."

"Trust me."

Aunt Vi grabbed Lola. "Are you Ava's best friend? Did you know you're the spitting image of Liza Minelli?"

"Really?" Lola frowned. "Oh, dear."

"The drink'll do ya no good, my girl," Aunt Vi tsked. "No good at all. Look what happened to Speed Bump."

"Excuse me?"

"Speed Bump. Now there's a sad case. Got loaded one night and didn't Buddy Whatzhisname from up the road run him over with his brand new truck. Yep, a real sin."

"He was killed?"

"No, my dear. He got up off his arse and went back to the Legion, but he's never been the same since. I feel sorry for his mother."

Ava had enough. "Excuse me, but I haven't even had a chance to ask you about my mother."

"Oh, she's right good today," Uncle Angus smiled. "Ain't that so, Vi?"

Aunt Viola patted Ava's hand. "She is, my love. She's hanging on to see her baby."

Ava felt her eyes begin to well up. She quickly turned to Lola. "You get the car sorted and I'll meet you outside."

Uncle Angus looked shocked. "What do you mean? You're coming with us, surely?"

Ava hesitated. "Ah, no." She waved Lola away. "Go. Go."

Lola went.

Aunt Vi and Uncle Angus glanced at each other. Ava said hurriedly, "Lola's my assistant."

"Your assistant?" they said together.

Rose was close enough to overhear the conversation. "Lord flyin' dyin'. Imagine that. I need to get me one of those."

Ava smiled at her. "I'll lend her to you."

"Deal."

"Look, I appreciate the fact that you came to meet me, but I'm tired and I need to get myself sorted before I go and see Ma. Can we meet at the hospital in an hour?"

Rose spoke first. "She's not there anymore. She's at home."

"But I thought..."

"She wants to die at home, Libby. With her pain medication and the V.O.N. coming in, she's much more comfortable in her own bed."

"I see. Well, I'll meet you back at the house as soon as possible. Tell her I'm coming." Before anyone could object, Ava pushed her way through the crowd of excited relatives. Then, to her horror, she realized the press was there, with another gang of on-lookers and fans. She turned back and looked to her sister. "I thought I told you not to tell anyone I was coming?"

"I only told Myrtle Beaver at Bingo."

Ava couldn't believe it. "Megaphone Myrtle?"

"Oh, get over yourself," Rose frowned. "You know damn well you can't keep a secret like this, so why try?"

"Fine. Never mind." Ava pulled her cashmere shawl closer around her shoulders and made a dash for it. Lola was outside beside the limo's open door. She waved Ava on, as if she were coaching third base. Ava jumped in the car, Lola right behind her. The adoring fans mobbed the vehicle, but at least the screaming was muffled.

Ava sank back into the leather seat. "Oh my god. What am I going to do? I'm trying to visit my dying mother and suddenly this has turned into a publicity tour."

"Who let the cat out of the bag?"

"Rose, of course. She never could keep her mouth shut."

"I hate to say it," Lola smirked, "but it seems to run in your family."

"Don't I know it," Ava sighed.

❈

Elizabeth Ruby MacKinnon, a.k.a. Ava Harris, was the baby in a family of nine, with seven years between her and her next sister, Rose. She'd known from a very early age that she was "the change" baby. She used to lie awake at night and wonder what that meant, exactly. It didn't sound very good and the fact that her mother was often impatient and cross with her didn't help matters. Rose would tell her not to worry, that of course their mother loved her. But there was always a niggling doubt that pulled at Ava's thoughts. Try as she might to ignore it, it coloured everything.

Things became worse when her father was killed in the mine when she was eight. He was the only one in the house who never said a word to her. Everything Libby did was okay by him. Not that she saw him much. For a few minutes after he'd scrubbed the coal dust off his body and had a hefty plateful of Ma's homemade beans and corn bread. She'd sit on his lap in his rocking chair and inevitably, just as things got interesting and everyone was filling him in about their day, she'd be whisked off to bed.

Despite her protests, her father would kiss the top of her head and tell her to listen to her Ma. "Goodnight, Peanut," he'd say. Usually it was Rose who pulled her up the stairs and tucked her in.

But Libby never stayed under the covers for long. She learned to move silently through the house, often hiding in closets if one of her siblings charged up the stairs or down the hall unexpectedly. Once she hid under the dining room table to listen in on a heated conversation between her parents and one of her older brothers. She couldn't believe they didn't see her. They walked right by as if she were invisible. She made funny faces at her mother the next morning to see if she really was invisible. A quick cuff on the ear and a "smarten up" set her straight.

The day their father died, she curled up in her father's rocking chair and screamed blue murder when her siblings tried to take her upstairs to bed. They eventually had to leave her there. She slept in that chair for a month, until finally, at her wits' end, her mother threatened to throw her fairy doll in the wood stove if she didn't stop her nonsense.

The thing that bothered Libby the most was when her mother came to school for some reason. Most of her friends had young, pretty mothers. Libby told some girls in her class that her Ma was really her Nana. Somehow it got back to her brothers and sisters and she got in trouble. There wasn't much she didn't get in trouble for, or so it seemed. With so many siblings expressing their opinions about her misdemeanors, she always felt she was letting someone down, no matter how she handled a situation. It was exhausting.

※

Ava got out of the shower and wrapped a towel around her head. She slipped on the hotel bathrobe and walked back to the king size bed. She threw herself on the mattress, face first, and groaned.

Lola shouted from the open door of the adjoining suite. "That doesn't sound too encouraging!"

"Kill me."

"Sorry, if I do that, I'll be out of a job and you know I'm up to my eyeballs in debt."

Ava turned over on her back and smirked. "And whose fault is that?"

"Yours."

"Oh?"

"Yippers. You look so damn good I have to spend a fortune to keep up appearances."

Ava tugged at her hair, looking for split ends. "What a lot of horseradish. The only reason I look good is Maurice, and he's not here at the moment, so you have no worries on that score."

"True that."

"Besides," she laughed, "when I'm around, no one looks at you anyway."

A pillow sailed through the door and landed on Ava's head. Lola followed suit. They tousled with the pillow for a moment but Ava won. She put it over her own face. "Do it. End it all."

Lola tore the pillow away from her. "No. I'm dying to meet your family properly and see where you grew up. It can't be as awful as you say."

"Oh, yes it can."

"So, who cares? I'm still dying to see it. Did you live in a big house?"

"No. It's about the size of my bedroom closet."

"Then it's gigantic."

"Hush up, Lo. I don't want to go back there."

Lola stopped clowning around and sat up against the head board. "Why? It's your family. You sound like you're afraid of them."

Ava stared at the ceiling. "I guess I am."

"Don't be silly. They love you."

When she didn't answer, Lola shoved her with her toe. "I'm right."

"They don't know me well enough to love me."

"That's because you don't let people in."

"Not this again." Ava sat up. "I let you in, didn't I?"

"And you regret it enormously."

"You took the words right out of my mouth," Ava smiled. "I've got to get dressed. What should I wear?"

"Something black."

"She's not dead yet."

"Then something white, it might cheer her up."

"I'll look like an angel come to take her to the other side. I don't want her to have a heart attack on top of everything else."

"Wear what you want," Lola shrugged.

"I can see now why I pay you the big bucks. You're indispensable."

Lola got off the bed and sauntered into her room. "Remember that when my Christmas bonus comes around." She shut the door behind her and left Ava to fend for herself.

Ava tried on a half a dozen outfits and got annoyed that she was dithering about it. Standing in front of the mirror didn't help. "Just put something on and get it over with." She walked over to the window and looked out on a typical Cape Breton winter day in February. Everything she had wasn't warm enough. She'd have to buy a winter coat or she'd freeze.

In the end she wore a pair of jeans and an oversized sweater, with her hair in a ponytail. She wanted to be as inconspicuous as possible. Trouble was, with her suede Steve Madden platform booties, Burberry trench coat, and Louis Vuitton handbag, she wasn't fooling anyone. Putting on oversized sunglasses didn't help matters.

Lola came out in a pinstriped pantsuit and did a double take. "You're wearing that!?"

Ava looked down at herself. "What's wrong with this?"

"It's pretty casual, don't you think?"

"So?" She grabbed her hotel key. "I don't want a big fuss."

Lola sniffed as she grabbed her purse and coat. "No worries then, because no one will make a fuss over you in that."

"Why do I keep you in my life?"

Lola pinched Ava's cheek. "Because you love me."

Ava yanked the door open and walked through it. "Don't be so sure."

Following her out and down the hall to the elevator, Lola said, "Listen kid, if it weren't for me you'd be a mess. We can't have you believing your own press, can we? Who else is gonna tell you the truth?"

Ava punched the elevator button and then put her arm through her friend's, her head resting on Lola's shoulder. "I know. Thank God you're here. Thank you for coming with me, I couldn't have done it alone."

Lola patted her hand. "That's the second time you've said that. Don't worry, I'm not going anywhere."

When they got off the elevator a crowd of teenaged girls accosted them.

"Oh please, can I have your autograph, Miss Harris?" they all said at once.

Ava put on her fake smile and murmured, "How sweet. So kind."

That was Lola's cue. She put her hands up. "Girls, it's lovely of you to come out tonight, but Miss Harris is here on personal family business. It's a sad occasion, so I'm sure you understand. Thank you." Then she pulled Ava along through the protesting girls and managed to hustle her into the car.

"Sometimes I get tired of this," Ava sighed.

"And sometimes you don't, you little diva."

Ava watched the scenery go by on the twenty-minute car ride to Glace Bay. Most of it was familiar, but there were a lot of changes, enough to make her realize she was away a long time. Ten years, a significant portion of her life—she was only twenty-eight. (Though Trent insisted her official biography read twenty-three.)

New businesses had popped up everywhere along Welton Street, with big box stores built in and around the Mayflower Mall. There were more fast food restaurants than she remembered. She was happy to see The Tasty Treat still going strong. They always did have the best ice cream.

They passed the drive-in theatre, now closed for the winter. The huge ratty old sign board read "_lose_ for th_ sea_ _ _."

When they drove by the cut-off for the town of New Waterford, more memories crowded in, ones she wanted for forget, so she tried to erase them from her mind by concentrating on the cemetery to her right. Forest Haven looked especially peaceful on this particular day, a vast expanse of undisturbed white snow covering the brass grave markers on the ground. Her grandparents were buried there, but she couldn't remember where exactly.

"Will you stop that?" Lola said.

Ava was aware of her heart beating too fast. "Stop what?"

"Biting your nails. You ruin every manicure you get."

"Sorry." Her hands were in her lap for about ten seconds before she started again.

Lola shook her head and looked out the window. "It's so funny here."

"Funny?"

"All the houses are made of wood or vinyl siding. I don't see any brick anywhere."

"I never really noticed."

Lola pointed to a half a house. "And what the heck is that?"

"That's what they call a company house. For the miners. Two units were built side by side. If one side falls into disrepair, sometimes they bulldoze it and leave the other half standing."

Lola continued to gawk. "But one side of that house has shutters and a porch and the other side doesn't have anything. And to make matters worse, they're not even painted the same colour. I love this place!"

They turned up Water Street, a winding narrow road that followed the harbour's edge. The houses were built facing in every direction because of old laneways that dissected some of the properties.

Ava broke out in a cold sweat as they approached her father's house. She looked at the harbour, expecting it to be changed as well, but everything was exactly the same. Bright colours adorned the fishing boats tied up on shore for the winter. Seagulls looked like security guards as they stood on the wharf watching for anything that might resemble food. But it wasn't until she got out of the car and smelled the sea air that she realized she was home.

"Is this it? Why, it's a sweet little house," Lola cried. "Just like a movie set!"

Ava tried to see it through Lola's eyes but wasn't very successful. It was an ordinary shingled house in need of a fresh coat of white paint. A small porch led to the front door that no one ever used. To make your way in, you had to go around back, by the coal shed and garage. The house had two stories and a pitched roof and it was about as nondescript as it could be except for the large iron anchor that marked the property's edge. The anchor, from her great-grandfather's Cape Islander boat, now did duty as a signpost. The block of wood hanging from it read, The MacKinnons. It had been crooked when she left and it was still crooked.

"It looks like Anne of Green Gables' house!" Lola said.

"Don't be ridiculous."

"Well, maybe not, but is sure looks homey."

"I can't believe eleven people lived in this house," Ava said. "It's so small."

The words were no sooner out of her mouth than the back door opened and out flowed the family.

"If it's big enough for this lot," Lola laughed, "it can't be that small."

They were swarmed and hustled inside, with Aunt Vi letting loose on some of the neighbours who gathered with their video cameras to catch a glimpse of the local girl who made good. She stormed across the yard, shooing people away as if they were chickens. "Git, the lot of ya. No use gawkin'."

Her next-door neighbour, Thelma Steele, got a lip on. "Oh, stop being so bossy, Vi. It's only natural people want to have a peek."

"She's come to visit her dyin' Ma, Thelma. She's not traipsing around for your gratification."

Thelma got huffy. "No harm done if I just stand here."

"Oh, go way with ya." Vi turned around and practically ran back to the house. Thelma yelled to her. "Are you on sweets at Club on Wednesday?"

"Is the Pope Catholic?" Vi yelled back before she disappeared from sight.

Ava and Lola were ushered into the kitchen by way of a small back porch. Ava knew it was like no entranceway Lola had ever seen. There was an ancient washer and dryer on one side, with laundry piled up on top of it, on hangers above it and hanging off brooms and mops—something even hung on the nail holding up a calendar. The area was filled with boots and shoes of all sorts, the cat's dish with dried goop in it, the kitty litter box shoved to one side, raincoats, overalls, baseball bats, the dog's rawhide chew, a box of potatoes and a crate of apples. For some reason, there was even a lemon pie in a cardboard box.

Then it was on to the kitchen, but it was hard to see what it was like with the number of people in it. The one great thing about it was the smell. Fresh baking sat on racks everywhere. Lola was in heaven.

"Look at all these goodies. Did you do all this?" she asked Aunt Vi.

"This? Holy Moses, this ain't much. Let me grab you a plate," she said as she bustled off. Uncle Angus tried to steer

Ava towards the rocking chair in the corner but she managed to slip from his grasp.

"Lord, child. You're like a slippery eel."

"Sorry, Uncle Angus. I'd prefer to take a look around. Not much has changed, I see." She took off her sunglasses and her eyes swept the kitchen. Her family looked at her. Rose reached up and touched her hair. "This is a fantastic colour. It's like honey. What's the name of it? I should get a box."

"It's about fifteen different shades," Ava grinned. "It takes Maurice three hours to work his magic. No box involved."

Her nieces all gave a collective sigh. "Who's Maurice?" one of them asked.

"My hairdresser and makeup man."

They sighed again. Before they asked her anything else, she cut them off. "I'm having trouble putting names to some of the younger kids. Who's who?"

Not that she could remember them all, but she did listen carefully as each of her brothers and sisters proudly pointed out their offspring and listed the ones absent. Her eldest brother Johnnie had two sons, almost her age. Lauchie had one daughter, Hugh three boys, Sandy two girls. Gerard never married, but declared he had offspring in every town on the island. Bev had a boy and a girl, Maryette two girls, and Rose two of each.

Quite a few of them looked like their parents as Ava remembered them when she was growing up, so it wasn't as difficult as she imagined keeping everyone straight. Vi insisted that they sit at the kitchen table for a cup of tea and a quick bite before venturing upstairs to see Ava's mother. At first Ava wanted to object, but she thought the better of it. She realized she hadn't eaten all day and maybe that was why she was feeling lightheaded.

Lola raved about the food. "Mrs.—sorry, I don't know your last name—"

"It's MacIntosh dear. But call me Aunt Vi. Everyone else does."

"Well Aunt Vi, I say we bundle you up and take you back to California. You'd make a killing with these delicious desserts. Wolfgang Puck could use you as a pastry chef."

One of the kids laughed. "Wolfgang Puck is a person? Who'd name their kid Wolfgang?"

"Mr. and Mrs. Puck, obviously," Lola laughed.

"Do you have a mansion?" one of the girls asked Ava.

"No. It's nice though. It's in Malibu."

This elicited more squeals. Then one of the boys spoke up. "How come we never go and visit you?"

The room became quiet. Ava had a hard time swallowing her blueberry cake, so she took a gulp of strong tea. "I guess that's because I'm not home too often."

"Why?"

"I travel a lot. Movies are made all over the world now."

Rose's daughter Vicky spoke up. "I saw your picture in People magazine. You were on their 50 Most Beautiful People list. Were you excited?"

Ava spoke to her plate. "More embarrassed than anything."

Aunt Vi, who had her hands in the sink washing dishes, turned around and wiped them on her apron. "Don't be so foolish, child. Look at ya. Why, anyone can see you're a looker."

"She wasn't when she was a kid," Gerard teased. "She was as homely as a hedge fence."

Everyone booed him down. Uncle Angus held his hands up. "Hush now. Mamie's upstairs."

Ava suddenly stood. "I better go see her now. Are you coming, Lola?"

Lola looked horrified. "Of course not. She doesn't want to see me. I'll meet her another time, you go ahead."

Ava stayed rooted to the spot. It wasn't until Rose came over and put her arm around her shoulders that she took a step. "It'll be all right, Libby. It's only Ma. She's so anxious to see you."

Ava had no choice but to go along with her sister. Walking up the back stairs, her feet seemed to get heavier with each step and her courage seeped away. By the time they stood in front of her mother's bedroom door, she was breathless. Rose turned to look at her. "Now it's going to be a shock, Libby. You haven't seen her in ten years and she's gone downhill pretty fast these last few weeks. But I'm right here, okay?"

Ava nodded. Rose opened the door.

CHAPTER THREE

Downstairs, the family turned their attention to Lola, who was busy chowing down on Aunt Vi's baking. Eventually she noticed there were about twenty-five pairs of eyes on her, if you counted the dog and various cats milling about. She coughed on the last bite of a pineapple square and took a sip of tea, then patted the napkin against her red lips and balled it up on a plate.

"Oh my, that was out of this world."

"Did you like your lunch, dear?" Aunt Vi asked.

"Lunch?"

"That's what you had."

"You call eating desserts lunch?"

Uncle Angus sat in the rocking chair. "Well then, my girl, what would you call it?"

"A diet crisis, but never mind, it was worth every mouthful."

At that point most of the family left to go home and make their own suppers—as though with Ava out of the room there wasn't much point in sticking around. Aunt Vi and Ava's sisters Bev and Maryette, however, rushed to sit at the table with Lola. Their teenage daughters hung around the edges, hoping they wouldn't be sent home with their fathers and brothers.

Lola looked at these female relatives of Ava's and saw the family resemblance. They were all fair haired and none of them were what you would call big people, except of course for Aunt Vi. A few of them had red hair and almost all of them had a smattering of freckles—the same freckles Maurice said were the bane of his existence. Of course, they looked as if they could do with a little pampering, but on the whole, they were a pleasant-looking bunch. The one thing they did have in common was Ava's lovely smile. But there was a big difference: They smiled a lot more then Ava did.

Aunt Vi clasped her hands and put them on the table. "Right now, girlie. I'd like to ask you something."

"Shoot."

"Is Libby happy?"

Lola was taken aback. "Goodness. You cut right to the chase."

"No use mincing words, as they say."

She had to think fast. "Of course she's happy. Why? Don't you think so?"

Aunt Vi looked at her nieces. "What do you think, girls?"

Bev and Maryette exchanged glances. Bev spoke first. "It's hard to tell of course, since we've only seen her for a few minutes, but I'm not sure. I hoped to see her as she was before she left us."

"And how was that?" Lola wanted to know.

"Bubbling."

"She was like a fairy," Maryette grinned.

Rose's daughter Vicky spoke up. "Mom always says that too."

Maryette continued. "Oh yes, she was a fairy, all right. Never in one spot too long, always flitting about, smiling and happy. And that laugh. She had a sparkling laugh."

Uncle Angus rocked and sucked on his pipe. "I remember we used to tell her jokes or tickle her so we could hear that laugh. It was like music."

An unsettling feeling came over Lola. "I never knew that."

"What do you mean?" Bev said. "You must know if you're her friend."

Lola cleared her throat. "Oh, I do. I do. She does have a great laugh. I mean, she never told me about you trying to trick her, that's all."

The others seemed satisfied with that, but Aunt Vi didn't look fooled. "She doesn't laugh much, does she?"

Lola was stuck. She floundered for something to say. Aunt Vi reached out and gave her hand a pat. "You're not betraying her, dear. We aren't her public. We're family and we're concerned about her."

"But why? Why are you concerned? That's what I don't understand."

Aunt Vi sighed, as if impatient with such a question. "Girl, what do you call running away from home and never coming back? Does that sound like someone who's happy?"

There was nothing else she could say. "No."

Rose's daughter Vicky spoke up again. She actually raised her hand, as if she were in class. "But I don't understand. Why wouldn't she be happy? She lives in Malibu, she's hot, she goes out with all kinds of super hot guys and she makes millions. I'd be happy, wouldn't you guys?" She looked at her cousins and they nodded furiously.

Aunt Vi dismissed her with a wave of her hand. "What's that got to do with the price of eggs?"

"Huh?"

"Child, you're too young to know what you're talking about."

Vicky looked peeved. "Well, if she isn't happy, then she's nuts."

Bev leaned towards Lola. "Does she have a boyfriend? Someone other than her co-stars?"

Lola shrugged. "From time to time."

"But they don't last, do they?"

"Not really."

"Why?"

Lola shrugged again. "It's a hard life, believe it or not. You never know whether a man wants you for you or for the actress on the screen."

"That's a problem?" Bev's daughter Samantha snorted. "Who cares? She's dated Toby James for heaven's sake!"

"Who hasn't?" Lola muttered.

Samantha's mother got cross. "Okay Sam, will you girls go somewhere else, please? This isn't your concern. We shouldn't be discussing this in front of you anyway."

Samantha and her cousins huffed off into the living room with complaints of always having to leave when the going got good. Once they were gone, Lola couldn't resist.

"What happened to make her run away? She's never said a thing to me about it. Not a word."

Ava's sisters looked at their Aunt Vi, who in turn looked at Uncle Angus. He nodded ever so slightly. She leaned closer to Lola and whispered, "A romance gone sour."

"A romance? When she was seventeen?"

The ladies nodded knowingly.

Lola didn't believe it. "Come on. No one runs away because of a high school crush."

"This was no ordinary crush," Maryette frowned. "We tried to tell Ma that, but she wouldn't listen."

"Well, what happened?"

Bev shook her head. "No one knows. That's the strange part about it. One minute they were so in love it was scary. The next minute...poof! She was gone."

"Well, not the next minute," Maryette corrected her. "She

was here that summer after Seamus went to New Brunswick. She was sad when he left. She didn't want him to go."

"She was sad before he left," Bev added. "She wasn't quite herself, probably because she knew he was going."

"Who was he?"

"Only the most gorgeous boy you ever laid eyes on," Maryette sighed. "Even we were jealous of her and half of us were married!"

"What was his name?"

"Seamus O'Reilly."

Lola laughed out loud. "You're making that up."

They looked at her in confusion.

So they weren't kidding. "I'm sorry," she stammered. "It's just that he sounds like someone from a Harlequin romance..."

Uncle Angus kept rocking. "No, my girl. There's lots of O'Reillys around here. And Seamus is a good, old-fashioned name. Lots of Scots and Irish in this part of the world."

"What happened to him?"

"There's a sad story," Aunt Vi tsked. "I'll never forget when his mother came up to the house to speak to Mamie, saying her son's heart was broken and who did that little madam think she was? Girl, the fur was flyin' that day. Mamie had her finger in that poor woman's face telling her it was all her son's fault her daughter run off and how she'd never let another O'Reilly cross her threshold ever again. Then I think she went after her with the broom."

"It was the coal shovel," said Uncle Angus.

"You're right, Angus, it was the coal shovel. Chased her halfway down Water Street. Lord have mercy, what a sight."

Lola couldn't believe her ears. "Good heavens, it's like a bad movie. But where is Seamus now?"

Maryette crossed her arms and leaned back in her chair.

"He's still around, but we hardly ever see him."

"Did he marry?"

"Yes," Bev replied. "A nice little girl, Sally Hooper. A shame about her, too."

Lola was reeling at this point. In the back of her mind she saw a Hollywood script in the making. "What about her?"

"She died after their second child was born."

"Are you serious?"

Aunt Vi gave her a look. "Why do you think we're lyin' to you all the time?"

Lola put her hand on Aunt Vi's arm. "I'm sorry. It's not that I doubt you; I just can't believe all this. It sounds so…"

"Dramatic?" Maryette volunteered.

"Yes, I guess that's what I mean."

"Everything about Libby's life is dramatic," Bev smiled. "I guess that's why she's such a great little actress."

Lola had to know. "So Seamus is raising two children by himself?"

"His sister helps out," Aunt Vi said. "Now there's a nice girl. Kids of her own, but she's always there when he needs her."

"Does Ava know about Seamus…about his wife, I mean?"

Aunt Vi frowned. "Well, Rose opened her big gob and told her he was married, but no, we never told her Sally died. Too afraid I guess. She's never asked about him. It's best to let it be."

"He lives out Mira," Bev continued. "And I think that's a shame. I've never understood why he doesn't come into town with those babies and be closer to folk. It would make his life a whole lot easier."

"Maybe he's afraid of running into all of you," Lola said.

Aunt Vi and her nieces looked at each other and suddenly

Lola was sorry she opened her big mouth. "I didn't mean that. I'm sure that's not it."

Aunt Vi slapped the table. "You've hit the nail on the head, girlie! Why didn't we think of that before?"

Uncle Angus chuckled. "We never were too bright."

All of them laughed, so Lola joined in as well.

❀

Upstairs Ava and Rose sat on either side of their mother's bed. Mamie was fast asleep, which was just as well, because the minute Ava laid eyes on her, she put her hand up to cover her mouth so she wouldn't gasp out loud.

Rose put her arm around her. "It's okay, Libby. Sit down."

Ava did as she was told. She couldn't have stood much longer anyway. It was a shock to see her loud and bossy mother lying faded and weak on her pillow.

"She looks so old."

Rose chuckled as she sat down herself. "She is old, honey. She'll be eighty in a week, God willing."

Ava shook her head. "I can't believe it. I thought she'd live forever. I never thought she'd get sick."

"Sorry to disappoint you, but we're all ten years older than the last time we laid eyes on you."

Ava glanced at her sister before looking at her hands. "I know. I'm sorry. I always meant to come home, but there never seemed to be enough time."

Rose didn't answer, but one look at her face told Ava what she thought about that statement.

"I always missed you," she added.

"And we missed you," Rose replied. "It's a terrible shame that you only come home when one of us is dying."

"Don't. Please."

"It's the truth, isn't it?"

"I know, I know. I just can't deal with it all at once." Ava reached over and grabbed a handful of tissue from her mother's bedside and began to shred them into little pieces. "I feel badly about it."

"Why, Lib? Just tell me why. You don't know what it was like here, after you left. Ma was so hurt. She read that letter over and over and asked us what she did wrong. It was awful."

Ava's heart was heavy, so heavy she had to take shallow breaths. But there was also something else below the surface. "You're telling me the only time she paid any attention to me was when I was gone?"

Rose looked shocked. "Is that what you think?"

Ava didn't trust herself to speak, so she shrugged.

Rose shook her head. "Libby..."

"Ava."

"I can't call you Ava. Ava is the girl I saw at the movie theatre last Friday night. Libby is my baby sister and I want to tell her to grow up."

Ava clenched her teeth. Here it comes.

"You've been saying that so long, I think you actually believe that Ma was never there for you."

"It's true, Rose, and you know it."

Her sister pointed her finger right in her face. "Stop thinking about yourself and start thinking about what it was like for her." Rose paused to look at her mother. "I've got four kids and I can hardly see straight. She had nine! Nine kids to bring up and suddenly her husband dies horribly and leaves her to cope with everything on her own. It wasn't easy. She'd be so tired at the end of a day, she couldn't move, let alone speak, and all you remember is that she didn't play patty-cake with you? She was in her sixties when you were a bratty teenager. Are you honestly telling me that you felt cheated somehow? You had four mothers! Maryette, Bev, and I looked after you like you were a baby doll. No, my girl, I don't know where you ever got the idea that you were neglected, but it sure wasn't in this house."

Ava wanted to run. Anywhere. Her head was going to explode if she sat for one more minute.

"Hush now."

Both heads turned at the sound of their mother's voice. "Leave the girl alone, Rose."

Ava reached for her mother's hand. "Ma? It's so good to see you again. I'm sorry…"

Her mother smiled and squeezed Ava's fingers. "You look the same. You hardly look a day older."

"That's because your eyesight isn't that good, Ma," Rose laughed.

"That's true, but it's good enough for me to see her father in her."

At the mention of her father, Ava began to cry, startling both her sister and her mother. But there wasn't a thing she could do about it. She leaned over and laid her head on her mother's breast.

"It's okay, let it out," her mother said. She rubbed Ava's back and made soothing noises. Then she looked at Rose. "Why don't you leave us, Rose? I think Libby needs to be with me for a while."

"I'll be downstairs if you need anything."

They didn't answer. She crept out of the room and closed the door quietly behind her.

"Please don't die," Ava hiccupped into her mother's nightie. "Not now."

"I'll try not to," her mother smiled.

"Why didn't you call me when you found out? I would've come right away."

"Because I wanted you to enjoy your moment in the sun. There would have been nothing for you to do but drag me to doctor's appointments, and your sisters were perfectly capable of doing that."

Ava's back began to hurt, so she lifted herself up and took more tissue to wipe her wet face. "I've been stupid and selfish to stay away so long. I hope you can forgive me."

"I forgave you a long time ago. I think it's time you forgave yourself."

"That may take a while."

Her mother closed her eyes, and for a minute Ava thought she went back to sleep. It was hard to look at her face. Her cheeks were hollow and her once thick hair was now wispy and shapeless, but what was worse was looking at her hands. They were nothing but bones and sinew, with blue veins and age spots covering her thin skin. They seemed almost transparent, as if the life force that once ran through them was disappearing.

Mamie spoke but kept her eyes closed. "Are you ever going to tell me why you left?"

Ava stayed awake many nights, trying to think of an explanation that would satisfy her family's curiosity, but she'd never come up with anything believable, so there was nothing to do but lie.

"I wanted to see the world, I guess. I felt stifled here."

"You left a lot of people behind."

"I know."

"Seamus, for one."

It was the first time in years she'd heard his name spoken out loud. It made him real again and she nearly stopped breathing altogether. Now it was her turn to close her eyes, but it was no good. His face swam before her, the face that had haunted her dreams for ten long years. Would it ever be over? Could she ever be free of him?

At that moment, she'd have give anything to be the one in bed dying.

CHAPTER FOUR

When Ava walked back into the kitchen, she found Lola holding court at the kitchen table. She had the family in stitches over something. Ava envied her easy manner. She looked like she belonged and she only knew them an hour. It was a talent Ava would never possess.

As soon as Rose saw her, she came over and put her arms around her. "I'm sorry for giving you old heck five minutes after you walked in the door."

"Doesn't matter. I deserved it."

"Are you okay?"

She nodded. "Ma's gone back to sleep."

"She sleeps a lot now. It's the pain medication."

Aunt Vi hopped out of her chair. "Come sit, me darling. You look like you've seen a ghost."

Ava was grateful for the seat. Two seconds after she sat down a cup of tea was placed in front of her along with another plateful of goodies.

"Oh, I couldn't eat another bite, Aunt Vi."

"Go way with ya. That there cake won first prize at the fair last fall. I got the recipe from Una Murchison. That woman knows her way around a Bundt pan."

"Well, you come a close second," Lola said.

"Learned everything I know from my mother. Now there was a woman who knew a thing or two about baking. I was making bread by the time I was eight."

"I'd love to make my own bread," Lola confessed. "But I'd only eat it."

"Well, what else would you do with it?" Uncle Angus chuckled. "You Hollywood people are mighty strange."

"You've got that right," Lola laughed. "Doesn't he, Ava?"

Ava nodded and took a sip of tea, pretending not to notice everyone glance at each other. Let them think what they want. She wasn't feeling up to small talk and the family must have sensed it, because the conversation resumed without her. Ava was eternally grateful that Lola was there to deflect the attention away from her. It was beyond the call of duty, but then Lola seemed to be having a good time. It almost made her envious.

Ava, on the other hand, felt as if she were underwater. Muffled voices droned on around her and everything seemed out of focus, everything but her father's rocking chair. As Uncle Angus rocked back and forth over the floor cloth worn away by the constant motion, she heard the faint squeak, and if she closed her eyes, it was as if her father had come back to her.

If only that were true.

Someone put their arm around her shoulder. She looked up. It was Aunt Vi.

"Pet, you look wore out. I'll go make up the spare room. There are twin beds in there for you and Lola. Uncle Angus and I are in your old bedroom because it's closer to your mother's room."

For a brief moment Ava forgot that her aunt and uncle lived in the house now. They'd decided years ago that it didn't make sense for Mamie to be rattling around by herself. It was a wise move financially, to combine their households, since Vi and Angus were always over helping out Mamie anyway.

"That's sounds great, Aunt Vi..." Lola started to say, but Ava interrupted her.

"I think I'll stay at the hotel if you don't mind."

"In heaven's name, why? You're throwing away good money. You can stay here for free."

"Money doesn't matter," she sighed.

"Well, excuse us, Miss Moneybags," her sister Bev snorted. "For your information, money does matter around here. You don't need to be rubbing our noses in the fact that you can afford anything you please."

This visit was rapidly turning into a bad idea. "I didn't mean it that way."

"But it doesn't make much sense," Rose said. "You're here for a visit but you're going to stay in a hotel? We can't be traipsing into Sydney every day. We have families and jobs. It would be a whole lot easier if you stayed here."

"I know Mamie would love it, dear," Aunt Vi nodded. "She's talked of nothing else for days."

It was a losing battle. "All right, all right."

"Don't do us any favours," Bev grumped.

Maryette turned on her sister. "Leave her alone. Today couldn't have been easy, all of us swarming her the way we did."

Ava gave her a faint smile.

Lola jumped in. "We really must go back tonight to collect our things. But we'll return tomorrow after lunch, how does that sound?"

Aunt Vi clapped her hands. "Oh, it will be so much fun having young people in the house again!"

Uncle Angus got out of the rocking chair. "What on earth are you talking about, woman? We've got youngsters crawling all over this place. They never leave us alone."

"That's because they know a soft touch when they see one," Rose teased him.

"Don't be so foolish." But with the next breath, he took the change out of his pocket and hollered, "Who wants a loonie?"

The kids galloped into the kitchen.

Soon after that, the sisters and their children bid Ava and Lola goodnight. There were kisses all around. Aunt Vi invited everyone over for a roast chicken dinner the next day. They told her it was too much, that she had enough to do with Mamie. She wouldn't hear of it, so the girls each said they'd bring a dish.

Lola asked if she could bring a dish too.

"Go way with ya," Aunt Vi laughed. "We've got plenty."

Lola would not be dissuaded. "Let me bring something. There must be a bakery around here."

"There's nothing a bakery has that I don't make better myself, so there's no sense wasting your brass."

Lola held up her hands. "Okay. I've been warned. But I'm still going to bring something. A big dinner sounds like fun."

Uncle Angus took his pipe out of his mouth. "Were you an only child, by chance?"

"Yes, how did you guess?"

"Fun isn't exactly how I'd describe a big dinner."

"It's a lot more fun for you than it is for me," Aunt Vi sniffed. "You sit back and eat a bellyful while I slave away over a hot stove."

Uncle Angus put his arms around his wife's so-called waist. "I'm a lucky man, what am I?"

She slapped him away. "Get off, you old fool."

On the way back to the hotel, Ava hardly said a word, while Lola prattled on about how wonderful her family was. She nodded at the appropriate moments and even smiled a few times.

Ava knew when Lola became fed up with her, but it couldn't be helped. She looked out one window while Lola looked out the other. The rest of the ride was silent.

When Ava got back to the hotel room, she told Lola she was going to take a shower and she'd see her in the morning. Lola was about to say something, but Ava gave a little wave and closed the door. Throwing her purse and trench coat across the room, she practically ripped the clothes off her body before turning on the shower faucets full blast. As soon as the water was hot, she stepped in and let the water rain down over her head.

It was too much. Her mother, her father, the ten years she'd missed with her siblings, and now Seamus.

Seamus.

It was always about him.

With her head pounding, she eventually turned off the shower and climbed back into the bathrobe hanging on the bathroom door, then towel-dried her hair before wiping the fogged-up mirror with it. Her eyes looked swollen. If only the gossip rags could see this, she thought. Wouldn't they have a field day?

She reached for the expensive moisturizer on the counter and soothed it over her hot and blotchy face. Everything ached. Grabbing a couple of painkillers, she swallowed them with a handful of water from under the tap, and then turned out the bathroom light, threw off the bathrobe and crawled into bed. She desperately wanted to sleep but couldn't. Trying not to think of Seamus kept her awake. He was in this city somewhere, married to Sally. Maybe they had children by now. She wondered if he ever thought of her. Finally, in desperation, she gave in and let him come to her, remembering the first day she laid eyes on him. Their school was hosting a skating party and a bunch from the high school in New Waterford came into the rink together. Her friends were excited at the thought of seeing a few new boys. She thought they were crazy and told them so.

"They're going to be the same as the boys in our high school. New Waterford isn't on the other side of the planet. It's fifteen minutes from here."

"That's not what my Dad says." Her friend Marilyn tied up her skates as she spoke. "He says they're nuts, but I think that's because my Uncle Charlie lives there, and he's crazy."

"So everyone in New Waterford is nuts because of your crazy Uncle Charlie?"

"Apparently, but my dad is a bit queer too. You know fathers. Oh, sorry, Libby. I forgot."

"That's okay." But it wasn't okay. She always felt hollow when someone mentioned their dad. Fortunately, a commotion at the door saved her from brooding. A group of about ten boys walked in, laughing and talking. Her friends preened and started to whisper behind their hands.

Libby kept very still. She picked him out the second he walked through the door. Everyone else walked in real time but he was in slow motion. It registered with her that he was tall and had brown hair and eyes, but it was his smile that made her heart pound, and the way he walked and the way he filled out a pair of jeans. His hair was long, brushing the collar of his hockey jacket. He was simply the nicest-looking boy she'd ever seen. And she knew by the squeals from her friends that they thought so too.

"Who is he?" Marilyn cooed. "He's adorable. Look at his skin. He doesn't even have a pimple."

"I bet he has a girlfriend though," said another. "Why couldn't it be me?"

Libby didn't open her mouth. It was so dry she couldn't say anything anyway. And then it became impossible.

He looked right at her and stopped dead. The boy behind him careened right into him.

"Omigod," Marilyn whispered. "Libby, he's looking at you. Do you see him?"

She wanted to tell her friend that she couldn't see anything but him, but her voice was still gone.

His friends followed his stare and started to tease him and shove him about. A few wolf whistles rang out. He suddenly turned around and told them to knock it off. They gave him a hard time, so he went right past her and up into the stands to put on his skates.

Marilyn told her to hurry up and get out on the ice, but Libby needed to get away from them for a minute. She had to think. The girls' bathroom seemed like a safe haven, but walking towards it, she was aware of him watching her every move out of the corner of his eye. When she looked in the bathroom mirror and saw her cheeks were blood red, she splashed cold water on her face and patted it dry with a paper towel.

Libby felt lightheaded and it threw her for a loop, but she knew exactly why that was. This was desire. She'd never felt it before, but she knew from romance books that this is what happened when you fell in love.

She couldn't stay in the bathroom all afternoon, but she was almost afraid to go back out. What if she was mistaken? What if he ignored her? How on earth would she get through life without this boy she'd never even met?

He was skating when she reappeared. She decided the best course of action was to ignore him and pretend to have a good time. Stepping onto the ice, Marilyn skated past her and gestured for her to join her, but she couldn't keep up. She wasn't a very good skater.

A group of her girlfriends came by and one of them grabbed her hand. "Hang on!" Libby found herself at the end of a line that was going to whip around and then let go. She let out a yelp and tried to stay on her skates. She went faster and faster and knew she was going to fall. They released her and she sailed into the boards—or would have if that good-looking boy hadn't stopped her first.

He put his arms around her and lifted her off her feet, going around and around before he stopped.

"Are you okay?"

She nodded.

He grabbed her hand. "Come on."

He took off and pulled her around the ice. He was going too fast for her to skate, so she kept a tight hold on his arm. She felt as if she were flying—through the rink and out beyond the stars. She never wanted it to end.

When he finally slowed down, he took both her hands and started to skate backwards.

"What's your name, little skater?"

"Libby," she laughed.

"Libby."

When he said her name she felt a tingle go through her body. She was aware of Marilyn going by with a big smile on her face, giving her a thumb's up.

He finally said, "Don't you want to know mine?"

"Yes, please."

He laughed out loud. "It's Seamus."

"I like it."

"I want you to love it."

She smiled at him. "Okay then, I love it."

He pulled her to him and kept her hands in his. "And I love yours. So I'll make you a promise, little skater. Tonight, when I'm alone in my room, I'm going to whisper your name before I go to sleep and I'll keep doing it until the day I can whisper it in your ear."

No one had ever talked to her like that before. She stood with her mouth open and tried to think of something wonderful to say too, but she couldn't think. She was aware only of his warm hands.

He gave her the sweetest smile. "Do you want to go round again?"

She suddenly found her voice. "No. I want to kiss you." And she reached up and put her arms around his neck. Her mouth found his and she tasted his Juicy Fruit gum.

✺

"Libby, I love you."

She was suffocating. He held her by the door and over the desk and in the stairwell. She wanted to run but she couldn't and now there was rain pounding against the roof. It was dark and she was frightened, so very, very frightened. The rain got louder and louder and suddenly lightning flashed and in that split second, she saw him.

She screamed.

She screamed when Lola crashed through the door into her room, brandishing a shoe.

"I've got a gun," she yelled. "Where is he?"

Ava sat straight up in bed and then realized she had nothing on. She gathered the sheet in front of her. "My god, who's here?"

"You tell me. The way you were yelling, I thought you were being ravished!"

She ran her fingers through her knotted hair. "You scared me half to death."

Lola threw the shoe away and plunked herself on the bed. "You were screaming like a banshee, so what was I supposed to do? Did you have a nightmare?"

"I guess I must have. I don't remember."

Lola yawned. "Well, you can just bet some little chamber maid will say you had an orgy in here and it will be front page news by tonight."

"Naturally. Pass me that bathrobe, would you?"

Lola stretched over the bed and grabbed it off the floor. Ava put it on and then lay across the bed on her side, holding her head in her hand. "Sorry about last night."

"No biggy," Lola shrugged. "You had a pretty emotional day."

"I never realized it would be so hard. I thought family reunions were happy occasions."

"I'm sure they are, but they are also a cesspool of memories, good and bad." Lola got off the bed and went to the window. "Looks like a nice day out there."

"Are you sure you want to stay with me? Wouldn't you rather be on Rodeo Drive buying some fabulous outfit?"

Lola jumped back on the bed. "Hell no, this is fun. I love your family. What a bunch of characters."

"But to stay there…"

"You say that like it was some flea-bitten motel. I'm dying to eat Aunt Vi's cooking. What a treat."

"I suppose so," Ava sighed. "I've got to stop being selfish and do my share. I'm sure Aunt Vi could use the break from running up and down stairs all day."

Lola patted her arm. "Today will be better. I think it was nerves yesterday. Let's face it; it must have been hard to see your mom."

"You have no idea. I felt so guilty!"

"Guilt is stupid. I hate guilt. I've decided to declare myself a guilt-free zone. Who's with me?"

Ava jumped up and hugged her friend. "That's why I love you. No one can be sad around you."

They ordered room service and ate way too much, then showered, dressed, and made arrangements to rent a car. One could hardly sneak around town in a limo. They packed their bags and were on their way by noon.

Ava felt decidedly better after coming to the conclusion that if she had to be here, she might as well enjoy herself. She'd missed enough time with her family already.

But first things first. Lola wanted to pick up something for Aunt Vi. "I could buy dinner rolls."

"She'll have made them already."

"How do you know?"

"I know."

"But she has your mom to look after too."

"Doesn't matter."

"Okay then," Lola sighed. "What do you suggest?"

"Well, you can't buy baking, because as you know it will be a pale imitation of hers. You can't buy pickles or chow because she'll have tons of it in the pantry. You can't buy jams or jellies."

"Okay then, how about wine?"

"They don't drink wine."

"They don't drink?"

"I didn't say that. Uncle Angus likes a drink of rum and Aunt Vi loves beer."

"All right. Let's load them up with some booze."

"Okay."

Off they went to the liquor store. Ava put on her sunglasses and tucked her hair up in a scarf. When they got in there, they bought enough liquor to keep the family going for months. The old fella in the line-up behind them shook his head. "How ya go about gettin' an invite to this here party?"

"I'll have my people call your people," Lola said.

"Huh?"

Ava told her to behave. They had a young clerk help them to the car with their purchases. Ava handed him a twenty-dollar tip.

He looked at it for a moment. "You made a mistake."

"No mistake. Thank you."

"Thanks!" He walked away with a big smile on his face.

"No one would ever question a tip in L.A., no matter how big it was," Lola smirked.

"People are honest here."

"Amazing. It's like another world."

"I know. I'd forgotten that."

They enjoyed their ride to Aunt Vi's. Lola couldn't get over the cars stopping for pedestrians or letting other cars in ahead of them. "I'm in a time warp," she declared.

Just then a funeral procession came towards them from down the street. Ava pulled off the road with the other cars. Two men out for a walk stopped and took off their ball caps until the hearse and the family cars went by.

Lola's mouth dropped open. She was speechless.

Ava smiled at her. "Welcome to civilization."

❀

Aunt Vi's roast chicken dinner was one for the books, in Lola's opinion. Once it was over Ava was sent upstairs to give her mother a cup of tea. The rest of them stayed downstairs and helped with the dishes.

Ava propped her mom up a little and put the china teacup to her lips. "It's hot, be careful."

Mamie nodded and took a sip, then laid her head back onto the pillow. "Nothing like a cup of tea. Your father always loved a good cuppa."

Ava smiled at the memory. "I remember he used to let me put in the sugar."

"Did he? I'd forgotten."

Ava sat a little further in on the bed and hugged her knees. "How did you and Daddy meet?"

"Oh goodness, it's so long ago now. He was my older brother's friend. He used to hang around our house all the time. I remember I always liked him, until the day he threw a snowball at me."

"He must have liked you a lot," Ava laughed.

"I was mad. I flew off home and wouldn't speak to him for days."

"You old meanie."

"You're darn right. Don't ever let a man think he's got ya for good. Always keep him guessing. Do you have a man?"

Ava shook her head. "No, no one special."

"Good lord, child, you're twenty-eight. You better get moving. I had five children by the time I was your age. Don't you want babies?"

Ava shrugged. "I never really thought about it. I've been so busy."

"Well, one day you won't be and you'll look around and wonder what it was all for."

Ava didn't answer, just picked at her thumbnail instead. She knew her mother was looking at her and it was unnerving, as if she was transparent and her mother was privy to everything under her skin. Ava turned the tables on her.

"Did you like being a mother?"

"Of course I did," her mother frowned. "Why?"

"No reason." Ava continued to pick at her fingers.

"Are you happy in Hollywood? Is that the lifestyle you want?"

"It's okay. I know it's artificial."

"What happens when you get wrinkles and your bosom sags?"

"Ma!"

"Well, you have to think of these things. It seems to me they only want them young and pretty, and then it's out with the trash."

"I have a few years left before that happens."

"It happens in the blink of an eye, my girl."

Ava's cell phone rang. "Oh, sorry Ma." She got off the bed and held the small device to her ear. "Hello?"

"Who's the sexiest girl in the world, then?"

She smiled. "Hayden."

"Is that all I get? No, 'Gosh I miss your body Hayden' or 'Come right now and do me, please, Hayden, please.'"

She turned away from her mother and covered her mouth with her hand. "Stop it."

"Oh, I can't stop. I don't wanna stop. Don't stop Hayden, don't stop!"

"I'm going to kill you," she whispered.

"Not before I take you to bed, sugar lump."

In spite of herself, Ava wanted him to go on. It was a silly game, but it cheered her up.

"I'd like that."

"You would? How about that? Usually I have to beg. So when are you and your delicious body coming home?"

"I'm not sure."

"Oh come on, sexy baby, you can't leave me like this. I may have to call room service and have them send someone up."

"Well, I'm not coming tonight, so I guess you'd better."

"No, you're not, are you?"

Ava turned around. "Excuse me, Ma. I'll be right back." She closed the bedroom door behind her and stood in the hallway. "You can't talk like that in front of my mother."

"I'm not talking to your mother. I'm breathing in your ear, sexy girl. But I have a good idea. Why don't you call me when you go to bed and we can have a nice little private session?"

"I'm sleeping with Lola tonight."

"You are? I always wondered about you two."

"Stop it, you nut. We're sleeping in the same room because we're staying at my old house."

"Do you have three-way calling?"

"Hayden, you are completely immoral."

"I know. Isn't it fun? Well, if you're going to be a party pooper, maybe I can fly in, shag you, and go home. How does that sound?"

"Good, actually," Ava sighed.

"Done."

"Sorry, I can't. You know that."

"I'll sneak in. No one will know."

She laughed out loud. "No one will know? The hottest star in television? Believe it or not, babe, they do watch TV up here."

"I'll wear a fake nose and mustache. Come on Ava, I'm dyin' here. You've been gone for two days."

"My mother…"

"Yeah, yeah, I know. Your mother's dying. Well, tell her to hurry up…I'm sorry, I'm sorry. I didn't mean that."

"You stupid bastard."

"Come on Ava, I was joking."

"It's not funny."

"I know."

"Goodbye Hayden."

"Don't hang up! I need you."

Ava fired the phone down the stairs, marched into the bathroom and promptly threw up. Then she washed her face, brushed her teeth, and went back to her mother, who was asleep. She sat on the edge of the bed and held her hand until Rose peeked in and said they were leaving, so she got up and said goodbye to her siblings. After telling her aunt and uncle that she was really tired, she kissed them and went upstairs to bed. Lola said she'd be up in a minute.

Ava rooted through her suitcase to get her nightie. The first one she picked up was one Hayden bought for her. She went to the window and threw it out into the night. The rest of them all looked too flimsy, too see-through or too short, so out they went as well. She opened the closet and found an old, soft, worn flannelette nightgown. She threw it over her head and crawled into the creaky twin bed. Lying there, listening to Lola and her aunt and uncle downstairs, was like being a kid again. Suddenly she wasn't tired anymore.

Ava popped out of bed and snuck over to the door, tiptoeing down the hall to peer into the hall grate, where she saw Uncle Angus's bald head rocking back and forth. She wondered if she could get downstairs without making the stairs creak, like she used to. Taking her time, she gingerly stepped on various spots down the stair treads and was amused that she remembered exactly where to place her toes. She was so busy congratulating herself that she didn't hear the others say they should hit the hay. They almost caught her as they came through the kitchen.

Lola found her with the blankets up to her nose. She tossed the cell phone on the bed. "You dropped something. From a great height, I might add."

Ava kicked it off the bed with her foot. "I hate it."

Lola rummaged through her suitcase. "What did that poor old phone ever do to you?"

"Hayden was on the other end of it."

"Ah, the boy wonder. How is the spoiled brat?"

Ava turned over on her side. "He wants my mother to hurry up and die so I can go home and screw him."

Lola stopped in mid-search and turned to face her. "Tell me you're kidding."

Ava shook her head.

"Shall I hire a hit man?"

"Yes."

"I'll get right on it." She went back to her rooting. "I wish I'd brought more practical clothes. I feel like a bit of a freak."

Ava pointed to her nightgown. "See. I found this in the closet. I love flannelette. Why did I ever stop wearing it?"

"Because your image would suffer, my dear."

"Who cares?"

"Your accountant, your lawyer, your studio, your staff..."

"Bullocks."

There was a knock on the door and Aunt Vi poked her head in. "You girls have everything you need?"

"You don't have another nightgown like Ava is wearing, do you?"

"That old rag! My drawers are full of them. I'll go get you one." She disappeared and in a flash was back with three suitable choices. "This here one is the smallest I've got. You'll swim in it." She passed it to Lola.

"I love it, it's perfect." Lola gathered her bag of toiletries, took the nightgown and headed for the bathroom. Aunt Vi sat on the end of Ava's bed.

"Are you all right, my love? You look pale. I'm afraid this

is going to be too much for you. You never were a strong girl."

Ava got up and sat cross-legged on the bed. "I'm fine. You worry too much."

"It's a hard, hard thing, to lose your mother. A once in a lifetime event. Doesn't matter how close you are, or how much time you've spent together, it's the end of a connection that will never be replaced."

Ava swallowed hard. "What was my grandmother like?"

Aunt Vi picked at her bathrobe sash. "She was a stern woman, a very hard worker. She had your Ma and me well trained by the time we were married."

"Was she fun?"

"Fun? No. Mothers were teachers in my day. They weren't your best friend, like they are today."

"Didn't you ever wish she could be your best friend?"

"No, not really. I had your Ma and she was enough."

"You're going to miss her," Ava whispered. "Probably more than I will."

Aunt Vi reached for a tissue in her pocket and wiped the end of her nose. "Yes, I daresay that's true. I was always closer to her than my older brother. You know how sisters are. You're lucky to have three of them."

"I don't know them very well."

"That can change, honey. You don't always have to be the outsider. You can let them in anytime you choose."

Ava nodded and looked up at Lola, who stood in the doorway. "Ta da!" Lola twirled around to show off her faded pink flowered nightgown. "This is so comfortable. I wonder if we can get Vera Wang to start selling these things. She'd make a fortune."

"Vera who?" Aunt Vi asked.

"A designer. She's famous for her wedding gowns, but she makes everything now."

Aunt Vi pointed to Ava. "Well, tell this one to make an appointment with this Wang woman real soon. Libby is on the verge of being an old maid." She patted Ava's leg affectionately. "Love ya anyway." She got up and gave Lola a quick squeeze on her way out the door. "Have a good sleep, girls."

"Aunt Vi, if Ma wakes up, I can go to her. You should get some sleep while you can."

"That's real nice of ya, honey. We'll take turns. Good night."

"Good night," Ava and Lola said together.

As it turned out, Ava was up three times that night with her mother, but it didn't matter, since she wasn't sleeping anyway. She didn't have the heart to wake up the snoring Aunt Vi. She'd probably get heck for it in the morning, but Ava knew her aunt needed the rest. Besides, her mother seemed to take comfort from her presence, and that was a good feeling.

She went back to bed for the last time just before dawn and woke around eight o'clock. Lola's bed was empty. Ava looked in on her mother and went downstairs. Aunt Vi had Lola up to her armpits in bread dough.

"Look Ava, I'm making bread!"

"Will wonders never cease? Let me get my camera." She raced back upstairs and came down with her small digital camera. She pointed it at Lola. "Say cheese."

Lola gave her a big grin, "Cheese and bread!"

"She's a natural, I can tell," Aunt Vi laughed.

"How so?" Lola asked.

"You've got strong hands. I'm afraid Libby here would be useless."

Ava looked at her hands. "Hey, according to this family, I'm useless at everything."

Aunt Vi hugged her. "Don't mind us. Come and get a cup of tea. You've had a long night, you little scamp. I told you to wake me."

"That's okay, it was no trouble." Ava sat at the kitchen table and looked out the window. The woman next door was in her living room window with a pair of binoculars trained at the house. "Good grief, is that Geranium?" She waved. Geranium waved back.

Aunt Vi put a plate of hot biscuits and homemade jam in front of her. "The very same."

"She never changes."

"Are you talking about a plant or a person?" Lola asked as she kneaded the bread.

"A person."

"That's her name?"

Aunt Vi laughed. "No, my darlin'. She's called Geranium because she's always in the window."

Ava cut her biscuit in half and slathered butter on top. "Everyone has a nickname around here. Isn't that so, Aunt Vi?"

"Oh gosh yes, couldn't do without them."

"Like what?" Lola said.

"Angus had a friend who was always scratchin' his bum. They called him Archie Itchy Arse."

Lola gave a shout of laughter. "No way!"

Ava took a bite of her biscuit. "Oh yeah. I love the guy who was really religious. The other miners called him Pope, so his son became known as Little Pope and his grandson was Poop. It's a science. Someone who's bald is called Curly, someone who's tall is called Stump."

Aunt Vi poured her own cup of tea. "Then there are names for the whole clan, like the Biscuit Foot MacKinnons and the Bore Hole Macdonalds."

"Stop! I can't breath," Lola gasped.

They took to giggling. The back door opened and in walked Uncle Angus. "Look what I found on the lawn." He held up Ava's nighties. "Can't for the life of me figure out what they're doin' in the rose bushes."

"They're my nighties, Uncle Angus."

"Nighties! They look like hankies."

"Exactly. That's why I threw them away. Fire them in the coal stove."

Aunt Vi grabbed them. "You'll do no such thing. If you don't want them any more, give them to your sisters or your nieces. They'd love them."

"You're right. Sorry, I should've thought of that."

Uncle Angus went to the sink for a glass of water. "It's a fine winter day out there. No snow on the roads. I think I'll take a run up to Sobey's. Anything you need at the store, Vi?"

"Oh dear, lots of things."

"Why don't you go with him, Aunt Vi?" Ava said with her mouth full. "You probably never get out of this house. Lola and I will hold down the fort for a few hours."

"Oh my, I'm not sure," Aunt Vi hesitated. "What if your mother wants something? And the nurse is coming by in an hour."

"I'll get whatever Ma needs and I'll be here when the nurse comes. I'd like to talk to her anyway. If it makes you feel better, why don't you take my cell phone and I can call you if something comes up. That's if it's still working."

Aunt Vi took off her apron. "Okay then, I don't see why not. I'll just be a minute, Angus."

Ava followed her aunt upstairs and picked the cell phone up off the floor. She flipped it open, and lo and behold it was still functional. She gave it to her aunt, but not before slipping three one hundred dollar bills in her hand. "Please take this. We can't be eating you out of house and home."

"You eat like a bird."

"Please. Don't make a fuss, just take it."

Her aunt took it. "Thank you, dear. I don't mind tellin' ya, it comes in handy."

❋

Vi and Angus left the house, feeling a bit guilty that they had some free time together but enjoying it all the same. Of course they didn't get too far up the first aisle in the grocery store before someone beetled over to talk about Ava.

"Is she as pretty in real life as she is on the screen?" Tootsie Wadden wanted to know.

"She's prettier," Angus said loyally.

"Oh my," Tootsie squealed. "Do you think she'd mind if I came over to say hello?"

"She might not, but I do," Vi said. "My sister is ill and needs her rest. We don't need the likes of you showin' up."

Tootsie stomped off.

Then there was Ethel Snow. "I'm bringing round a mess of cod tongues for your dinner. Will Ava be there?"

"You've never brought a mess of anything round to our house, Ethel. I wonder why you'd pick now, eh?"

"Bein' neighbourly."

"Go way with ya. I don't have time for you or your tongues." This time it was Vi who marched off. There was nothing for Angus to do but tip his ball cap. "Ethel." He hurried after his wife.

At the check-out counter, Ava's picture was on the front of the TV Guide. Angus picked it up. "We should buy this."

"Suit yourself."

The cashier rang it in. "Isn't she your niece?"

Vi nodded proudly. "That she is."

"Wow. Can you tell her I'm her biggest fan? I've seen like every movie she's ever made at least three times."

"I will, dear. What's your name?"

"It's Debbie."

"I'll tell her, Debbie."

"Thank you. Oh, this is so exciting."

"This here's her money. She gave it to me this morning." Vi passed over the bills.

"It is? Oh my gosh." Debbie stroked the bills. "My hand is touching where she touched. I'm so lucky!"

"Calm down, dearie. It's dirty old money."

"No it isn't," Debbie sighed. "It's her money."

Vi and Angus walked out of the store and put the groceries in the back of their truck. Angus settled behind the wheel. "That young girl is a lunatic."

"We live in a nutty world, that's for sure."

"Let's go get a Tim's and a Boston cream doughnut before we go home. I could do with some warming up."

"Okay," Vi said happily.

On the way to get their coffee the cell phone rang. Vi fumbled for it in her purse. "Oh gosh, I hope nothing's wrong at home. How on earth do you open this thing?"

"I believe it unfolds, at least that's what I saw on a commercial once."

Vi opened it. "Hello?"

"Don't hang up! I love you and I miss you like crazy. You have to forgive me, okay?"

"Who is this?"

"Who's this?"

"Vi."

"Vi who?"

"Who are you?"

"Hayden. Is Ava there?"

"No, she isn't."

"Why do you have her phone, then? Is she okay?"

"Of course she's okay. I'm her aunt. Now tell me who you are."

"I'm her boyfriend."

"That so? She never mentioned a boyfriend."

"Didn't she?"

"No."

"Well, she has one and I'm it. I'm trying to get in touch with her. I said something really stupid last night and I want her to forgive me. Will you please tell her I called?"

"I'll tell her, but if you really want a woman to forgive you, you should send her flowers."

"That's a great idea. Do you have an address?"

"I'll give it to you." She told him.

"Thank you. I appreciate your help, Vi. I hope I get to meet you one day."

"Well, you just never know, do you? Gotta go. Bye."

She closed the phone. "That was Libby's boyfriend."

"I didn't know she had one."

"Can't be too serious. She never mentioned him."

Naturally, at the coffee shop they ran into about six people they knew and had a great gab, everyone asking about Ava Harris. Aunt Vi bragged about her niece and felt very important.

And then it was time to go. They climbed back into the truck and stopped at the entrance to wait for traffic to go by. It was a busy intersection and Uncle Angus had to swivel his head back and forth to see who was coming. Aunt Vi gave him the all clear on her side and he revved the truck forward. He never saw the car speeding through the red light until it was too late.

CHAPTER FIVE

The phone rang. Ava was washing the dishes, so she grabbed a dish towel to dry her hands and walked over to the phone.

"Yes, hello?"

"Ah, yes. This is Constable Murrant with the Regional Police Department. Does an Angus or Vi MacIntosh live there?"

Ava's mouth went dry. "Yes, is something wrong?"

"I'm sorry to have to tell you this, but there's been an accident."

"An accident?" Ava whispered. "What do you mean?"

Lola got up from the kitchen table and came over to stand beside her.

"There was a car accident. Are you a relative?"

"Yes, yes, I'm their niece. Please tell me, are they all right?"

"They've been taken to the Regional Hospital."

"Oh, my god. Are they badly hurt?"

"They do have injuries. Do you have someone who can take you to the hospital?"

"Yes, yes. I'll go right now."

"We'll be in touch about the accident report. Charges may be laid. A teenage boy ran a red light. It wasn't your uncle's fault."

"Oh, no. Thank you for calling."

"It's a tough situation. I'm sorry."

"Yes. Goodbye."

Ava hung up and grabbed Lola. "Oh my god, Aunt Vi and Uncle Angus are in the hospital. There's been a car accident!"

Lola hugged her tight to keep her from shaking. "I'm sure they'll be fine."

"I have to tell Ma."

"No, don't do that yet. Let's find out their condition first. There's no sense in upsetting her until we know all the facts."

Ava put her hand to her forehead, trying to think clearly. "Yes, yes, you're right. What do I do?"

Lola picked up the address book that was by the phone. "Call your sister Rose and get her to take you to the hospital. I'll stay here with your mother. The nurse is upstairs now. Don't worry, we'll take good care of her."

Ava hugged Lola again. "What on earth would I do without you?"

"Hey, that's what friends are for."

Ava called her sister at work and Rose came as fast as she could to pick her up. Lola waved them goodbye. "Let me know as soon as you can."

Ava called back, "We will."

Rose zoomed out of the driveway. "What happened?"

"I don't know. The police said a kid ran a red light and crashed into them."

"Oh my god, this is horrible. I can't believe it. It's not fair. They're the sweetest people alive. Why did this have to happen?"

Ava buried her head in her hands. "I told her to go. If only I hadn't done that."

"It's not your fault, Libby. Don't think that." Rose reached into her purse. "Here's my cell phone. Everyone's number is in there. Call as many as you can while I drive."

By the time they reached the hospital, almost all the relatives had been called. Rose parked the car in a no-parking zone and the two of them flew into the lobby and raced to the front desk.

"My aunt and uncle were involved in a car accident. The police said they were sent here, Angus and Viola MacIntosh."

"Just a moment, please." The woman left her desk and went to talk to someone. A few minutes later she came back. "They're still in the emergency department. I'll take you there."

"Thank you."

Rose took Ava by the hand and the two of them walked through several doors, oblivious of the people they passed. There was a bit of a buzz when they went by and someone called out Ava's name, but they kept going. Soon they were in a crowded annex, with the nurses' station in the middle and curtained cubicles surrounding it. There were several rooms off it as well.

The woman who escorted them left them then, saying, "Someone will be with you in a moment."

They nodded and stood there, scared to death and set adrift. They didn't know where to look for help. They watched nurses and doctors go about their business. If one approached them, they went rigid, afraid of what might be said, but they inevitably walked on by. Finally a young doctor with horn-rimmed glasses and a stethoscope around his neck approached them. "I'm Dr. Richardson. Are you the MacIntoshes' relatives?"

"Yes," Rose said. "Please tell me they're all right."

He looked at his chart. "According to the police, they're very lucky it wasn't worse, but it's still considerable trauma for people of their age. Mrs. MacIntosh has a broken ankle and wrist…"

"Oh no."

He continued. "Mr. MacIntosh has a badly broken arm. He'll have to be operated on, as he needs pins to fix it. They both have considerable bruising and Mr. MacIntosh needed several stitches to sew up a nasty gash over his eye. He also has a dislocated knee. All that said, I'm sure they can make a reasonable recovery, as long as they have plenty of help for the next few months."

"Don't you worry about that," Rose said. "There are plenty of us to pitch in."

Ava nodded. "I can stay for as long as necessary."

Rose looked at her. "Are you sure?"

"I don't care. Can we see them now?"

"Only for a minute." The doctor smiled. "They are more concerned about each other. Please assure them they are in good hands."

"Oh, we will."

He escorted Ava and Rose to adjoining rooms. "Remember, only a few moments. They've been through an ordeal."

"Thank you, doctor," Ava said.

They went through the door and pushed back the curtains. Aunt Vi lay still on the bed, her face black and blue, hooked up to an I.V. Her eyes were closed, whether by bruising or by choice, it was hard to tell. They approached quietly.

"Oh dear," Rose moaned. "Her poor face."

Ava took her hand gently in her own. "Aunt Vi, can you hear me?"

She fluttered her eyelids. "Yes."

"I'm sorry," Ava choked. "I should've gone instead."

"Nonsense. How's Angus?"

Rose stroked her hair. "How about I go see and I'll be right back."

"Okay," Vi nodded. "Tell the old coot I love him."

Rose and Ava looked at each other. "I think she's going to be all right," Rose whispered before she tiptoed out of the room. Ava kept Aunt Vi's hand in her own.

"Don't worry now. Everyone will take care of you. I'm going to stay."

Vi shook her head slightly. "No dear. You be here for your Ma, but don't stay on account of me."

"You're more important than anything."

"Silly girl." Vi moaned. "This is mighty sore, I can tell you. And you know the worst part?"

"What?"

"I bought you a box of Timbits, and now they're all over the road."

Ava gave her hand a squeeze. "Timbits make you fat anyway."

"Don't tell your Ma. Not yet."

"She'll have to know soon."

"Well, don't make out it's so bad. Tell her I'll be home in a couple of days."

"You might be here a little longer, but don't worry about Ma, we'll handle her."

Just then Bev, Maryette, and Gerard showed up. They couldn't all come into the room at the same time, so Ava backed out and let them have a turn. Rose met her in the hall.

"Uncle Angus is fine, but he's pretty woozy. I think we better let him be."

Dr. Richardson made another appearance. "I'm afraid we can't have any more visitors. We'll let you know when the surgery is going to be and you can wait in the visitors lounge. After that, they'll be assigned their rooms."

Ava stepped forward. "May I speak to you a moment?"

He nodded and stepped away from the others, but before she could open her mouth, he said under his breath. "I'm sorry, but are you Ava Harris?"

"Yes."

He suddenly stammered as if he were fifteen. "I've seen all your movies."

"Thank you."

"I couldn't get your autograph, could I?"

Ava wanted to spit. "Of course."

He handed her a pen and his prescription pad. "My name is Brian."

"Brian." She took the pen and wrote, 'To Brian, Thank you for everything. Ava Harris.'

She passed it back to him.

"Thanks a lot. My wife will be very excited."

She gave the doctor her professional smile. "I wonder if it would be possible to have my aunt and uncle in the same room. I know it would make them feel much better. I'll pay for it, of course. I'd also like to hire private nurses, to help with their care while they're here. My brothers and sisters have to work and they have families to look after. On top of everything else, my mother is in the final stages of cancer, so everyone has a full plate at the moment."

"I'm sure something can be arranged. I'll contact the administration office and they can help you."

"Thank you."

"My pleasure. If there's anything else you need, I'd be glad to help."

She reached out and shook his hand. "You've been very kind. I appreciate it." She flashed the famous smile again and Dr. Richardson floated away. As soon as he was gone, she frowned and went back to her family.

They spent the whole day at the hospital. When they called home Lola assured them that Mamie was fine, that she'd slept through most of the afternoon. Uncle Angus's surgery was performed and everything went well, so the clan left finally. Their uncle would spend the night in I.C.U. and Aunt Vi was resting in their private room, knocked out on pain killers. A private nurse would be there in the morning.

Rose drove Ava back to the house. They went in together and broke the news to their mother, glossing over the details. Mamie was upset, of course, but they assured her that everything went smoothly and Vi and Angus would be back before she knew it.

After giving their mother her medication and settling her for the night, they finally went downstairs and collapsed into the kitchen chairs.

"I'm pooped," Rose said.

Ava yawned. "Me too."

Lola came out of the pantry with a plateful of homemade bread. "Here. Have some of my specialty. White bread hard enough to break your teeth."

"Can I have a cup of tea with it?" Ava asked. "To wash it down."

"I've already made some." She went to the stove and poured the tea, bringing the mugs back to the table. Rose took her first bite and chewed for a while.

Lola looked at her hopefully. "It's not too bad, is it?"

"No. I've had worse."

"Well, its better than the first batch," Lola sighed. "I put the loaves to rise in the warming oven and they were glorious. They puffed up like magic."

"Can't we have some of that, then?"

Lola shook her head. "Sorry. When I cut them open, there was no bread inside."

"What?"

"It rose really high. It must have used up all the dough."

They started to laugh. It felt good after such a horrible day.

Despite the chewy nature of the bread, Rose and Ava ate two pieces each. They hadn't eaten since breakfast, so it filled the hole in their stomachs.

Rose downed the last of her tea and looked at her sister. "Did you mean it when you said you could stay here?"

Lola gave Ava a surprised look.

Ava nodded. "Of course. I need to make a few phone calls though." She turned to Lola. "Trent will have a fit but I don't care. I know I can't get out of the New York gig, but that doesn't start until the end of August. Do you remember when?"

"You have to be in New York on the twenty-fifth," Lola told her. "But what about the promotional tour for your new movie? That was going to take a couple of months at least, and wasn't there a Broadway play?"

"Promotional tours and Broadway plays can get along without me. There are about five big-time actors in this new release, so for me not to show up on TV talk shows is not a great loss. And the understudy for the play will kiss my boots."

"Trent won't be a happy camper," Lola frowned. "And Camilla will be scrambling."

"Fortunately I'm five thousand miles from her office, so she can scramble away."

"If you do stay here," Rose said, "you'll be worked off your feet."

Ava shrugged. "It's payback time."

"Do you want me to stay too?" Lola asked. "I don't want to be in the way but maybe you could use an extra pair of hands."

"I couldn't let you do that," Ava said. "You've done enough. Go back home and have a vacation. You've earned it, chasing me around 24/7."

"That's okay..."

"No, really. I can't take you away for months. That's ridiculous."

"Well, let me stay for a couple of weeks anyway, until you get your aunt and uncle sorted."

"All right," Ava conceded. "But I need you to do something first. Would you mind going back to Malibu for a few days to pack some of my clothes and sort out the house? Tell Mercedes and the gardener to take a paid holiday. And cancel that decorator, too."

"God, you live in another world, don't you?" Rose said.

"It's not as glamorous as it sounds. People underfoot all day."

"Oh shut up. That is so not true," Rose laughed.

Ava laughed with her. "I know, just thought it would make you feel better."

"Sure, I don't mind going back," Lola said. "I better go now, while Aunt Vi and Uncle Angus are still in the hospital. You'll need more help when they come home."

"It's settled, then."

"Well, that's great," Rose sighed. "Thanks a lot, you two. This will be a big help. Who knows how long Ma can hold out? It's so upsetting."

Ava patted her hand. "Let's get through one day at a time, eh?"

"I must go. I've got to drive Vicky to school tomorrow. She's excited; they're practicing their Grand March routine."

"Vicky is graduating from high school this year?" Ava said. "I can't believe it."

"What's a grand march?" Lola asked.

"All the graduating students gather before the prom and parade around the school gym in formation," Rose explained. "It's set to music, which makes it very festive. It's a chance for the parents to see the kids in their finery. In a small town, most people know all the kids, so it's a lot of fun. Samantha and Emily are graduating too."

"Imagine," Ava sighed. "The prom is such a magical night in a young girl's life."

"It might have been for you," Lola frowned. "Mine was a disaster. The stupid jerk barfed all over my dress."

"Mine was pretty bad too," Rose laughed. "Not yours, Libby. You looked like a princess that night."

"I felt like a princess, too."

"You must have gone with Seamus." Lola quickly covered her mouth with her hand.

Ava looked at her. "How do you know about him?"

"Sorry." Rose looked sheepish. "I told her about him the night you arrived."

Ava stood. "That was none of your business, Rose. Why can't you ever keep your mouth shut?" Then she turned to Lola. "When were you going to ask me about him? Or were you going to pretend you didn't know a thing about it?"

"No one meant any harm. It came up in the conversation."

"Well, stop talking behind my back. I'm going to bed. Good night." Ava walked out of the kitchen. Lola and Rose were left looking at each other.

"God, I'm sorry. I didn't mean to get you in trouble."

Rose waved her away. "She's right; I do have a big mouth. But you know what bothers me? She's way too touchy about Seamus, which leads me to think that she's not over him."

"Maybe," Lola nodded. "She never keeps a guy for long."

"Is there anyone in her life now?"

"She's dating someone but I think she gave him the boot last night."

"Is he famous?"

"Ah...he's a bit of jerk."

"Handsome, I bet."

"Yeah, but he's not that nice."

"You must meet a lot of cool guys because of her."

"They don't look at me when Ava's in the room."

"Doesn't that bug you?"

"No, I'm happy being around her."

Rose stood and grabbed her keys. "Well, enough of this, we better get some sleep."

"You're right." Lola put her hand on Rose's arm. "Please drive home safely."

"Don't worry. I'll crawl home."

Since Lola was the only one downstairs, she locked the back door and put on the outside light, then made sure the stove burners were shut off before she turned out the kitchen lights. Careful not to wake Mamie, she crept up to bed. Ava was pretending to be asleep when she entered the room.

Lola sat on the twin bed. "I'm sorry. I didn't know what to say, so I figured I wouldn't say anything."

Ava didn't answer her.

"Okay. Good night then. If you need any help with your mother during the night, wake me up."

Ava turned over. "I didn't mean to yell at you."

"That's okay."

"No, it's not. I find it hard to talk about him."

"How come you never told me?"

Ava didn't answer at first, so Lola waited. "It was so long ago," she said finally.

Lola took her watch off and put it on the bedside table. "Are you sure about that?"

"What do you mean?"

"It's not like you to fly off the handle about something so trivial."

"Well, it's been a long day, hasn't it? I'm tired." She turned away from her friend. "Good night."

CHAPTER SIX

The March wind blew off the water in a north-easterly direction, which made the air bitterly cold and damp—the kind of wind that went through you not around you, as his mother used to say.

Seamus finally brought the kids inside, because making a snowman isn't much fun when fingers and toes are chilled to the bone. He helped them take off their wet snowsuits and boots in the back porch and said it was Jack's turn to kick their gear downstairs. It was a great game, as long as Seamus remembered to pick the stuff up off the basement floor and throw it in the dryer before he went to bed.

Now he had to think about dinner. The cupboard doors were already open, and they didn't reveal anything appetizing, so he looked in the fridge. That's when Jack held his nose and pointed at his little sister.

"Poohy! Sarah stinks!"

"Yeah!" Sarah confirmed. Her father grabbed her and tucked her under his arm. Jack demanded the same treatment, so all three of them headed for Sarah's room. He dropped Jack on the bed and Sarah on the dressing table.

That's when he heard the back door open.

"It's only me," his sister's voice rang out.

"Hi Colleen, I'm in Sarah's room."

"I've got a pot of spaghetti sauce. I'll put it on the stove."

Seamus smiled at his baby girl as he changed her diaper.

"Aunt Colleen made you some pisgetti."

Sarah clapped her hands. "Yum."

Jack jumped up and down on his sister's bed. "I don't want pisgetti."

"It's good," his father informed him. "Better than mine."

Jack nodded. "Yeah, yours is poohy."

"Hey mister…"

Colleen poked her head in the door. "Hi guys. Where's my hug?"

Jack bounced off the bed and straight into his aunt's arms. "Have you got a treat?"

"Don't I always?" She reached into her coat pocket and pulled out a small Caramel bar.

"Oh boy. Thank you." Jack ran off with it.

"Wait until after supper," his dad yelled after him, knowing it was a lost cause.

Sarah held her hands in the air. "Mine?"

Colleen poked her niece's belly button. "I've got one for you too, don't worry."

Seamus picked Sarah up and put her on the floor. Her aunt placed the treat in her hands.

"Tanks." She ran after her brother.

Colleen leaned in the doorway. "You look tired."

"Sarah was up a couple of times last night. I think she's coming down with a cold."

"Have you got stuff in? Cough syrup and the like?"

He rolled his eyes. "I'm not stupid, you know." He picked up the dirty diaper and walked into the kitchen with it, lobbing it into the garbage can like a basketball player. "Yes! Three points."

"You should empty that thing a little more often."

"Nah," he grinned at her. "The cat would starve."

"You're hopeless." She sat at his kitchen table, still covered with the breakfast dishes. "I have to go in a minute. Just wondering if you want me to take the kids tomorrow. Are you on night shift?"

He removed the lid from the saucepan and smelled the sauce. "No. I'm home."

"Okay. By the way, I went to see Dad today."

He put the lid back and went to the fridge for a Coke. "Want one?"

"No. Did you hear me?"

"Yeah, I heard ya."

"Don't you want to know how he is?"

Seamus twirled the kitchen chair around and straddled it. Then he picked the tab of the Coke can and pulled it back. "I know how he is. Drunk."

"He wasn't, actually."

Seamus downed a half a can before he spoke. "Well, that is news."

Colleen rubbed her forehead. "I hate being the go-between."

He looked at his sister. She seemed tired as well. "I'm sorry, Coll. But you can't change him and I don't know why you try."

"Because he's the grandfather of your children, even if you don't like to admit he's your father."

"He's been drinkin' his whole life and now that Mom's dead, he's trying to kill himself with it. If that's what he wants, you should leave him alone."

"He's weak," Colleen sighed. "He feels bad about it."

"Not bad enough to quit."

"Okay, I'll shut up." She got out of the chair.

"Sit for a minute, don't run off."

She sat. "What?"

"How was your day, anyway?"

Colleen brushed her hair back with her fingers. "Lousy. I had a fight with Dave before I went to work, the kids were cranky and then, to top it off, I saw a horrible accident by Tim Horton's in Reserve Mines on my lunch hour."

"Jesus. Was everyone okay?"

"No, an elderly couple was taken away by ambulance."

"Do you know who they were?"

She looked down and shrugged. "I'm not sure."

It was the look on her face that alerted him that something wasn't quite right. "You know who it was."

"It doesn't matter."

"Why are you keeping it from me? What difference does it make?"

She crossed her arms in front of her. "It was Angus and Vi MacIntosh, if you must know."

Her family. He downed the rest of his Coke. "I hope they're not badly hurt."

"So do I. They have enough to contend with, what with Mamie on her deathbed."

He got up and went to the sink, rinsed out his can and looked out the window. A full minute went by. Neither of them spoke. Eventually his sister said, "I didn't know whether to tell you or not, but you might as well know. She's in town."

His throat seized and suddenly he had to remind himself how to breathe. He tried to keep his wits about him, because he knew Colleen was watching his reaction. A shiver crawled along his spine. He turned around. "Is that so?"

"I didn't want you to run into her on the street and be surprised."

He grunted. "Does she walk on the street like the rest of us? I assume she's chauffeured wherever she needs to go."

"I have no idea."

"Don't worry, I won't run into her."

"Well, I hope I do," Colleen frowned. "I'd love to tear a strip off her."

"She's not worth it. Leave it alone."

"No, Seamus. One of these days I'm going to tell her exactly what I think of her, whether you like it or not."

He held his hands up in front of him. "Okay, okay, Sis. Down girl."

She smiled and got up again. "I have to go. Call me if you need anything." She walked over and gave him a quick kiss. "Go to bed early. Try and get some rest."

He nodded. "Same goes for you."

"Bye, kids," she hollered.

They hollered back, "Bye!"

Seamus fed Jack and Sarah, gave them their baths, read them a story, and kissed them good night. He did the dishes and put the snow suits in the dryer before he locked up for the night. After a hot shower, he crawled into bed. Only then did he let himself think of her.

She was here. Only twenty minutes away.

He put his hands behind his head and stared out the window at the night sky before he reached over and picked up Sally's picture, kissed it and put it in the bedside table drawer.

Returning to his memories, he went to his favourite—the night of the prom. When Libby came down the stairs into the kitchen, he thought he'd burst with love for her. She was the most beautiful girl he'd ever laid eyes on. Her dress was simple and she wore her hair long, unlike most of her friends. When they got to the dance, he was aware of guys looking at her, but she only had eyes for him. He wondered what he'd ever done to deserve her.

Everyone headed for Mira to party at some of the bungalows there. They went along, but soon got bored with the drinking and carrying on. It was a beautiful moonlit night, so he took her by the hand and they walked along the beach.

She ran through the surf in her bare feet, holding up her gown. "You can't catch me."

Of course he did, as she knew he would. He carried her up through the dunes, laid her down on the edge of the field, and got down beside her. She reached up and put her hands through his hair.

"This grass is full of wild strawberries. Can you smell them?"

He nodded.

"I love wild strawberries," she whispered. "Almost as much as I love you."

He kissed her then. All he could remember afterwards was how soft her skin was, how sweet her mouth was, how stars and strawberries and the saltwater breeze made him drunk with desire. His breathing became ragged and he groaned with the wanting of her, but before he could fall over into that heavenly darkness, she stopped it.

"No. Not here."

He wanted to scream with frustration. "Why? I love you, Libby."

She held his face in her hands. "I know that, Seamus. But not like this. This beach is probably crawling with drunken fools doing it with anybody who'll let them. We deserve better."

And in spite of his protesting body, he knew she was right. She was better than this. And she was worth waiting for. He gave her one last kiss, then stood and pulled her up into his arms. They held each other at the edge of that beach for a long time. It was the best moment of his life.

Suddenly in need of air, Seamus got up off the bed and grabbed a sweatshirt, pulling it over his head as he walked out the front door and onto the deck. It was quiet in the frosty air, the wind finally let up. He heard the waves lap on shore. The moon shone down on the beach where she ran, her hair cascading down her back. He could actually see her. He rubbed his eyes; sure that he was going crazy. Then he heard her magical laugh as she ran through the surf.

"No. Please go. Please."

He opened his eyes. She was gone.

He was up with Sarah twice that night before he caved in and took her to bed with him. He lay propped up with her on his chest. She snuggled in and was comforted, her stuffy nose causing her to snore against his skin. Kissing the top of her head, he eventually closed his eyes.

In the morning, he found Jack sprawled on the bed beside him. He got the two of them ready for daycare and was out the door by eight o'clock. When he dropped them off, he handed one of the caregivers a bottle of Sarah's medicine. "If she gets too stuffed up, you can give her some of that."

"Oh, don't worry about Sarah, we'll take good care of her." She batted her eyes at him. Some of the women dropping their kids off seemed to do that too. Apparently there was something sexy about a man bringing up two small children on his own. They'd twitter at his attempts to control Sarah's unruly hair, or tease him about Jack's mismatched socks.

His friend told him it wasn't the kids. "It's the uniform, you big goof." Roger had a theory for everything. "Women love authority figures. The gun and the handcuffs are a big turn on too."

"You are so full of shit."

"Hey, I get laid quite frequently."

"You're married, you jerk."

"Oh yeah."

Seamus went out on patrol and had a pretty ordinary day—a couple of speeding tickets, two fender benders, someone caught shoplifting and a ton of paperwork in between. The final call was about a drunk woman staggering up George Street. There weren't many people he didn't know, being raised in this neck of the woods, so he hoped the woman wasn't anyone he was acquainted with. It was always an uncomfortable situation when he had to deal with someone he knew.

At George Street, he stopped the patrol car and got out. He approached the intoxicated woman—sure enough, it was a girl he'd gone to school with.

"June."

She turned and threw her hands up in the air. "Oh boy," she slurred, "this is my lucky day. How the hell's it goin', Seamus?"

"Pretty good. I think you better come along with me. We need to sober you up."

She shook her head and wagged her finger in his face. "No, dearie. We don't need to. I feel just fine." With that she turned away from him and started to weave down the sidewalk. A couple walked by, giving her a look.

"Whatcha lookin' at, ya goddamn goody two-shoes?"

They hurried away, as he walked over to her and grabbed her by the arm. "Come with me, June."

She struggled at first, but ultimately relented. "Aw, Geez. You always were a tightass."

Smiling, he lowered her head while settling her into the back seat of the car. He shut the door and got into the front seat. "I'm taking you to the lockup. You can sleep it off there."

She gave him a wicked grin. "Are you sleepin' with me?"

"Not today."

"Shit. You always were stuck up."

"I'm a stuck-up tight ass. Anything else?"

"Yeah. You're still fuckin' gorgeous."

He laughed out loud. "You were a babe in high school. Get off the booze and you could be again."

She dismissed him with her hand. "Nah, you broke my heart. I got nothin' to live for." She cracked herself up with that observation and he laughed again.

June was quiet for a moment as she looked out the window.

He thought she'd fallen asleep, but she suddenly blurted, "She's here, ya know."

His stomach went tight because he knew what she meant. He didn't answer, and June went right on talking. "Yeah, I saw her at the airport. A couple of us went down to sneak a peek. She's still friggin' beautiful, the stupid bitch. Of course, she's stuck up too, just hurried past us without a glance, like we was dog shit. Gets in her big fancy car. You should've saw the plane she was on. Right out of the movies, it was. Stupid bitch."

Seamus was aware that his jaw was clenched. He needed to stop reacting every time someone mentioned her.

"How come she dumped ya, anyway?"

He kept his mouth shut.

"Well, I think she used ya. She was sleeping with everyone in town, you just didn't know it. My brother had her, said she was great."

He slammed on the brakes and turned around to face her. "Shut your mouth this instant or I swear, I'll make sure you get jail time."

Her eyes widened. "Geez, I'm only saying what everyone else said. It was no big secret."

He pointed his finger at her. "I'm warning you."

She folded her arms. "Fuckin' cops." She kept quiet though.

He took her to the station and was glad to be able to dump her there. His head was pounding so he bummed a couple of Tylenol from one of the clerks. She looked at him.

"You don't look good."

"I'm okay. Just a headache."

"Darn. I was going to ask you if you wanted to get something to eat later."

"Thanks, but I've got to get home."

She looked resigned. "I knew you'd say that. Oh, by the way, can you give this accident report to Roger. It's the one from yesterday, near Reserve Mines."

Seamus couldn't get away from her or her family. "Sure." He picked up the report and tossed it on Roger's desk as he passed by, then got undressed in the locker room and stashed his uniform. Out to the car, he turned the ignition and headed for the daycare centre. Pulling up to the front of the house, with its crayon shutters and its alphabet fence, Seamus noticed another dad arriving to pick up his kids. He looked familiar, but Seamus couldn't recall the man's name. He thought he might have been on one of his hockey teams at school.

"Hey man, how are ya?"

Seamus nodded his head. "Good."

"I didn't know your kids were here."

He shrugged. "There aren't too many daycare centres around."

His friend chuckled. "True. So what's new?"

"Nothin' much."

They approached the front door. The guy said, "Hey, did you hear Libby's back in town? Or Ava, I should say."

Why did everyone keep mentioning her?

"Yeah, I heard."

"You were lucky, man. Can't imagine having her."

Moron, thought Seamus, as he went through the door and escaped into the confusion of the front porch, with parents and staff trying to get children into their jackets to go home.

Jack came running up to him. "Hi Daddy, I made a monster." He held up a lump of clay.

"Scary. Where's your sister?"

He pointed. "She's in there."

Seamus went into the main room and looked around, unable to locate Sarah at first. A small flutter of unease settled on him for a second, but suddenly the sun came out because there she was, her hair in an untidy mess of curls. She sat at a small table with a pot of paint, brushing the paper with large swipes.

"Sarah. Come on, baby."

She turned and her face lit up. "Daddy, look." She ran over with the soggy piece of paper and handed it to him. "See."

He knelt down and looked at it. "It's beautiful." He picked her up and she waved the wet picture about. "It's a doggy."

"Good." He went back into the porch. "Come on, Jack."

"I'm coming." He and the monster ran up and followed him out the door.

The moron from high school was still in the porch. "Nice seein' ya, Seamus."

"Yeah, you too."

Thinking the exchange was over, Seamus moved to pass, but the man opened his mouth again. Seamus stiffened, bracing himself for another comment about Libby.

"By the way, I was sorry to hear about your wife. A damn shame."

This caught him off guard. "Oh, yes. Thanks."

"Your little girl looks like her."

Seamus wanted to get out of there. "Yes, she does. See ya." He practically ran down the stairs and over to the car. He put the kids in their car seats and got behind the wheel. His head was still throbbing, despite the painkillers. He rested it against the steering wheel for a moment.

"Are you okay, Daddy?" Jack asked.

He lifted his head. "Yeah, buddy. I'm okay."

"Can we go to Burger King?"

"Sure."

He knew Colleen thought he fed his children too much junk food, but he didn't have the energy to peel carrots and potatoes tonight, so he herded them into the restaurant, bought them their chicken nuggets and fries, and ordered a cheeseburger for himself. They sat at a table near the windows and Jack told him about his day. Sarah nodded a lot and said "Yeah" every few minutes. She spilled her milk and then her dipping sauce. Her nose was runny and her face was dirty and he got a few looks from mothers with kids in pristine condition. Seamus ignored them.

They wanted ice cream, so he bought them some and they ate it in the car. He was about to go home when he realized he needed a few groceries, especially diapers.

"We have to go to the store."

"Do we have to?" Jack whined.

"Sorry, pal."

"That's poohy."

He looked at his ice cream–soaked son in the rear-view mirror. "That's your favourite word lately, isn't it?"

"Yeah!" Sarah said happily.

Once more, he hauled the kids out of their car seats. He held their sticky hands as they went in the store. Sarah wanted to get into the little seat at the front of the shopping cart and Jack wanted to get into the cart itself. He held their messiness away from him as he lifted them in. Off they went, down one aisle and up the next, while he threw things in at intervals, trying to remember what was in the fridge. His guilty conscience got the better of him, so he headed back to the fruit and vegetable aisle. Jack wasn't impressed.

"I hate onions."

"I ate onons," Sarah mimicked.

"I hate turnips."

"I ate ips."

"I hate broccoli."

"I ate bocci..."

"It's good for you."

"I don't care," Jack yelled. He rubbed his eyes. "I wanna go home."

Sarah nodded. "Home."

"Just a sec, you two. I'm almost done."

Jack wasn't having any of it. "This is poohy." He picked up a stalk of celery and threw it out of the cart.

"Jack! Stop it this instant."

Seamus picked up the celery and put it back in the cart, though he had no intention of buying it. Jack started to cry.

"Me tired," Sarah said.

Seamus gave up. "All right. Let's go."

He hurried around the corner and bumped smack into someone else's cart.

It was Libby.

CHAPTER SEVEN

She nearly died.

She actually took two steps backward. He looked as shocked as she felt. She took in everything in an instant. The boy she loved was now a man. He'd filled out and his hair was shorter, but he was still gorgeous. He always would be.

Then her eyes focused on his babies. They were dirty and looked tired and cranky but they were adorable—just as she always imagined their children would look someday.

"Libby," he said.

The last time she heard him say that name was the night before he left for New Brunswick. It was like salve on a heartbreak that had lasted ten years. She couldn't find her voice for a moment, and then she whispered, "Seamus."

Neither one of them spoke; they stared at each other. She wanted to cry and then she wanted to scream and then she wanted to reach over and take his face in her hands and kiss him for the rest of her life. But she did none of those things. She had no right.

"I was sorry to hear about Vi and Angus. Are they going to be all right?"

She cleared her throat. "Yes. It will be tough going for a while, but yes."

"And your mother?"

"She's very ill."

"I'm sorry."

"Thank you."

His little boy reached over and pulled his father's shirt. "Can we go now?" But his daughter held out her fist and said, "See."

"What honey?"

"See. See."

"She wants to show you something," Seamus said.

Ava stepped closer. "What is it?"

The girl opened her chubby fist to reveal a grape. "Ape."

Ava wasn't sure what to do, but his daughter seemed intent on giving it to her, so she took it. "Thank you."

"Sarah likes to give people things."

"Sarah is a beautiful name. And your son?"

"This is Jack."

"Hello, Jack."

"Poohy."

She smiled in spite of herself. Seamus looked horrified. "Jack, behave yourself."

"Sorry. You're pretty."

Ava felt her cheeks burning. "Thank you."

Seamus looked straight at her. "Like father, like son."

Her knees went weak, but she was ashamed of herself when she remembered his wife. Not wanting him to think the wrong thing, she said, "How's Sally?"

The look on his face was one she wasn't expecting.

"You don't know about Sally?"

"Know what?"

Seamus glanced at his kids and looked flustered. That's when Jack said, "My mommy's in heaven."

"...eaven," Sarah chimed in.

Ava looked open-mouthed at Seamus. She stammered, "I'm sorry, Seamus. I didn't know. No one told me."

Just then she was surrounded by a group of giggling girls. "Excuse us. Can we have your autograph?"

Seamus looked away. "I have to get the kids home. It was nice seeing you again."

She nodded miserably. "And you."

Ava ignored the notebooks thrust at her so she could keep Seamus in sight. He walked to the check-out and soon disappeared behind racks of magazines and customer traffic.

"Please," one of the girls said.

Ava shook her head to clear it. "What?"

"Sign my book."

Automatically, she took the book and scratched something that looked like her signature. She couldn't stand it any longer. "I'm sorry, I have to go."

"Oh, please," the other girls whined, unable to believe they'd gotten this close to Ava Harris only to leave empty-handed.

Abandoning her cart, Ava ran out of the store. He was still in the parking lot, putting the kids in their seats. She hurried over to him. He looked up as he opened the front door.

"Seamus."

He stood still.

She gulped the huge ball of misery in her throat. "I have no right to talk to you, I know." She thought he would say something but he didn't, so she had no choice but to continue. "I owe you an apology, but this isn't the time or the place. I need to speak to you, because I may never get the chance again." Here, she faltered. "I'm sorry. I don't know what I'm saying. I feel so badly about Sally."

"We'll talk someday, Libby, when I'm not..." He struggled with his own words, and she understood.

"Yes. Someday."

He got in his car and drove away. She stood in the parking lot, oblivious to the stares and people pointing and the friendly smiles as people recognized her. It was as if she were alone in the universe. A car beeped to move her out of the middle of the driving lane. Ava came out of her stupor and realized she'd been sent on a mission to get some supplies and she couldn't very well arrive home without them. As she hurried back into the store, she vowed she wouldn't say a word about meeting Seamus. Her sisters would breathe down her neck until they sucked every bit of information out of her, and she couldn't share him with anyone. She needed to digest the awful news that his wife was dead. Poor Seamus. Her heart broke for him, and those dear children, losing their mother. Why hadn't someone told her?

When she got back to the house, her brothers Sandy and Hugh were in the kitchen. It was Sandy's turn to look after Ma. Hugh brought mussels for dinner.

"I hope I don't have to cook them," she said as she threw the grocery bags on the table.

"Lord almighty," Hugh complained. "I suppose we have to shuck them for you too."

"Would you?"

"You always were a spoiled brat." He took the mussels and dragged them out to the cooking pot in the garage. Sandy helped her put the groceries away. "Maryette and Rose said they'd be over after supper to help you bathe Ma. I bet you'll be glad when your friend gets back, what's her name?"

"Lola." Ava shrugged off her coat. "I've missed her. She's flying in tomorrow, which is good timing because the hospital called this morning and said Aunt Vi and Uncle Angus can come home in a couple of days."

"Good. I'll pick them up then."

"It'll be easier if they come home by ambulance. I've already arranged it. Did you see the hospital beds I bought? I'm putting them in the living room, so they don't have to go upstairs for the first while."

Sandy looked around. "It looks like you've been buyin' a lot of things for the house. Are you sure Aunt Vi wants all this new-fangled stuff?"

"I'm sure she will."

"You don't have to buy our affection."

Ava couldn't believe her ears. "I'm not. I'm trying to help out. And by the way, any one of you could've helped me by telling me that Seamus's wife was dead."

"Seamus? Why would we talk about Seamus? You left him ten years ago. That's all in the past, isn't it?"

Ava looked away. "Yes, of course, but it was embarrassing to run into him and ask him how his wife was."

"I'm sure he understood." Sandy looked uncomfortable. "I'll go see if Hugh needs a hand." He was out the back door before she said another word.

Ava sat hard on a kitchen chair. She couldn't seem to do anything right. Not about Seamus, and apparently not about buying things for her family. She either bought too much or not enough. She didn't know how to bridge the financial gap. If she gave them her clothes, they'd think it was charity. If she didn't offer to pay for everything, she felt guilty because she knew she made more money in a day than they made combined in a year. She was fed up with trying to do the right thing.

Her cell phone rang and she looked at the number. "Oh god." It was Trent. He'd called several times in the last few days, but she refused to answer the phone. She was trying to figure out what she'd say to him. Well, she couldn't avoid him forever. She put the phone to her ear.

"Hello?"

"Where have you been?!" Trent yelled.

"I'm with my dying mother, Trent. Or did you forget?"

There was a pause. "Oh right. How is she?"

"She's dying."

"Give her my best."

"Sure."

"When are you coming home? I'm fielding fifty calls a day from movie producers and television executives all trying to sign you. We're missing valuable time. By rights you should be traipsing around the country being interviewed by news shows on how you feel about winning the Oscar. Did you know that Pearl Tanner wanted you on her after-Oscar show the next day? That's huge!"

"I don't know when I'm coming home, Trent, because my mother hasn't given me her scheduled time of death."

"I'm sorry," Trent sighed. "That was callous. But is there anyway you can give me an idea of when you might be back? A rough estimate?"

Ava cleared her throat. "I'm staying here with my mother until the end and as long as my aunt and uncle need me. They were in a car accident and they need help over the next few months. I want to be here for them. They've been looking after my mother and they are elderly themselves. I owe them."

There was complete silence.

"Trent? Are you there?"

"Repeat that for me again?" His voice was low and dangerous.

"You heard me. If you can't understand why this is necessary then you're not the man I thought you were."

There was more silence before he said, "You're very clever, Ava, to put the burden on me, to make me out to be the bad guy. You have commitments. You said you'd be available to go on a promotional tour for your new movie. You also said you'd be on Broadway for the summer, not to mention the charity work you planned to do down in New Orleans."

"Charity begins at home," Ava reminded him. "Trent, all you have to do is go to these people and tell them that I have a family emergency. I think they'll understand. Believe it or not, actors are people too and we can't control our lives any more than anyone else can. If your parent was dying, I wouldn't expect you to keep working. Think about it."

Now his voice took on a whining quality. "But what about World-Wide Pictures? What am I going to say to Forrest Kavanaugh?"

"Now that I'll be taking some time off, tell him I'll consider his offer once my shoot in New York is done. Is that fair?"

"I suppose so."

"Thank you. I know you work hard on my behalf, Trent, and I appreciate it. But these things happen."

She heard a big sigh. "Fine. I'll deal with things here, but I think you should call Camilla and give her some kind of statement she can dole out to the press about your absence. She's been inundated with media, but she didn't want to phone you considering the circumstances."

"All right. I'll call her now. Thanks for this. I appreciate it."

"Yes, okay. I'll get back to you. Sorry about your mother."

"Bye, Trent." She closed the phone and immediately flipped it open again to call Camilla.

"Darling!" Camilla shouted. "Are you all right? I've been terrified to call."

"I'm okay. It's hard, obviously. And to top it off my aunt and uncle were in a car accident."

"Oh no! Are they all right?"

"They will be. But because of that I've decided to stay on here for a while, to help out my family."

"Dare I ask if you've told Trent this news?"

"I just got off the phone with him. I'm not his favourite person at the moment but he'll live."

"Remind me not to call him for seventy-two hours. Now what do you want me to say to the newspapers and so on? I take it you haven't been reading the rags. Otherwise you'd know the outlandish reasons they've come up with for why you've disappeared from sight."

"I've hardly disappeared."

"Sweetie, you're not in L.A. You're not in California. You're not in New York. You're not even in the States. So as far as everyone in the entertainment industry is concerned, you've vanished into thin air or rocketed into outer space!"

Ava laughed. "And you have no idea how good that feels."

"Have you had Hayden Judd's baby yet? Of all the excuses they've come up with the last few days that one takes the cake, seeing as how when you received your Oscar you looked about as pregnant as a pin."

"They found out about us?"

"You did jump into his arms at the Vanity Fair party in front of the Gossip News reporter."

"Damn."

"They've also had you running off to elope with Jasper Jones. But how you could do that and be lying on a beach in the Mediterranean with Prince William beats me."

"Tell them my mother is ill and I hope they'll give me and my family some privacy at this very difficult time. You know the drill."

"Fine. I'll do my best to get it out there, but there are a few loose ends."

"Camilla, I've had a rough day. Can we do this another time?"

"Of course. Why don't you give me a call when you have a chance? In the meantime, wish your mother all the best. And take care of yourself, sweetie. I worry about you."

"I'll be fine. I'm with my brothers and sisters and I can't tell you how wonderful that is. Oh, and Camilla? Could you call Maurice and Harold and tell them I love them and I'll call them soon?"

"Righto. Bye bye!"

"Bye."

She no sooner got off the phone than someone knocked on the back door.

"Come in," she shouted as she made her way to the door. There stood a delivery boy holding an enormous box tied with a red ribbon.

"For Miss Ava Harris."

"Oh thank you." She reached out for the box and took it. The guy grinned like a Cheshire cat. "I love you, Miss Harris."

This struck her as funny. "Do you?"

"Yes. My mother thinks you're the greatest thing since sliced bread. She said so just the other day."

"Come in for a minute." She turned away and put the box on the kitchen table, then reached into her purse and took out a twenty. She also grabbed a notepad and pen by the phone and turned to him. "What's your mother's name?"

"Florence."

She scribbled, "To Florence, You have a very nice son. All the best, Ava Harris." She folded it up and passed it to him along with the money. "Here. Tell your mother I said hello."

His face lit up. "Thanks! She'll freak."

"I hope not."

He walked backwards out the door. Ava was afraid he was going to bow. He stumbled down the steps and hurried back to his truck. She went to the table and opened the box. A glorious arrangement of exotic flowers lay in scented tissue paper. The card read, "I'm a wicked man and a foolish one. Please, please forgive me. I love you. I love you. I love you. Hayden xoxoxo."

She didn't want to smile, but she did. At least someone loved her—or thought he did. While her brothers were out of the house and before her sisters arrived, she quickly ran upstairs and checked on her mother, who thankfully was sleeping comfortably. She'd had a good week. Everyone said so and the family was sure it was because the baby had finally come home.

Ava crept to her room and called Hayden. He answered on the first ring.

"Do you forgive me?" he said, before she had a chance to say anything.

"I'm not sure."

"I love you, baby."

"So you say."

"I really, really mean it."

"You always mean it."

"This time I'll prove it to you."

She lay back on the bed. "How do you propose to do that?"

"I'm here."

She sat back up in an instant. "What?"

"I'm here, on this glorious island in the middle of nowhere. I flew in this morning. I've been holed up in a hotel room waiting for your call. Please say you'll come to me."

She didn't know what to think. She was a bundle of conflicting emotions.

"Please come to me," he whispered. "I'll make you feel good. You must be lonely and upset with everything that's happening with your family. I thought you could use a big hug."

She felt her resistance start to disappear.

"You don't have to tell anyone I'm here. I'll go away as soon as you want me to. Just let me hold you in my arms for a little while."

"Okay," she said quietly.

"I'm at the Delta, under Charlie Chaplin. Room 502."

"You're a dope," she laughed.

"I know."

"I'll be there in a couple of hours."

"Thank you, baby. Thank you."

She closed the phone and fell back on the bed. Why did she say yes? She was a fool. He didn't love her any more than the delivery guy did. But he was good fun when he wanted to be—why not take what was on offer and worry about it tomorrow? Besides, how else would she get through the evening after the shock of seeing Seamus? And knowing he was now a widower didn't help the situation. Maybe Hayden could erase him from her mind for a few hours.

After a quick shower, she greeted her sisters when they arrived for the evening and even ate a few of Hugh's mussels. Then said she needed to get out of the house for a bit. Would they mind terribly?

They told her to go ahead. Before she lost her nerve, she grabbed the keys for the rental and drove out of town, taking the long way in, through Mira. She told herself it was to sight-see a little, to take in the miles of fir trees and the little clapboard cottages nestled along the shoreline, but she soon found herself parked by the side of the road, walking across the highway to look down onto one of the beaches that circled Mira Bay. She stared out to sea for several minutes, remembering a night a long time ago.

Why did she tell Seamus to stop? She had regretted it ever since and now she'd never have that moment back again.

This way of thinking was doing her no good. She turned around and got back into the car, churning up gravel as she put her foot to the floor and sped towards Sydney. Or was it rushing away from that beach?

On went the sunglasses before she got to the lobby of the hotel. She looked down at the floor and rushed passed the reservations desk. Thankfully, the elevator was empty. She was in front of his door in no time. She knocked softly.

Hayden, the ridiculous man, answered the door in a tuxedo. The lights were dimmed, music played, and a bottle of champagne chilled in an ice bucket. The room was full of roses. He never said a word, just took by her hand and locked the door behind her. He took off her sunglasses, then reached behind and released her hair from its clip.

She was content to do and say nothing.

He led her into the middle of the room and put his arm about her waist. He started to dance slowly and she let him lead. Keeping his eyes on her, he reached over to hand her a glass of champagne. She took a sip while he grabbed another glass. He emptied his, and so did she.

Hayden danced her over to the bed and then took his hands away and started to undo her satin buttons. She didn't move until he drew the sleeves of her blouse down her arms. That's when she put her head back. He reached behind and undid her bra. That too slipped down her arms like silk.

He helped her take off the rest of her clothes before she lay back on the bed. He never took his eyes off her.

And that's when she knew she was in trouble. She only saw one face looking back: Seamus.

He made love to her and she let him. He never even noticed that she was silent for most of it, and that she had tears in her eyes from a sorrow that threatened to overwhelm her. The only way she felt him was to pretend that it was Seamus kissing her body and Seamus moving on top of her. Oh God, if only.

Her body responded as it should, but it was an automatic reaction brought on by someone who was undeniably an expert on how to pleasure a woman. He plied all his tricks, and just when she thought it was over, he'd take her in his arms again and make her moan in spite of herself.

Only much later did Hayden speak. He pulled her up over him and did what he always did, traced her jaw line with the back of his finger. "So, little one. Do you believe me now when I say I love you?"

She nodded.

"Good. When you need reminding, I'll come back and we can do it all over again."

She closed her eyes. He took her face in his hands and kissed her eyelids. "Say it."

She stayed quiet.

"Say it." He crushed his mouth against hers. When he finally let her go, she whispered, "I love you."

"Oh, baby, that's better."

He rolled her onto her back and took her again.

Ava left the room at two o'clock in the morning, barely remembering the drive home. She snuck in the house after finding the door open. A note on the table instructed her to "Lock up, please." She did, and then climbed the stairs as quietly as she could. Rose was in Lola's bed. Off went Ava's clothes, on went her nightie, and under the covers she slipped, to fall into a dead sleep.

In the morning, she could hardly lift her head from the pillow. She ached, almost as if she had a hangover. On top of that, it looked about noon, judging from the splash of sunlight that fell across the bed.

"Oh God. I'm an idiot." Ava slipped into the bathroom and took a long, hot shower. Now she was a sore prune. She put on a bathrobe and went downstairs in search of strong coffee. Two of her sisters were in the kitchen. One was making a casserole of some kind and the other was ironing.

Ava shuffled into the pantry in search of a mug. "Morning. Sorry I slept in. Shouldn't you guys be at work?"

"Lucky for you, I'm back shift," Rose said.

"I called in sick," Maryette said unashamedly. "They can do without me for a day. There's a fresh pot of tea on the stove."

"I need coffee this morning," she croaked. She poured water into the coffee maker and added about ten scoops of ground java. Then she came back and sat on one of the kitchen chairs. "How's Ma this morning?"

"She's okay," Rose said. "Had a bit of a rough night. I'm surprised we didn't wake you."

"I didn't hear a thing."

"What the hell time did you get home?" Maryette asked before she threw another shirt on the ironing board. "I called Rose at midnight and you still weren't in."

"Sorry," Ava sighed. "I lost track of time."

"I can just bet," Maryette smirked.

Ava looked at her. "What do you mean?"

Rose threw a can of tomatoes into her concoction. "What she means is it's all over town that you bumped into Seamus yesterday."

Ava blinked a couple of times, trying to get her head around this information.

"You've been away too long, girl," Maryette laughed. "Everyone knows your business in this town. Did you think you could keep it a secret?"

"It wasn't a secret. I bumped into him at Sobey's, which is about as romantic as cutting your toenails, so I don't understand why all you busybodies around here get off on it. And speaking of that, thanks a lot for not telling me his wife was dead. I felt like an idiot when I asked him how Sally was." She jumped out of her chair and went into the pantry to wait for the coffee to drip through.

She was livid. Typical bloody small-town crap. She'd suffocate in a place like this. Gossip and untruths thrived like mosquitoes in this environment. For a few minutes she considered taking the car to the airport and jumping on the first available plane. But when she poured the coffee, her shoulders slumped. She couldn't run again. They'd never forgive her.

There was nothing for it. She emerged, coffee in hand, and sat back at the table. The other two didn't say a word. They looked sheepish and that was fine with Ava.

It was Rose who spoke first. "If you remember, when I told you Seamus was married you said in no uncertain terms that you didn't need a blow by blow of his life and then you hung up on me. So I never said another thing."

"Surprisingly," Ava muttered. She realized they were waiting for her to say something. "I wasn't with him last night, if that's what you think."

Rose came and sat down at the table. "You weren't? What did he say to you, anyway?"

"Nothing. We said hi and he introduced me to his kids. That was all."

Maryette turned off the iron and sat too. "That's it? I don't know why I thought there'd be more…"

"Fireworks?" Rose volunteered.

"Yeah, fireworks."

Ava took a sip of her coffee so she wouldn't tear the face off her sister. She counted to ten in her head before she opened her mouth. "How do you think I felt, Maryette? I was in hell if you must know, and he was too. Then a bunch of kids came up clamoring for my autograph and they chased him away. It was horrible."

Maryette looked away. "I'm sorry; I shouldn't have asked you that."

Ava put down her mug because it was suddenly too heavy to hold. "Don't be. Of course you'd want to know." She sighed. "It was awful. He looked so good and he wanted to talk to me, I could tell, but his kids started to whine and then these stupid girls showed up. I wanted the earth to swallow me up." She put her face in her hands.

Rose reached over and patted her arm. "We're sorry, pet. We had no idea."

"God. This is terrible," Maryette said. "We'll keep our mouths shut from now on."

Ava looked up and shook her head. "It's okay. It actually helps to talk about him. I always feel as if I'm carrying him on my shoulders and everyone knows he's there and I can never put him down. I need to put him down."

They nodded sympathetically. She regained her composure and took a big gulp of coffee before letting out another big sigh.

"So where were you last night?" Rose ventured, but quickly added, "If you don't want to say, that's okay."

"It doesn't matter anymore. I went to bed with someone."

Their mouths hung open. She went in for the kill. "Hayden Judd."

Rose and Maryette jumped up from their chairs and bounced around the kitchen, screaming. Ava started to laugh and couldn't stop. She laughed and laughed at her sisters in their near-hysteria.

This was the scene that greeted Lola as she walked through the door.

*

Ava was happy to have Lola back. She had missed her cheery sidekick, with her down-to-earth manner and comforting presence. The unhappiness that threatened to overwhelm her eased when Lola was around.

Lola assured her that things were fine at home, and for a moment Ava was confused—she never thought of the Malibu beach house as home. She lay awake that night thinking about it. What an eye-opener: living somewhere for eight years and never becoming attached to it. It was sad.

Happily, two days later Aunt Vi and Uncle Angus were brought home. Ava and Lola ran out to greet them, carrying blankets to make sure they didn't get cold on their way into the house.

Aunt Vi was unloaded first. "Lordy, lordy. How in the heck are you going to get me up those stairs? You'll need a forklift."

"Don't worry, Mrs. MacIntosh," one of the medics smiled. "We've never needed one yet."

As they wheeled her towards the back door, Ava covered her aunt with the blanket. "We're so happy to have you back!" She kissed her even as they were moving.

"I'm happy to be back," Aunt Vi confided. "If I had to endure one more day of that hospital food, I'd have gone crazy. Good thing my stomach is made of cast iron."

There was no room for all of them on the back stairs, so Ava got out of the way, just in time to hear Uncle Angus moan about people driving over his tulip beds. Lola reassured him that the bulbs were perfectly safe underneath the frozen ground. Then Uncle Angus spied Ava. "I keep telling these people I'm perfectly capable of walking myself."

Ava had to smile. The cast on her uncle's arm was at a ninety degree angle, jutting out and in the way of everyone and everything.

"This is for your own protection, Uncle Angus. We can't have you slipping on the ice."

"I don't like being hauled around like an old bag of turnips," he grumbled.

Ava and Lola grinned.

After much maneuvering and grunting, the gurneys were brought into the kitchen. Ava pointed towards the living room. "Aunt Vi, I've got two hospital beds set up in the living room, to save you and Uncle Angus from having to climb the stairs with casts and crutches and canes. It's only for a little while."

"Goodness gracious! I'm going to be in my nightie in the parlor? My mother would roll over in her grave."

"I'm sure she'd understand." Ava nodded at the paramedics. "If you could you help her in, please, that would be great."

They reached down to help Aunt Vi off the gurney and held on to her as she hobbled into the living room. All the furniture was pushed back to the walls except for a large end table, which was positioned between the beds.

"Oh my," Aunt Vi said. "You didn't have to go to all this trouble."

They helped her into bed. "It was no trouble," Ava said. Then it was Uncle Angus who was escorted in. Lola pointed. "Uncle Angus, this is your bed."

He sat on the end of it and looked around before picking up the television remote with his good hand and turning on the TV. "Now ain't this something. We can watch our shows and lie in bed, Vi!"

"Looks like that's all we can do, seeing as how we can't make whoopee. Geranium will be spying on us through the curtains."

The others tried to keep straight faces. The idea of the two of them in a clinch with their heavy, awkward casts was too funny.

Once the gurneys were taken away, the downstairs didn't look quite so claustrophobic. Luckily Uncle Angus converted an old closet off the main hall into a powder room a couple of years before. They'd have to endure a few weeks of sponge baths, but they'd manage the inconvenience.

It turned out to be a lot of work having three patients in the house. Ava and Lola ran up and down stairs all day. If Ava thought she'd neglected her family all these years, she certainly made up for it in the weeks that followed. It was a wonderful opportunity to help these much-loved elders of the clan. But if she were honest, it wasn't the only reason why she kept moving. Ava needed to stop thinking about Seamus, a man who with one look could blot out everything and everyone else in her world.

CHAPTER EIGHT

For the next two weeks, Seamus did his best to put Libby right out of his mind. He had no intention of upsetting his kids, which is exactly what he did the day he bumped into her at the grocery store and the morning after. Both of them cried that night when he told them he wasn't reading two more books. "Knock it off and go to bed!" he said in a tone angrier than usual. They cried when he left them at daycare the next day because he forgot to kiss them goodbye.

When he picked them up that evening, they didn't run out to meet him and that's when he knew he had to get his act together and forget all about her. It wasn't fair to them. They were innocent victims and their welfare came first, he reminded himself.

He filled his days with all the fun things he could think of. He took them to the park after work. They went to the movies, even though Sarah was a little young to be in the theatre. But it turned out she really liked it. She sat quite content with a big bag of popcorn and yelled, "Yeah," every time Shrek came on the screen.

The trips to the movies stopped the day Libby suddenly filled the screen one afternoon during the previews. Jack grabbed his sleeve. "Daddy, isn't that the lady from the store?"

Seamus was hardly aware that Jack spoke, because his entire body was rigid with longing. The trailer showed her in period costume, a long dress with a bonnet tied under the chin.

Flashes of her walking down a cobbled street being kissed by some Hollywood star was bad enough but worse was a shot of her running along a shoreline, laughing, her hair cascading down her back as a man galloped towards her with a horse. He scooped her up and they rode off together towards the horizon. The last shot was of her in a wedding dress, running down the steps of a church.

❀

Seamus continued to struggle with remaining focused on his kids when all he thought of was her. He needed to cut loose, so one Friday night when Roger suggested they go to the Steel City Tavern and have a few brews, he accepted. His sister offered to pick up the kids at daycare and have them spend the night with her. He knew the kids would welcome the chance to spend some time with their older cousins.

Seamus, Roger, and a couple of other cops gathered after work and had a steak along with their beer. They laughed and joked around, and before he knew it, Seamus was drunk. He didn't care.

Some women came into the bar and more drinks were ordered. One of the women took a liking to Seamus, practically throwing herself in his lap. He didn't care about that either. After a while she asked him if he wanted to go home with her. He said he didn't care.

She pulled him outside, though Roger came after him and said he'd drive him home. Seamus smirked and told him to go babysit someone else and stop worrying. The woman told Roger to bugger off. In the end, he had no choice but to leave them alone.

She drove him back to her place, a rundown apartment in Whitney Pier. "My roommate's gone for the night. We have the place to ourselves."

"Ya gotta drink?" he slurred.

"Sure baby. I've got just the thing." She took out a bottle of rum and mixed it with diet Coke. It was flat and warm. Seamus took a gulp, spilling most of it on the floor.

"Hey, sorry."

She pushed him onto the living room couch. "Never mind. I know how you can make it up to me." She straddled him and started to unbutton his shirt. "I need some lovin'."

"Don't we all," he grinned.

"I bet you're great in the sack, aren't you?" She kissed him before he could answer. Her breath smelled like garlic. He turned his head. She kissed his ear instead. "Come on, baby. Let's play." She reached down and grabbed his crotch.

He pushed her hand away. "Hey, take it easy."

"I don't wanna take it easy. I like it rough." She pulled off her sweater. "Take off my bra with your teeth."

At this, he burst out laughing. He suddenly sobered up a bit.

She looked put out. "What's the matter? Don't you like to talk dirty?"

"I don't know what I like lady, but I have a sneaking suspicion it's not you. Where's your phone?"

She jumped off his lap and held her sweater in front of her. "You're an asshole, did you know that?"

"Yep. Where's your phone?"

"It's in the kitchen, you jerk. Don't let the door hit you on the way out." She stormed off to the bathroom. He stumbled out to the kitchen and sat on a chair, trying to stop his dizzy head. What the hell was he doing here? He must be losing his mind. All he thought of was Libby. All he wanted was Libby. Why wasn't she here? He pressed his fingers against his temple trying to get the pounding to stop.

"I know. I'll ask her," he said to no one. "No harm in asking." He got up, went over to the phone and dialed the number he knew by heart. It began to ring once, twice…

"Hello?"

"Libby? Is that you? Please say that's you."

"Seamus?"

"Yep."

"What are you doing? Where are you? Are you all right?"

"No, I'm not all right. I haven't been all right in a long, long time."

"Oh god, Seamus. Stop."

"Stop what?"

"You sound drunk."

"I am drunk. Care to join me?" She didn't respond. He thought maybe she hung up. He whispered, "Libby, are you there?"

"I'm here."

"Don't cry."

"I can't help it."

"Ah shit. I'm always fucking up."

"No, no. It's not your fault. Don't ever think that."

"I don't know what to do. I saw you the other day."

"Yes, in the store."

"No, not in the store. You were on the screen and someone was kissing you."

"It's only make-believe."

"It wasn't me kissing you. How come I can't kiss you anymore? I'm sorry for whatever I did to make you go away."

"I have to hang up, Seamus. Go to sleep and I'll talk to you again, okay?"

"Promise?"

"I promise."

"Can I kiss you?"

There was a long pause. "Good night, Seamus."

Seamus heard her hang up the phone. He replaced the receiver as his mind reeled. Needing desperately to escape the dingy apartment, he reached for the phone again and called Roger, telling him only that he was "somewhere in the Pier." Then he let the phone drop and fumbled around until he found the apartment door. Staggering down a narrow flight of stairs, he tripped over the threshold and out into the street.

He walked, and kept walking until Roger drove up beside him, reaching over to open the side door and let Seamus in.

The next morning found him on the living room couch at home with a colossal headache. Panic set in because he couldn't remember how he got back. He prayed to God he didn't drive himself, but the memory of rolling out the passenger side door of Roger's car came back to him. Good old Roger picked him up off the ground and dragged him into the house.

Seamus managed to get up and make his way to the bathroom, where he stood under a cold shower for quite a while, to punish himself for being so stupid. While he shaved he found it difficult to look at himself in the mirror. In this state, he looked like his father and that made him sick. Seamus hated drunks.

He took a couple of Tylenol and opened the fridge in search of a Coke. He reached for the phone and suddenly stopped. Did he talk to Libby last night? Oh shit.

He looked at the cat, who sat by the garbage can. "Dexter, please tell me I didn't." Dexter was no help. He looked up accusingly, not because of anything Seamus did but because it was past breakfast and nearly lunch. Seamus got up in search of a can of cat food. When he couldn't find any, he opened a can of tuna and placed it on the floor.

He called Roger.

"Ah, he's in the land of the living," Roger laughed when he picked up the phone.

"I'm in rough shape. What the hell happened?"

"You had a lucky escape, my friend."

"What do you mean?"

"I mean, you were dragged off by the bride of Frankenstein. I hope all your parts are in good working order."

"Oh Christ, why didn't you stop me?"

"I tried, but she almost broke a beer bottle and went at me. I like ya and everything, but not that much."

"How did you find me, then?"

"You eventually called me and I drove around until I spied you wandering up Victoria Road."

"Can I ask you something?"

"What?"

"Did I mention talking to Libby last night?"

There was a long pause on the other end of the phone. His heart sank.

"Look man, I feel badly for you, but yeah, you called her."

Seamus rubbed his eyes to lessen the pain of this throbbing head. "I'm such a loser."

"You were drunk. We all do stupid things when we drink."

"Have you ever called up a famous actress and begged her to come back to you, because I have a feeling that's what I did."

"Maybe she will."

"Yeah, I'm sure she'd swap her digs in Hollywood and come live in Catalone with me. I mean, wouldn't you?"

"Don't know what to tell ya, buddy."

"Well, thanks for last night. I owe ya one."

"No prob. See ya Monday."

"Yeah. See ya."

Next, he phoned Colleen and told her he'd be over in a couple of hours to pick up the kids. She invited him for supper. Hoping he'd be able to stomach food by suppertime, he accepted. The rest of the morning was occupied with cleaning up, which was a lot easier to do when Jack wasn't riding the vacuum cleaner and Sarah wasn't on a chair in front of the sink helping him do the dishes. When he was finished, the place wasn't Martha Stewart clean, but the crushed potato chips were sucked up and even the bag in the garbage can was changed.

Stepping outside, the sunshine made him wince, so he went back in the house for his sunglasses and more Tylenol. "This is stupid. I'm never drinking again." Blasé, Dexter blinked at him and looked out the window.

Colleen lived in Louisbourg, a ten-minute drive away. Naturally, the temperature when he got there was a lot cooler than at his house, because the fog lay heavy on the coast. The foghorn worked overtime.

"Ah, shit." His father's car was in Colleen's driveway. He wished she'd knock off the Florence Nightingale routine. Some people couldn't be saved.

He got out of the car and walked into the house. Colleen was on her way downstairs with a load of laundry. "Hi."

"Why didn't you tell me he'd be here?"

"Because you wouldn't have come and that's ridiculous. Act your age." She continued down the stairs.

He took off his sunglasses and put them on the kitchen counter. "Hi, kids."

Jack and Sarah shrieked from somewhere and then ran into the kitchen and hopped into his arms.

"Guess what?" Jack said.

"What?"

"I didn't go to bed until eleven."

"You're kidding!"

He nodded proudly. "We watched Finding Nemo. It was good."

Sarah grinned. "Yeah."

He kissed them both and put them down. Their cousins Liam and Courtney came into the kitchen. "Hi, Uncle Seamus."

He reached out and ruffled Liam's hair. "Hey, squirt."

Liam reached up and pushed his hand away. "Stop it."

Courtney hugged him. He cupped her face in his big hand. "Hiya, sweetheart. Thanks for looking after the kids for me."

"That's okay."

Jack was offended. "She didn't look after me. I'm big."

Sarah nodded. "Yeah. Big."

"You're right. Sorry."

Jack ran out of the kitchen. "Come on, Liam. Let's play pirates."

The four cousins zoomed out together. Seamus sat at the kitchen table and waited for Colleen to come upstairs. No truck in the driveway meant Dave wasn't home. His father cleared his throat in the living room. Damn Colleen. She was staying downstairs on purpose.

Seamus reluctantly walked into the living room. "Hi Dad." He took in his father's ruddy cheeks and puffy face. He'd put on weight and it didn't suit him. In fact, it made him look about fifteen years older than he was.

His father got up from the couch and held out his hand. "Son."

They shook hands, and then Kenny sat back on the couch. He had a glass of something on the end table. Seamus pointed to it.

"A little early in the day, isn't it?"

Kenny took a drink. "It's Pepsi."

Seamus rubbed his hands down the front of his pants and looked out the window. He finally had no choice but to sit. His father looked about as comfortable as he felt. "So what's new?"

Kenny shook his head. "Not much. I've been fixin' up the shed. The roof just about tore off during the last blow we had."

"Yeah, it was a bad one." Seamus leaned forward in his chair and rubbed his hands together, itching to get up and walk out. "You're feeling well?"

"Aye. My hip gives out now and again, but ain't nothing worth worryin' about."

"Good."

He took another drink. "The kids are growin' I see. Jack's goin' to be a big fella someday. Bigger than you."

Seamus knew he'd say that. "Yep. He'll be bigger then me. Smarter too, probably."

"Aye. Sarah's got the look of her mother. Do you ever bring them over to Sally's people?"

"Of course, I do. They love to go."

"Her folks see the kids more than I do then, I guess."

"Yeah, Dad. No doubt."

"Shame."

Finally Seamus heard Colleen on the stairs. She entered the living room. "Well, this is nice. All of us together." Neither her father nor her brother said anything. She kept smiling, walked over to the armchair and sat down. "Did you know, Seamus, that Dad's going to AA? Isn't that right, Dad?"

"Aye."

"What's it been, now? Six weeks?"

Kenny took another drink. "About that."

Colleen looked at him. "Isn't that great, Seamus?"

He nodded. "Hope it works."

His father grunted and downed his drink. Shaking the ice cubes in his glass, he got up. "Think I'll have another." He walked out and into the kitchen.

"You could give him a little encouragement, you know," Colleen frowned. "It wouldn't kill you."

"He's not going to do it; you know that, don't you?"

"You can't give up on people, Seamus."

"No?"

"Oh, all right. Be as stubborn as he is." She got up and started to leave. Seamus stood too and grabbed her arm. "I'm sorry, Colleen. I know how much you want this to happen. I hope for your sake it does."

She had tears in her eyes. "I miss Mom and we have such a little family, Seamus. I want us to get along. Is that too much to ask?"

He gathered his big sister in his arms. "You're right. You've been wonderful to me and I don't make it easy. I promise I'll try to do better."

"Thanks," she sniffed.

He patted her back and then let her go. She started for the kitchen. "I have to stuff the salmon."

"Can I help?"

"You can peel some potatoes."

Dave finally came home from a trip to Central Supplies. Seamus helped him bring in four sheets of plywood. The visit got easier after that. Dave, who had an easy way about him, was quite the talker and he had everyone laughing before supper, teasing his father-in-law and giving Colleen's rear end a pinch every time she went by. She finally had to threaten him with a potato masher to get him to stop. Once the kids joined in the festivities at the table, Seamus began to enjoy himself.

He and his father exchanged a few jokes. It was worth it for the big smile on Colleen's face.

Finally the kids drifted away to go back to the pirate cave of blankets and towels. The four adults sat at the table, drinking their tea and enjoying second helpings of Colleen's famous strawberry and rhubarb pie.

"God, this is good," Seamus said with his mouth full.

"I'll give you the recipe," she teased.

"You do that," he smiled.

"Didn't know you could get strawberries in March," her dad said.

"I think they're from California. I got them at Sobey's."

Dave obviously wasn't thinking when he blurted out, "Hey, a guy in the shop said he saw Ava Harris in Sobey's a couple of weeks ago."

The silence was deafening. He backtracked. "Oh, shit. Sorry."

Seamus pretended it didn't matter. "Don't be sorry on my account. I couldn't care less." Colleen looked at him and bit her lip. He shook his fork at her. "Really, it's okay."

His father growled at the other end of the table. "That bitch better not come near me."

The hairs on the back of Seamus's neck stood at attention. He swallowed hard. "No need for name-calling."

"She's a bitch and she always was."

Seamus dropped his fork to his plate. He saw Colleen and Dave give him worried looks but he didn't care. "Don't call her that."

"I can call her whatever I want," his father scowled.

"It's none of your business."

"Isn't it? She made your mother's life miserable for a long time, so I guess it is my business."

"Leave her alone."

His father threw his napkin on the table and pointed at him. "No. You leave her alone. If I hear of you going anywhere near her, I'll have your hide."

"Dad, please…" Colleen interjected.

Seamus got up from the table. "If I want to go over there tonight, I will. And not you or anyone else can tell me otherwise."

"Then you're a damn fool."

"Maybe I am." He turned to Colleen. "Sorry, I better get the kids home. Thanks for the great meal."

Seamus walked out of the dining room, called his two protesting children and bundled them into the car. They whined all the way home, so he made it up to them by popping popcorn and letting them watch Shrek for the seventh time. Soon after that they were snuggled into bed.

When all was quiet, he went out onto the deck and watched the beach for the longest time, gathering his courage. He looked up into the night sky. "I'm sorry, Sally. Please forgive me. But I've always loved her."

He went to the phone and called Libby.

The phone rang and rang. He was about to chicken out and hang up when a breathless voice answered. "Sorry, hello?"

"Ah, yes. Is Li…Ava there?"

"Who's calling please?"

"A friend."

The voice became business like. "I'm sorry, but unless you identify yourself I can't summon Miss Harris to the phone."

He looked at the receiver. Who on earth was speaking?

"Tell her it's Seamus."

"Ohhh. Oh my. Sorry. I'll go get her."

It seemed like ages before she came to the phone. She spoke his name softly. "Seamus."

"Libby. Someone told me I called you last night."

"Yes."

"I'm sorry. I was drunk and I apologize for anything I might have said that was inappropriate."

"Nothing you said was inappropriate."

He wiped the sweat off his brow. "I can't really remember."

"That's okay."

"I'm a jerk."

"No. Never."

"Sorry."

"Don't ever be sorry, Seamus."

"I don't know what to do."

"Maybe we should talk."

"Yes, but where?"

"You could meet me for coffee, maybe."

"And have everyone in town see us together?"

Ava sighed. "You're right. I could meet you some afternoon at Wentworth Park. By the fountain?"

"All right. How about this Monday? I can take an hour off work."

"Fine. I'll be there at two. That is of course unless something comes up with my mother. I can't stay long because I'm here to help Aunt Vi."

"Of course, of course."

"I'll see you then, Seamus."

"Yes. See you then."

Ava hung up the phone and went up to her room. Lola was on the bed and this time she was the one biting her fingernails. "Oh god. It was him, wasn't it?"

Ava nodded. She flopped down on the bed and pulled the hair off her face. She stared at nothing.

"Are you sure you know what you're doing, Ava?"

"I have no clue."

"Do you want to see him?"

"Yes. No. Yes."

"Maybe you shouldn't."

Ava made a face. "Why would you say something like that?"

"I don't know," Lola shrugged. "I have a bad feeling about this."

"Wonderful. That makes me feel better." She bounced off the bed and said over her shoulder, "I'm going to see Ma."

Lola continued to gnaw at her nails and tried hard to make the bad feeling go away, but it wouldn't budge.

Ava sat with her mom for a while. They talked a little, but mostly Mamie lay quietly with her eyes closed. The doctor said she was in a bit of a remission, seeing as her health stayed the same for the last couple of weeks. Of course, none of them got their hopes up, but it was a relief that she seemed stable and they were able to control her pain.

Ava did notice that her mother watched her when she didn't think Ava was looking. She wondered why. If she turned her head suddenly, she'd catch Mamie closing her eyes. It was a strange little game and Ava wasn't sure what it meant. She mentioned it to Rose, but of course her sister said she was foolish and blamed it on an over-active imagination.

Ava decided to test her theory by emptying the wastepaper basket. Ma definitely opened her eyes and followed her about the room, but when she turned to go sit in the chair by the bed, her mother's eyes were closed.

She sat down. "Ma?"

"Yes?"

"Why are you looking at me?"

She opened her eyes. "I wasn't."

"Yes, Ma. You were."

Her mother gave her a bit of a grin. "You caught me. You always were a smart little thing."

"Was I?"

"Yes. You were the smartest of the bunch."

"You never told me that before."

"I'm telling you now." Her mother started to cough and Ava grabbed the glass of water on the bedside table and put the bent straw to her lips.

"Thank you," Mamie whispered when she'd taken a small sip.

Ava decided not to bother her with silly questions. She didn't want her to use up too much of her energy, but it was her mother who spoke first.

"I look at you, because I can't for the life of me figure out where you came from."

Ava tilted her head. "What do you mean?"

"Can you keep a secret?"

"Yes."

"I was always a bit afraid of you."

Ava didn't know what to say. "Oh?"

"Mmm. Strange when you think of it, a grown woman being afraid of a small child."

"Why?"

"You were bright. You saw things. You'd look at people as if you could see right through them, and it was…uncomfortable, for want of a better word."

"I didn't know that."

"And you were talented. Everyone said so. You'd play

make-believe and grownups had tears in their eyes watching you, because you really believed that you were a fairy or a star or the donkey in the Nativity play. It was almost frightening."

Ava's mouth went dry. She'd never heard her mother talk about her. Ever. And now this outpouring. She wasn't sure what to make of it.

"I was afraid something would happen to you. You felt too much. You felt much too much."

Ava didn't want her to keep talking, so she rose out of the chair, but her mother turned her face towards her. "Sit."

Ava slowly lowered herself back in the chair.

"Why did you leave?"

She shook her head.

"You're never going to tell me, are you?"

She looked at the floor.

"All right. I'll leave it be." Her mother closed her eyes. Ava got up quickly and went to the door, but before she went through it her mother said, "I know you still love him."

She stood very still.

Her mother opened her eyes again and looked right at her. "Don't hurt him again."

Ava fled.

But she got only as far as downstairs before duty called. Aunt Vi hollered from the living room. "Libby, darlin'. Bring me the hot water bottle, there's a good girl."

She wiped her eyes on the arm of her sweater. "Sure. I'll be right there."

"And get me the Post," Uncle Angus chimed in. "It should be here by now."

Ava ran to fill the hot water bottle and bumped into Lola going down the stairs. "I'll get the paper for you," Lola said.

"Thanks." Ava went to the bathroom sink and turned on the hot water tap. While she waited for the water to heat up, she looked at herself in the mirror. A very frightened face looked back at her. She mouthed her mother's words. Don't hurt him again.

She and Lola got supper ready for their three patients. Both Aunt Vi and Uncle Angus got along fairly well, considering all they'd been through, but they never would've managed on their own. They both had one arm and one leg out of commission, so moving about was awkward, and their unwieldy casts were uncomfortable. Their bruises had faded to that sickly colour both yellow and ghastly. Deciding Aunt Vi needed makeup to cover the worst of it, Lola gave her the full treatment. When she was done, Uncle Angus gave his wife a quick glance.

"You don't need all that muck on your face. You look better without it."

"You heard the man," Aunt Vi said. "Take it off."

Lola's eyes widened. "Do you always do what he tells you?"

"Girl, ya gotta keep your man happy," Aunt Vi said.

Lola passed her some tissue and a jar of Nivea cream. "I could learn a thing or two from you."

Of course Lola should have gone home days before, but she kept making excuses not to leave, so Ava dropped the subject. She felt safe with Lola around, and her Aunt Vi loved having such an avid student. Her friend sat on the end of Aunt Vi's bed every morning and wrote down everything she had to say about cooking and household hints and how to hang out clothes properly. She'd "ohh" and "ahh" for hours, and Aunt Vi's chest swelled more and more each day.

Ava's brothers Johnnie and Lauchie arrived after supper for a visit. Johnnie moved the hospital beds closer together in the living room so they could have a game of Tarbish.

Ava begged off from playing cards with the rest of them. Her excuse was she had to do the dishes. She was drying her last plate when Rose came through the door with her daughter Vicky and nieces Samantha and Emily. Rose went upstairs to sit with their mother for the evening. Ava was relieved to have three young girls to talk to. It kept her from thinking too hard.

They put their elbows on the table in unison and began peppering her with questions.

"What's it like kissing all those gorgeous actors?" Vicky asked.

"It's a lot of work."

"No way," Vicky laughed. "I don't believe you."

Ava folded her arms. "Okay, answer me this. What if you had to walk into your class, with everyone watching, and kiss someone you've never met before? And not just kiss him once, but over and over, while some of the other students fussed around you, telling you to tilt your head a little more, or drop your chin. And this person you don't know has bad breath, but you have to kiss him as if you love him and make everyone believe it. And then after three hours in the same spot, someone says cut and the guy you were kissing pushes you away and complains long and loud about having to kiss someone with small tits, when there are plenty of other students around with bigger boobs."

The girls looked at each other. "Gross!" was the general consensus.

"So you see, girls, everything is not what it seems up on the big screen."

"Still," Sam sighed. "You get to have someone do your makeup and hair. That must be fun."

"It is fun when you're going to parties or premieres, but

when you have to sit in a makeup chair for a couple of hours before one scene, it gets a little dreary."

"But all your clothes," Emily said. "Do you get to keep them?"

"Yes. It's in my contract."

The girls got excited again, making Ava laugh.

"Your mother tells me the three of you are graduating this year. I can't believe it. You were little girls when..." She looked away.

"Yes, it's going to be great," Vicky said. "Joey asked me to go with him."

Ava looked at Vicky's cousins. "Do you two have a date?"

They nodded. Sam said, "Like, you have to hook up by at least the end of March. Otherwise you're dead. No one will take you."

"Oh dear. That sounds dreadful."

"Mom says I have to have my dress made, so it won't cost too much," Emily sighed. "I'll look like a freak."

Ava stood straight up. "Girls. I know what I can give you as a graduation present."

"What?" they said excitedly.

"I'll buy you each a prom dress. The most beautiful prom dresses anyone has ever seen!"

They started to jump up and down and scream their heads off.

"And wait!"

They held each other and didn't move.

Ava clasped her hands together. "I'll fly Maurice in from Hollywood to do your hair and makeup!"

The shrieks of delight were deafening. Everyone in the house yelled, "What's the matter?" Rose ran down the stairs. Lauchie and Johnnie burst in from the living room with Lola on their heels, while Uncle Angus and Aunt Vi had to yell from their beds, "What's going on?!"

The girls ran over to Rose but they were talking at the same time so she still didn't know what had transpired. Finally, Lauchie gave a loud whistle. "What in the name of jumpin' jahosiphats is goin' on in here? You sound like a bunch of cacklin' hens."

Eventually the story was relayed, and then relayed again to Aunt Vi and Mamie. The girls ran upstairs to call every girl in town and tell them about their wonderful fairy godmother.

Ava took Rose aside. "I'm sorry, I should've asked you first. It just popped in my head. I hope Maryette and Bev don't mind. I want you to come with me when we pick out the dresses. It can be a mother-daughter outing."

Rose gave her a hug. "It's wonderful. You've given them something they'll never forget." She pushed Ava away but kept her hands clasped on her shoulders. "But you know what the best thing is?"

"What?"

"For a second there, you looked like you did when you were a little girl."

Ava hid her face in her sister's neck and stayed there for a long time.

Her nieces' delight over her brilliant idea gave Ava great satisfaction. These were the moments she missed out on over the years. She wanted to make it up to her family, because their happiness had a direct bearing on her own. The trouble was the warm, fuzzy feeling didn't last for long. She was meeting Seamus in two days and her mother's warning of not hurting him again kept playing over and over in her head.

Ava didn't sleep most of Sunday night. Instead, she stared at the ceiling and went over what she would say to Seamus.

She even spent a few hours thinking she should call him back and cancel the whole thing. Perhaps her mother was right. It might be best to slip out of his life before she had a chance to slip back in.

In the morning, as they made their beds, Ava told Lola she had to go out in the early afternoon and asked her to keep an eye on things.

"You're meeting him, aren't you?"

"Yes. We have to talk."

"Are you sure?"

"Lola, I can't leave it like this. I owe him something. I'm not sure what, but I do."

"Are you telling your sisters?"

"No. Please don't say anything."

"I won't, but I'm worried about you."

Ava smiled at her. "If everything's a disaster, I'll come crying home to you, how's that?"

"I can't wait."

The morning hours seemed to crawl by. She looked at the clock at least a hundred times an hour. She washed the floor, did the dusting, and even made a meat pie for supper, and it was still only noon. She finally went upstairs to get ready.

How do you dress to see someone you love but really don't know anymore? Maybe she was kidding herself. It might be like an awkward blind date. She didn't know what to expect.

Unable to sit still, she left the house a half an hour early. She drove along the Sydney–Glace Bay highway and then on to the Sydney bypass. Wentworth Park was at the bottom of Hardwood Hill. In the summer it was a leafy green oasis with a duck pond, the huge trees creating a canopy of leaves. In late March, however, the leaves were still nowhere to be seen, so the overall impression of the park was rather drab, and the large gnarled branches looked like witch's fingers scrapping against the grey sky.

Ava parked the car along one of the side streets and walked towards the fountain. Her heart turned over when she saw him sitting on the cement fence, gazing in the other direction. He looked lonely. How she longed to walk up to him, put her arms around his waist, and feel him hug her close. To press her cheek against his coat and be tucked under his chin.

Seamus turned and saw her. He stood then and waited for her to come to him. At the last minute he walked towards her. "Hi."

"Hi," she said.

They stood awkwardly for a few seconds. She put out her hand and shook his, using it to pull him toward her so she could reach up and kiss his cheek quickly before letting him go.

She looked around. "Where shall we sit?"

He gestured behind her. "I think the park bench is a little warmer than this fence."

"I imagine it would be." Ava smiled.

They sat together on the bench, not too close to each other. They both looked at their feet, neither one of them saying anything, until at the exact same moment they turned to each other and said, "So."

"This is ridiculous," Ava laughed. "You'd think we were thirteen years old."

"I feel about thirteen."

She smiled at him. "Let's start over. How are you, Seamus?"

"I'm fine. And you? Oh god, that was a stupid thing to say. Of course you're not fine."

"I'm okay."

"How is your mother?"

Ava clasped her gloves together and sighed. "It's hard. It's been so long since I've seen her."

"Yes."

"Of course you know that. It was a shock to see her at first. I wasn't prepared. But we've had some wonderful moments together this last while and that's as much as I ever hoped for. Maybe she can fight this thing a little longer. We're keeping our fingers crossed."

"Perhaps you wouldn't mind telling her I'm thinking of her."

"I'm sure she'd be happy to know that, Seamus. And how's your mother?"

Seamus glanced away for a moment. "She died five years ago. A sudden heart attack."

"That's awful," Ava frowned. "I'm sorry, I didn't know. She was a lovely woman."

"It was terrible. Colleen in particular had a hard time. You know how close she was to Mom."

"Yes, I remember."

They looked at each other then. Ava finally said, "I have to tell you again how sorry I am about Sally. What a dreadful shock for you."

"It was a nightmare. She developed an infection shortly after Sarah was born. Everyone thought she had the flu. By the time the doctors figured it out, she was dead. The only thing that kept me sane was my kids."

"You're lucky to have them. They're beautiful children. Of course, their mother was striking. I remember her. She was a grade behind us, wasn't she?"

Seamus nodded. "Yes. Yes, she was beautiful."

Neither one of them said anything for a few moments. Ava broke the silence. "I came here today to ask you to forgive me. I hurt you and you didn't deserve it. I apologize from the bottom of my heart."

He looked at his gloves. "Okay. Are you ever going to tell me why?"

Ava quickly stood. "I'm sorry. I think this was a bad idea."

Seamus stood too. "You said you wanted to talk."

"I know." Ava looked at the ground. "But we're sitting here pretending we know each other and we don't. We're trying to bridge a gap of ten years in ten minutes and it's too much. I'm confused, what with Ma and everything. I wanted to say I'm sorry and now that I've said it, I better go."

She started to walk away. He ran after her. "Wait a minute. Wait."

Ava turned to him. He put his hand on her arm. "You don't have to be afraid me. You don't have to tell me anything. You don't owe me anything. It was just a question, but it doesn't need to be answered right this minute."

Ava didn't want to cry in front of him. She nodded. "Okay."

"I won't lie to you, Libby. I still have feelings for you, but I know this is a totally inappropriate time to talk about it. Please, don't run away from me. I'll leave you alone, just don't go."

"I won't. I can't. My family needs me."

"Okay. Maybe down the road we can meet again and it won't be so hard. You wanted to apologize and I've accepted your apology and now it's over. We can start fresh. Maybe you can tell me what you've been doing all these years."

They both laughed then.

"You know what I've been doing, you silly man," she smiled.

"Well, you can tell me what it's like to win an Academy Award. That's not something I get to ask too many people."

She wiped her bangs away from her eyes with the back of her gloves. "Okay. You've got a deal."

"All right. I'll talk to you again."

"Yes. We'll talk again."

Ava turned to go but before she'd gone even two feet he said, "Libby?"

She slowly turned around.

"You never married, did you?"

She looked at him sadly. "No. I never did." And then she walked away.

CHAPTER NINE

Now that spring was in the air, it felt to Ava as if she'd never left home. The slower rhythm and pace of life started to seep into her bones again. Gradually, even with the emotional upheaval, she found herself loosening up, not hopping around from room to room anymore. She even noticed that her bad habit of clenching her teeth was disappearing.

"I know my mother is practically on her deathbed," she said to Lola as they folded laundry in the kitchen, "but I feel at peace somehow. Does that make sense? I feel better here than I have in years, even with all the upset."

Lola nodded. "Well, no wonder. Look at the life you lead. You barely have five minutes to yourself. I have to tell you, I could get used to this."

They walked towards each other, holding out either end of a flat sheet. When they met in the middle Lola took it from her and continued to fold. Ava started on a pillow case.

"I feel guilty about keeping you here, you know," Ava said. "You should've gone home two months ago."

"And done what? Twiddled my thumbs in my dinky apartment while inhaling L.A. smog?"

"You do have some people who must miss you."

Lola shook her head. "Surprisingly few, as it happens. You've chased them all away."

Ava threw a facecloth at her. "I have not!"

"All right," Lola laughed. "I concede a few people still come around, but I think they get tired of tracking me down. We aren't in L.A. all that often anymore. We're too busy flying around."

"I still think you should go home. Or go visit your parents."

"I'm happy right here."

Ava threw her hands up in defeat. "Fine. Stay as long as you want."

"I don't need your permission," Lola smirked. "Aunt Vi and Uncle Angus said they're adopting me."

"Then we'll be cousins!"

At that moment Aunt Vi hobbled into the kitchen on her cane. She and Uncle Angus had graduated to the second floor now that the cast on Vi's ankle was off. Uncle Angus had a new cast on his arm, one that was easier to manage. "Who wants raisins?"

"I said, 'cousins.'"

"Dear lord, I'm going deaf on top of everything else. Why don't you two do me a favour and take me out to the coal shed and shoot me? It would save a lot of bother."

"I'd be lynched by the family if I did that, Aunt Vi."

Aunt Vi sat at the kitchen table with a sigh. "This bandage is too tight."

"Let me re-do it." Ava unwrapped several feet of beige bandage and rolled it back around her aunt's swollen ankle. "How's that?"

"Better dear, thank you. Libby, one of your brothers asked me to talk to you about something."

Ava and Lola looked at each other. Ava sat in the chair next to Aunt Vi. "Have I done something wrong?"

"Of course not, child. It's your brother Hugh. Apparently one of his boys is doing a school project on making movies. You know Hugh. He doesn't like to put people on the spot.

Doesn't seem to mind if I do, though." Aunt Vi grinned. "Anyway, he wondered if there was any way his young fella could take your Academy Award to school during his presentation."

"Is that all? God. I thought it was something serious!"

"Well, isn't it?" Aunt Vi asked. "I thought you might have it locked up in Fort Knox or something."

"It's on my bedroom dresser, as it happens. I'll get Mercedes to go to the house and wrap it up. She can send it UPS."

"Well, that's mighty kind of ya, darlin'."

Ava cupped her chin in her hand. "You know, I haven't even thought of it, to tell you the truth. I like the idea of having it here in Cape Breton. Then everyone can see it, not just me and the housekeeper."

Ava called Hugh that night and he put his son on the phone. The poor kid was beside himself with excitement. He ran off to tell his buddies on MSN. Hugh got back on the phone, thanking her profusely. If only he knew how happy it made her to be able to do something for one of her brothers.

The statue arrived three days later. A small crowd of Ava's nearest and dearest came over for the unveiling. Her brother Hugh opened the box with a box cutter, but it was Ava who unveiled it for all to see.

Even standing on Aunt Vi's plastic kitchen tablecloth, Oscar looked impressive. Everyone took turns picking it up and had exactly the same thing to say. "It's heavy!"

Hugh and his son swore upside down that they'd take good care of it. Hugh planned to drive his son to school and pick him up afterwards, just to make sure. They would return it immediately. Ava laughed and told them to take as long as they needed.

Before they left for the night, Ava took the award upstairs to show her mother. Mamie didn't know it was coming. Ava thought she'd surprise her.

She knocked lightly on the door and entered her mother's bedroom. As always, the slight smell of sick, stale air hit her in the face. Nothing they did seemed to get rid of it. How Ava wished she could throw open the window and sit her mother right in front of it, but she was so often cold now. Ava tried not to see her mother going downhill, but there were small signs every week. She pushed the inevitability from her mind.

"Mom, are you asleep?" she whispered.

Her mother stirred. "No, just resting my eyes."

Ava approached the bed with the statue behind her back. "I brought someone to meet you."

Mamie's eyes popped open. "Oh heavens, child, I thought you had someone in the room. You could've given me a little warning."

"I do have someone with me." She reached behind and brought out her prize. "This is Oscar."

Her mother smiled and reached out to touch the golden figure. "Oh my. Isn't that something." She touched it all over while Ava held it. It was too much for her mother to hold by herself.

"Well child, you should be well pleased with yourself. That's quite an honour and very well deserved. Your father would be mighty proud of you. Mighty proud indeed. As am I."

Ava reached for her mother's hand. "Thanks, Ma. That means a lot."

❀

Now that Ava was getting into the groove of a more relaxed atmosphere, she decided she needed to buy some normal clothes—jeans and tops she could buy at the Mayflower Mall.

The outfits she brought with her were completely inappropriate for life in Glace Bay, and she didn't want people thinking she was showing off by wearing designer clothes. And besides, she'd come in the winter and now spring was in the air. The fact that their mother was still with them was a wonderful bonus she'd not thought possible when she arrived home that cold day in February.

Good old Lola stayed home with the three invalids, which seemed to be where she wanted to be anyway. Ava said she'd only be a couple of hours and they waved vaguely in her direction, so she gathered she wouldn't be missed.

She found a parking space close to the main entrance of the mall and hurried through the crosswalk to let the cars go by. A man opened the door for her and she smiled. "Thank you." He tipped his hat and kept going. She took off her sunglasses as she entered the mall and rooted through her bag to find the case. As she did, she noticed a tall man standing in front of the cash machine. She looked again and her heart beat a little faster.

"Seamus?"

He turned around. When he saw her, he gave her a big smile. "Oh, hi, Libby."

She resorted to a stupid question. "What are you doing here?"

He looked down to put his cash in his wallet. "Colleen sent me on a mission."

"Sounds exciting."

He pulled out a piece of paper from his pocket. "She told me in no uncertain terms my kids needed new pajamas as well as new underwear and socks. I've got their sizes here. I'm to look for size 6X for Jack and 3 for Sarah."

"The kids aren't with you?"

Seamus laughed. "If you ever saw the way I shop, you'd understand why Colleen keeps the kids with her. She thinks I'm going to lose them one day. It's safer for me to go with a list." He paused. "What about you?"

Ava looked down at herself. "I'm off to buy normal clothes. Stuff I can wash the kitchen floor in."

"I see."

They looked at each other and smiled. Neither one of them made a move to go anywhere but it was obvious one of them had to do something.

Finally Ava said, "Well, I better let you get to it. It was nice to see you again."

Seamus cleared his throat. "You wouldn't want to get a cup of coffee before we start?" He pointed to the other side of the door, where the food court was.

She pulled her purse back up to her shoulder and smiled. "Okay. That sounds great."

They stood in line at the counter. Seamus asked her if she wanted anything to eat.

"No, thank you. I'm putting on weight as it is, thanks to Aunt Vi's recipes."

Seamus looked her up and down. "If you are, then you needed it, because you look awfully tiny to me."

"Didn't you know that actresses ideally should be a size two these days, if not a zero?"

"Zero? What a lot of hogwash."

She laughed at him. He paid the girl and took both cups. They walked as if by some silent agreement to a table near the back of the food court. Once again, out of habit, she chose the seat that faced the wall. The first minute was taken up with getting their coffee lids opened and taking that first sip. Then there was nothing to do but look at each other.

"So what do we talk about now?" Ava said.

He shrugged and smiled. "You were going to tell me what it was like to win an Oscar."

"Ah, yes. Well, it's scary. People walk on your gown. You don't remember your name being called. You don't remember a thing you said or a thing you did and then a whole lot of people ask you a whole lot of questions and you're dragged from party to party with no time to eat or drink so you end up with a huge headache. And if you're like me, you faint dead away in the middle of a dance floor and wake up to find six TV cameras trained on you. Yeah, it's a blast."

"Wow. Remind me not to get nominated."

Ava took another sip of coffee. "I'm sure it's wonderful if your family is with you and you don't find out your mother has cancer on the same night. I have a pretty skewered take on it."

"You found out that night?"

"Rose had to call me. They kept it a secret from me for three weeks because my mother didn't want to 'ruin' it for me. Can you imagine? I was so upset when I found that out."

Seamus shook his head. "You know mothers. They protect their kids at all costs."

"But I hadn't seen my mother in ten years. Three weeks is a long time to lose when you don't have much time left."

"Ten years is a long time."

"So what do you do now, Seamus?"

He blinked at the rapid change of subject but followed her cue. "I'm a police officer."

"Wow. I never would have guessed that."

"Why?"

"I don't know. You planned on going to university."

"My plans changed that summer."

A dreadfully awkward silence ensued.

"This isn't going to work," Ava sighed. "Our conversations are filled with landmines at every turn. Maybe we should quit trying."

"No. Please. That was stupid of me. I should've said that I liked the idea of helping the community and it was a great excuse to go live in P.E.I. for a while and get away from my dad."

Ava took another sip of her coffee. "Tell me about your children."

It got easier after that. Ava found out that Jack loved dinosaurs and hated vegetables and his favourite thing was to go fishing with his dad. Sarah loved everything except going to bed and her vocabulary was limited yet to only a few words. Seamus told her about his niece and nephew and about his cat, Dexter. Dexter thought he was a dog and liked to go for walks with Seamus along the beach.

Then, their coffee was finished.

"I guess I shouldn't keep you any longer," Seamus said.

"That's okay. It shouldn't take more than a few minutes to do what I have to do."

Looking at his list, Seamus grinned. "I may be here till this place closes. I'm hopeless at this sort of thing. I get confused at the sizes. But Colleen believes in tough love. She says they're my kids and my responsibility. It would take her ten minutes to do this, but she won't."

"She's right. She's trying to make you self-sufficient. What if she ever moved away?"

"My kids would be naked."

Ava laughed. "I know! Why don't I help you? I don't have kids, but I do have a lot of nieces and nephews and I've shopped for their gifts every birthday and Christmas. We won't tell Colleen and she'll think you're a genius."

"Okay. Why not? Lead on."

They spent a good hour rooting through the children's sections at various stores. She explained the sizes to him and any time he picked up anything just because it was the right size, she tried to steer him to more suitable choices. She said she doubted Sarah would want to wear robot pajamas and maybe she'd like Dora the Explorer instead. When Ava spotted new bathing suits for both of the kids, Seamus turned to the pile in his cart. "I think I'm at my limit. Summer's not here for a couple of months."

She put her hand on her hip. "Spoken like a typical man. By the time you come back here in two months everything will be picked over."

"Well…"

"Oh Seamus, let me buy them. Please? It would give me such pleasure."

"You don't—"

"I know I don't have to, but I'd love to."

He smiled at her. "All right then. Have it your way."

Ava was positively giddy taking the bathing suits to the check-out. When the girl ran them through, she tucked them into Seamus's shopping cart. "There. Colleen will thank you."

"I thank you. It's been a wonderful afternoon."

They stood by the door to the parking lot, out of the way of the shoppers coming in and going out.

"It has been wonderful. I'll never forget it."

Seamus looked around and then leaned in closer. "Look, Libby, is there any way we can get together and be alone?"

She bit her bottom lip before saying, "Do you think that's wise?"

"What's to stop us? Our past? The past is over. We should be able to be friends and enjoy each other's company. I miss talking to a woman."

"I'd like that. But where?"

"Why don't we meet at Gooseberry Cove? Just name the day."

"Friday. I'll meet you Friday at six."

"Six it is."

"Goodbye, Seamus."

"Bye, Libby." He leaned down and kissed her cheek. And then he was gone.

It was only when she got home that she realized she forgot to buy anything for herself.

✢

It was a long week waiting for Friday to come. Ava tried to keep busy. The house was spotless and she spent a great deal of time with her mother, telling her stories about her travels all over the world or reading to her for hours at a time. Often her mother slept while she read, but Ava hoped that the sound of her voice would bring her mother comfort.

One day her mother grabbed her hand and kissed it. "Thank you, Libby. Thank you for being so kind to me."

Ava closed her eyes and tried not to let guilt overwhelm her. She knew she'd stayed away too long and she'd give anything to get that time back again. At least it did her heart good to know that Aunt Vi and Uncle Angus were feeling better. She took them to the doctor, who was pleased with their progress. They were still sore, of course, and moved slowly, but their good spirits had returned. Aunt Vi even insisted on making bread pudding one day, saying if she didn't bake something soon, she'd forget how.

Finally Friday came and Ava spent the day puttering and humming to herself. That is until her agent Trent called with some bogus excuse to reel off more projects that might be coming her way—if only she'd come home sooner rather than later.

She was polite but firm, and Trent was thwarted yet again. She had to give him points for trying, though.

And then something happened that she never saw coming. There was a knock at the back door.

"Someone get that!" Uncle Angus hollered. "And if it's Boots Boutlier, tell him to get the jesus in here. I'm bored outta me gourd."

"Okay!" Ava shouted back. She was in the pantry rolling out cookie dough. She wiped her floury hands on her apron and walked to the back porch. Who was standing on the outside steps but Hayden. Ava was dumbfounded. She could have kicked him.

He waved at her. "Darling, aren't you going to let me in?"

She stormed over and opened door. "What on earth are you doing here?"

"Enlarging my fan base." He waved to Thelma Steele and Geranium and the half-dozen other women running toward the house. "I best scoot in now, before I'm mauled." He pushed past her and straight into the kitchen. He looked around. "My, how…country."

Aunt Vi yelled from the living room. "Who's at the door?"

"No one!" To Hayden, she whispered, "You have to get out of here."

"But why? I've come to take you and your family out to dinner. I'm sure your sisters will be thrilled." He shouted out, "Where is this wonderful Aunt Vi I keep hearing about?" He made for the living room before Ava could stop him. Ava heard Aunt Vi shriek, "Mother Mary and all that's Holy! Are you who I think you are?"

"The very same."

Ava ran up the stairs and grabbed Lola, who was on her knees scrubbing the bathtub. "You'll never believe who just showed up."

"Who?"

"Hayden."

"Good God. I didn't think he knew where Canada was."

"He's been here before, remember?"

"Oh yeah! Well, that's typical behaviour. Give him an inch and he takes a mile."

"He wants to take us out to dinner. What am I going to do? Oh damn. Today of all days."

Lola got up and looked out the bathroom window. "His arrival has been noted, I'm afraid. There are two ladies, and I use the term loosely, outside fighting over who gets the milk crate so they can stand on it and peek in the window."

Ava hopped up and down in frustration. "My sisters will hear about this and dash over here after work, but I can't go to dinner, I have to meet Seamus."

"Your very famous boyfriend arrives in town and wants to take the whole clan out for a bang-up meal and you're not going to be with them? How in God's name are you going to explain that?"

"I hate him!"

"Who? God?"

"Shut up, Lola."

Ava ran to the hall table and rooted around in the pile of magazines and found a phone book. She took it to her room and looked up Catalone, but it didn't seem to be in the phone book—then she remembered to look under Port Morien. She searched through the O's, and since there weren't that many, it took only a second to realize his number was unlisted. She had no way of getting in touch with him. She didn't dare call his family. Why hadn't she asked him for a phone number? She threw the phone book across the room.

There was nothing she could do but go downstairs. Hayden

had Aunt Vi and Uncle Angus enthralled with his tales of Hollywood nightlife. (There was nothing Hayden liked better than a captive audience.)

The phone rang and Ava hoped against hope it was Seamus, but it turned out to be a CBC reporter who wanted to confirm that Hayden Judd was visiting the area and whether it was possible to get an interview. Ava slammed the phone in his ear.

As predicted, the whole clan started arriving one by one, after fighting off the mob outside. Ava had to introduce them one at a time. Hayden was charm personified and everyone thought he was fabulous. Her sisters spent most of their time giggling at him. For her part, Ava wanted to gag.

Hayden told everyone that he'd booked an entire restaurant for them and everyone was invited, children as well. He looked at his watch. "How about we meet in front of Governor's in an hour. Ava will need at least that long to put on her face. And it's such a beautiful face." He pulled her to him and kissed her in front of everyone. The family tittered. It took all her willpower not to kick him in the shin.

Everyone took off in twenty different directions and Hayden dragged her into the seldom-used front hall. He put his arms around her.

"You don't seem very happy to see me."

"It's not that. I don't like surprises."

"I'm trying to help; to give your family something to smile about. If it makes them happy just to turn up and take them to dinner, then it's worth the five-hour flight to get here."

"You're right. I'm sorry," she sighed.

"Of course I'm right. Now kiss me."

She gave him a peck.

"Not like that."

"Hayden, I have to get ready."

"Kiss me."

She kissed him and he pulled her in tight. He wouldn't let her go. He pressed his mouth against hers until it hurt. She struggled against him but he was too strong. Panic welled up inside. That's when she realized there were people looking in the windows at them. And he knew it. The stupid jerk knew all along.

Since she couldn't fight him, she went limp instead. He groaned, as if relishing his victory. He took his lips away. "See, baby? You love me."

She caught him by surprise when she pushed him away. "You can stop acting for your audience now."

Pretending he didn't know what she was talking about, he turned to look out the window. "Goodness. All these people."

"You're sick."

He rolled his eyes. "Ava, stop being so touchy. It's a bit of fun. What better way to brighten up dreary lives than to put on a free show starring two of Hollywood's finest?"

"You are so full of yourself."

"Calm down, I'm joking. Ava, please don't make a big deal out of it. I apologize."

He looked contrite, but then again, he was a good actor.

"May I go upstairs and get dressed now?"

"Of course."

She ran up the stairs wanting nothing more than to wash her face, but there was a lineup for the bathroom, what with everyone getting ready for their night out. Lola told them she'd stay with the elders, so they could enjoy themselves. Auntie Vi called her "a little darlin'." As much as she would've liked to have gone, Aunt Vi was content with her private audience earlier. No one wanted her to fall and break her other ankle.

As she waited, Ava saw how much this night out with Hayden meant to them. It made her feel small and foolish. He flew all this way to make her family happy and they were. She had to make this sacrifice. She'd explain it to Seamus. Hopefully he'd understand.

When six o'clock arrived, Ava was in a limo. They went out on the town and everyone had a wonderful time. Hayden was the life of the party and her family was in love with him. They couldn't believe how thoughtful he was. He'd hired a trio of musicians and he danced with all the ladies and the young girls. The looks on their faces told Ava it was worth it. She was one and they were many. How often did something like this happen to them? When she danced with Hayden herself, everyone clapped.

That night, as they drove home, she genuinely meant it when she thanked him. This time he was sweet, kissing her cheek chastely. "The gig in New York this September will be wonderful. You and I playing lovers. Great typecasting, don't you think?"

She nodded.

"Take care of yourself. And if you need me for anything, I'll be back on the next plane. I'm going to miss you, beautiful."

He held her close and she let him, then he kissed her hand and said goodbye. She got out of the limo and walked into the house. It was midnight.

CHAPTER TEN

He waited until ten.

The day before Seamus had imposed on Colleen yet again, asking her to take the kids for the night. She gave him a bit of a look, but knew better than to ask what he had planned. It was the usual sort of day at work, nothing too exciting happened; near the end of his shift, he caught a drunk driver. Nothing gave him more pleasure than pulling the bastard off the road.

The day done, he hurried home to give the place a quick tidy-up, telling himself she wasn't going to come back to the house with him, but if she did, he didn't want to embarrass himself.

After a long hot shower and time spent trying to figure out what to wear, he finally chose a white denim button-down shirt and a pair of jeans. He threw on a brown leather jacket at the last minute and slapped on some of the cologne Colleen gave him for Christmas. Looking at himself in the mirror, he was satisfied. He wanted Libby to know that he'd made an effort.

For the last half hour, Seamus sat in a kitchen chair shaking his leg nervously. When he couldn't stand it any longer, he hopped in the car. Gooseberry Cove wasn't far away. He pulled down the narrow rutted road and parked to one side. He got out, locked the doors and walked along the grassy cliffs, looking out over the huge black rocks where waves broke in spectacular fashion, white foam flying into the air.

Seamus loved it here. It was quiet and away from everyday life. The blue sky was full of enormous white clouds and as he sat on one of the grassy knolls, he watched the gulls swirl about in the air. He was lucky enough to spy not one but two eagles, so high up he could hardly make out their white caps. It was a blustery day, but as the minutes passed, the wind died down a little and he didn't have to squint against the on-shore breeze.

The first hour he waited, he laughed to himself, because the Libby he knew was always late. It was comforting to know she hadn't changed. They would agree to meet and inevitably he was left to cool his heels. When he first went out with her, he'd panic and think she wasn't coming, but after a while, he came to know all her excuses. There was a chickadee that followed her and she didn't want to leave it. A spider was building a web. There was a rainbow shining in the sky and if she were a rainbow she'd want someone to stop and look at her. The best one was the day she told him she'd found a snake run over by a car and all its babies were drying out in the sun on the hot pavement, so she had to take them to a shady spot, hoping they'd live. She was close to tears when she told him.

The second hour, he was concerned about her. What if someone gave her a hard time about meeting him? He didn't think she'd tell anyone, but maybe someone found out. Then he wondered if she had an accident. She wasn't used to these narrow back roads anymore.

The third hour, he worried that he'd pushed her into something she wasn't ready for. He was an idiot for calling her up while he was drunk. What kind of impression did that make? She was being polite, that was all; didn't know how to tell him to leave her alone. She always was a big softie.

The fourth hour, when the sun had long since disappeared behind the horizon and the stars came out; he concluded that she didn't want him. She left him again. How many times did he have to be told? If she wanted him, she'd be here. He looked around the isolated landscape. He was alone. Wasn't that proof enough?

Seamus was angry by the time he reached home, more at himself than at her. What a complete fool he felt. She was famous. Libby was someone else now. He was her high school boyfriend, a first love hankering after something that wasn't real. He was in love with a memory—the memory of a girl laughing in the surf on a moonlit night, her hair dancing around her face as a gown of shimmering white flew around her.

Seamus got out of the car and went in the house, throwing his keys on the table. Off came his jacket, tossed over a chair. He went to get a Coke, but grabbed a beer instead, downing it as he stood in the light of the fridge. He tossed the can in the sink and grabbed the rest of the six-pack and took it into the living room with him. He switched on the TV and drank steadily as he flipped through the channels.

The local evening news came on. At the end of it there was a fun story about how famous actor Hayden Judd shocked the residents of Glace Bay by showing up unannounced, to escort his girlfriend, local sweetheart Ava Harris and her family to dinner. A reporter asked a few of the excited citizens on the street if they had a chance to have a quick glance at the handsome leading man.

Two women, one with a hair full of curlers, nodded enthusiastically. "He was bee-uu-tiful," one of them said. "Ain't that right, Theresa?"

"My gawd, he looked right good. Good enough to eat." Theresa grabbed the mike. "He almost ate the face off her, so he did."

The reporter asked, "Off who?"

"That there Ava Harris, eh. They was smoochin' up a storm. I never saw the like of it. It was somethin' awful."

"There you have it," the reporter said. "A live witness account of…"

Seamus clicked off the TV angrily and stared at the black screen.

Eventually, he got up and took his last two beers out on the deck. He finished them in about three swallows before he took the cans and hurled them as far as he could into the night, grunting with the effort of it.

Then he fell back into a deck chair and stayed there until the sun came up.

❁

Ava got up at the crack of dawn. She put on a pair of old jeans and a hoodie belonging to her niece Vicky, piling her hair up loosely with a clip and pulling the hood over it. She grabbed the car keys and tiptoed out of the bedroom after leaving a note for Lola saying she'd be back in a couple of hours.

Careful to close the door quietly behind her, she hopped in the car and drove out to Catalone. She had a general idea of where he lived and knew that one of the locals would be able to point her to the exact house. But she was nervous to approach anyone in case they recognized her. She had to risk it.

In the end, she went to the Albert Bridge gas station and asked the young fellow who worked there if he knew where Seamus O'Reilly lived. He wasn't sure, so he went into the store and asked someone, coming back to tell her it was a house on the edge of the beach and that she couldn't miss it. It had a big deck in front and it was grey with blue shutters.

Ava thanked him and went on her way. She found it quickly and it was just as they said. It brought a smile to her face because Seamus always told her that if he ever shingled a house, he'd never stain it because he liked a weather-beaten look. The house looked like a large fisherman's shack. She liked it very much.

It was difficult to be there, because it was above the beach. Their beach. But she had to see him and explain. She couldn't leave it one more second.

Pulling up behind the car already in the driveway, she got out of the rental and walked towards the house. Her sandals crunched on the gravel beneath her feet. She wasn't sure which door to go in, finally choosing to walk up on the deck. There, Seamus was sound asleep in a deck chair, curled up, with his hands tucked under his arms. He looked frozen. Ava didn't know what to do at first. She didn't want to scare him, but his lips looked blue. The morning was cold.

She approached him, taking a moment to gaze at his sweet face. How she loved that face. He looked like a little kid. She touched his arm gently and whispered, "Seamus."

He never moved. She shook his sleeve a little. "Seamus, wake up."

God. Maybe he'd frozen to death in the night, she thought. She started to panic and raised her voice. "Seamus, please. Wake up."

He bolted out of the chair, seemingly unaware of his surroundings. "Wha? What is it?"

"It's me."

He looked at her with his eyes half closed. "Who?"

"Libby." She pulled the hood off her head.

His face registered shock and then he started to shiver uncontrollably.

"Please, Seamus. We have to get you in the house. You're freezing." She took his arm and steered him towards the door. He looked at her as if he still didn't understand exactly who she was or why she was there.

"Is this a dream?"

"No. I'm quite real. Let's get a blanket around you." She pulled him through the door and made him sit in an armchair. She grabbed an afghan off the couch and put it around him. "I'm going to get you something hot to drink."

He stared at her.

She soon had a kettle boiling and after a search through the cupboards, found some tea. Then she went into his bathroom and looked under the sink for a hot water bottle. She found one and filled it with hot water from the tub. Next, it was on to his bedroom where she opened bureau drawers looking for socks. She grabbed a pair and finally pulled the comforter off the bed and dragged it into the living room behind her.

Back in the kitchen, she filled a mug with the hot tea and added a little milk. She took everything back into the living room. Without saying a word, she handed him the hot water bottle and then tucked the comforter around him. Off went his shoes and on went another pair of thick socks. Then she passed him the tea.

"Put your hands around it and you'll get warm. Be careful, it's hot."

He took a drink and then two. After a few minutes, his lips lost their blue tint and his cheeks turned from white to red. She sat on the ottoman in front of him.

"Seamus, I couldn't come to you yesterday. I'm sorry. I wanted to. I wanted to very much."

He looked at her and took another drink.

"Why were you out on the deck? Please tell me that wasn't because of me."

He cleared his throat. "No, of course not. You're not that important."

She winced.

"I had too much to drink and fell asleep that's all."

"Oh."

"You didn't have to come here."

She looked away. "No, I guess I didn't." She took a deep breath and stood up. "Anyway, I'm glad I did, because maybe I saved you from pneumonia, if nothing else."

"Yeah, thanks."

"Sure. I should get back home. Can't leave Lola alone with three patients for too long. She'll have my hide."

Ava walked to the door. "Take care of yourself, Seamus."

She had her hand on the knob when he said, "Heard about your boyfriend on TV last night."

She didn't turn around but she heard him get out of the chair. "Yeah, it was all over the news, how Hayden Judd came into town to neck up a storm with his girlfriend, a certain famous actress. Imagine kissing in front of a whole crowd of people like that. Did you get off on it?"

She turned to face him. "It wasn't like that."

"Wasn't it?"

"No. If you'd let me explain..."

"There's nothing to explain. You said you'd meet me and you didn't. Instead you made out with your boyfriend in front of the whole town. A real public way of saying, get lost Seamus. I just wish you'd had the decency to say it to my face."

Her breathing became shallow. "I wanted to get to you. You have to believe me."

"I don't believe you, Libby, because actions speak louder than words."

"Think what you want, then." She turned to go and tried to open the door but struggled with the lock. In those few moments, he came up behind her, grabbed her shoulders and turned her around.

"You were supposed to be kissing me last night."

"Leave me alone."

"Just tell me why. Why do you leave me?"

"I don't want to leave you. I've never wanted to leave you."

"But you do. You do, Libby, and I don't know how much more I can take."

She couldn't stand it anymore. She reached up and put her hands on his face, looked at his mouth and brought her lips to meet his. It wasn't soft and slow. It was angry, hard and searching. She bit his tongue and licked the small drop of blood that formed. He sucked her top lip, then her bottom. He lifted his head and with his hands moved her face first one way and then another, giving her kisses that were fast and deep and intense. They both moaned, aching for each other. Just a moment more...

The phone rang.

They parted, both of them panting. Neither of them spoke. The phone rang again.

"Wait," he said.

"I have to go."

Another ring. "Please, two seconds."

He raced to the phone, "Yes?" He listened but never took his eyes off her. She rubbed her bruised lips against the soft fleece of her cuff. Her heart rate slowed and the pulse in her ears quieted.

"An ear infection? Are you sure she's all right? Okay, I'll phone the doctor. Thanks. See you in ten."

He hung up the phone.

"Sarah?"

"Yes. Colleen was up with her all night. I'm taking her in."

"Can I do anything to help?"

He shook his head.

She backed up to the door. "I'm sorry."

"Me too. We'll talk."

"Okay."

With the door finally open, she ran to the car, started it up and roared out of the driveway. She sped away from the house as fast as she could, but stopped at the look-off in Port Morien to sit for a minute and try to understand what had happened back there. She was ashamed and excited all at the same time. It was almost as if they were dueling, trying to hurt each other with their bodies, expressing their anger the only way they could. But she was exhausted. She knew she'd reached the end of her emotional rope. Life was slower here but so far the trip had been a roller coaster and she wasn't sure how much more she could take. And that was frightening because she knew it meant hurting him again.

When she got back to the house, everyone except Lola was still asleep. She was on the bed reading a magazine.

"Bloody hell. Were you in a fight?"

"Sort of."

Lola put the magazine down. "You are driving me around the bend. What is going on?"

Ava plunked down on the bed and covered her face in her hands. "I think I need to get out of here. I'm ruining everyone's life."

"Rubbish. Everyone's glad you're here. You're a regular Suzy Homemaker, and you've made life a whole lot easier for everyone since you've arrived."

She looked up and smiled. "I don't think I'd have stayed if you weren't here. I have no right to ask you to stay on."

"I told you before, I love it here."

Ava took off her sandals and sat back against the headboard. "Why? Why do you love it here?"

Lola's face lit up. "Because the people are real. When they say something they mean it. You don't have to wonder if someone's telling you the truth. They take pleasure in their friends and they can party like no one else. Hey, they can make music with two spoons. How great is that?"

Ava smiled, though it hurt her swollen lips.

"And I've never laughed so much in all my life. You have a wonderful family, Ava. You don't need to run away from them."

"I didn't run away from them."

"What happened to you?"

"Seamus and I kind of beat each other up."

"I don't mean today, I mean when you left the first time."

When she didn't say anything, Lola sighed. "Okay, what happened to you today? He didn't hit you, I hope."

"He kissed me."

"Wow. He should patent those kisses. Women everywhere pay good money to get bee-stung lips. He'd make a fortune."

"Don't make me laugh. It hurts."

"Stop bragging. I better go get the porridge on. Uncle Angus will be banging his bowl before too long." She got up and left the room.

Ava sat for a long time, absentmindedly tracing her lips with her forefinger. She could still feel him pressing against them. He left a permanent mark. She'd always have it and was grateful for it. Did he feel the same way?

What would've happened if the phone hadn't rung? She almost blushed thinking about it. So she thought about it some more. She snuggled into the blankets and made love to him in her mind. It was something she was good at—she'd been doing it for years.

CHAPTER ELEVEN

As if by some secret pact, they stayed away from each other after that. Ava was grateful for the chance to get back a sense of normalcy. And besides, the end of June was rapidly approaching and she had a date with her nieces. The day after she mentioned her idea, she placed a call to Maurice and asked him if he'd help her out.

"Anything for you, dumpling. What is it? Oh, just a minute." She heard him shout at Harold. "Tell that walking-stick of a client that I can't poof her hair up. She'll look like a Q-tip." He came back on the line. "You were saying, darling?"

"You wouldn't like to take a little side trip, would you?"

"You sweet thing. Where are we going now? Morocco? Paris, please God."

"Cape Breton, Nova Scotia?"

"Cape where?"

"You know. Where I live."

"You live in Malibu."

"Maurice…"

"Oh. You mean Canada, where the Inuit and the Mounties do play?"

"That's right."

"Pardon my French, darling, but isn't it fucking freezing there?"

"Of course not, it's June. Granted, it's not California hot."

"I'll wear my pink long johns. So what am I doing for you?

What fabulous event is so important that I have to fly to the other side of the earth?"

. "Um, I'd like you to do my nieces' hair and makeup for the prom."

"Say what?"

"You know, the prom. A magic night in any young girl's life. It's important and they were so excited when I mentioned it."

"They?"

"There are three of them."

Maurice hollered, "Harold! Get my smelling salts."

"Please? Please? With sugar on top?"

"Replace the sugar with Hugh Jackman and you've got a deal."

"Thank you so much. I love you!"

"That's what they all say." He hung up on her and she kissed the phone.

The day arrived when Ava, her sisters and nieces traipsed into Sydney to look for prom dresses. Lola tagged along as well, after Sandy's wife told them she'd be glad to babysit the old folk for the afternoon. At first Ava offered to fly them to Halifax for the day, to look at some of the formal-wear shops there, but everyone seemed happier with the thought of staying close to home, mostly in case Mamie took a turn for the worst.

When their entourage arrived at Jacobson's, they trooped up the stairs to the bridal salon. The sales ladies did a double take when they realized Ava Harris was in their shop.

The girls went wild and so did their mothers. Ava and Lola fairly hopped with glee. Sam, Vicky and Emily each headed for a different dressing room and came out again and again to model their choices and get feedback. Ava beamed watching them. Their fresh faces instantly transformed into young beauties as they twirled around in a sea of sparkling silk, taffeta and organza. But what was even more wonderful for Ava was the joy in her sisters' faces as they gazed upon their baby girls.

The girls were delighted with their choices and each of them ran to their Aunt Libby to give her big hugs.

Ava summoned one of the salesladies, who looked overwhelmed herself with all the excitement. "Get the girls to pick out the most expensive shoes and whatever else they need."

"Can I have a tiara?" Vicky whispered.

"Of course you can. And gloves and wraps and little satin bags...whatever your heart desires."

"Even jewelry?" Emily squeaked.

Her mother said, "That's enough, honey. She's spending way too much as it is."

"Nonsense. Choose whatever you like and we'll have them wrap it up."

The girls flitted off to try on satin and rhinestone high heels, and then hurried to the jewelry counter to ohh and ahh over necklaces and earrings.

"Oh god," Bev tsked, "this is way too much Libby. You've already spent eight hundred dollars each for their dresses."

Ava grabbed her hands. "Please let me. I don't have children of my own. Who else do I have to spend my money on?"

Lola raised her hand. "I'm at your service."

They wrapped up their incredible afternoon with a lovely lunch at Goodies and then scooted home to show everyone their purchases. But as incredible as that day was, it was nothing compared to the excitement generated by the arrival of Maurice and his entourage.

Aunt Vi could hardly contain her excitement. "I'm real glad

this is hair central. Wait till them fellas get here. Geranium will have a stroke."

Uncle Angus rocked in the rocking chair. "I'll leave once them fairy fellas show up. But I have to see one up close."

Ava put her hands on her hips. "How do you know they're fairy fellas?"

He snorted. "What sort of man plays with makeup? I'm not stupid, ya know."

Aunt Vi concurred. "Everyone knows them Hollywood hairdressers sit to pee."

Lola laughed out loud. "Oh Aunt Vi. I love you."

Ava knew the jet was landing at eleven o'clock. She arranged for a car to pick them up, so estimated they'd arrive around eleven thirty, which would give them a chance to catch their breath and also have a bite before the girls showed up. Under Aunt Vi's tutelage, she and Lola prepared a nice lunch of lobster rolls, tea biscuits, potato salad, and pasta salad. There was fresh strawberry shortcake with whipped cream for dessert.

The car pulled up bang on time. Maurice, Harold, and their assistants, Lars and Philippe, disembarked with the dazed look of people who'd been dropped on another planet. Maurice wore a multi-coloured scarf around his neck with what looked like a purple Stetson on his head. His suit was impeccable.

Harold, in his oversized mirrored sunglasses, clapped his hands at the driver in an obvious attempt to get the man moving with the bags. Ava and Lola rushed out to meet them.

Ava ran into Maurice's arms. "Oh, I've missed you! Thank you for this."

He hugged her and lifted her off her feet. "Good God, you're enormous. You fat pig."

"I know," she smiled. "It's my Aunt Vi's cooking."

"Where is the beastly woman? She mustn't go unpunished."

He delivered a quick peck to Lola. "You're looking as vile as ever."

"Ditto," she retorted.

Maurice looked around and sniffed the air. "What is that foul odor?"

"The fish plant over there."

"Ah. Tell them to move it." He looked around and then peered from under his glasses. "There's a woman with a telescope leering at us."

"Wave. That's Geranium."

He waved and Geranium disappeared. She no doubt fell to the floor in a dead faint.

Harold rushed up, Lars and Philippe on his heels carrying the bags. "Ava, it's so good to see you!" He grabbed her and gave her a big kiss before turning around and ordering the other two about. "We're on an impossible schedule, darlings, so chop chop. We have to be in the air by seven."

Maurice held up his hands. "Harold, calm down. Genius takes time. We don't want to rush the little creatures. Apparently, it's a big night in their lives, so Ava informs me. And speaking of Ava, sweetie, you need drastic emergency work on your roots. I'm surprised people don't flee in disgust when they see you."

"Never mind me. Come meet my family."

They headed for the house. Inside, they took off their sunglasses simultaneously.

"Oh my," Maurice sniffed. "How adorable."

"Quaint," Harold agreed. Lars and Philippe were too stunned to speak.

Ava pulled Maurice along. "Maurice, this is my Uncle Angus and my Aunt Vi."

Maurice held out his hand, as if waiting for someone to kiss it. "Charmed."

Uncle Angus reached out and waggled his index finger. "Nice to meet you."

"Thank you, kind sir. And this is your lovely wife. Enchanté, madam."

Aunt Vi dismissed him with her hand and giggled. "Lordy, ain't you a sight for sore eyes."

"That's what people tell me."

Ava ushered them into the dining room where their lunch was laid out. "I thought you could do with a bite before the girls get here."

"Oh darling, you know I never eat."

"Is that so?" Uncle Angus said. "Is that some kinda rule?"

"Excuse me?"

Lola jumped in. "No one eats in Hollywood, Uncle Angus."

"Remind me not to go there."

Maurice took a second look at the scrumptious feast. "Well, one has to be polite. I'll make an exception."

Not a crumb was left by the time they served the tea.

The girls and their mothers arrived, excited and nervous. The minute they saw Maurice and his entourage, they became unnaturally quiet. They looked completely overwhelmed, like lambs to the slaughter.

But Maurice wasn't famous for nothing. He instantly engaged his famous charm and made the girls feel at ease. Ava was grateful that he took the engagement seriously. He pondered and discussed the merits of one hairstyle over another, then consulted with the girls about what kind of colour they might like and even took a folded piece of paper that Samantha gave him with a picture of Britney Spears on it, pretending to examine it closely.

Harold, with Maurice's guidance, supervised the mixing of colours for the streaks. All the women watched the process with fascination. Uncle Angus excused himself and went to watch *The Price is Right*. Soon their tools—hair dryers, huge rollers, and flat irons—were spread over the kitchen table. At one point the girls looked like TV dinners, they had so much foil on their heads.

The facilities weren't ideal, but everyone kept their sense of humour. Once the colour was done, Maurice rolled up his sleeves and gave every one of them a five-hundred-dollar haircut. The girls couldn't take their eyes off one another.

Vicky clapped her hands. "Joey is gonna die when he sees me."

Maurice gave them beautiful up-do's, placed their tiaras in their hair and shook glitter over them. All that was left was the makeup, and Maurice took his time with each of them. When they were done, the girls were speechless. They took turns hugging Maurice and thanked him from the bottom of their hearts.

Maurice dabbed his eyes with his scarf as they left. "Those darling children. They were so grateful! I've been jaded by dreary socialites. I really must get out more."

Ava and Lola put on fresh tea and brought out the tray of squares always on hand in Aunt Vi's kitchen. As Lars and Philippe did the dirty job of tidying up, Maurice and Harold sat at the kitchen table and delivered the scandalous news from tinsel town. Ava was brought up to date on who was having sex with whom, who had a court order against the paparazzi, who'd gone into detox and who'd had breast augmentation.

Aunt Vi's eyes grew bigger by the minute. She said, "Go way with ya," every two minutes until Maurice asked her if she really wanted him to leave. She thought that was great.

The instruments of beauty were eventually packed away and a tired-looking Maurice said it was time to go. He kissed everyone goodbye, even a shocked Uncle Angus.

Ava walked out to the car with him, arm in arm. She said goodbye to Harold and the others while Maurice lingered behind.

"So, my love. Are you all right? You look a little peaked."

Maurice had been her soft shoulder for eight long years. She hugged him again and sighed into his label. "I'm so confused."

"About the boy?"

"Yes."

"You know what I say, little one. It all comes out in the rinse water. What is meant to happen will happen, so take your time."

"I love you."

"Of course you do. Who wouldn't?"

She gave him a squeeze. "Thank you for today."

"For you, anything." He kissed her and started for the limo but before he disappeared, he blew a giant kiss to Geranium. Down she went again.

Ava waved them off. She was lonely when they were gone.

But she didn't have time to linger. There was the Grand March to get to. She and Lola decided to go when Thelma Steele next door said she'd pass the evening with Vi and Angus and Mamie. As much as Ava wanted to go, she didn't want to upstage the girls. She told her sisters that if there was a scene caused by autograph hounds, she'd leave. It was their night with their daughters and as much as she wanted to be there, they came first.

Thankfully, no one made a fuss. They were too interested in their own flesh and blood, so she and Lola sat like all the others, soaking up the sight of young people in their finery. As Vicky, Emily, and Samantha went by at regular intervals with their dates, they threw her big smiles and she gave them a little wave. Like every year, when it was time for daughters to dance with their fathers, and boys with their mothers, there wasn't a dry eye in the joint.

A million pictures were taken and then the adults were ushered out and the kids were let loose to make their own fun at the dance. Parents lingered in the parking lot, remarking on how fabulous everyone looked. A great many of her sisters' friends came up and remarked how pretty the girls were, but Ava thought, in the end, they really looked like all the others. Maurice hadn't gone overboard and Ava was grateful for that. They were young girls, not actresses.

And then it was over. All that excitement, all the waiting and planning and shopping. It was a bit of a let-down.

When Ava and Lola returned home, they entertained Aunt Vi and Uncle Angus with some of the shots from Ava's digital camera.

"Why don't you go upstairs and show your Ma? She'd love to see it." Ava went up to relieve Thelma. As Thelma left, she whispered, "I'm not sure she's so good tonight. She seemed a little short of breath, but then I haven't seen her that much."

Ava thanked her and told her not to worry; they'd take care of it, even if it meant calling the doctor. She sat by her mother and held her hand. Mamie fluttered her eyelashes but her eyes remained closed. She spoke so softly, Ava could hardly hear her.

"How did it go?"

"It was beautiful." She felt her mother's forehead. "Ma, I think I better call the doctor. You're a little pale and Thelma said you seemed to have trouble breathing."

She squeezed her hand slightly. "Please don't."

Ava wasn't sure what to do.

"Don't leave me."

She remained where she was, holding her mother's hand. Mamie smiled a little and whispered, "You were born during a snow storm, did you know that?"

"No."

"It was an awful night, and we couldn't get to the hospital. I had you right here on this bed."

"You did?"

"All the kids were down in the kitchen and when the midwife handed you to your father, he took you downstairs and sat in the rocking chair so everyone could see you."

Ava bit her lip.

"They all suggested names. Gerard wanted to call you Old Yeller, because you cried a lot."

"Typical."

"We were very happy you came into the world."

Ava lowered her cheek on the back of her mother's hand. Mamie reached out with her other hand and placed it on her daughter's head.

"Life and death in this old bed. And all that's in between is the love."

Ava's tears fell.

"Be happy, child. Find peace."

"I will Ma. I'll try." She lifted her head and looked at her mother's face. It seemed different. Her heart raced a little. "I think I should call someone."

"Don't. Please. Just sit with me."

She sat for an hour. Her mother stopped talking, breathing in and out with shallow intakes of air. And then suddenly she gave a little gasp.

"What is it, Ma? Please let me get you some help."

She was barely audible. "Your father's here."

Ava didn't move. No. This couldn't be happening. Not with just her in the room. What about the others? They'd want to be here. But before she could get out of the chair, her mother's face turned to the wall and she stopped breathing.

Ava stared in disbelief. In the end, her mother wanted only her in the room. A very old dam burst then and there and she howled with the pain of it. Great sobs racked her body.

She didn't have to summon anyone. They came running to her.

CHAPTER TWELVE

Seamus didn't want to admit it to himself, but he was badly shaken by what had transpired between the two of them. Trouble was, he didn't have a chance to examine his own heart closely because real life kept interfering.

There was the rush to get Sarah to the doctor. She was miserable and feverish when he picked her up and he felt terrible that she cried in her car seat all the way in. She wanted a hug but he had to drive. Colleen offered to come too, but it was more helpful for her to watch Jack. A dose of antibiotics did the trick eventually, and she was right as rain, but Seamus felt guilty dropping Sarah off at daycare. When the kids were sick, he always worried that he didn't know enough and that he'd let Sally down. These were the days when he missed his wife the most.

Seamus found himself at the cemetery one day after work. He often went, always with a few flowers. He wished there was a bench to sit on so he didn't have to kneel awkwardly in front of her or stand feeling useless above her.

"I'm sorry, Sally. I love you. I'm so confused. She means nothing and she means everything. It's complicated. But it doesn't take away from you. I'm forever grateful that we found each other, because what would I do without Jack and Sarah? They were meant to be. I know that."

He kissed his fingers and touched the grass in front of the headstone. He was about to leave when he saw Sally's mother,

Lynn, coming between the rows. She was a nice looking woman, sort of round, with flyaway graying hair she tried to keep in a bun. She had daisies and buttercups in a little container.

"Hi, Seamus."

"Hi, Lynn. How are you?"

"Never good when I come here."

"No."

She placed the flowers on the ground and patted it, as if to say, I'll be with you in a minute. Lynn straightened up and smiled. "How are my beautiful grandchildren?"

"Sarah had an ear infection earlier in the week. It's better now."

"Thank goodness. Sally used to get ear infections, I remember. Must run in the family."

Seamus nodded.

Lynn looked at him. "Are you all right, dear?"

"I'm okay."

"You know, Sally's father and I will take the children any time you need us. As a matter of fact, I wanted to ask if I could have them for the weekend. Our dog had puppies and now that they're a few weeks old, I thought the kids would like to see them."

He cleared his throat but his voice was husky. "That would be great."

"Honey—"

He held his thumb and forefinger over his eyes to try and get himself under control.

Lynn put her hand on his arm. "There, there, pet. I know. I know all about it."

He stepped backwards and held his cuff to his nose.

Lynn reached in her pocket. "I always have tissue. I can't come here otherwise." She passed it to him.

"Thanks."

"I know it doesn't feel like it, but it's better to let your emotions out."

"I guess so."

"Is there anything I can do?"

He shook his head.

"You must miss your mother."

Seamus looked over the field of headstones. "I miss her a lot. Seems like all the women in my life leave me."

Lynn looked concerned. "I'm sure that's how it must feel." She looked out over the horizon too and didn't say anything for a few moments. "You know, Seamus, I've been meaning to have a word with you. I have a feeling I know what you're upset about."

He felt a chill. "Oh?"

"I hear Libby MacKinnon is back in town, or Ava Harris, or whatever she's called now."

He nodded but stayed quiet, unsure where she was going with this.

She gave a big sigh and clasped her hands in front of her. "I feel I can say this, because I have a vested interest in it. Not because I'm Sally's mother, but because you're the father of my grandchildren."

"Go on."

"Everyone in this town knows about you and Libby. Certainly Sally was more than aware of it and was quite insecure about it, if the truth be told."

"I loved Sally."

She held her hands up. "Oh, I know, dear. I'm not saying you didn't. I just know that Sally felt very lucky to have you because she knew how much you loved Libby. So what I'm saying is, you're not betraying her memory if you talk to Libby again or associate with her."

Seamus looked at his feet. He felt a rush of relief and his shoulders sagged. He was unaware that he had been as stiff as a board.

"Life is for the living, dear. You're a handsome young man, only twenty-eight. Do you honestly think I'd expect you to never marry again, or have other children? I'm not crazy. And I'm not worried that Jack and Sarah will never know us. You've proved that from day one. They will always be a part of our lives and it gives us great pleasure to see Sally alive in them."

He looked at her. "Thank you. It means a lot."

Lynn looked down at her daughter's grave. "I think she meant for us to meet today. What do you think?"

"I think that Sally's mother is as wonderful as Sally was." He reached over and kissed Lynn's cheek. She patted his back. "Good. So bring those kiddies by after work on Friday. I'll make a batch of Rice Krispie squares. Off you go now. Sally and I are going to have a natter."

He smiled and walked back to the patrol car. He was an incredibly lucky man and sometimes he forgot that in the day-to-day events that threatened to drown him at times. Lynn would never know how much that meant to him.

But of course, as is the way of life, two steps forward, one step back. When he went to work the next day, one of his colleagues, Reg, had the early morning Post. He was reading the obituaries. "See here, Seamus. Libby's mother died."

He jerked his head up. "Did she? Let me see that." He took the offered paper and read it through. The wake was at Patten's the next night and the following day. The funeral would be at Knox United Church, with burial in Black Brook Cemetery. There was a picture of Mamie as she looked about ten years earlier. She always was a handsome woman.

"That's going be some turnout," Reg said.

"What do you mean?"

"What do you think I mean? It's goin' be around the block so people can have a boo at Ava Harris."

"You don't honestly think people will go to a wake just to see her?" Seamus frowned.

"Are you crazy? I'd go."

"You think someone grieving for their mother is a spectator sport?" He threw the paper back at him. "You disgust me."

Reg got out of his chair. "Take it easy. No offense, man."

"Then don't treat it like a joke. Have some decency, for Christ's sake."

Afraid he would punch the man, Seamus decided the best thing to do was to leave. Of course, she was on his mind all day. And everywhere he turned, he heard people talking about it. The more he heard them talk, the more he wanted to protect her. But he didn't want to call the house. Not now. He had no other way to get a hold of her.

Seamus knew her family might not appreciate it, but he had to go to the wake. Just so she could see he wasn't indifferent. That he cared about her.

He went to Colleen's for supper that night, and naturally, almost the first thing out of her mouth was about Mamie MacKinnon.

"So the poor soul finally died. I guess that means Libby will head back to California soon."

Seamus sat at the kitchen table with Sarah on his lap. She had a knot in her shoe that was annoying her for some reason. She grunted and pointed to it with her chubby finger. Seamus did his best to undo it. When it was finally loose, she yelled, "Yeah! Me tell Ack."

"Jack is in the bedroom, honey. Go find him."

She jumped off his lap and ran out of the kitchen. Seamus

looked up at his sister. "You'd like that wouldn't you? For her to leave."

Colleen opened the microwave to take out the defrosted hamburger for the sloppy joes she was making for dinner. "Yes, quite frankly, I would."

Seamus stared at her for a moment. "Why do you dislike her so much?"

She rolled her eyes and sat at the table. "I guess you don't remember how much you suffered when she left."

"Everyone keeps saying that. Well, maybe it was me. Did you ever think of that? I left that summer to work in the woods in New Brunswick."

"Only because you were trying to save money for school like the rest of us. What was wrong with that? Everyone's entitled to a summer job."

"She begged me not to go, begged me to find something here. But I thought she was being her over-dramatic self and ignored it. It was hard for me too. I told her that."

"Well, she didn't wait too long after you left to start running around on you."

He looked at her and blinked.

Colleen jumped up from the table. "I'm sorry, I don't want to hurt you, but you have to face facts before you start up with her again. She's nothing but trouble. I don't want you being made a fool of twice."

"You're the second person lately who's made that accusation. I want to know why I've never heard it before, if it's true. No one said anything to me ten years ago. No one."

"Because you were heartbroken," Colleen said. "No one wanted to torture you, obviously. Why do you think Mom and Dad were upset with her? Have you ever asked yourself that question? Maybe because they had reason to be."

"You're lying."

"Fine, I'm lying," she sighed. "Never mind, it doesn't matter anymore. Do what you want. You're a big boy." She busied herself with cutting up an onion. Just then Dave came home from work and the conversation was dropped.

Before he left for home, Colleen came up to him. "You're right. What happened ten years ago doesn't make any difference. You were a kid. So was she. I know you care enough about her to at least show up at her mother's wake. We've been through it. We know how much it means. If you'd like me to go with you for moral support, I will. I swear I won't say a word, other than to tell her how sorry I am for her loss. How's that?"

He was still smarting from her earlier comments, but he knew he'd have a cooler head if his sister was with him. "Okay. If you wouldn't mind, we'll go tomorrow."

He was awake for hours thinking about this new information. It rattled around in his head with no place to go. Libby slept around? She didn't even sleep with him and they were in love. Why would she suddenly be with everyone else? It didn't make sense. The rumours had to be wrong, no doubt started by jealous people. There were a lot of kids in school who used to give them a hard time because they were the golden couple. Not that they wanted to be. Or maybe she was so upset by his desertion, she went over the edge. He knew it was a possibility—she always was a highly emotional person. In the end, he had himself befuddled; he dropped it and turned on Jay Leno for a little mindless entertainment.

The next evening, he dropped the kids off with Dave when he picked up Colleen. They drove to Glace Bay in silence. They knew where they stood on the issue. There was no point rehashing it endlessly.

Just as Reg predicted, there was a long lineup of so-called mourners waiting to troop in the door of the funeral home.

"Oh God. Look at these people. Bastards."

"Good lord," Colleen tsked. "They aren't all voyeurs. There are nine kids in that family and Mamie lived here her whole life. A lot of people know them."

"Yeah, I guess so." He quickly saw the sense of having Colleen beside him.

They joined the end of the queue and people rapidly came up behind them. One thing about long waits to offer condolences was that friends and neighbours who hadn't seen each other for a while got caught up on their own news. Quietly, of course, but because there was a celebrity in the midst, there was a bit more chatter than usual.

Two women behind them obviously didn't realize Seamus stood in front of them. They gossiped back and forth and it began to get under his skin. He glanced at Colleen and she made a face that meant "Ignore it."

"I'm dying to see her up close. I wonder if she's as beautiful in real life."

"I'm sure not today, her mother just died."

"True, poor dear. I remember her in high school. God, all I wanted to do was be her."

"I know. The guys were crazy about her. It drove me nuts."

"It wasn't just the boys."

"What do you mean?"

"I saw the drama teacher kissing her once. He practically had her on his desk."

"What?"

"Oh yeah. They broke apart in a hurry and she was pretty upset that I'd caught them, but at least I got an A in drama that term."

She giggled but not for long. Seamus turned around.

"Are you quite finished?"

The two women froze, wishing for all the world they had the power to disappear.

"Oh God, Seamus. I'm sorry. I didn't mean anything by that."

"You make me sick." He turned away but was aware when they took off like scalded cats and stood at the end of the line to avoid him.

Seamus and Colleen neared the room where Mamie's coffin was on display. In true Cape Breton style, it was open, with small corsages lining the satin interior, to represent her grandchildren. Her children were lined up by the coffin in a line, standing oldest to youngest. Aunt Vi and Uncle Angus were at the front of the pack.

As he and Colleen inched closer, he noticed Libby peek over at him. He thought she looked awful, pale and worn out. He wanted to rush over and take her in his arms. She quickly looked away from him but every so often threw quick glances at him, measuring how soon he would be in front of her.

Her siblings saw him too and Rose switched spots and put Ava between herself and Maryette, as if to protect her from all sides. The only thing Seamus was aware of was the rushing sound in his ears as his heart beat out of his chest. It slowly occurred to him that a great many people were looking at him and he heard his name whispered over and over.

The bastards were waiting. They were waiting for him to go up to her, to see how they behaved, how the two old sweethearts reacted when their hands met. He'd been so worried about Libby that he never thought how his presence would create a dramatic little vignette for the whole town to see.

He grabbed Colleen's arm and whispered, "I'm sorry. I can't stay here." He rushed out of the room.

❀

People looked at each other when he left. Colleen was unsure whether to run after him or proceed, but the smirks on people's faces and the "I told you so" looks made her stay put. She knew they were dying to get outside and tell everyone what happened when Seamus and Libby's eyes met. Well, she wasn't going to give them the satisfaction of seeing two O'Reillys run out of the room. She had to do her best to represent him.

It took all her willpower to remain calm. This was a girl who hurt her baby brother. Sometimes she forgot that he was now a man. When she thought of Seamus and Libby together, she saw them as the teenagers they were back then.

As Colleen got closer, she watched Libby accept the condolences of family and friends. She seemed incredibly fragile, as if she'd disappear if you so much as blew on her. Colleen was used to seeing her on a huge movie screen, where everyone was larger then life. A childhood nickname that Seamus told her about seemed very appropriate. She was like a fairy.

Libby's big eyes watched her approach. Colleen shook Rose's hand first. "I'm very sorry for your loss."

Rose nodded, "Thank you."

Colleen took one step closer and Libby was in front of her. She looked scared to death. "I'm sorry about your mother, Libby. I know what it's like and I wouldn't wish it on anyone."

Libby squeezed her hand and her bottom lip trembled. "Thank you, Colleen."

It was that fast. Then it was on through the line. All the siblings were grateful for her appearance, appreciated the fact that she took the time to show up. They never mentioned

Seamus leaving. At last she faced Aunt Vi. "So good of you to come, duck. It will mean the world to our Libby. Did Seamus not come?"

"He was here, but he left."

Aunt Vi nodded her head up and down. "God love 'im." She leaned in closer. "It's such a shame, Colleen. Such a shame. My heart bleeds for the both of them."

Colleen wasn't sure how she should respond, so she nodded politely. Then it was a quick glance at poor Mamie and she was free to go. She was dizzy with the effort she'd just made, not realizing how much it had taken out of her. As soon as she squeezed by the throngs of people still waiting to get in, she knew she had to head for the ladies room or she was going to be sick right there on the rug.

Colleen pushed on the bathroom door; thankfully no one was in either stall. She didn't throw up so much as gag. It was too hot and sticky and her head ached. She needed some air. When the door opened and someone walked in, she flushed the toilet and grabbed more toilet paper to blot her face. She opened the stall door.

Libby was standing there.

They looked at each other for what seemed like an eternity. Everything was said, and yet no words were spoken. Colleen broke the trance by going to the sink and splashing water on her face. She pulled down the paper towels and patted it dry.

"I saw you come in here and I had to talk to you, if you don't mind."

Colleen wiped her hands and threw away the towel. "All right."

"Why did he leave?"

"Why do you think?"

"I don't know."

"Libby, Seamus is a very private person. You're a very public person. Maybe you're used to having people look at you all day long, but this has been excruciating for him. Your presence alone conjures up so many old memories. How do you think he felt when he walked in that room and suddenly everyone's eyes are on you two? All he wanted to do was tell you he was sorry about your mother, and look what happened. It became a freak show."

Libby stood with her head lowered.

"Look," Colleen sighed. "I don't want to make you feel bad on today of all days, so why don't we drop it? I assume you'll go back home in a few days and this will be a bad memory. Let him get on with his life and you get on with yours."

Libby lifted her head to meet Colleen's sharp gaze. "Whatever you think, Colleen, it's not as easy as you make out. This isn't the first time I've seen him since I've been here."

"I know about your meeting in Sobey's. He told me."

"Did he tell you about our meeting in the park, or at the mall, or what about the morning Sarah was sick?"

Colleen felt her insides knot. "No."

"So you don't know everything, do you? I think you should leave him alone and let him make up his own mind about whether he wants to see me or not."

Colleen was flustered and she knew it. He hadn't told her everything and that hurt. She knew she should walk out and not say another word, but the image of Seamus crying in his room when he knew Libby was gone forever was still a powerful memory. It was now or never.

"Listen here, Libby, I've been waiting ten years to say this to you. What you did to my brother was unforgivable. The minute his back was turned that summer, you were all over town with every other guy. I heard the rumours about the drinking and partying. Everyone thought you were this sweet little miss but you weren't, were you? Why, just outside someone talked about the time she caught you kissing your drama teacher. That goes to show what kind of woman you really are."

Libby started to shake. "That teacher...that man attacked me. He came after me. He was always after me. I could never get away from him."

"Why should I believe you? You've hurt Seamus once, but by God, you're not going to hurt him again. Not if I have anything to say about it."

Libby backed up against the wall of the restroom. Colleen thought she was going to fall, so she reached out to steady her.

"DON'T!" Libby shouted. "Don't touch me. Don't ever touch me." Her hands slipped on the walls behind her. "You don't know everything. Everyone thinks they know everything, but you don't know anything. Nothing, do you hear me? Nothing!"

Colleen was shocked. Libby was out of control and she didn't know what to do. Just then a woman with black spiky hair came in. "Rose sent me to look for you. My god. What's wrong?" The woman turned and shouted at Colleen. "What did you do to her?"

"I didn't do anything..."

"Get out of here, you stupid bitch, and leave her alone."

The woman reached for Libby and caught her before she hit the floor. Colleen turned and ran out of the bathroom. People looked at her as she pushed them out of the way in her haste to escape. A few called after her, "Colleen, are you all right?"

She ran as fast as she could back to the car and tore the door open. Seamus was waiting. "Drive. Drive as fast as you can."

"What's wrong? What's happened?"

Colleen put her face in her hands. "Stop asking me! Just get me out of here."

He drove her away.

CHAPTER THIRTEEN

He'd picked her up after drama class, just happened to be in the parking lot when she and her friend Terri were walking home from school.

"Want a lift, girls?"

"No, that's okay," she said.

Terri ran over. "Sure. I'm sick of walking."

He opened the front door of the truck and Terri sat next to him. Reluctant to get in but feeling she had no choice, Libby took the seat by the window. They chatted about school and how well the play had been received two nights before. He smiled, "School's pretty much over for another year. Hard to believe."

Libby assumed since she was next to the door, he'd drop her off first, but he didn't. He made some excuse about having to go to the store and if he was going that way anyway, he might as well drop Terri off first. So he did. She was going to get out with her friend but Terri scrambled over her when he said, "Can I talk to you for a second, Libby?"

"See ya tomorrow, Lib." Her friend waved goodbye.

"I should go home. Ma will be worried."

"Nonsense. It's a nice day. Let's go for a drive."

They didn't talk after that. Not until she realized he was driving out of town.

"Where are we going?"

"A nice little place I know."

"But I have to get home."

"You will get home. I'll drive you back myself."

"I have to meet Seamus after."

"I'll make sure you do. Relax. It's just a drive."

She remembered she looked out the window and saw a dog by the side of the road. He was out for a walk, she supposed. He didn't seem to be in any hurry. She remembered wishing she was that dog.

They drove all the way out to Marion Bridge and further still. "I think this is far enough."

"We're almost there."

He pulled into an old country road that got narrower as they went on. The truck bounced in the ruts. They came up to a small, run-down house. "Who lives here?"

"It belongs to a friend. He won't mind if we use it." He turned off the engine.

Her heart started to race. "What are we using it for?"

That's when he grabbed her arm and jerked her over and out the driver's side door.

"Please! What are you doing?"

"Don't talk."

He yanked her behind him, up the steps. She dragged her feet and grasped one of the porch rails. She pulled against him with all her might but he snatched her around the waist and picked her up like a feather.

"Let me go! You can't do this. Why are you doing this?"

He hauled her in the door and locked it behind him. Then he dragged her through the house and into one of the bedrooms, where he threw her on the bed.

"Please. Don't hurt me."

"I'm not going to hurt you. I'm going to love you."

"Seamus! Help me!" she screamed.

He reached across the bed and slapped her face. "I am so fucking sick of hearing about your fucking Seamus!"

He pulled her hair and brought her face close to his. "You little slut. I'm gonna show you how a real man does it." He grabbed the back of her neck and covered her mouth with his own. He kept it there even as he ripped off her skirt and tore off her panties. He pushed her back on the bed.

She screamed and screamed until he punched her. That's when she stayed quiet.

She retreated to a small brown stain on the ceiling. She kept her eyes on that stain until he turned her over. Then she stared at the crack in the wall. As long as she kept her eyes on it she was in a small safe place. So small she couldn't see it. But if she were to lose sight of it, all would be lost.

She remembered being driven back to town in the dark and keeping her eyes on the windshield wipers swishing back and forth. He acted like nothing happened, as if she'd imagined the whole thing. She began to think maybe she had. It was her imagination. Lots of things were. That was it, it never happened.

But then he had to go and ruin it. He stopped three streets from where she lived. He never touched her. Instead he smiled at her. "If you ever say anything about this, I'll tell Seamus. I'll tell him everything we did, and I'll tell him you loved it. Do you understand me?"

She nodded.

She opened the door and got out. He drove off. She walked home in the dark. She walked and walked and it was still dark, so she walked some more and it was still dark. Why was it dark, she wondered? Stop being dark. Stop the dark.

"STOP IT. STOP IT. STOP IT. STOP IT."

"Libby, Libby, darlin', it's okay, it's okay. You're safe."

Ava's eyelids were so heavy she couldn't open them, but she thought she heard Aunt Vi's voice. Then she heard someone say, "She's coming round."

The light hurt her eyes. She squinted and nothing was in focus. She blinked and saw a few faces swimming in front of her. She picked out Lola's face. That was Lola.

"Hi."

Lola looked frightened. "Oh sweetheart, I'm glad you're awake."

"What happened?"

"You fainted, that's all. You just fainted."

"Where am I?"

"Never mind that, honey," Aunt Vi said. "We're taking you home."

She looked and saw her sisters and then all kinds of people in a doorway. She was in a white place. She was in a bathroom. "What's happening?"

Rose bent over and grabbed her hand. "There's nothing to be afraid of, Libby. We're at Ma's wake and you got a little emotional and fainted, that's all. There's nothing wrong with you."

"Oh, that's good. We're at Ma's wake? She must have died then." She saw everyone look at each other. "I can get up."

Rose pushed her back down. "No, honey, you need to rest."

"But Ma—"

"Ma will understand. Johnnie, lift her up. Gently now."

Her brother came into the bathroom and smiled at her before he lifted her off the floor as if she were a rag doll.

"It's okay, child. I've got ya."

Ava rested her head on her big brother's shoulder. She felt safe and warm and sort of dreamy. Maybe this was a dream. She'd have to tell Lola when she woke up. She saw people all around and yet when they walked by, the people stepped back, as if they were frightened of her. Oh well, it didn't matter. Johnnie would take care of her.

Lola wrapped a sweater around her and they went down the steps. People lined the stairs. This must be a premiere, but she couldn't remember what movie it was. She wondered if she should wave.

Ava was bundled into the car. Lauchie drove and Johnnie kept her on his lap. He patted her and told her to hush. The car stopped and he carried her out and into the house. She heard the voices of her sisters and Lola. They were coming up the stairs behind them. So strange that everyone needed to go upstairs at the same time.

Johnnie laid her on the bed.

"We'll take it from here," Rose said.

"Thank you Johnnie. You're so nice to me."

"That's okay, baby." He turned from the room.

Then all these women fussed over her, got her into pajamas and wiped her face and made her drink tea laced with something. Then they wanted her to take a bite of toast, but she had no appetite. Finally they let her lie down and Rose sat by her side and stroked her hair.

"Sing me that song, Rosie. You know the one."

"'You Are My Sunshine'?"

"Yes. That's it."

Rose was still singing when she fell asleep.

❀

Seamus couldn't get Colleen to tell him what had happened.

"Well, something must have happened. Look at you. You're a mess."

"It doesn't matter," she sobbed. "Just leave it."

"One of her brothers didn't say anything to you, I hope, because I'll wring their necks if they did."

"No. No. It wasn't like that."

"This is ridiculous. I have a right to know."

She turned on him. "You left me there. You ran out and I had to stand there with everyone looking at me. It was hard, okay?"

He felt terrible. Her face was flushed and tear-streaked and she looked miserable.

"I'm sorry. I never thought of that. You should've come with me."

"You never gave me the chance, did you?" She turned away from him and leaned her head on the side door window. "I want to go home."

"I'm sorry, Colleen. I never should've asked you to go. I knew how you felt. It wasn't fair."

"Nothing about this damn situation is fair. I never want to discuss it again. You do what you want. Talk to her, date her; fuck her for all I care. I don't give a shit. I never want to hear her name mentioned again. Have you got that?"

He was speechless. His sister didn't swear often. She was terribly upset and it was his fault. He wanted it to end.

The next day at work he had coffee with Roger. He poured them two mugs and put them on the table in the lunch room. Roger reached for his. "Thanks."

Seamus pulled open a couple of creamers and poured them in. Then he stirred his coffee with a Bic pen.

"I hear it was pretty bad at the wake last night."

"Someone told you I ran out of there, did they? Goddamn it. Don't people have anything better to talk about?"

"No, I mean about Libby."

Seamus was about to take a sip of his coffee, but he put it down. "What do you mean?"

"Apparently she had some sort of breakdown. Her brother had to carry her out of the funeral home."

"What?"

"I'm surprised Colleen didn't tell you. She was in the bathroom with her when it happened."

Seamus froze.

Roger looked at him. "Are you okay?"

He didn't answer.

"Hey, I hope I'm not speaking out of turn. The only reason I know is because Julie was standing in line at the time. I heard about it briefly on the radio this morning too, about Libby being helped out of the building."

Seamus stood. "Call me off sick." He turned around to leave.

"Hey, hey buddy! Look, I feel bad. I didn't mean to upset you."

"You didn't. Someone else did," he said over his shoulder.

Seamus got in the patrol car and drove straight out to Colleen's. He saw her anxious face in the kitchen window when she looked out and saw it was him. She was standing with her back to the cupboards when he burst through the door and threw his keys on the table.

"When were you going to tell me?"

"What do you mean?"

He slammed his fist on the kitchen table. She jumped.

"You know damn well what I mean. What did you say to her in that bathroom?"

"Nothing."

He slammed his fist again. "That's bullshit! Give me some credit. She was fine when she went in that bathroom and a mess when she was carried out. Don't you dare lie to me and tell me nothing happened."

"I told her to leave you alone," Colleen yelled.

"And?"

"And that…and that…"

"Tell me the truth, Colleen, or I swear to God, I'll never speak to you again."

She had a hard time getting the words out. "I told her that what she did to you was unforgivable, partying with boys that summer you were gone."

"There's something else. I know it."

Colleen slapped her hand on the counter. "I told her what those two women said outside, about her being with the drama teacher. I said it showed what kind of a woman she really was."

"And what did she say when you made that sweeping judgment of her character?"

Colleen suddenly deflated. "She said he attacked her, that he was always after her. That he never left her alone."

"He assaulted her?"

Colleen continued as if he hadn't spoken. "I swear, that was all I said and the minute she told me that, she sort of fell into the wall and I tried to help her, but she screamed at me not to touch her and then her friend came in and called me a stupid bitch and told me to get out. I didn't mean for it to happen. It's like she fell apart. It was scary. I was afraid." She covered her face with her hands. "I'm sorry. I should never have spoken to her."

"You've got that right."

She looked up at him accusingly. "You wanted me to go. You put me in a terrible position."

"That's right, Colleen. It's my fault. It's her fault. It's everyone's fault but yours. She drove you to it, because she's such a nasty piece of work. You accused her of something that two strangers happened to mention and used it as a weapon against her, even though you had no proof. Did you ever think it might be a painful memory? No. Because you automatically assumed she was a slag and sleeping with not only every boy in town but all the teachers too."

"I'm sorry."

He couldn't contain his anger. He turned around and punched the wall.

"Seamus, don't!"

He looked back at her, hardly able to see her for his rage. "You know everything, don't you, Colleen? You and this fucking town know everything." He jabbed his finger in her face. "She didn't even sleep with me. Me! The boy who loved her more than life itself. The boy she loved more than anyone. And you and these sanctimonious busybodies all delight in malicious gossip that no one can prove. You make me sick. You all make me sick."

He spun around and grabbed his keys. He heard her shout, "Don't go, Seamus. Don't go. I'm sorry. I never should have..."

He didn't hear anything else, just ran to the car and slammed the door behind him. He revved the engine and pulled out of the dirt driveway, causing gravel to fly everywhere. He had to see her. He had to see her right this minute. It didn't matter what he'd say. She needed to be in his arms because she was alone and needed protecting. Nothing else mattered. He wanted her. Seamus had wanted her his whole life.

He pulled into the MacKinnon yard, got out and walked up to the door. He knocked on it louder than he should have. It was Rose who walked toward him and opened the screen door.

"Rose, I need to see her."

Rose came towards him, so he had to back up.

"I'd like to speak to you for a moment, outside."

He had no choice but to do as she said. She got right in his face and she wasn't smiling.

"If you or your sister or any of your family ever come near that girl again, your life won't be worth living. Do I make myself clear?"

"What Colleen did was unforgivable. She just told me what happened. I'm as upset as you are."

Rose folded her arms across her chest. "Oh, I don't think so. I think there are a whole lot of people who are more upset than you are. And I'm glad you know what happened in that bathroom, because we sure don't. You know why?"

"Why?"

She pointed her finger at him. "Because we haven't been able to get any sense out of her since it happened. She's in bed now, practically unconscious since yesterday. The doctor says it's nervous exhaustion, that she may be in bed for a while." Rose poked him in the shoulder. "If anything happens to her, I'll never forgive you. I'll haunt you for the rest of your life."

"Rose, I love her. I've always loved her. I'd never hurt her in a million years. You know that."

"I don't know anything, anymore. All I know is that your family has had a vendetta against her since she left. Yes, she went away and you were hurt. It was upsetting, but it wasn't a crime. It's not something she should be punished for forever, is it?"

"Of course not."

"You moved on. I assume you loved Sally, you married her and gave her children. We felt awful when she died, but you can't come here and ask Libby to replace her and feel that you're entitled to do so."

That was the one thing she said that hit him right between the eyes. He looked at the ground and his heart turned cold. "You're right, Rose. You're absolutely right."

When she didn't say anything, he looked back up at her. "Please forgive me. Please forgive Colleen. As hard as it is to believe, she was trying to protect me. She's not a mean person."

Rose nodded. "We know that."

"Please tell Libby I only wish her the best. But if you feel it's better to say nothing, then that's fine. I promise you. I won't bother you or your family again."

"Thank you, Seamus. I appreciate that. As you can imagine, we're all a bit raw at the moment, what with Ma and everything."

"I know. I know what that feels like, and it's not good. Goodbye, Rose."

"Goodbye."

He walked down the steps and out of the yard, though his heart stayed in the small upstairs bedroom, with her where she lay.

❀

Afterwards, they told her she slept for three days. Ava didn't believe it. But when she tried to get out of bed, she had so little energy, she knew it must be true. She didn't remember what had happened, just took it on faith that she was at her mother's wake, was suddenly overcome and fainted. It's not like that was unheard of. Lola told her everyone handles grief differently and it was too overwhelming.

"So what you're saying is, I'm not nuts," she laughed.

Lola laughed too. "Well, I never said that. You've always been nuts. Let's just say, you're not a raving lunatic."

"Oh good. I'm reassured."

"Listen, babe," Lola said, "while everyone else is out of the room, I want to get your opinion on something."

"Okay."

"I've given this a lot of thought, so it's not a harebrained idea."

"Are you going to tell me?"

Lola took a deep breath. "I don't think you should go back to California yet."

"You don't?"

"I shudder at the thought of you roaming around that big empty minimalist box you call home. And then I worry about the social life you'll be dragged into by your so-called friends. I don't think you're up to it. I know Aunt Vi and Uncle Angus don't need us anymore now that they're feeling better. Your siblings can certainly handle their creature comforts. And obviously with your dear mother being laid to rest, our mission of mercy is over. I think it's more a case of us needing them."

Ava was about to say something, but Lola cut her off. "I've already discussed this with them and all of them, every last one of them, want us to stay here until you go to New York. Just spend the summer doing nothing but swim and lie on the beach. Doesn't that sound heavenly?"

"But I can't drag you..."

Lola hit her hands on her thighs. "Will you shut up about you dragging me and making me stay in some backwater! I have no bloody life other than you. I'm Gayle and you're Oprah."

"But what will Trent and Camilla say?"

"I'm going to tell them that you're ill. You've been through a lot and you need rest. I don't think you'll get it in Malibu. As much as Trent would say he'd leave you alone, he wouldn't. And Camilla would pop in for a quick cup of coffee but bring her briefcase with her. You're safest here." Lola grabbed her hand. "My one concern is with you-know-who. Perhaps you'd like to get away from all that."

"I carry him wherever I go. It really doesn't matter."

"Well, if that's the case, will you take my advice and give yourself a true vacation? A few months in the sun with your brothers and sisters and nieces and nephews? I think you've earned it, babe."

"I think you're right."

Lola grabbed her chest. "I can't believe it. It's a breakthrough! Ava actually said yes to one of my ideas. Hurray!"

"Keep it up and I'll hit you with my orange."

Lola jumped up. "I'm outta here." She ran down the stairs, yelling, "Aunt Vi, guess what?"

Ava lay back into her pillows. A whole summer with nothing to do but sit and watch the waves roll in. It was her idea of heaven. She didn't even think of Seamus. She had no energy to think about him any more. It was as if something had changed in that bathroom. She knew Colleen was with her, but she couldn't remember their conversation. Yet, it didn't seem to matter. She wasn't afraid of them any more.

CHAPTER FOURTEEN

It was the best summer of her life. It took a while to get started, since she didn't have the energy to do much for a couple of weeks. She was either in bed or, now that Aunt Vi and Uncle Angus were back upstairs, on the sofa in the living room or on the front veranda sitting on the porch swing her uncle insisted on buying. For once, she was in no hurry to go anywhere. She let everyone come to her. And they did, in droves. The colour began to return to her cheeks.

Vicky, Samantha, and Emily often came over with their latest Seventeen magazines and went through the questionnaires to find out if they were sexy, organized, had fashion sense or the right haircut. Bathing suits to fit all body types were discussed ad nauseum. They asked her what she thought.

"I like one-piece suits, but of course I'm a firm believer in imagination. I like to leave a little."

They'd nod and take it all in. Then they'd kiss her goodbye and walk away in their low rise jeans with their belly buttons showing. She'd laugh to herself.

One morning, because Hayden was supposed to be the guest, she and Lola watched the Regis and Kelly Show. They sat in their nightgowns with their feet on the coffee table. They had on thick pit socks and both had terrible bedhead. They drank their tea and feasted on two huge bowls of homemade porridge with brown sugar and cream, all the while making rude comments about everything and everyone.

The credits came up. "Aunt Vi. It's on!"

Vi limped in from the kitchen on her cane. "Look at the pair of ya. Ya look like bums."

Lola grinned. "I know, isn't it great?"

"If you say so." Aunt Vi hobbled over to the armchair and dropped into it. "How on earth can you two eat hot oatmeal in the middle of the summer?"

"I love your oatmeal." Ava licked her lips. "It's making me fat. Isn't that what you want?"

"True."

Lola pointed at Ava with a spoon. "You're going to be so fired when you show up on that movie set in New York. They're gonna kick your big fat ugly butt outta Manhattan."

"Like I care."

Aunt Vi spoke up. "Would you two mind if I had Club here tomorrow night?"

"Of course not, silly," Ava said. "It's your house. Why are you asking us?"

"Because you've been planted down here for the last week, looking like somethin' the cat dragged in. I want to make sure you at least put on a brassiere when the ladies get here."

Lola scraped her bowl with her spoon. "What's Club?"

Ava wiped her mouth on her sleeve before she answered. "It's this thing where all these old ladies show up in one old lady's house, and they pretend they're doing stuff, like making plans to bake cupcakes for the church bazaar and knitting mittens and things, but what they really do is sit around and talk about the one member who didn't show up, and then stuff their faces with tiny sandwiches and squares that they wash down with gallons of strong tea. Have I got that right, Aunt Vi?"

"Yep."

"Wonderful," Lola smiled. "I can't wait."

Applause alerted them to the fact that Hayden Judd was being introduced.

"Oh hush, here he is." Ava turned up the volume.

"He looks fatter on television," Aunt Vi observed. "He's still cute though."

They listened to the dreary pablum of movie promotion, where the actor grins and answers stupid questions with stupid answers. Then they cut away for a film clip and cut back to show that the hosts and guest were so cool that they didn't watch the clip because they were too busy chatting amongst themselves.

Regis just finished thanking Hayden for being there, when suddenly Hayden turned to the camera. "Before I go, I want to say a big hello to someone near and dear to my heart. Hi Aunt Vi!" He waved into the camera.

Aunt Vi's mouth dropped open. Ava and Lola laughed with delight.

"Land sakes! How did he know we was watching?"

"Cause I talked to him a couple of days ago. I said you'd get a kick out of it."

Aunt Vi put her hands up to her cheeks. "Lord love a duck. I can't believe it. Wait till Club hears about this."

The phone rang.

"I think they already know." Ava grinned.

The phone didn't stop ringing all morning. Aunt Vi was a celebrity for a day, a mantle she wore proudly.

Ava and Lola took special pains to look well groomed the next night, so as not to shame the woman they loved best. They played hostess and passed around double-decker egg and Cheez Whiz sandwiches. Lola went back to the pantry for more while Ava assembled the china teacups and saucers on the dining room table. She went into the kitchen to make sure the water was boiling.

"Are there any more sandwiches in the fridge?"

There was no answer. Ava was sure Lola was in the pantry. She walked in and Lola quickly turned around to hide the platter. She couldn't hide the fact that she had a wad of sandwich in her cheek.

"Hey, stop eating those." Ava grabbed the plate from her.

Lola started to chew furiously. "I can't help it," she mumbled. "These are like the most divine sandwiches I ever ate. Why can't they serve stuff like this at award shows?"

"Because people would get fat and Hollywood would crumble into decay because of it."

"Gimme another one."

Ava pulled the tray out of Lola's reach. "They're for Club."

"I'm in Club. I'm an honorary Club member, for your information. Aunt Vi said so."

Ava passed her the plate. "Well then, go to town."

Once their business was done and the lunch was devoured, the Club members felt free to sit around for a while. They obviously wanted to talk to Ava. Especially Thelma and Geranium.

"So. What's that there fella like in real life?" Geranium asked.

"What fella?"

"The fruity one with the scarf."

"He's delightful. As a matter of fact, I'm thinking of inviting him for a few days."

"Do you think he'd come?"

"You never know."

"Oh my." Geranium tugged at the collar of her blouse. "He blew me a kiss you know. I thought that was kind."

"You'd think it was kind if he coughed in your direction," Thelma sniffed.

"Did he blow you a kiss, Thelma Steele?"

"Of course not. I don't sit in my living room window all day with binoculars like some I could mention."

"I'm an avid bird watcher, I'll have you know."

"The only birds you're watching, honey, belong to the milkman and the mailman."

"Well, I never!"

"No. That's your trouble, dear. Maybe you should."

Lola and Ava quietly got up at the same time and walked out the living room door. Then they bolted up the stairs and threw themselves on their beds, trying to stifle their laughter by covering their faces with pillows. When they finally looked at each other, they were hot and sweaty.

"You know what?" Lola gasped. "Being in this house is better than having sex."

"Maybe you should tell Geranium. Might make her feel better."

That started them off again.

Finally it was time to go a little further a field. The doctor, besides suggesting rest and nourishment, told Ava she should get a little exercise. Nothing like her trainer's idea of exercise, but out for a walk every day and maybe some yoga.

Ava and Lola would set their alarm for six a.m. and take a walk before breakfast, when there weren't a lot of people around so they could keep up a steady pace and not be interrupted by well-meaning fans. It was pretty slow going at first and they didn't go far, but after a while, they'd walk down Water Street and head for South Street and then walk all the way to the Glace Bay General Hospital and back.

It was on one of their outings that Ava spied a puppy. He was a friendly little thing.

"Look at this little guy. He looks like a teddy bear. You don't think he's lost, do you?"

Lola shrugged. "He doesn't look like he's starving to death, but then again, he's pretty young to be away from his mother."

Ava reached down and picked him up. He licked her face all over. "Oh, you are so sweet. What should we do?"

"Maybe we should ask a few people around here if anyone has lost a puppy?"

They went to a few doors in the neighbourhood and knocked. One woman nearly fainted upon finding Ava Harris on her doorstep. She managed a scream and her family ran down and crowded behind her. She stood in the front porch and jumped up and down.

"Am I on Oprah? Is this Oprah's 'Dream Come True' show?" She looked behind them for the cameras.

"No. I want to know if this little puppy belongs to you."

"No," she frowned. "That mutt's been hangin' around for the last few days. Once you start feedin' them, you never get rid of them."

Ava frowned. "Never mind." She and Lola hurried down the stairs. The woman shouted. "Are you sure you're not with Oprah?"

They walked down the street and thought better of asking anyone else. The puppy squirmed to get down. Ava put him on the sidewalk. "I don't want to leave him here. What if it rains?"

The puppy bounced into the grass and then stood with a stunned look on its face. "Oh look, Lola. He's peeing."

"Dogs do that, you great dope."

Ava walked towards him and the puppy ran to her. Then she walked ahead of him and he trotted happily behind her. "Let's see how far he comes."

He followed them all the way up to Blackett Street.

"Okay, that's it. He's mine." She reached down and picked him up. "You, little guy, are coming home with me."

"What if he belongs to someone?"

"I'll put an ad in the paper. If no one answers, problem solved."

She kissed his face and he licked her back.

"What are you going to call him?"

"Teddy Bear."

Ava and Lola got all sorts of exercise after that. No one called about the dog, so they took him to the vet, spending a fortune on needles, shampoo, doggy treats, and chew toys. He was outfitted first with a flea collar, then with a nice red collar with rhinestones and a leash to match.

Uncle Angus shook his head when they returned. "A collar with diamonds on it?"

"They aren't real," Ava laughed. "He's going to be a Hollywood dog, so he better get used to it."

They took a big tub out in the yard and gave him a soapy bath. The house cats and Uncle Angus's mutt, whose name was Dog, sat back and watched the procedure. Teddy Bear looked mortified. Just to punish his new mother, he wiggled out of her soapy arms and headed right for the pile of fish bait Johnnie had stacked in the yard.

Once he came out of his second bath, they dried him with fluffy towels and finished him off with a hair dryer. Aunt Vi took to laughing when they came in with him.

"Lord save us. He looks like a dandelion fluff."

"Isn't he beautiful?"

"He's somethin' all right."

So Teddy Bear became a regular on their morning walks too. Ava would take a plastic grocery bag with her, to clean up his poop. One day they headed in the other direction, down Brookside Street. There were a bunch of ragtag kids hanging around their porch in bathing suits, their front door wide open to the street, no doubt because they didn't have an air conditioner.

"Maybe we should take them home and give them a bath too," Lola whispered.

They nodded to the kids and kept going. A boy of around eight said, "That your dog?"

"Yes."

"I gotta dog."

"That's nice." Ava pulled on Teddy's leash a little to make him come faster. But naturally Teddy decided to do his business right in front of the kid's door. The boy's dog came out and, not to be outdone, did the same thing.

Ava rolled her eyes. "Wonderful."

She reached down with her hand in the plastic bag and scooped up both poops, just to be polite. She couldn't very well take one and leave the other. She turned the bag inside out and tied a knot in it.

The kid looked at her in horror. He ran back onto his porch and yelled in the door. "Ma! Ma! Come here. Some lady's pickin' up Lucky's shit."

A shrill voice came from inside. "What the Christ are you talkin' about? Where's she at?" A woman with great sagging boobs and a stomach to match marched out of the house. As soon as she spoke, they saw she had no teeth.

"What the frig do you think you're doin' lady? Don't ya got enough shit of your own? Are ya that hard up ya gotta take our dog's shit?"

Ava backed up and so did Lola. "I thought I was doing you a favour, that's all."

"By picking up stinkin' dog shit? How were you brought up, girl? Now get the Jesus outta here before I call the cops. No good useless tramp."

Lola looked at Ava. "Let's run, ya no good useless tramp."

They turned around and booted up Brookside Street as fast as they could. The woman was still mouthing off. And then Lucky ran after them, as if to chase them down and demand his poop back. Lola grabbed the bag out of Ava's hand and threw it at him. "Here ya go." And didn't the stupid dog pick it and take it home. Needless to say, they never went up Brookside Street again.

The next day Ava insisted on taking Lola out for a drive. "I need to show you another side of Glace Bay and Sydney. Believe it or not, not everyone calls you a no-good useless tramp when you're walking down the street."

She showed her some of the beautiful old homes that made up the landscape, the grand churches, the stores and the parks. Lola was suitably impressed, but by the end of the day she said, "Can't we go home to Aunt Vi's kitchen? That's the best place of all."

Very early one morning, Ava's cell phone rang. She fumbled for it on the bedside table.

"Mmm. Yeah, hello?" All she heard was a very loud party going on. "Hello?"

"Darling. How's my girl?"

"Maurice?"

"The very same."

"Where are you?"

"Getting smashed at a party, darling. What else?"

"What time is it?"

"It's only midnight. I just got here."

"Oh." She yawned.

"Don't you remember midnight, precious? Or are you totally indoctrinated to a healthier way of life?"

"I go to bed around nine."

"In the morning? I am impressed."

"At night, you doofus."

"Oh my god. We have to do something about that. Listen, Harold and I thought we'd like to come see you for a few days. I've been missing you terribly and we have a window of opportunity between a celebrity wedding and some stupid awards show. Actors really feel the need to congratulate themselves a lot, don't you find?"

"Uh huh."

"Fine. Go back to bed then. Hopefully, I'll be doing the same in an hour or so. There really is the most delicious specimen at two o'clock but don't tell Harold."

"My lips are sealed. Come when you want. You know where to find us."

"Could you ask Aunt Vi to make more of those heavenly lobster rolls?"

"I have a better idea. It'll be a surprise."

"Ciao, meow. Love you." He hung up before she could say anything. She folded the phone and shoved it back on the table, then burrowed into the blankets, but not before a very sleepy Lola grunted, "Who was that?"

"Maurice. He's trying to get laid at a party."

"That's the only reason I go to parties."

"Go back to sleep."

❀

Their friends arrived one very hot morning in late July. Ava and Lola had plans to go to the beach that day. They sat on the porch swing convincing themselves they should get up and put on their bathing suits.

When the limo pulled up, Maurice and Harold stepped out looking every bit like royalty. Ava and Lola jumped up and ran through the kitchen. "Aunt Vi, the queens have arrived!" Lola shouted.

Ava reached them first. There was a grand reunion, with kisses and hugs a plenty. The driver put their luggage beside the driveway. Uncle Angus hurried out of the house, eyeing the bags. "How long are ya stayin'? A year?"

"Uncle Angus! It's delightful to see you again." Maurice kissed him on both cheeks. Ava looked over in Geranium's window. She clutched her chest.

Uncle Angus wiped his cheeks. "Well now, ya best come in. How are you, Harriet?"

"Harold."

"Sorry."

There was a grand reunion with Aunt Vi. They made her sit down and open up at least a dozen presents, everything from a perfume atomizer to a fancy heating pad for her sore ankle. She was thrilled to say the least. They didn't forget Uncle Angus either. Maurice gave a bit of a presentation before they revealed his gift.

"Now," Maurice said, "Ava tells me that during hunting season you have to wear orange so you don't get killed by beastly hunters when you're out in the woods. Well, Harold," he paused to blow him a kiss, "found this wonderful vest in Prada that you can wear when you go out for a walk." He opened a box and shook it out like a bull fighter. "Ta da!"

They gazed at Uncle Angus's new vest. It was a beautiful shade of burnt umber and looked super expensive. The workmanship was impeccable. Everyone clapped and made appreciative noises. Uncle Angus tried it on and it fit perfectly. He thanked them very much and only after Maurice and Harold were busy talking to Aunt Vi, did he sidle up to Ava. "When ya get a minute, maybe you could rip off the feather collar. I'll look like a duck and be shot for sure."

Aunt Vi told them under no circumstances were they to book a hotel. There was plenty of room. Ava and Lola glanced at each other.

"The girls can sleep on the hide-a-bed in the living room and we'll put you upstairs in their room," Aunt Vi smiled. "I'm not taking no for an answer."

Maurice clapped his hands. "What an adventure, Harold! This is better then our trek along the Great Wall of China."

"Indeed," Harold said soberly.

"I don't suppose there are any lobster rolls going, are there, Aunt Vi?"

"We've got a special treat for you, darlin'. Just hold your horses."

The rest of that morning and afternoon were spent fixing all the rooms, changing bed sheets, and doling out towels. Ava and Lola threw their suitcases under the window at the end of the upstairs hall. They only wore their threadbare nighties and bathing suits anyway.

Just before supper, Aunt Vi and the girls got the table ready. They pulled out the two extensions and laid a plastic sheet over the top. The table, which they layered with newspaper, took up most of the kitchen. A couple of rolls of paper towels stood at the ready and boxes lined with garbage bags were positioned on the floor at each corner of the table. A load of knives and even a hammer and a couple of pairs of pliers were thrown on the newspaper.

Harold whispered to Maurice. "Maybe they're planning to kill us."

"I think we're ready," Uncle Angus declared.

"For what?" Harold asked.

"Go outside and see for yourself."

Everyone trooped out to the yard. Johnnie and Lauchie were in the doorway of the garage with a huge pot of boiling water.

"How's she goin', b'y?" Johnnie nodded at them.

Maurice and Harold returned with a polite, "How do you do."

"What is all this?" Maurice asked.

Lauchie took the cigarette out of his mouth. "This here's what you call a lobster boil."

Maurice clapped his hands. "Oh my!"

"Ever seen a live lobster, me son?" Johnnie smirked.

"I thought they came out of a can," Harold said.

Johnnie and Lauchie smirked at each other. "No way, b'y. This here's a lobster." He opened up the huge plastic container he took from the wharf. Dozens of green lobsters squirmed inside.

Harold screamed and jumped into Maurice's arms.

"There's nothing to be afraid of, Harriet. These here ain't gonna hurt ya." Uncle Angus reached out and grabbed one. "Its claws got bands on them." He put the crustacean on the ground and it wiggled around.

Harold got down and pointed. "Look. Its antlers are moving."

That's when Ava thought Lauchie and Johnnie were going to die laughing. "They're called antennae," Ava informed him.

Harold was still distressed. "How come you don't have pretty red ones? The ones I've seen with an entree are red."

Lauchie picked up the lobster and removed the bands. "Ya want red lobsters, you got it." He took the lobster and threw it in the boiling water.

Harold put his hands over his face. "Oh, I can't watch. How barbaric."

Maurice patted his back. "Think of it as an adventure, Harold. We're in the wilds of Nova Scotia. We're practically living off the land. It's so exciting."

"If you say so."

While the fellas cooked up a mess of lobsters, everyone else went inside and put the rest of the food on the table—big baskets of homemade rolls, bowls of melted butter, potato salad and jars of mayonnaise. There was also a big cooler filled with ice and beer.

Maurice was practically salivating. "I'm tingling all over."

"For someone who don't eat, you're mighty anxious," Uncle Angus laughed.

"This is real food. Not that low-fat, low-carb crap we eat."

They heard the men come into the kitchen. "Everyone sit," Aunt Vi ordered. They took their places around the table.

Harold looked up. "Where are the plates?"

Lauchie dumped a whole pile of cooked lobster on the table. "Don't need plates."

Ava's brothers instructed the guests on how to shuck a lobster. Johnnie tore the claws off. The boys did too. Then he ripped the tail off. They followed suit. But when he smashed the claw open with the side of his fist, the demo hit a snag.

Maurice pursed his lips. "How manly."

"Go ahead," Johnnie said.

Maurice and Harold both tapped the lobster lightly with the palms of their hands. "It doesn't seem to be working."

"That's because you're spanking them. Smash 'em, by God."

They raised their manicured hands and hit them. "Ow. Ow. Ow." They shook their wrists. "I don't think this is going to work."

"Try something different, then." He picked up the tail and squeezed the back shell between his hands, prying the two halves apart and tearing out the entire tail. He dipped it in a big bowl of butter and stuffed the whole thing in his mouth, saying, through his mouthful, "Now that's eatin'."

Maurice and Harold tried to do the same without much luck. "We're going to starve to death," Maurice wailed.

Uncle Angus pointed at his nephews. "Shuck some for the girls...ah...the boys." In no time at all, a pile of lobster meat sat on the newspaper in front of them. They copied Johnnie and dipped their lobster in the melted butter. Everyone waited to hear the verdict.

Maurice flapped his hands around as he swallowed his first mouthful. "My god! It's better than an orgasm."

Johnnie and Lauchie gave a great shout. Johnnie took a huge swig of beer and wiped the butter off his chin. "If you think that there's better than an orgasm, me son, then I think you better stop messin' with the boys and get yourself a woman."

"I think I will!"

Everyone hooted. Then it was down to business. There was no talk, just the sound of grunting and smashing and chewing. Lobster shells flew through the air into the plastic lined boxes at their feet. Paper towels were used to wipe off messy hands and faces. The rolls were gone, the potato salad bowl was licked clean and there wasn't a lobster to be seen by the time they were done.

Maurice sat back and groaned. "I've been around the world three times but I have to tell you that was the best meal of my life. Thank you gentlemen, I'll never forget it. Never."

"It was," nodded Harold. "It truly was."

Ava saw that her brothers were well pleased with the compliment. "Lobster season was over on the fifteenth, but maybe you boys would like to come out jiggin' for mackerel some day."

"I don't know what that is, but we'd be delighted, wouldn't we, Harold?"

Harold nodded, but not quite as enthusiastically as before.

There was nothing left to do but sit and have a cup of tea. No one could face the thought of dessert. Once they'd given their bodies a bit of a breather, the women took the implements and the bowls off the table, and their guests watched in fascination as they took the plastic sheet from the corners of the table, rolled up the mess and threw it in one of the boxes. The fellas took the boxes and put them in the garbage outside and what looked like a gigantic mess two seconds earlier was wiped away clean, as if it never happened.

Harold was fascinated. "My God, Maurice. That's how we should host our next dinner party. Newspaper. The tablecloth of the twenty-first century."

They all went to bed at nine and slept like the dead.

The first sign of impracticality about their guests staying in the house instead of a hotel was revealed the next morning. No one could get in the bathroom and by the time Maurice and Harold had had their showers there was no hot water for anyone else. It didn't help matters that Uncle Angus got a real fright when Harold walked out of the bathroom with a shower cap on and a face full of cream. Both came down for breakfast in silk lounge wear and absolutely raved about the porridge. They were nearly overcome when Aunt Vi brought hot tea biscuits and scones to the table with her fresh strawberry jam.

"Guys, it's going to be a hot one today," Ava said. "I've got to get to the beach. Would you like to go?"

"Wonderful," Maurice gushed with his mouth full.

"Great. Lola and I will pack a picnic lunch. We leave in an hour."

"One hates to be greedy, but what's on the menu tonight, Aunt Vi?" Maurice smiled as he licked jam off his fingers.

"Well, I've got a mess of scallops that need to be eaten. I fry them in butter with a coat of seasoned bread crumbs and we'll have new potatoes, fresh green beans from the garden and then we'll finish it off with apple crisp and whipped cream for dessert."

Ava thought they were going to weep.

Soon they were on their way. The girls carried a towel, a blanket for lying on, a beach umbrella, and the picnic basket. Maurice and Harold each carried a very large tote bag. Aunt Vi kissed them goodbye and away they went.

Ava decided she'd take them to Mira Gut Beach. She'd love to have gone to the wilder Kennington Cove, but decided she didn't want to scare the life out of them first thing. Besides, the water wasn't as cold at Mira Gut.

They made quite a little procession as they crossed the sand to claim their spot amid the other bathers. Lola shook open the blanket and laid it on the sand, then unfurled the umbrella and put the picnic basket in its shade. Throwing their towels aside, Ava and Lola ran to the water.

"Get back here and put on some sunscreen!" Maurice hollered. "I have no intention of dealing with sun-damaged skin when you get back to work."

"Oh, brother." The two of them trooped back and lathered up. Since it took their guests a good fifteen minutes to prepare themselves for sun exposure, the girls got fed up and once again ran down the beach. They jumped right in the water. When Maurice and Harold finally decided they were ready, they tiptoed down to the water in their designer swimwear. Both had straw hats on with silk scarves tied around the brim. They got some funny looks from kids playing in the sand.

"I can't wait," Maurice hollered to Ava. Harold echoed the sentiment.

Then each put a big toe in the water. They both screamed and ran back up under the umbrella.

"For heaven's sake," Ava cried. "Don't be such cowards."

"I can't feel my toe," Harold yelled. "Is that bad?"

"You have to get used to it. Come on."

They reluctantly went to the water's edge again and did a back and forth dance, trying to avoid the small waves cresting on the beach. They eventually got up to their ankles, but of course a jellyfish happened to float by and that was the end of that. They headed for the blanket and stayed there. The girls had a better time once the cowards were safely back on dry land.

They floated around and did the breast stroke every so often. It wasn't swimming, it was more like squatting on the bottom and swishing water about, but it was glorious, because the sky was a bright, almost baby blue, and the ocean was navy with a tint of green, the far shore a dark smudge in between. The sun blazed and soon the people on the beach were black shadows against the taupe sand. The salt air and the cool breeze that every so often blew across their hot shoulders was all the medicine Ava needed. It took her back to an innocent time, when her sisters took her to the beach. While they flirted with boys, she'd play in the sand quite happily by herself and, more often than not, stayed in the water too long until one of them realized her lips were purple and her skinny body was covered with goose bumps. They'd beg her not to tell Ma as they wrapped her tightly in towels. She'd be too busy shivering to answer but she'd nod her head and, true to her word, never say a thing.

"I think I'll go in," Lola said.

"Okay. I'll be there in a minute. Get the boys their lunch."

"I'm going to dazzle them with my egg and Cheez Whiz sandwiches," Lola said.

Ava turned away and looked out on Mira Bay. Although everyone's lives were pretty well back to normal, and they were able to laugh and carry on, there was still a pall of sadness. Her mother had been gone for a month now. It was hard to believe. Sometimes Ava forgot she was dead. It was easier to think of her as she did when she lived in Los Angeles. She was just away.

But there were moments when great waves of guilt washed over her. How could she have let ten years go by? All that time wasted. The last few months with her mother were the best they'd ever spent together. To sit on the bed and talk quietly was a gift Ava didn't deserve and she deeply regretted the hurt she'd caused her mother.

Of course when she thought of guilt, she only had to slip her eyes to the horizon on the right. Seamus lived there. She hadn't thought about him since the funeral, had no desire to, but maybe because she was feeling stronger now, her thoughts drifted to him more frequently. She hoped he'd be happy one day. That was the one thing she truly wished for him. He deserved to be happy, and since it was becoming obvious that their lives were not meant to be entwined, it was all she had to give him.

Feeling a chill, Ava realized she'd been daydreaming far too long, so she left the water and wrapped herself in a towel. The others waited for her, not wanting to have their picnic without her. It was fun to talk to her three dear friends. They were her family in California. These were the people who truly cared about her and they were hard to find in a place like Hollywood. It delighted her that they seemed to take to her family.

And why wouldn't they? Once upon a time, when she was first caught up in the glamour of the movie business, she did think of her family as something to be ashamed of. But she was young and unsure of herself then. She'd lie awake at night and cringe at the thought that the National Enquirer would find her brother Gerard and take a picture of him with his missing front tooth. Gerard might look like a country hick, but he was the gentle giant of the family, a person who would run through fire for her. She was the one who should be ashamed.

Ava tried to shake off these upsetting thoughts and enjoy the rest of her day, and she did for the most part, but she asked her friends if they'd mind if she stopped off at her mother's grave on the way home.

They drove into the country cemetery, where giant poplar trees shaded the ground. Mamie was buried in a newer section, so the trees weren't as big, but with loving care it would be very pretty someday. They'd come out here as a family about three weeks after their mother died to lay sod around her newly in-stalled headstone, and the girls made a flower garden in front of it. Their mother loved flowers and hummingbirds, so they hung a feeder from the tree and were delighted to see these perfect little creatures show up to keep her company.

The other three headed back to the car to give Ava a mo-ment alone. "One day, Ma, I'll come back here and tell you everything you wanted to know. But not yet. Be a little more patient." She touched the headstone. "I love you. I'm glad you and Daddy are together."

They were a tired bunch worn out by the sun and surf when they arrived home. Maurice and Harold yawned every minute and a half. They couldn't understand why they could barely keep their eyes open.

"It's probably the fresh air," Aunt Vi laughed. "You haven't had any in years."

She put their supper on the table and they waxed poetic about their meal. Aunt Vi got the greatest kick out of their praise. She'd been serving similar suppers for fifty years and no one had ever thanked her like these two. It did her heart good.

The rest of their stay was filled with sightseeing. Ava and Lola took Maurice and Harold over the Cabot Trail, to take in some of the most spectacular scenery in the world. They went whale watching. True to their word, Johnnie and Lauchie took the boys mackerel fishing, setting them up with their own jigs. Harold got his hooks caught in his new argyle vest and was quite distressed. They showed Maurice how to haul the jigs up and down through the water. He could hardly lift his arms after a while. "This is the most grueling cardio workout I've ever had."

Johnnie squinted through the smoke of the cigarette that was stuck to his lips. "Ya don't say."

While Lauchie helped Harold untangle his jig, Maurice felt a tug on his line. "Oh my, I think I caught a shark."

"If ya caught a shark, son, you'd be waterskiing through the waves."

Johnnie helped him reel it in. A small mackerel flipped from one of the hooks. Maurice was disappointed. "I only caught one."

"Better than wakin' up to a frozen boot," Johnnie said. Maurice had no idea what this meant.

Naturally, when Johnnie took his jig out of the water, there were all kinds of fish at the end of the line.

"That's no fair," Maurice cried.

Lauchie laughed at him. "Johnnie's always been luckier than a dog with two dicks."

"Sounds delightful," Harold said.

In the end, they weren't sure who enjoyed it more. Johnnie and Lauchie couldn't wait to regale the other fishers with Maurice and Harold stories, and the other two couldn't wait to go home and tell their friends of their adventures on the high seas.

The week went by and it was time to pack up. Maurice and Harold were teary through the entire process. They hauled their luggage downstairs and put it in the middle of the kitchen floor. Aunt Vi, who looked mighty weepy herself, walked out of the pantry with a few tins.

"Now, there are date squares in this one and Fat Archies in this one." She placed the tins of goodies in their hands. "I also have some recipe cards here. I wrote down all the recipes of the dishes you've had since you were here. Take them home and when you're cookin', think of me."

Well, that did it. They were a mess. Ava and Lola joined in and there was a giant group hug. This is how Johnnie and Lauchie found them.

"In the name of all that's holy," Lauchie shouted, "Knock off the racket."

"What are you doin' here?" Ava sniffed.

"Came to say goodbye to our buddies here." They shook hands with Maurice and Harold.

"Remember what I told ya," Johnnie said. "You need any lobster for one of your big shin digs, give me a call and I'll ship em to ya right quick. Impress those friends of yours."

Maurice tried to give him a hug, but Johnnie quickly picked up the bags. Lauchie did the same. "We'll take these for ya. There's a big car outside. Must be yours."

Uncle Angus was out in the garden when they marched down the stairs. He hurried over with a couple of Sobey's bags. "I picked ya some green and yellow wax beans and some carrots. There's a bunch a peas and a few onions. Threw in lots of little red potatoes, too." Uncle Angus wasn't fast enough. They grabbed him in a choke hold and squeezed him tight.

Neither of them could speak when it came time to say farewell. Aunt Vi had to give them a wave and hurry back into the kitchen. She hated long goodbyes. They hugged the girls and Maurice whispered to Ava, "You're the luckiest girl in the world, did you know that?"

"I do."

CHAPTER FIFTEEN

It was the worst summer of his life, not counting the first one without Sally. The week after he left the MacKinnons' yard, he was numb, going about his everyday life but almost as an observer. Colleen called every day but he didn't answer the phone. The kids whined constantly to see their cousins but he couldn't bring himself to reach out.

He called Sally's parents if he needed help and they were more than happy to provide it, although he knew that Lynn was concerned, afraid to get in the middle of a family feud. Not that he told her there was one, but she wasn't a stupid woman. In the end he didn't have to tell her because she took him aside one day and said that Colleen called her, very upset.

"I can't help it if Colleen is upset. That's her problem."

"You're not speaking to her, obviously. I know it's none of my business why, but if you ever need to talk, I'm here. You know that, don't you?"

He gave her a tight smile. "I do know that, and I'm grateful, but this is something I have to work out for myself."

"All right, dear. Have it your way."

Roger broached the subject one day by mentioning that Seamus didn't seem himself, but quickly dropped the matter when Seamus told him to mind his own business.

Then one day out of the blue, his father called him. His father never called him—the last time he phoned was to tell him his mother was on the floor, unconscious.

"Seamus."

"Dad?"

"Your sister is upset."

"So I've heard."

"I think this has gone on long enough, don't you?"

"What do you know about it?"

"Only what Colleen tells me. That you had a quarrel and you stopped speaking to her. I think your temper tantrum has gone on long enough."

"Do you?"

"Your sister has been there for you." He paused. "Unlike myself."

"Well, that's true."

There was silence. "I know we've never been close, but I do know it would break your mother's heart if she knew her two kids weren't speaking to each other. So I hope you reconsider your actions. There's been enough hurt in this family."

"You're right, Dad. And most of it was because of you."

"I probably deserved that," he sighed. "I'm trying to turn my life around."

"Too late for Mom to see it."

"All right, Seamus. I can see I'm not having much luck. Just be a man and call your sister." He hung up.

The person who did get through to him was Dave. He dropped by one Saturday afternoon and brought the kids with him. The cousins were delighted to see each other. Seamus felt like a heel when he saw their faces light up.

Dave accepted a beer and the two men sat out on the deck and talked about work, baseball, the usual guy stuff. But there was an uncomfortable atmosphere and Seamus couldn't stand it.

"Say what you've come to say and get it over with."

Dave finished off his beer and put it beside his deck chair. "How long have we known each other?"

"Since elementary school."

"How often have I interfered with anything that's gone on with your family, since I started going with Colleen?"

"Never."

Dave nodded. "And it hasn't been easy. You guys had a lot of problems. Alcoholism can destroy families. I think the only reason you and Colleen are as sane as you are is because of your mother."

Seamus hung his head. "That's true."

"Colleen is very much like your mother. She's got a big heart and she tries to protect the ones she loves. It's not easy for her. She misses her mom. You're the only family she has, because we both know your dad is not someone she can count on."

Seamus peeled the label off his beer bottle while he listened. He didn't want to look up and see Dave's face.

"I've spent the last week listening to the woman I love cry her heart out over you, and I've come to tell you that it's not right, and it isn't fair. She's the only reason you were able to take care of these kids. In those early days after Sally died, she was the one who took them under her wing. You and Sally's parents were destroyed at the time. But she took Jack and that little baby girl and loved them as her own."

Seamus stopped peeling.

"I want you to go and tell your sister that you love her and appreciate what she's done for you. And accept her apology, because she feels very badly about what happened to Libby. Very badly."

Seamus looked up. "You're right. I've been a shit." He rose from his chair. "Thanks, Dave. You've been a good friend to us." He held out his hand and Dave shook it.

"Go to her now. I'll watch the kids. That's why I'm here."

Seamus got in his car and drove the ten minutes to Colleen's house. She looked out the window and ran down the porch steps. He got out of the car and she jumped in his arms. They never said a word. They didn't have to.

And while he was glad to have the spat with Colleen over with, if the truth be told, it didn't relieve the misery he felt when he thought of Libby. He worried about her health, her mental and physical health. She wasn't a strong person. He spent that July remembering their times together when they were kids, happy and carefree. One night he thought about the day he first saw her. He loved to skate, and was anxious to get on the ice with his friends. They went as a large group in case the Glace Bay boys gave them a hard time, as often happened between the two communities. There'd been animosity for years—his old man would regale him with stories of the fights, seeming to relish the telling. Seamus was never impressed. He thought it was juvenile.

When he walked in the rink he didn't see her at first, and didn't know what made him glance over as he passed her. Not only his heart stopped, his feet stopped as well, and he remembered being mortified that his friends made fun of him. But the only thing that really stood out at that moment was her. She was slender and dainty, with perfect features. He remembered the colour pink. Her blonde hair was held up by a pink ribbon and her cheeks and lips were soft pink as well. She had on a pink sweater and white jeans.

And then suddenly he was pushed forward by his stupid friends and he had to pretend it didn't matter that she was the most perfect creature he'd ever laid eyes on. When she turned and started to walk away, his heart was in his mouth. He thought she was leaving, but thankfully she soon returned to the ice. From that point on, their meeting was inevitable because he promised himself he wasn't leaving without speaking to her.

When she reached up and kissed him that first time, it was like a dream. He was sure he had imagined it. But when her cold sweet breath mingled with his own, he knew he'd never be the same again.

They skated together all afternoon and made plans to meet later that night. Before his friends could drag him away, he caught her by the hand and took her into the corridor behind the team bench. They kissed each other over and over. He couldn't get enough of her. She was the one who finally put a stop to it by placing her index finger on his lips.

"No more."

"Just one more."

She shook her head. Then she kissed her finger and put it back against his lips. "Sometimes when you wait, kisses are sweeter."

"Nothing could be as sweet as this."

She laughed and slipped out of his grasp, then out of his hands and disappeared. He sagged against the wall. He was afraid he imagined her. When he went home for supper that night, his mother took one look at him and smiled. "Is she pretty?"

He had only the strength to nod.

The trouble with remembering her, however, was that it took a lot out of him. He finally figured out by week two that he wasn't doing himself any favours. Once again his buddy Roger seemed to sense the dilemma. They were on patrol together that day.

"You know what your problem is, don't you?"

"What's that?"

"You need a little 'forget all about her' sex."

"And what is that, oh wise one?"

"It's pretty self-explanatory. You go on a date with a nice woman and have your way with her. You'll feel better. Trust me."

"I think you're right. I'm starting to look at the lingerie section in the Sears catalogue."

"Surely to God you've got reading material a little more imaginative than that?"

"Nah. Jack might find it."

"He's only five. How's he going to get at it on the top shelf of your closet?"

"Is that where you keep yours?"

"Partly."

"I'll think about it."

"I'd do more then think about it. Listen, Julie has a friend who has the hots for you. I told Julie the only reason this woman hangs around with her is to eventually get close to you, so let's do her a favour and put her out of her misery. The four of us can go to dinner and you can see how it goes."

"I'm not sure…"

"She's not a dog, if that's what you're thinking. I'm your friend; I'd never hang you out to dry."

"You let the bride of Frankenstein drag me away."

"That was a mistake that will never be repeated."

"Okay, I guess."

"Down, boy, your enthusiasm is getting the better of you."

"Sorry."

"She's got a nice rack."

"That's something to look forward to."

Roger shook his head in despair.

Colleen was thrilled to take the kids for the night. She

didn't even ask why he was going out, and because she didn't, he told her he had a blind date. She tried to keep the smile off her face. He told her not to get her hopes up.

Seamus showered, shaved and dressed with as much enthusiasm as someone going to the gallows. He never even looked at himself in the mirror. He drove to Roger's for the meet up. Roger lived in a nice bungalow in Sydney. His kids' playthings were sprawled over the lawn, giving it the air of a happy home. It must be nice to have a wife and kids and be normal, Seamus thought as he pulled into the driveway. Seamus had that for just long enough to know that he missed it.

He walked into the kitchen, able to tell right away that Julie was as nervous as her friend. From the looks of it, they'd had a couple of glasses of wine already.

Roger got to him first. "Hey buddy."

"Hey."

Julie came over and gave him a kiss on the cheek. "Hi, Seamus. I'm glad you're here. I'd like you to meet my friend Jennifer."

He reached out his hand and shook hers. "Hi Jennifer. Nice to meet you."

"And you." She smiled at him. Roger was right; she was very pretty and nicely dressed. And she did have a great body.

"Like a drink before we go?" Roger asked him. "Since we're driving, you and I have to stick with the boring stuff."

"How often do I get to have a glass of wine?" Julie said. "It's our turn tonight, isn't it, Jen?"

Jen smiled and took another sip.

"I'll have a Coke," Seamus said.

"One Coke, coming up."

They sat out on the back deck, since it was too hot in the

house. It was very pleasant. Jennifer didn't talk too much or too little. She asked him all the right questions. He started to relax a little. He returned the favour and inquired about her situation. She told him she worked in a law firm and had a young son. She was divorced—had been for a couple of years.

The time came for them to go out to eat and they decided to go to Huang's for Chinese food. It was an enjoyable evening together and they had a lot of laughs. They talked about their kids and he and Roger regaled the girls with some of the antics that went on at the station.

Seamus thought Jennifer was a nice person. It was pleasant to be around a woman who was friendly and interesting. He surprised himself when he asked if she'd like a drive home. Roger and Julie beamed like happy parents. "Knock it off," Seamus growled when Jennifer went in the house to get her sweater. Julie and Jennifer kissed each other goodbye and had a small giggle together.

They got in his car and waved goodbye to the matchmakers. Seamus drove down the street.

"They're great, aren't they?" she commented.

"They are. Roger's been a good friend for a lot of years."

"Did you go to the Police Academy together?"

"Yes, over in P.E.I. We didn't know each other growing up. You'd think New Waterford and Sydney were in separate provinces."

She laughed.

"Would you like to go for a cup of coffee, or do you have to get home?"

"My son's staying at my mother's tonight, so I'm in no hurry."

At the coffee shop, they sat together and talked about a lot of things. He found her easy to be with and ended up telling her more than perhaps he should have. He talked about Sally and how he missed her and how difficult it was to bring up the children without their mother. She made all the right sympathetic noises.

"I'm not sure if Roger told you," Jennifer said, "but I've wanted to meet you for a long time. Being a friend of Julie's, I've heard about you and knew you to see you on the street. I was heartsick when I heard about your wife. I'm glad you feel good enough to start dating again. Maybe you'll be able to move forward now."

He nodded and looked at his hands.

She reached over and covered one of his with her own. "I understand this can't be easy, but I want you to know that I like you very much and if you think you're ready to be with someone again, I'd be happy if it was me."

He cleared his throat before he spoke. "You're sweet. I'm not certain if I'm ready or not. That's probably the reason why I've stayed away from women."

She gave his hand a squeeze. "Well, why don't we find out?"

He looked at her then. She smiled.

"Okay."

He drove her to his house and they went inside. He wasn't sure what to do next, but she seemed to know exactly what she was doing. She took his hand and led him to bedroom, closing the door behind him.

"You don't have to say anything," she said. "We'll go as slow as you want."

He nodded.

She reached out with her arms and touched his chest through his shirt. She left her hands there for a few moments before she came closer and put them around his waist. She spread her palms across his back and brought her face close to his. She kissed him softly, once, twice, three times, before he kissed her back.

As soon as he did, she pulled him to the bed and made him sit down on the edge of it. "Stay very still," she said.

He swallowed. He stopped thinking with his mind and started to listen to his body. She stood in front of him and did a slow strip tease. She somehow knew this was best. She didn't touch him, didn't demand anything from him, just slowly took off her clothes only inches away from him.

When he reached out and pulled her down onto the bed with him, he wasn't frightened anymore. She helped him remove his clothes and when their bodies came together, the touch of skin on skin was one he remembered. It did feel nice to hold a woman in his arms again. She smelled good. That was something he missed the most—the scent of a woman, how her hair and her skin and her lips all seemed to have their own perfect perfume.

But as soon as he started to make love to her, his neglected body betrayed him and it was over much too soon. Seamus was embarrassed. She told him to hush, that it was only natural. He was reassured by her quiet manner. She talked to him in the dark and after a while she reached for him again. This time he was able to make her feel good—his own small victory.

They fell asleep then, but some time a few hours later, Seamus woke up. He wasn't sure where he was at first—he felt a body beside him and for one delirious moment he thought it was Libby. But because he thought of her and not his wife, he felt he betrayed Sally. Here he was in their bed, making love to a stranger, yet dreaming of his first sweetheart.

He groped on the floor for his jeans, put them on and walked out of the bedroom. Closing the door behind him so as not to wake Jennifer, he walked into the living room, where the moonlight over the still water of the bay cast a dreamy glow. He thought how beautiful it looked. A night for lovers.

Seamus sat on the couch and tears came unbidden. As much as his body had released its energy, so now did his heart. He thought of the women in his life, the wasted years, the happy years, the unbearable sad years. It was too much.

He was gradually aware that he wasn't alone. Jennifer stood in the doorway with a sheet around her. He turned to her.

"I'm sorry."

She looked sad. "I understand. I wish it was different, but I understand. I can't compete with a memory."

He didn't correct her.

CHAPTER SIXTEEN

One morning in early August, Lola got a phone call. She took it upstairs. When she didn't come back downstairs after forty minutes, Ava crept up the steps to listen and see if she was still talking. She heard Lola crying instead.

Ava opened the bedroom door slowly. "Are you alright? What's wrong?"

"That was my Dad," Lola sniffed. "Mom's been told she has breast cancer."

Ava went to her and took her in her arms. Lola cried on her shoulder as they rocked back and forth. After awhile, Lola calmed down long enough to wipe away her tears.

"I'm sorry. Here I am crying my eyes out and my mother is still alive."

"Well, of course you're crying. You have every right."

"I've seen firsthand what it's like for someone to lose their mother and I don't think I can stand it."

"Sweetheart, I think you're jumping the gun. There are a million things they can do to help women these days. It's not an automatic death sentence anymore."

"You're right," Lola nodded. "But Dad was so upset."

"Well, of course he was. He needs you. Your mother needs you. You have to go, Lola."

Lola looked at her friend. "I don't want to leave you, but…"

"Don't be ridiculous. As you can see, I'm well taken care of. You should get home to your parents right away."

"Well, it's still almost a month before you have to go to New York. If things work out, I'll be able to meet you there."

"Of course. But if you need to stay longer, do it. If there's one thing I've learned in the last couple of months, it's never to squander time with your family. It's the most important thing in life."

They went downstairs and broke the news to Aunt Vi and Uncle Angus.

"Oh, you dear child!" Aunt Vi hobbled across the kitchen to give Lola a hug. "We'll miss you something awful, but your mother needs you."

Uncle Angus rose from the rocking chair and Lola ran over to him next. He gave her a big hug too. Then he put his hand in his pocket and took out a handful of change. "You're gonna need a couple of loonies for the parking meter at the airport. The bastards are always scrounging money for no goddamn reason." He picked through his coins and handed her four loonies.

"I'm calling you Uncle Loonie from now on," Lola said through a grin.

"You can call me whatever you like," Uncle Angus said. "Just as long as you call me."

Lola started to tear up again, so she quickly ran upstairs. Ava followed.

She packed her bags and Ava drove her to the airport for the first flight that would take her to Halifax and, from there, to Toronto and on to Chicago. As they waited, they remembered their arrival all those months before.

"I feel as if an entire lifetime has elapsed since we walked through those doors," Ava said.

"I remember how nervous you were. Nervous and edgy and angry, if the truth be told."

"You're right, I was. I was afraid of them; afraid that I'd be a disappointment or that they'd hate me."

"You've been proven very wrong, haven't you?"

"Very."

"It's at times like this that I wish I was lucky enough to have a brother or sister."

"You have me. I'm your sister in everything that's important. We don't have to share the same chromosomes."

Lola grabbed her hand. "Yes, you are. And I thank God for that everyday."

Her flight was called and they rose to their feet. They hugged each other for a long time.

"Thank you for everything, Lola. I'll miss you so much, but I'm glad you're going."

"Me too. I'll call you when I get home, after I've talked to Mom."

"Yes, please. I'll be waiting."

As Lola went through security, Ava went over to the same window her own relatives had stood in front of the night she arrived. With only one gate at Sydney Airport, she was able to watch Lola walk to the small jet that sat on the runway. Lola went up the steps and turned around to give Ava one last wave, then ducked her head and disappeared.

It was as if the sun had gone behind a cloud.

Lola called later that night to tell them that she arrived safely and her mother felt much better now that her own little family was together again. She promised to call often and keep them up to date on her progress.

When Ava turned in that night, she felt sorry for herself. The bed next to her was empty and she was lonely. Without Lola to distract her, she was aware of how alone she was. She was desperate enough to place a call to Hayden. A woman answered his cell.

"Is Hayden there, please?"

"He's around somewhere. I think he may be in the shower. Can he call you back?"

Rattled, Ava dithered for a moment before the voice said, "Oh never mind. Here he is. Sweetie, it's for you."

"Yes?"

"Hayden."

"Babe! How are you?"

"Not as good as you."

"Why Ava, I didn't know you were the jealous type."

"I'm not."

"Doesn't sound like it."

"Never mind, you're busy."

"I was busy. Not anymore."

"You've already screwed her then."

"Don't be nasty."

"Sorry."

"Listen, babe, we both agreed we're free agents when we're away from each other."

"Did I actually agree to that?"

"Yes, you did."

"I was nuts."

"I thought it was quite clever of you."

"You would," she laughed.

"What can I do, Ava?" he sighed. "They throw themselves at me all day long. A man can only resist so long."

"Fine. Go enjoy yourself."

"Don't be mad at me. I remember a night not long ago when I made you very happy for a quite long time. And I promise you, I don't do that for everyone."

She didn't say anything.

"I'm right. Say it."

"You're right."

"You loved it. Couldn't get enough of it, you sexy thing. Actually, that's what turns me on the most."

She lay back in bed. "What?"

"How you have this little miss innocent demeanor, but you're a very accomplished lover. Always willing to be just slightly naughty. God, thinking of it now, I'm getting myself quite worked up."

"Are you?"

"Mmm. What are you wearing?"

She looked at her ratty old nightgown and lied. "Nothing."

"Good. Just the way I like you. You do have the most gorgeous body. You are aware of that fact, I hope."

"It's not getting much attention, I'm afraid."

"If I was there, I'd be giving it a great deal of attention. Especially my favourite spots."

"And those are?"

"Well, besides the heavenly obvious ones, that little mole on your bottom right-hand rib has a way of making me dizzy with desire."

She covered her eyes with her arm. "Oh god, you have no idea how lonely I am."

"I don't want you to be lonely. Why don't you come home? I'll make you feel better in no time."

Her heart sank at the prospect of heading back to Los Angeles. "I'll be there soon enough. Don't mind me, I'm fine." She changed the subject. "So what's new with you?"

He droned on about himself, as she knew he would. Finally she said she had to go.

"Sweet dreams...of me," Hayden laughed.

"Good night, Hayden."

She hung up the phone and curled into a little ball.

It felt different being in the house without a friend or her mother. Aunt Vi and Uncle Angus were slowly getting their lives back and they had their own friends, who dropped by to help or take them somewhere. It was as if the early summer had been a lovely dream with Lola and Maurice and Harold and then, suddenly, it was back to real life.

Her sisters and brothers had their families and some of them were away on vacation or busy with soccer practice and baseball games. Mothers with children to entertain and keep out of trouble were on double duty in the summer when their kids were out of school. They called often and invited her along and she did go on some outings, but the day she went to see her nephew play baseball, the women in the bleachers all wanted her autograph and created a bit of a fuss. She saw her nephew gesture to his mom as if to say, is she here to see me or be a star? She told Bev she had a headache and had to go. Bev almost looked relieved.

After a few days of wandering around like a lost soul, she thought she'd go to the beach by herself. She packed her own lunch and headed out for Kennington Cove, but when she drove by Mira Gut, she was surprised to see the beach not as crowded as usual, so she decided she might as well take advantage of it.

It was a nice day, but not a scorcher. The tide was very low. Ava was content to take her blanket and umbrella and sit in the sand. She had a good book with her and spent a nice couple of hours reading, then ate an apple and got a little drowsy. She wasn't sure how long she was dozing when she felt a cold little finger poke her. Ava lifted her head and saw a small black shadow against the sun. She shielded her eyes from the glare and gradually a little girl came into focus. She was trying to give her something.

"Hello."

"Ell." She opened her fist and held out a sandy seashell.

"For me?"

"Yeah."

Ava took it. "Thank you. It's very pretty."

Then she heard a man call out, "Sarah?"

"Yeah?"

He ran over. "There you are. You scared me to death." He took his daughter's hand. "I'm sorry. She likes…"

Ava sat up. "…to give people things."

He took a step back. "Libby."

"Seamus."

He looked like he was having trouble finding something to say, so she helped him. "She's beautiful, especially in that bathing suit."

Seamus smiled. "Yes, she loves it."

She had a hard time taking her eyes off his body. It was a man's body. Someone she didn't know. She noticed he never took his eyes off hers.

"Do you come to this beach often?"

"Yes, at low tide. It makes it easier for me to watch them." He looked a little sheepish. "Although I wasn't doing a very good job a minute ago." As if he suddenly remembered he had another child, he turned around quickly and called Jack's name. Jack waved. He was digging a big hole and was quite content.

"Are you here by yourself?" he asked her.

"Yes, my friend Lola had to go home, a family emergency."

"That's too bad."

"I miss her."

"I'm sure you do. How are you feeling? Better?"

"Yes. I'm much better."

Sarah wiggled out of his grasp and ran back to her brother. Without her there, it felt awkward, as if a barrier had been removed and now there was nothing between them. It felt dangerous. Ava closed her eyes and sighed. "I'm tired of this. It's ridiculous. Why do we feel as if we're doing something wrong, just standing here?"

"I'm not sure."

"We're old friends. Why can't we be again?"

"I was told in no uncertain terms to stay away from you."

"By who?"

"Your sister."

"Let me guess...Rose?"

He nodded. "Although Colleen isn't crazy about the idea either."

She shook her head. "It's such a waste, Seamus. I've wasted enough time. Losing my mother has made everything else seem trivial and petty."

"You're right. Would you like a sandy peanut butter sandwich?"

"Yes, I would," she laughed.

They spent the afternoon together not talking about anything important, just listening to the kids prattle on about silly things. They made a sand castle with them and Ava went up into the grass and found some daisies. She showed Sarah how to make a daisy chain and put a little crown of flowers on her mess of curls. Sarah walked around with her tummy sticking out, trying hard to keep it on her head. Her father laughed and laughed when he watched her. Ava felt good that she'd made him happy.

The sun was going down and the wind became still, the most beautiful time of day on the beach. Both the children were asleep on their towels and Ava knew they should go, but it was hard to part. It had been a lovely day.

"I've enjoyed this," he said to her. "You have no idea."

"Me too."

"It must seem a little boring for you. I know you jet-set all over the world. I saw you at the Cannes Film Festival on TV once, and you were so glamorous, with all these beautiful people around you."

"I always sound as if I don't appreciate the opportunities given to me, but a day posing for the cameras in a faraway exotic place doesn't hold a candle to a day like today." She looked out over the water. "That day, I'd flown in from L.A. I was hot and tired and cranky. The only reason I wasn't completely nuts is because Maurice can fix my hair and makeup while I sleep in a chair. Harold picked my outfit and they dressed me like a mannequin. I couldn't eat anything or the dress wouldn't fit. I was paraded around on this dock with other celebrities, most of whom I didn't know. You kiss them and pretend you do. You smile as thousands of cameras flash at you and all you can hear is your name shouted from four hundred different directions and you're not sure where to look."

"Sounds delightful."

"Since I don't drink like a fish or smoke or do drugs, I'm not much fun at a party, so I usually skip those to play monopoly with Lola and Maurice and Harold."

He smiled.

"Then on my way down to breakfast the next morning, I found myself in an elevator with a very famous actor who pushed the stop button. He thought he'd feel me up and expected me to be grateful for the opportunity."

"Are you serious? What did you do?"

"I kneed him in the nuts, pushed the button, and continued down to breakfast."

"Atta girl," he laughed.

She gave a great sigh. "I've missed this island. I've missed it with every fibre of my being. The land, the water, the sky, all of it. Whenever I get lonely in some strange part of the world, I picture it in my mind and feel better."

"Do you get lonely, Libby?"

She looked at him. "Very."

"Me too."

He reached out and held her hand. They sat like that for a long time. Eventually she said, "We better go. You don't want the kids to get a chill."

Ava helped him carry them up to the car. She took Sarah's sweet little body and held it close. Sarah nestled into her neck. As she waited for Seamus to put Jack in his car seat, she swayed slightly back and forth with Sarah in her arms. She closed her eyes and kissed those messy curls.

When Ava opened her eyes, Seamus was watching her hold his daughter.

"Sorry, I just wanted to hold her for a minute."

"You're beautiful, Libby."

She closed her eyes again. She couldn't look at him. "Take her."

He lifted Sarah out of her arms. She turned around and went back to the beach to collect their things, but it was really to keep him from looking at her anymore. Picking up their belongings gave her a moment to gather her wits. She crossed the beach and walked back to his car, quickly passing over the children's toys. "I think I have everything."

"Thank you for today," he said.

"You're welcome. Thank you for sharing your children with me. They're delightful company."

"As are you."

"Goodbye Seamus." She turned to go.

"Libby."

She looked back.

"Can you meet me here tomorrow?"

She nodded and ran to her car.

He was on vacation that week and the next, so they spent every day at the beach. She'd often bring Teddy Bear too—the kids loved him. It was as if they needed the kids and the dog there, so they wouldn't be tempted to repeat what happened the last time they were alone. And Ava was grateful for it, because as much as they liked to think they knew each other; they had a lot to catch up on. Their days were filled with stories of friends and adventures they'd had.

One rainy day, they decided to be bold and go to town. The kids wanted ice cream so they headed for the Tasty Treat. They sat in the car and ate their waffle cones. Sarah was completely covered in sticky ice cream by the time she was through. Ava said she'd take her into the bathroom and tidy her up. She and Sarah ran through the rain to get the key for the outdoor facilities but they told her it was in use so they waited outside under the overhang. Seamus waved her to come back, but she shook her head. She and Sarah were having fun jumping in the puddles.

The door to the bathroom opened and out walked Colleen and Courtney. Sarah gave a delighted shout to her cousin. "Cory!"

Colleen looked at Ava and then at Sarah and then over her head to search for Seamus's car.

"Hello, Colleen."

"What are you doing with Sarah?"

"I'm cleaning her up."

"Is Seamus here?"

"Of course he's here. Do you think I kidnapped his daughter?"

She didn't say anything.

"May I have the key?"

Colleen passed it to her.

"We're having ice cream, Colleen."

"Yes."

They both saw Seamus start to get out of the car. "Wave to him and let him be. Please, I beg you."

Colleen waved, then grabbed Courtney's hand and ran to the other side of the building, where her car was parked. Ava gave him a smile and a quick wave and took Sarah into the bathroom. When they were finished, they hurried back in the car.

"What did she say to you?"

"Nothing."

"Nothing?"

"She asked what we were doing here and I said we were having ice cream and she said, have fun."

"She did?"

"Yeah."

"That was nice." Seamus smiled.

"Yes, it was."

They bought a pizza and took it back to his place. They ate it while they played Go Fish with the kids. Jack got fed up with Sarah always saying "yeah," when she didn't have anything, so he went off in a huff. He came back when they bribed him with a video. When both kids fell asleep on the couch halfway though the movie, Ava decided she'd better be going. Seamus got up with her and walked her to the door. She hurried out on the deck.

"It's been a nice day," he said.

"It's been a lot of nice days. I've had such fun."

He looked at her. "May I kiss you?"

She looked away.

"I promise I won't get carried away like the last time."

She smiled. "Oh my, if it's going to be a boring, chaste kiss then I suppose I can risk it."

He reached out and took her hand, pulling her close, raising her chin with the crook of his finger. He touched her lips softly with his own and then looked at her. "More?"

"A little more."

He bent his head and parted his lips. She reached up and did the same. It was a nice, slow, deep kiss, as if they had all the time in the world.

And then Jack woke up. They heard him through the open window. "Daddy! I have a tummy ache."

Seamus groaned and took her face in his hands. "Sorry."

"Don't be."

"Will you come to me soon?"

She hesitated.

"We don't have to do anything but this. Please let me do this."

She nodded. He kissed her once more.

"Daddy!"

He dropped his hands and walked back in the house. Ava had to hold on to the railing to get down the stairs. Her heart pounded in her chest. She got in the car and laid her head back on the headrest. "Oh god, what am I going to do?"

CHAPTER SEVENTEEN

Seamus was happier than he'd been in a long time. He whistled everywhere he went. Unfortunately his vacation was up and he couldn't spend every day with her anymore—but it didn't matter. He had enough memories of their two weeks together to keep him going for a while.

He was so shocked to see her on the beach that day he couldn't remember what he said at first. All he knew was that he couldn't stop looking at her. When she sat beside him and shared their sandwiches, his eyes lingered over her collarbones. She had beautiful shoulders and the small hollow in front of her neck was vulnerable and delicate. He was dying to put his mouth on it and kiss his way up under her chin.

It took a lot of concentration not to spend the entire time fantasizing about the feel of her body under him. He had to shake his head sometimes and ask her to repeat what she said. She laughed at him, as if she knew what the trouble was. But the moment that got to him the most was when she held Sarah in her arms and rocked her gently back and forth. She closed her eyes and leaned her head against Sarah's curls and it seemed right. It was perfect. He never wanted it to end.

Their last night together before he went back to work, they took the kids to the drive-in. The kids loved it. Excited about being allowed out of their car seats, they stayed awake for almost two movies. They ate too much and bounced from the front to the back seat, until that novelty wore off. Finally, they curled up in awkward positions in the back seat and slept like babies.

"I suppose we should go," Ava said.

"Not yet. It's our last night together."

"I'm not going tomorrow."

"I mean my vacation's over."

"Oh."

He hated to be reminded of her leaving. "When are you going again?"

"In about a week."

"You have to go, I guess."

"Yes," she sighed. "I signed a contract."

"Break it."

She laughed at him. "Okay. Have you got about ten million dollars so I can get out of it?"

"Good lord."

"It's a weird business."

He reached for her hand and rubbed his thumb against her palm. "I don't want to talk about it, anyway."

"Neither do I."

"What does this remind you of?"

"Right now?"

"Mmm."

"The time we came here with a bunch of friends and you ended up locking everyone out of the car so you could neck with me."

They laughed.

"I know. It was great. Don't think the others were too happy about it though."

"Gee, Seamus, I wonder why. They had to sit in other people's cars and I'm sure the couples in those cars were happy to see them."

"I know. It was rotten. Fun, though."

"Do you remember what you said to me that night?"

"Did I talk?"

"Moaned mostly, but when you did come up for air you told me that you wished we could run away together. Just take the car and drive."

He bowed his head and kept rubbing her hand. "Why don't we?"

"What?"

"Take the kids and get the hell out of here, away from prying, judgmental relatives and nosy friends and neighbours. Just you, me and the kids."

"You couldn't take them away from Sally's parents, or your sister, for that matter."

Seamus stopped holding her hand and grabbed the steering wheel with both of his. He laid his forehead against them. "I know, I know. But my whole life I've done what was best for other people. When am I going to be happy?"

"You were happy with Sally, weren't you?"

He kept his head down but he turned his face to her and whispered, "I loved Sally. I always will. But I'm in love with you and that will never change for as long as I'm alive."

"Oh, Seamus."

"Don't talk, Libby. I don't want to talk."

She slid over beside him and she let him kiss her for a long time. He kissed her throat and ears and the spot on her neck he was dying to taste, before he got up the courage to put his hand under her sweater and hold her waist. He touched her ribs. She didn't pull away when his hand traveled upward and cupped her breast. She kept kissing him so he reached under her bra and held her breast against the palm of his hand. A shiver went through his body.

She whispered against his lips, "The children."

He took his hand away and the lovely sensation of her warm skin was lost. She went back to sit closer to the car window. The car was fogged up.

"We're like two teenagers again," she smiled.

He didn't answer her.

"What's wrong?"

"I don't know how much more I can take."

Now it was her turn not to say anything.

He got up the courage to look at her. "I ache for you. My whole body aches for you. You can't let me kiss you and then pull away."

She sounded annoyed with him. "You want to make love to me in front of your babies?"

"Of course not. Stay with me tonight."

"I can't."

"Why not?"

"Seamus, don't ruin this. Please. I couldn't stand it if you were mad at me."

"I'm not mad at you. I'm..."

"...mad at me."

That made him laugh. "Okay. I'm mad at you."

"Well, stop acting like a horny teenager. Don't ruin our time together. We have so little of it left."

They drove back to his place, where she gave him a quick kiss and then got in her car and went home. He knew she hadn't told her family she'd been with him, said there was no point in upsetting people if she didn't have to.

He decided she was right. He wasn't going to waste their last week together acting like a spoiled brat. He'd take her lead and enjoy her company. It was that or drive himself crazy, and he'd been crazy for much too long to want it to continue.

Naturally people noticed the difference in him. His sister especially. He dropped in to give her back a jacket Courtney left at his house.

"I wondered where that went."

"I found it under the bed."

"But when was she over there?"

"The day Dave told me to stop being a creep."

"Ahh. Trust her father not to remember she had a jacket on when she left the house."

"You know us fathers," he smiled and took a cookie from a baking rack on the kitchen counter.

"Leave those for the kids."

"I'm a kid. I'm your kid brother."

"Woe is me."

He snuck up behind her and put his hands on her shoulders. He pressed his cheek against hers. "You love me though."

"Fool that I am."

He let her go and sat at the kitchen table to finish his cookie. She looked at him.

"You're happy these days."

"Just a bit."

"No need to ask why."

"Is that a dig or an observation?"

Colleen put the dirty cookie sheet in the sink. "I don't want to get into trouble again so I'll keep my mouth shut."

"Oh Coll, don't be like that. I thought that nonsense was over. You told Libby to have fun when you met her at the Tasty Treat."

"She told you that?"

"Yes. Why? Didn't you?"

"Yeah. I'm not taking a jab at you. It's a topic we're too sensitive about, so let's pretend it doesn't exist."

"Fine by me."

"Can I ask one thing?"

"What?"

"What's going to happen when she leaves?"

"Maybe she'll stay."

She turned around and wiped her counter top with a dish-towel. "Maybe she will."

But his good mood soured when he met Jennifer a few days later coming out of the drugstore. He gave her a friendly wave and she kept right on going. Confused, he ran after her in the parking lot. "Jennifer."

She turned around. "What do you want, Seamus?"

"I thought I'd say hello. Isn't that what friends do?"

"We're friends, are we?"

"Aren't we?"

"No. I don't think so."

"I thought you said you understood."

Jennifer shifted her parcel to her opposite hip. "I did understand, when I thought I was up against the memory of your dead wife. What you conveniently forgot to mention was that you had Ava Harris in the wings as well."

"It wasn't like that."

"No? My brother saw the two of you picking up a pizza, looking extremely lovey dovey, I might add. I thought you were still in mourning for Sally. I didn't realize I was competing with a film star. I didn't have much chance, did I?"

"Jennifer…"

She fumbled in her purse for the keys to her car. "What I can't understand is why she hasn't helped you over your big hurdle of being with other women. I'm sure she's much better at it than me. I hear she's had a lot of practice."

"Please."

Her eyes filled with tears. "You fed me so much crap that night. How you weren't sure and you didn't know if you could be with someone else. And stupid me fell for it. How you must have laughed when I did my little strip tease. What an easy mark I was. You made me feel like a fool. You can't use people like that. Don't ever come near me again."

She turned on her heel, walked to her car and left him standing there. She drove off in a hurry.

He felt terrible. He sought out Roger after work but Roger wasn't his usual accommodating self. He seemed annoyed at him too.

"Great. Jennifer must have said her spiel to Julie, who then told you and now you're going to punish me too."

Roger put his stuff in his work locker. "Hey man, I'd like to stay out of this if I can."

"Shit. Why didn't you tell me she was upset?"

"Hell, I didn't know myself until a couple of days ago. I guess her brother told her something about you and Libby and she calls Julie and cries into the phone for three hours and then I get it in the neck for being your friend, and how could I have been so mean as to set you up. Then I had to remind Julie that she asked me to, but she seems to have forgotten that part of the conversation, so now I'm a shit. No, I've had enough grief, thank you very much."

"Well, this sucks."

"You're darn right it does. Jennifer's a nice girl. I don't think she deserved that kind of treatment."

Seamus slammed his own locker door. "What are you talking about? Weren't you the one who said to have 'forget about her' sex?"

"Yeah. But you conveniently forgot to tell me you're going out with Libby. I thought you were boohooing into your pillow alone every night. I didn't know you had someone with you."

Seamus was about to scream that he was alone every night, but he stopped himself. Roger wouldn't believe him anyway. Seamus couldn't believe it himself.

Roger closed his locker. "I'll see ya tomorrow."

Roger started to walk away but Seamus held him back when he grabbed his arm. "I'm sorry because I liked Jennifer. She's a lovely woman. None of this has anything to do with her."

"I'm not the one you should be telling that to." He shook off Seamus's grip and walked out of the locker room.

So Seamus wasn't in a real good mood for the rest of the week. It didn't help that Ava called to say she had to take her Aunt Vi to a concert at the Savoy Theatre because Uncle Angus refused to go with her and her sisters weren't available.

"We don't have much time left." He knew he sounded like he was whining. He heard her sigh.

"It's not easy for me either, you know. I'd like to be with you tonight too, but what's my excuse going to be? I've already told them enough lies to sink a ship. She never asks me for anything. I can't very well disappoint her."

"Can you see me tomorrow night?"

"I'll try."

That's as good as he could get out of her. He made plans in the back of his mind to make up some excuse for Colleen to take the kids. He didn't want them in the house for these last few nights. He'd also have to take two sick days, something he'd normally never do, but he was desperate. He hoped to be able to convince Libby to stay in Cape Breton. He knew in his heart it might be his last chance.

But before he did that, he had to speak to Sally. He took her roses and got down on his knees in the grass. "Please don't hate me, Sally. I don't want to disappoint you but I need her. If you were here with me it would be different, but you're not and I think that's just beginning to sink in."

He tried to explain it. "When I saw her hold Sarah one day at the beach, I realized how much the kids need a mother. Especially Sarah. She's in danger of becoming a tomboy and I'd like her to have someone she can look up to. And Libby would make a great mother, Sally. I know she would. She's loving and kind and patient. I know you'd like her. I think you would've been great friends, in some other lifetime." He looked up at the sky. "Please give me your blessing. Please tell me its okay."

He closed his eyes so he could hear her voice. There was nothing but the wind. He bowed his head. When he opened his eyes, there was a butterfly on her marker. It stayed there and dried its wings in the sun. It was just a butterfly that happened by, but he wanted it to be a sign so badly that he took it as such.

"Thank you Sally. I love you. I won't forget you. I'll tell Jack and Sarah about their beautiful mom for the rest of their lives. You don't ever have to worry about that." He got up off his knees, blew her a kiss and walked away. He didn't see the butterfly fly up in the air and disappear into the sun.

He phoned Colleen. "I have to work back shift tonight. Would you be able to take the kids?"

"Don't I always?"

"Did anyone ever tell you you're the best sis a guy ever had?"

"You better believe it."

Seamus spent the day cleaning his house. He put fresh sheets on the bed, just in case. He went into town and bought steak, champagne, candles, and a huge bouquet of flowers, and just before he went home he had a brilliant idea. He couldn't believe he didn't think of it before. He turned around and made one more stop.

When her car pulled up into the driveway, everything was ready. There was even soft music playing in the background. He was fresh from the shower and probably had too much aftershave on, but there was nothing he could do about it now. He wore new jeans and a new shirt that he realized too late should've been ironed.

When Libby walked in, he blinked a few times. He wanted to breathe her in. She had on a simple wrap-around dress that was a buttercup yellow and perfect against her sun-kissed skin. She'd put her hair up. She had delicate high heels on, and since he'd only seen her that summer in bare feet or flip flops, they were the biggest surprise of all. They made her taller. She came up to his nose instead of his chin.

And then he smelled her perfume. Surely she wouldn't go to all this trouble if she wasn't ready to give him a chance, he thought.

"Hi Seamus. You look very nice."

He looked down at himself. "I'm an idiot. I should've ironed my shirt."

"Yes. That would've been a good idea." She laughed then and so did he.

Suddenly he was as nervous as a schoolboy. What should he do? "Ah, would you like a glass of wine?"

"A small glass would be lovely."

"Sit down. I'll get it."

He zoomed into the kitchen and took the bottle of champagne out of the fridge. Eager to get back to her, he poured it into the wineglasses too quickly, which caused an avalanche of bubbles to overflow and pool on the kitchen counter. He quickly wiped off the glasses and hurried out to the living room. He passed her a glass.

"Thank you."

"You're welcome." He stood there.

"Aren't you going to sit down?"

"I think I'm forgetting something. There was something I had to do."

"Well, never mind. You'll think of it."

"You're right." He sat down and sprang back up again. "Now I remember." Putting his glass on the floor, he hurried away and re-emerged with a bouquet of roses. "I hope you like them."

"Seamus, they're lovely." She reached for them and gave them a sniff. "Thank you. Should we put them in water?"

"The girl said that's what those things are for on the bottom of each stem, to hold water. So they should be okay."

"You're right. Do you mind if I put them here?" She pointed to the side table.

"No, go ahead."

She put them down and turned back to him, taking a sip of her champagne. "It's very good."

"Is it? I don't know much about champagne." He put it to his lips and drained the whole thing.

"Feel better now?" she asked him.

"Yes. I'm fine."

She reached out and touched his knee. "You're wound up tighter then a drum. Relax. It's only me."

"I am relaxed." He pulled his collar away from his neck. "This is a little itchy though."

She laughed at him. "You silly man, why don't you put on another shirt? You look like you've been dissected in six places with those creases."

"I'll be one minute." He tore into his bedroom and grabbed his old white jean shirt. When he came back in, he found her with her shoes kicked off and her hair down. "The bobby pins were killing me."

"We're a fine pair. You can dress us up but you can't take us anywhere because we look like fugitives in a matter of minutes."

They laughed and suddenly the mood was a lot more relaxed. This he could handle. He told her he had rib steaks to barbeque and she asked if she could make a salad to go with it, so they ended up in the kitchen. She put a dish towel around her waist and rummaged through the fridge for some veggies.

"You don't have a whole lot here."

"I know. Jack hates vegetables, remember? I don't like to see them rot in the fridge week after week."

"Well, you and Sarah can eat them surely."

"I have a hard enough time making one meal at night. I don't need to be preparing two."

"Well, I'm afraid it's celery and carrot sticks with our steaks."

"I have onions."

"I'll fry some up then. You don't have any mushrooms by chance?"

"There might be some in a bag in the crisper."

She found it and took a peek, then showed to him. Petrified bits of what were once mushrooms stuck to the bottom of the bag.

"Onions will be fine."

They had a nice meal in spite of the lack of side dishes. He'd forgotten to get potatoes and offered her SuperFries instead, which she declined. Then he realized he hadn't thought about anything for dessert, so he rummaged in the cupboards and came up with a box of Arrowroots.

Finally they cleared up and washed the dishes and sat back

down on the couch. He put his arm over her shoulders. The moon was rising over the water.

"You have such a beautiful view."

"I chose this spot before I knew Sally. I built it myself."

She leaned her head on the back of his arm. "Is there anything you can't do?"

"Have you."

He felt her stiffen in his arms. "I'm sorry. I didn't mean to be glib."

"That's okay."

But he felt a slight change in the air and he didn't want the mellow mood to go away. "I have a big mouth."

She met him halfway. He guessed she didn't want to ruin the evening either. "You have a perfect mouth." She looked at his and waited for him to lean down and kiss hers and when he did, it was heaven. They parted and she looked back at the shimmering water while she snuggled against him. "I could sit like this forever."

"Me too."

"I wish I didn't have to go."

"Then stay. Stay with me."

"It's not that simple. I have a life. You have a life. We pretend it would be easy, but it might be harder than you think."

"You're always putting up roadblocks," he sighed.

She reached up and stroked his cheek. "I don't mean to. I really don't."

"Then prove it."

She took back her hand. "What do you mean?"

He got off the couch and knelt in front of her, putting his hand in his pocket and pulling out a small velvet box. He opened it and showed her the diamond ring inside. He reached for her hand.

"Elizabeth Ruby MacKinnon, I love you. I want to marry you. Please say you will. Please say you'll stay with me here for the rest of your life. You and Jack and Sarah and me. You'd make me the happiest man in the world."

The look on her face told him he made the biggest mistake of his life.

CHAPTER EIGHTEEN

"What's wrong?"

She couldn't meet his eye as she rose from the couch. "I have to go."

He couldn't believe it. "Are you serious?"

She slipped on her high heels and glanced around as if she'd forgotten something. She looked panicked and he didn't know what to do. He got off his knee and snapped the box shut. He threw it on the couch and stood in front of her.

"Libby, you can't do this to me."

She shook her hands as if they were on fire. "I can't."

He grabbed her shoulders. "You can't what?"

"Stay."

He shook her. "Why? Tell me why you can't stay."

She bit her lip and looked away. He kept a tight grip on her. "You're doing my head in. Is this a game? Some sort of weird fantasy you've dreamed up to keep me on a leash? You pull me in and then push me away, over and over and over again."

Still she wouldn't look at him.

"Thousands of men propose to women every day. It's not unheard of. From what I understand, most of the women jump in their arms and say yes. But not you. Not you, Libby."

He pushed her away. "I deserve an explanation and you're not leaving this house until you give me one."

She ran to the door and he yelled, "Stop!" She put her hands on the door but didn't turn around. "You walk out that door on me, and so help me I'll follow you. I'll follow you into town and into your house and into your bedroom until you give me an answer. Because this stops tonight—this crazy bullshit of letting me kiss you and hold you and then pushing me away."

She was crying now. He didn't care. He paced the living room. "I'm trying to think. Trying to think of why you would do this to me."

She leaned on the door with her fist against her mouth. She peeked at him with tears streaming down her face.

And then the light went on. Seamus stopped and pointed at her. "What am I talking about? You've done this before. The night of the prom you let me do everything to you and then at the last minute you stopped me. You wouldn't do it." He shook his head in disbelief. "It never occurred to me. This is your game. This is what you do best." He walked up, stood right beside her and then whispered in her ear. "But you know what, Libby? I want to know why you fucked everyone else in town but me."

He'd done it then. He could tell. He'd sent her over the edge. She leaned against the door with her open palms and slammed her hands against it. "You stupid boy. You stupid, stupid boy."

Then she turned on him and started to hit him. "It's your fault," she cried. "You left me. You should never have left me. I begged you to stay and you didn't. I begged you."

He was finally able to grab hold of her wrists. "Stop. Stop it."

"Let go of me. You're hurting me."

Seamus didn't let go. He shook her again. "Tell me. You have to tell me."

"I can't."

"Yes, you can."

"No. NO."

"It was that teacher, wasn't it? That drama teacher. Did he do something to you, Libby? If he did something to you, you have to tell me."

She fell on her knees and would have slipped to the floor if he hadn't been holding her wrists. Her head sagged in front of him. She whispered something.

"What? What did you say?"

She threw her head up and screamed at him, "He raped me. He raped me for hours. He nearly killed me. Is that what you want to know? Does that satisfy your curiosity? Do you feel better now?"

He got down on the floor in front of her and let go of her wrists, reaching out to take her in his arms. She grabbed him around the neck and buried her face against his shirt before she cried and cried and finally, when there was nothing left, she whimpered like a beaten dog.

He never let her go. He kept hold of her because if he didn't, he'd go out of his mind. He didn't want to think; he needed to quiet her breathing, needed her to stop shaking and needed to stop her heart from hammering like a wild bird in a cage.

They held onto one another for a long time before he picked her up and carried her into the bedroom. He lay her down and kissed her hands and told her he'd be right back, returning with a damp facecloth and towel. He sat beside her on the bed where she lay like a broken thing. Seamus wiped her sweet face. Her hair was wet from her tears and sweat, so he pushed back her bangs and held the cloth against her forehead, then dabbed her neck and picked up one arm then the other, wiping her fingers. He kissed her palms as he lay them back down. Drying her with a soft towel, he made hushing sounds, soothing, quiet sounds so she wouldn't be frightened.

Her eyes were closed, as if they were too heavy to open. When her breathing finally became even, he knelt by the side of the bed and kissed her brow, brushing his thumb against it softly.

"You're going to be all right, Libby. I'm going to keep you safe."

He barely heard her breathe, "Yes."

He pulled the quilt over her. They stayed like that for a long time, and then when he thought it might be okay, he went around to the other side of the bed and lay beside her. He gently put his arm around her and turned her towards him. They lay close together, side by side. He didn't dare move. This was enough.

Finally she spoke, so quietly he had to strain to hear her. "I didn't know what to do. I thought I'd done something wrong, that I somehow deserved it. I must have led him on. I didn't know how it could happen otherwise. He told me not to tell you."

"Oh god."

"He said if I did, he'd tell you that I wanted it and I loved it."

Seamus thought he was going to be sick, but he didn't dare move. He may never get her to talk about it again, so he swallowed hard and listened.

"I couldn't tell anyone. There was no one to tell. I was afraid no one would believe me. Then you went away and I didn't know what to do. I had nightmares and couldn't sleep. One night I went to a friend's house and there were some other people there drinking rum. They wanted me to try some, so I did. And it felt good after a while, like I could forget about what happened. So I started to go out every night and went to places where I could get liquor. Boys would buy me drinks because I didn't have a lot of money. And at first it was a kiss they wanted for a drink, but soon they were asking me to do other things. I needed that liquor to sleep. It wasn't so bad because I never remembered what I'd done the night before. I felt like a slut anyway. I was a slut. He told me I was, over and over. So I played the role. It was make-believe and if it was a role, I could disappear inside it."

She stopped talking for a minute. Seamus stayed quiet.

"And then one day a boy held out a glass of rum and told me I could have it if…you know the rest. I was very popular with the boys that summer."

He squeezed her. "It wasn't your fault."

"And somewhere inside I knew you were coming back and I didn't know what to do. How was I ever going to tell you that I'd been with—"

"It wouldn't have mattered."

"But it would have, Seamus. Two months after he raped me, I found out I was pregnant."

He stopped breathing for a moment. "Oh my girl. My sweet girl."

She started to cry then. "I couldn't face you. I couldn't think any more. I couldn't bear the thought of going to my mother to tell her I was having a baby. She'd be heartbroken. None of my sisters had babies before they were married. I would have shamed them."

"No."

"I didn't want it, Seamus. I didn't want it growing inside me. I had to get rid of it. So two days before you got back, I took money from my mother's secret stash and took a bus to Halifax to get an abortion."

"Oh god."

"A girl I knew let me stay with her after it was done. I was with her for a couple of months and then she and a friend decided they wanted to drive to California to become actresses. I tagged along so I could get as far away as possible from the memories of that summer. I went to my friend's audition and they asked me to read instead of her. I did and they gave me a job. That was the start of my career. It was perfect for me. I could be anyone else in the world but Elizabeth Ruby MacKinnon."

He held her head and rocked her. "I don't know what I can say to you that will ever make this hurt go away, other than I love you and none of this matters in the least. You don't have to hide from me anymore, Libby. I know everything now. Let me help you."

She finally rose up on the bed and held her hair back with her hands. "I'm tired."

"Stay here tonight."

She looked at him quickly. He grabbed her hands. "Just to sleep, sweetheart. You need to sleep and I'll be here to hold you if you get frightened."

"But what do I tell Aunt Vi?"

"Why don't you call her and tell her you're staying with Rose tonight? She'll never check. And that way you can go home in the morning after you've had a shower and something in your stomach and you can face Aunt Vi without looking…"

"As I look now."

He nodded.

"Okay. I don't think I have the energy to do anything else." He reached across the bed and grabbed the phone, handing it to her. She dialed the number and, proving she was a great little actress, told Aunt Vi she'd see her in the morning, that she and Rose were having a good old-fashioned chin wag. She nodded and said she loved her too and then bid her aunt goodnight. She dropped the phone on the mattress.

Seamus got out of bed. "I'm going to run you a bath. I think you need a hot soak. Then you can throw on one of my t-shirts and crawl into bed. You can sleep as long as you want. I won't wake you."

She nodded. He ran to the bathroom and filled the tub, grabbing a clean towel and the t-shirt for her. He left them by the bathroom sink, turned off the tap and helped her to the bathroom door. "I'm okay. Thank you." She closed the door. He sat on the edge of the bed and heard her step into the water, then scoop it up and splash it over and over again. He had to concentrate on these noises because he wasn't allowed to think. Not yet. He must take care of her first.

Finally, he heard her get out and let the water run out of the tub. She emerged shortly afterward with her damp hair combed back, wearing his shirt, which came down to her knees. He helped her into bed and tucked her in.

"I'll be here beside you all night. I'm not going anywhere. You're safe here."

She raised her hand and stroked his cheek with her finger. "Thank you, Seamus. You're so kind. You always were." She closed her eyes and pulled up the blankets around her.

He held his hand on her head for a moment and whispered, "My Libby."

He stayed in his clothes on top of the blankets on the other side of the bed, close to her, with his hand on her back so she'd know he hadn't gone anywhere. Eventually, he heard her breathing become heavier and even. She was asleep.

Seamus lay awake all night.

At five thirty, he got out of bed very carefully and shut the door behind him. He had a shower—he felt dirty somehow. He scrubbed his skin raw so the words she'd whispered to him last night would leave him. When he stepped out of the shower, he saw her dress, panties, and bra hanging on the back of the door. He wrapped his towel around his waist and reached over to take the dress off the hook. It was small and light, just a piece of gauze that wrapped around her perfect body. He held it to his face and smelled her perfume. Then he rubbed it against his cheek. So little, so defenseless. He thought his heart would break.

Back to the bedroom he tiptoed to put her things where she could find them when she woke up. Once dressed, he made some coffee and went out to the deck to watch the pink sky turn gradually white and then light blue.

He was numb. This revelation made a lot of things make sense; he couldn't understand why he never thought of it before. The worst part was knowing that he let her slip out of his life without bothering to make sure she was all right. Leaving town without a word should have warned him. That wasn't like her, and he blamed himself for not realizing it before this. He was so wrapped up in his own hurt, his own disbelief that she could vanish like that; he never gave any other explanation a thought. His family was anxious for him to move forward and forget the past; he allowed them to distract him. They talked of him starting over and said perhaps he should go away for a while, that it might be the tonic he needed.

So when the idea of the police academy came up, it sounded good to him. Anything had to be better than wandering around town and having people look at him with pity. And it proved to be the best thing he could have done. Seamus loved the discipline, the physical training, and the idea that there was right and wrong and people should obey rules. Rules gave him comfort.

Roger became a close friend and they formed a strong bond. They were lucky enough to get jobs almost immediately after coming home. That's when he made plans to build his own house. His father's drinking made life at home unpleasant and he wasn't prepared to put up with it any more.

He'd drive out this way time and time again, always gravitating towards the beach where he and Libby had been together. When a piece of property came up for sale, he went straight to the bank for a loan and bought it. His parents were concerned that it was out in the sticks and he'd get tired of being isolated. What they didn't know was that this was the one place that gave him the most comfort. Looking out over their beach was a touchstone for him. It meant she was real. She wasn't a figment of his imagination.

Of course, they never knew that.

And now what was he to do? How could he help her? He was adrift in uncertainty. This was something that was too big for him and he knew it. All he could do was hope that his love for her would eventually make everything all right. But who was he kidding?

He must have dozed off in the chair, because he didn't hear her until she had her hand on his shoulder. His eyes flew open and he sat up straight. "Is everything okay?" He shook his head to chase away the cobwebs.

"Hold me."

Holding out his arms, she crawled into his lap. She still had on his t-shirt. She snuggled under his chin and he put his hand over her hair to get it out of her face, then kissed the top of her scalp and pulled her tighter.

"I slept for a long time, didn't I?"

"Yes. I'm glad you did. Do you feel a little better?"

She nodded. They didn't speak for a few minutes.

"Thank you for being there last night."

"I should've been there ten years ago."

She lifted her face and placed her finger against his lips. "Shhh, I don't want to talk about it. I don't want to ruin today, too."

He kissed the pad of her finger. "Okay."

They sat and let the early morning breeze bring the smell of the ocean to them. The sound of the surf soothed them. She pointed at an eagle flying by in search of prey. They watched it until it disappeared from sight.

Everything was all right in the natural world that morning. Maybe the sense of calm and normalcy could infect their spirits too. The sound of chickadees and crows, blue jays and squirrels. There was even a woodpecker nearby. When he tap-tap-tapped on the tree, they looked at each other and grinned. Then Seamus's cat made an appearance, coming home after a hunting raid, no doubt. He strolled up the deck stairs and seemed surprised at the company.

"Hi Dexter. Any mice left in the neighbourhood?"

Dexter sat, blinked and then yawned. He plunked on the deck and rolled over a few times. He stayed on his back for a minute, but apparently no one was interested in giving him a belly rub, so he pretended he wanted to lie like that anyway. He dozed off.

"I wish I was a cat," she said.

"I'd rather be a dog."

"But a cat doesn't need anyone for their emotional well-being. They're happy as they are."

"You're right. We dogs are a desperately needy lot."

She threw back her head and laughed. It was a wonderful sound. She hugged him. "I love you."

Seamus didn't mean to do it. It just happened. He felt

himself losing control and he didn't have the strength to keep his arms around her. He leaned against her and let the tears fall as she held him tight.

"I'm sorry."

"Shhh."

"I'm sorry I wasn't there."

"It's not your fault."

"I should have come after you. I should've tracked you down and found you. But instead I let you suffer alone. I'll never forgive myself for that."

"We were kids, Seamus. We were just kids."

"I should've known you'd never leave without saying goodbye."

She wiped his face with the end of the shirt she was wearing. He put his head back against the chair and looked up at the sky. "I can't believe this happened to us. Why?"

"Why does anything happen? Why did Sally die? Life is good and bad, beautiful and ugly. It's all a game of chance."

He looked at her. "I want to give us a chance again. Is that possible?"

She got out of his lap then and walked over to the edge of the deck. She leaned against it and looked out over the water. "I think we need time, Seamus. And time is our enemy at the moment."

He got out of the chair and came up behind her, putting his arms around her. "We love each other. That's all that matters." She was still. He was afraid he'd said the wrong thing.

"If only it were that simple."

He turned her around. "Be with me. Let me show you."

"I do want to, but…"

"Trust me."

She looked at him and nodded ever so slightly. He picked her up and carried her into the house. He took her back to the bedroom and laid her on the bed. Her legs were bare and his t-shirt was so big it fell off her shoulders. She got up on her elbows. "I don't want to disappoint you."

"In a million years, that would never happen. Believe me. I just need to touch your skin."

He got down beside her in the bed and gathered her into his arms. She fit perfectly. They held each other for a long time before he gathered up the courage to kiss her. And the minute he did, he knew he was in trouble. It was one thing to kiss her on the porch or in a car, but to have her lying next to him was a completely different sensation. As his hand traveled under her t-shirt and felt the warmth of her satin skin, he knew he was lost. Too quickly he pushed her shirt up, and the sight of her naked body was too much. He stopped.

She opened her eyes. "Seamus?"

At that moment, he knew he couldn't control himself. He was terrified of making love to her. He turned his head and rested his cheek on her stomach. His face rose and fell with her breathing.

"Seamus?"

"I can't. I can't do this. I'm going to hurt you."

"No, you're not."

"I have to stop. You have to believe me." He pushed off her and, without looking back, walked out of the room. He went into the bathroom and turned on the tap, dousing his face with cold water before leaning over the sink and letting the water drip. He didn't know when he'd felt so miserable in his own body. It was at war with his mind and he wanted it to end. And now he didn't know how to go out and face her. His head pounded and his throat was parched. Maybe he was coming down with something. He felt sick, very sick.

And suddenly he was. He didn't make it to the toilet. He vomited all over the bathroom floor. Again and again, his stomach tried to get rid of the agony of the last twenty-four hours.

He heard the door open and she stood there in her bare feet.

"Seamus."

"Please, please leave me alone. I'll be okay. I just need a min—" He spewed over the floor again. "Go."

She shut the door. He bent over with his hands on his knees, saliva hanging down from his lips. He waited to see if that was it. He had to keep swallowing. She knocked on the door.

"What?"

"Seamus, do you need me?"

"No. Please. It's okay. I'm sorry. I'm sorry."

"Do you want me to go?"

"Yes. I'll be better then. Come tomorrow."

"Okay. I love you."

"I know. I..." He never got to finish his sentence. He was sick once more.

He eventually started to feel better once all that misery was on the floor instead of in him. He brushed his teeth and took great gulps of mouthwash to rid himself of the taste. It took him a long time to clean it up and by the time he was done, he was exhausted, so he limped into the shower and stayed there, letting the water pound the back of his neck and his shoulders. When there was no hot water left, he got out and, still wearing the damp towel, stretched across the bed and fell into a deep sleep.

At around suppertime the phone rang and woke him up. He wasn't sure where he was at first. He grabbed the phone. Maybe it was Libby.

"Hello?"

"Hi Seamus, it's me."

"Oh, hi."

"Listen, I didn't hear from you so I wondered if you wanted me to keep the kids again tonight?"

"I'm sorry, I should've called. I've been in bed all day. I think I have the flu."

"Oh dear. Well, obviously I better keep the kids for another night."

"That would really be a help. I think I'll stay in bed and try to get some rest."

"You do that. Lots of liquids now. And if your temperature goes up, you can always take Tylenol or something."

"I know, I know."

"Okay, well, if you're sure you're all right."

"I am. I'll call you if I need you. I promise."

"Okay then. Oh, Sarah wants to say something."

"Okay."

"Hi Daddy."

"Hi baby. Are you being good for Aunt Colleen?"

"Yeah."

"Daddy misses you."

"Me you too."

"Is Jack there?"

"No. He baseball."

"Okay, don't call him in. Give Aunt Colleen the phone and I'll see you tomorrow. I love you."

"Too."

"Hello…did you want me to call Jack in? He's playing outside."

"No. Just tell him I'll probably see him tomorrow."

"Okay, dear. Love ya."

"Love you too."

He hung up the phone and lay on the bed for another hour at least, not thinking of anything. Then he got up and put his bathrobe on. He was hungry but he wasn't. In the end he had some cereal. He fed Dexter then he went back to bed and turned on the TV. It was still on when he woke up the next morning.

Seamus felt much better because he knew she was coming today. They'd be able to talk about things more rationally. It had been too emotional to make any sense of anything before, but now that they had a chance to go away and think it would be easier.

He got dressed, tidied up, and made lunch. If it was like before, she'd come after she'd spent the morning with her aunt and uncle. He didn't want to think about it being her last day, had to put it right out of his mind. He wanted her to see that he looked a little more normal today.

The first hour after lunch he laughed to himself, because she was always late. The second hour he was concerned about her. Maybe her family found out where she was last night and were giving her a hard time. The third hour he thought maybe he'd pushed her too hard. He shouldn't have asked her to marry him, should have waited to make love to her. The fourth hour he still knew she was coming because she'd never leave again without saying goodbye.

At eight o'clock that night, he called the MacKinnon house.
"Hello?"
"Hi. Is Libby there?"
"Why no. She's gone. Flew to New York today."
That wasn't right.
"She was supposed to be leaving tomorrow."
"I know. We were pretty surprised and sorry to see her go. It's

been such fun, but she told us her agent called and said she had to leave today."

He held the phone to his ear and breathed into it.

"Who's calling, please? Would you like to leave a message?"

He couldn't move.

"Seamus? Is that you?"

He hung up the phone.

CHAPTER NINETEEN

She didn't blame him. He had every right to be sick. Sick about what she'd told him, sick at the thought of making love to her, knowing that she'd been used like tissue and tossed aside. Ava knew exactly how he felt. She'd felt it herself for years. What made her feel guilty was that he tried so hard for her. A loving and caring man who tried to help her but in the end couldn't mask his true feelings. They were plain to see splattered on the bathroom floor.

She had to go. It would be fairer in the end to step out of his life and let him get on with his. She knew he'd be upset for a while and then angry with her, but anger was good. Maybe anger would allow him to pick up the pieces of his life and move on. She refused to hurt him anymore. Loving him was a beautiful dream that would simply never come true.

The twenty-minute drive into Glace Bay was spent preparing for her role as loving niece and sister without a care in the world—who'd come back for Christmas and maybe even Easter, if her schedule allowed.

She drove into the yard and waved to Geranium, then took a deep breath and walked into the kitchen. "I'm home."

Uncle Angus was rocking in the rocking chair. He looked up from the paper. "Hello darlin'."

She bounced over and kissed him. "Hi. What's new with the state of the world?"

"Nothin' that a good kick in the arse wouldn't cure."

Aunt Vi came out of the pantry. "Good morning, honey. Did Rose give you breakfast?"

"You know Rose. I couldn't leave without stuffing my face."

Her aunt came over to her and lifted her chin with the crook of her finger. "You look peaked. You have bags under your eyes. Did you get enough sleep last night?"

"We were up pretty late, you know…girl talk."

"Hmm."

"I think I'll go have a shower."

"Okay, dear. Should be some hot water left."

She went upstairs and closed the bedroom door. Her clothes were as she'd left them before she went to him last night. Was it only last night or was it a thousand years ago? The shower beckoned because she had to think. By the time she was done she had a plan. But of course it would depend on whether she could keep from going out of her mind.

Back in the bedroom she picked up the cell phone and called Air Canada. There was a plane out of Sydney in the morning so she booked a first-class ticket to New York. Time to call her agent.

"Hi Trent."

"Good God, she's alive!"

"Sort of."

"You can see I kept my word," Trent said.

"What?"

"I didn't bug you all summer."

"Thanks. I appreciate it."

"Did you have a good one?"

"My mother died."

"Oh God, I forgot. Did I send flowers?"

"Your P.A. did."

"Shit."

"Doesn't matter."

"Mental telepathy is quite something. I was going to call you tomorrow because if I'm correct you're flying in the day after that."

"I'm leaving in the morning, actually. I wanted to let you know so you could book an extra night."

"Will do. Does the Plaza suit, or shall I…"

"The Plaza's fine."

"I do hope you're rested up dumpling, because the week is going to be filled with pre-production meetings and director's meetings. You'll have to meet with the producers."

"I thought all that was done."

"There have been a few changes."

"What?"

"Don't get panicky. Nothing drastic, but they fired the director and we have a new hot shot on board who's very ready to impress the studios. He's keen and he's full of ideas."

"Oh, spare me."

"Don't be like that, Ava. You're beginning to have a hint of a reputation for being difficult and if you get too pouty, it could keep you from earning the big bucks."

"Don't be ridiculous, Trent. A-list actors who earn the really big bucks are in another stratosphere altogether."

"But you're not far behind. That's what I keep trying to stress. Just a little more gas in that engine and you'll be off the charts too."

"And naturally, that's the only thing I want in life."

There was dead air.

"Sorry."

"I hope you're hormonal, because if you waltz into New York with this fucking attitude, your ass will be on the first plane outta there. The studios aren't putting up with shit from prima donnas. There are too many eager beavers in the wing, and I do mean beavers."

"What a disgusting thing to say. Is that all these young girls are? You think all of us sleep our way into a career. I thought you were classier than that, Trent."

"You're right, I apologize. But I am trying to make life easier for you. I know what they're like and it's getting meaner by the picture. I'm in your corner but you have to meet me halfway."

She rubbed her forehead. "Yes, I know. I'm just a little tired."

"I'll pick you up, then, the day after tomorrow and we'll head over there about ten. Okay by you?"

"Fine."

"Camilla will be coming a couple of days later. She's in Europe at the moment, organizing your upcoming appearances at various film festivals. Hopefully, they haven't forgotten you completely."

"Right."

"Be good, my little retirement fund."

She hung up. "Goodbye, jerk."

The next call was more difficult. She had to be strong for this one.

"Hey, Lola!"

"Hi sweetie! I was going to call you tomorrow."

"I was going to call you too."

"Only two more days. Can you bear to leave?"

She bit her knuckle. "Not really."

"Oh gosh, I don't blame you. I miss Aunt Vi and Uncle Angus so much."

"Well honey, they miss you too. Listen, how's your mother?"

"She's really good, thanks. She opted to have the

lumpectomy and she's having her radiation therapy now. The doctors are optimistic because she caught it early, so fingers crossed."

"And toes."

"As it looks now, I think I'll be able to make it, for a little while anyway."

"Oh honey, you don't have to do that."

"No, really. I'm going out of my mind, anyway. There's something about being almost thirty and living in your old bedroom that's sort of freaky. My mom still has my cheerleading trophies in here."

"Cheerleading? I don't believe it. My little rebel?"

"Teenagers always go through a hellish stage. That was mine."

"I've missed you," Ava laughed.

"Me too. Now what's today...Sunday? You're flying into New York on Tuesday, so how about I meet you there on Wednesday. I have a few things I have to do first."

"Wednesday will be fine."

"Maurice and Harold should be there by then. We'll have a girl's night in. At the Plaza, right?"

"Yeah."

"Who are you under this time?"

"I was thinking Geranium." Lola's laughter made her smile. "I can't think of a last name though."

"Easy. Potts."

"Perfect."

"See you soon! I can't wait."

"Me either. Love you."

"You too." She made kissy noises before she hung up.

Now all she had to do was tell everyone she was leaving a day early.

Her packing was finished in an hour. She left out clothes for the next day and put on jeans and a sleeveless blouse, since it looked like another hot day. It had been a great summer, mostly beach weather, which only reminded her of Seamus and the kids.

Sarah's shell was on the window ledge. When she picked it up a bit of dry sand fell out of it. She kissed it and tucked it into her jewelry case.

Then it was downstairs to break the news. She arranged her face into a woe-begotten look and walked into the kitchen slowly with her hands in her pockets. Her aunt and uncle looked at her.

"What's wrong?"

"You're not going to believe it."

"What?"

"My agent called and told me I have to be in New York tomorrow." It killed her to see their faces fall.

"But I'm having everyone over for dinner tomorrow. A grand send-off," Aunt Vi moaned.

"I'm sorry. I can't get out of it. I signed a contract and I have to be there when they tell me to."

Uncle Angus threw his newspaper on the floor. "Well, don't that just beat all. What on earth would one day matter?" He pointed at her. "You see! That's what's wrong with the world. The tail's waggin' the dog. No one gives a damn how people feel, so long as there's money to be made."

She suddenly remembered. "Oh my god, what about Teddy Bear!" At the sound of his name, Teddy rushed over from his bed by the window and jumped up on his mother. Ava picked him up and held him close, kissing his face. "I can't leave him in a hotel room alone. Why didn't I think of that before? What am I going to do?"

"He'll stay here with us of course, until you're ready to go back to California," Uncle Angus said. "Dog would miss him anyway, wouldn't you Dog?"

Dog thumped his tail at the sound of his name.

Ava reached down and kissed Uncle Angus's bald head. "Thank you. Thank you."

"I know," Aunt Vi said. "Everyone will come for supper tonight. It won't be fancy, but if everyone brings something, it won't matter."

"That's a great idea. I'll call."

"You do that. I have to make four pies."

"Am I going to spend my last day with you baking?"

Aunt Vi turned around. "You used to love to watch me bake. You can help me."

"I'd love to," she squeaked.

Her aunt hurried over, as fast as one can be with a cane. "Sweetheart, don't cry now. We can't waste the day in tears. Time enough for that tomorrow."

She nodded and sniffed.

Luckily, it didn't matter to the family whether they had their meal that night or the next, it was all the same to them, except that everyone hated to think they'd miss a whole day with Libby. Everyone came over earlier than they ordinarily would have, just so they could have a bit of a visit.

If she had been up for another Academy Award for her performance, she'd have won hands down again. She reassured them constantly that's she'd come back on a regular basis and if she couldn't get to them, they'd have to come to her. Her house was big enough to hold them all. But she knew in her heart she'd never return to the island again.

At the table that night, they laughed until they cried at Maurice and Harold stories.

"I've got a batch of oatcakes in the freezer and blueberry muffins. Can you take it to them, dear, or do you have too much to carry?" Aunt Vi asked.

"I'll put them with my carry-on luggage. They'd never forgive me if I left them behind."

Vicky stood up. "We have something for them too." She ran out of the kitchen for a minute and came back with a picture. "We made sure we took one of the three of us at the prom with our dates." She passed it to her aunt.

Ava touched the picture. Three beautiful young ladies with three boys—one too tall, one too short and one with a mouth full of braces smiled back at her. "They'll love it. I know they'll have this framed and treasure it. Thank you, darling." Ava's voice cracked. Everyone looked at her. Rose put her hand up. "Don't you dare cry or I'll be bawlin' like a baby."

"Me too," Bev said.

"Ditto," said Maryette.

"Ah geez, are we goin' to have boohooing in here," Johnnie complained. "I'm leavin' the table if that's going to start."

"I'll get dessert," Aunt Vi said. "There's banana cream pie, strawberry pie, blueberry pie, and a lemon meringue that Libby made."

"Oh well, I'll stay for that then," Johnnie said.

It was just as well most of them left together. It was obvious that Ava was having a very hard time with the idea of going, so they tried not to make it too difficult for her, which she appreciated. Rose said she'd drive her to the airport.

"I have to take the rental back anyway, so I might as well go myself."

Rose wouldn't hear of it. "Look, I know we can't all go to the airport tomorrow, it would be too hard. But I'll be damned if you're going to drive yourself there alone. I'll pick you up and Stan will drive the car in behind us. How's that?"

"Okay. Thank you."

They lined up as they hugged and kissed her goodbye. In the end, nothing was said. No one could talk, so they waved and smiled and hurried out the door.

When she was ready for bed, Ava stood in front of Aunt Vi's bedroom door and gave a little knock before she entered. "Only me."

They only just crawled into bed themselves. Uncle Angus flipped through the flyers as Aunt Vi put Jergen's Hand Lotion on her hands.

"I love that smell," Ava smiled. "Mom used that all the time, didn't she?"

"She did indeed. Want some?"

"Okay. A little squirt." She held out her hand. "It smells like cherries."

"And you remember this one." Aunt Vi pointed to her Avon Moisture Cream in the small green container on her bureau.

"I forgot about this." She reached over and took the lid off. The yellow cream was just as she remembered. "Mom used to let me put a little of this on sometimes, if I bugged her long enough." She took a whiff. "This smells like her." Suddenly her face went blank. "I forgot to go to the cemetery today."

"Never mind, child. You'll be back. Your mother never was one for a lot of sentimentality. She'd rather you'd spent your last day with your brothers and sisters."

"I'm so stupid." She felt sick.

"Nonsense."

"You're not stupid," Uncle Angus said, "This here store is stupid. Look at this. Chargin' an arm and a leg for toilet paper. Paper to wipe me arse costs more than a case of beer. I'll use their flamin' flyer for toilet paper before I pay that ransom."

"Well, the package is as big as the washing machine downstairs," Aunt Vi observed.

"Exactly. How the hell is a person supposed to get it through the bloody door?"

"Don't get your blood pressure up, Angus. You'll be tootin' all night."

If only they knew how much she'd miss them. She had to leave the room or she'd give herself away.

"Would you mind if I took this nightgown home, Aunt Vi?"

"Of course not, honey, and take Lola's. I washed it and put it in the drawer."

"Thank you. Thank you for everything. I—"

"Don't get yourself all worked up love. We'll have a nice bowl of porridge in the morning before you go. How's that sound?"

She nodded and kissed them both good night, then went down the hall and got into the little twin bed for the last time. Teddy Bear jumped up and cuddled next to her. "I'm going to miss you, Teddy." With her arms around him, she listened to the night sounds through the open window. The leaves on the big maple tree beside the house rustled every so often in the wind, and soon she heard the pitter-pat of raindrops falling from the eave against the sill. It was a lonely sound.

She whispered in pet's ear, "I won't see you again, Teddy. I don't want you to live in California with dogs who wear designer clothes and booties and have their nails painted. You belong with Dog and Aunt Vi and Uncle Angus. I know you'll be happier here."

Teddy tossed his head and hit her cheek with his rubbery wet nose. He slept. She didn't.

Ava was able to get up the next morning because she couldn't feel anything. It was better this way. She showered and got dressed, stripped the sheets off the bed and folded the blankets at the end of the mattress. She trooped downstairs with the luggage, managed to keep down her breakfast, and, last but not least, put Maurice and Harold's goodies in her bag before putting on her coat.

At nine on the dot, Rose arrived and honked the horn. Ava kissed her kin one last time, gave Teddy a final embrace, and walked outside, handing Stan the keys to the rental. He took her luggage and put it in the back of their car. Aunt Vi and Uncle Angus stood on the porch and waved, Teddy whining in Aunt Vi's arms. As Ava opened the car door she noticed Geranium in the window, so she blew her a kiss.

She didn't say much in the car with Rose and Rose made a valiant attempt to keep the conversation going. Ava would smile at her now and again and even laughed once, but it was unbearable to do more.

At the airport, Stan kissed her goodbye and went to deal with the rental. Rose stood off to the side as Ava went to the ticket counter and got her boarding pass. When all was done, there was nothing to do but sit side by side until it was closer to the flight time.

Ava looked at her hands and rubbed her thumbs. Rose finally put her own hand on top of them to keep them warm. They didn't speak. They didn't look at each other. But Rose must have looked at a few people, because once or twice someone approached her and suddenly backed off.

Finally, her flight was called. It was time to go. She got up and so did Rose. Ava couldn't look at her sister's face. She saw her hair, her neck, her white blouse, but not her face. Rose pulled her into her arms and held her tight. She tried not to shake but it was hard.

Rose kissed her hair. "If you need any of us, anytime, anywhere, you call and we'll be there so fast you won't know what hit ya."

Ava nodded and pulled away, picked up the bags and walked through security. When boarding was announced, she stood in line with the other passengers, showed her boarding pass and I.D. to the ticket agent, then walked outside to the plane. Behind her were Rose and Stan, waiting by the window to wave her goodbye.

As Ava climbed the stairs to the plane, she turned to them. Rose had her hand on the glass, as if trying to touch her. Ava held her hand up too.

Fortunately no one sat beside her. She put her head on the cold glass of the window and stared at the pavement and then the runway and then the trees as they lifted off the ground. She saw the Mayflower Mall and other familiar landmarks. Because of the prevailing wind, they circled before heading out, following the Sydney–Louisbourg Highway and the Mira River as it snaked its way towards the ocean. And finally she saw Mira Bay and his small house. It looked insignificant from up there in the sky, but it was her safe haven and it suddenly vanished into the clouds in a blink of an eye.

CHAPTER TWENTY

Rose was silent all the way home in the car with Stan. When they got out of the car she said, "Nuts to this. Give me the keys."

"Where ya goin'?"

"To Aunt Vi's."

"You'll only upset her."

"We're all upset, Stan, so what the hell's the difference?"

"Okay, okay." He threw her the keys. "Women."

She drove over to Water Street and parked in the driveway. Walking to the back door who did she see but that goddamn woman with her goddamn binoculars, so up went Rose's middle finger. Geranium jumped back. If Rose thought she could pull it off without being arrested, she'd moon her too.

She walked into the kitchen and Aunt Vi was at the table with a cup of tea. She held a handful of tissue and her face was mottled. She pointed at the stove. "I thought you'd be back. I put on the tea."

"Thanks." Rose poured herself a cup, adding evaporated milk to it, took a big swig and put it down.

"Was it awful?"

"It was worse than awful. That girl was paralyzed. She didn't talk, she didn't cry. It's like she was afraid to open her mouth in case something spilled out. I'm worried about her."

"Well, she seemed okay when she got back from your place yesterday and last night at dinner."

Rose's mug stopped halfway to her mouth. "Come again?"

"When she walked in yesterday morning, she seemed cheerful enough, although she did have dark circles under her eyes, now that I think of it."

"My place? She hasn't been to my place in a week."

Aunt Vi's mouth dropped open. "Why that little monkey. She called me on...what night was it...Saturday night and said she was staying at your house for a girls gab night."

"Well, she was gabbin' with someone all right, but it sure wasn't me."

"Why would she lie?"

Rose slammed her mug on the table. "I bet it was that goddamn Seamus."

"Oh lord." Aunt Vi heaved a great sigh. "What is it with those two? They're tearing each other to shreds and it's ridiculous."

"Yes, it is ridiculous and he deserves to have his ass whooped."

Aunt Vi put her hand up. "Now whoa there, Missy. He's only one side of the story. She's as involved as he is, so don't go blamin' him. She's the one who phoned and lied as bold as brass."

"Why can't they just leave it? Why?"

"Why can't they be together is what I want to know."

"You don't honestly want the two of them to get back together again, do you?"

"Why not? It's clear they're miserable without each other."

"I was here the day his mother came shootin' her mouth off about her precious son and how Libby was a right little madam. She had no business coming in here and upsetting Ma."

"Maybe when you get a little older you'll see things in a different light. Evelyn O'Reilly was as upset about her boy as your Ma was about Libby. Mothers protect their young. Just because he was a lad, doesn't mean his heart wasn't broken."

"Well, if they wanted each other so bad, why did she leave? She couldn't have loved him that much."

"She didn't so much leave as run."

Rose sat and thought about that for a moment. "You're right."

Aunt Vi blew her nose. "You know, maybe because I wasn't lucky enough to have any kids of my own I became over-involved with you lot, but I saw things that your mother didn't see, or didn't want to see."

"What do you mean?"

"Well, you fellas were all gone, married or as good as. Libby was alone here. She was so often alone."

"No, she wasn't. We had a whole house full."

Aunt Vi gave her an exasperated look. "Child, when she was six, you were thirteen. When she was thirteen, you were twenty. You might've thought you were around, but you weren't. You girls were in and out all day with your friends and your fellas. You'd pat her on the head and play with her for ten minutes and then off you'd go. She wasn't going anywhere. She was here with your ma."

"You make it sound as if we neglected her."

Aunt Vi took a sip of tea.

Rose felt her hackles rise. "Is that what you're saying?"

Her aunt put the cup down. "What I'm saying is that Libby was a difficult child. She didn't have a lot of friends because she was so often in her own little world. And it didn't help matters that she was the only one in school who didn't have a Da. That set her apart right off the bat, and you know damn well things like that matter."

Rose tried to put holes in her argument. "She had girlfriends. She was always popular."

"No. She had girls who wanted to hang around with her because that's where the boys were, like bees to honey. She never had a girlfriend who came and spent the night and giggled with her."

"Sure she did."

Aunt Vi got her dander up. "You listen to me Rose, because I know what I'm talking about. No one wanted to come here because it wasn't a fun house, with a young mother icing cupcakes with her daughter and her friends. Most of the time your ma told them to pipe down and go outside."

"Well, she was old."

"I'm not suggesting it was your mother's fault. She was a sad and lonely woman. She had her reasons for being moody, Lord knows. Left with so many kids and always worried about money. It ages a woman, not to have a man. It's not like it is today. Women have careers and such— they don't need a man. But in our day, you couldn't get a bank loan unless your husband put his signature on it too. You young ones seem to forget that our world wasn't like today's world."

"Wonderful." Rose sighed. "Now I feel miserable and guilty."

"Don't be dramatic. No one's blaming you or your brothers and sisters. You had a right to have a life too. But what I'm saying is, stop being in such a hurry to tell your baby sister what she should and shouldn't feel. Her upbringing was vastly different from yours. If she decides in the end she wants Seamus O'Reilly and he's the one man in the world who makes her happy, why should she be deprived of him, simply because you don't like him?"

Rose didn't say anything, so her aunt gave her another jab.

"Did anyone open their big mouth and give you an earful about marrying Stan?"

There. She'd been told. "You're right. Libby always did say my mouth was too big."

"Not only Libby."

Rose crossed her arms. "Thank you."

"You're welcome."

She sat with her own thoughts while Aunt Vi sipped her tea and looked lonely.

"I think I should call him."

Aunt Vi's head went back. "After I just finished tellin' ya…"

"…to mind my own business, I know. But I don't plan on screaming at him. I want to know if Libby's all right. Did they quarrel? Did they agree to part? Or has she run off on him again?"

Aunt Vi nodded her head. "Maybe she did run off. I mean, suddenly she has to go? Does that sound logical? No one calls here all summer and suddenly there's a huge rush to get her back to New York for just one day. I didn't think it made sense, but then again that Hollywood business is beyond me anyway."

"And if she is on the run…"

"What on earth is she running from?" Aunt Vi planted her elbows on the table and rested her head in her hands. "That poor boy. If she's done this to him again, I'm afraid it's going to kill him."

"Now who's being dramatic."

"Listen to yourself. He lost Libby once. He lost his mother. He lost his young wife and now he may have lost Libby again. What on earth has he done to deserve all that?"

"That's true," Rose nodded. "No one deserves that much heartache."

They looked at each other.

"Should I call?"

"Well honey, you're the one who said she seemed terribly upset when she left. Maybe we should find out if we need to be worried. I don't want her disappearing for another ten years, do you?"

"Of course not. But I don't think I can talk to him yet. I'm too emotional. I don't want to go off half-cocked and make it worse for her."

"You've got a point."

"I think I'll go home and call him tonight. I've got a headache anyway."

Aunt Vi patted her hand. "Okay, love. I think we should keep our heads down today. It's been a pretty emotional twenty-four hours."

Rose gave her aunt a quick kiss and hurried out to the car. She didn't even look at Geranium but gave her the finger again anyway. Once home, she tackled a mountain of housework to take her mind off things. Thank goodness it was her day off. She'd be useless anyway. Who knows what horrors unsuspecting hospital patients would've endured? She called her sisters and they had a chat about missing Libby, though Rose didn't mention the conversation she'd had with her aunt. That was something she needed to sort out in her head first.

She never saw it from Libby's point of view. Rose felt terrible about telling her off the first night she was here, actually cringed when she though of it. Damn her and her big mouth. She wondered if she had a problem serious enough to warrant getting professional help.

Once supper was out of the way and homework dealt with, she planned on calling Seamus, but her Aunt Vi phoned first.

"I think we were right about Libby running off."

"Why? Did something happen?"

"Someone just called here—I think it was Seamus. He asked for Libby and I said she was gone, that she'd flown to New York today. There was this terrible silence on the other end for the longest time and when I said, 'Seamus, is that you?' he hung up."

"That doesn't sound good."

"No, it doesn't. What should we do? Do you still want to call him?"

"I'm not sure. What do you think?"

"If it's true, he'll be so upset. Maybe we should let him be."

"But what if he knows something about Libby that we should know? Something that could help her? Obviously she's not confiding in us."

"That's true. Oh, Rose, I don't know what's best."

"I suppose the worst he could do is hang up on me."

"Okay. Call him and call me back. I'll wait by the phone."

"God. This is nerve-wracking."

"Good luck, dear."

Rose put down the phone and looked up his number, but it seemed to be unlisted. She forgot he was a cop. Most of them had unlisted numbers—and no wonder. That's all they'd need, people calling to tell them to shove their speeding tickets.

Rose didn't want to call his sister but she didn't want to talk to his dad either. She couldn't think of anyone else, so she looked up Colleen's number and punched it in.

"Hello?"

"Colleen?"

"Speaking."

"This is Rose Petrie."

"Sorry?"

"Libby's sister."

There was a long pause. Rose waited her out.

"What can I do for you?"

"I need Seamus's phone number."

"And why would you want to call him?"

"I'm sorry if I sound rude, but that's none of your business."

"It is my business. He's my kid brother."

"Excuse me, Colleen, but he's a grown man. Do you filter all his calls? If I run into him on the street and tell him I tried to get in touch with him but his big sister stopped me, what do you think he'd say?"

She knew she hit a nerve because Colleen didn't answer for a good ten seconds. Finally, she blurted out the number.

"Thank you."

"Don't hurt him. I'm warning you."

"I don't intend to. Goodbye."

She hung up and thought, no time like the present. She dialed his number and it rang six times before she heard a voice. "Yes?"

"Seamus?"

"Yes."

"It's Rose. Libby's sister."

"What do you want?"

"I wanted to know if you were with Libby on Saturday night. She told Aunt Vi that she was with me, but she wasn't."

"She was here."

"Oh. Well, I don't mean to pry but I'm worried about her. Is there anything I should know?"

"Know?"

"Yes. Was she upset?"

"No."

"Okay. She left a day early and we thought…"

"You thought that she was running away from me again?"

"Well…"

"No. We had dinner together and she told me she was leaving. We said goodbye."

"I see."

"Is there anything else I can help you with?"

"No. I guess not. I…are you all right?"

"Of course. Why wouldn't I be?"

"No reason. I'm sorry I bothered you."

"Yeah, okay."

When he hung up she looked at the phone. If Rose didn't know any better she'd swear she was talking to an automated answering machine. It made her feel worse than if he screamed in her ear. She called her Aunt Vi and told her what happened.

"Call his sister back and tell her. I don't like the sounds of that."

"Okay."

She dialed Colleen's number again.

"Hello?"

"Colleen, it's Rose again."

"God. Now what?"

"I think you should call your brother, or better yet, go over and see him."

Her voice was instantly alert. "Why? What's wrong?"

"Libby left for New York today."

"Shit."

"And he sounded like it didn't bother him in the least."

"Oh God."

"I know. You better go."

"Yes. Um…thanks for letting me know."

"Hey, you love him, we love her."

"Yes, I have to go."

She hung up the phone and Rose saw her in her mind's eye,

driving to Catalone to help her brother. If only she could get in a car and help Libby.

❀

Colleen yelled for Dave and told him what Rose said.

"Well, you better get over there."

She grabbed a sweater and looked around for the car keys. "What if he's in a bad way?"

"You know he's in a bad way. Just let him talk or whatever."

She raced to the door.

"Call if you need help and I'll leave the kids with Audrey next door."

"She'd love that, four more on top of her three. Wish me luck."

"Good luck."

Colleen drove, trying not to think, but her mind imagined all sorts of wild scenarios. He'd hang himself and Jack and Sarah would be orphans. He'd become a drunk like their dad. Or maybe Rose overreacted and he'd be pissed that she was interfering again. She was sick of the whole business. All she wanted was for him to have a normal life. Was that too much to ask?

She drove into his yard and nearly ran over Dexter. The stupid cat was asleep in the middle of the driveway. Dexter woke in a hurry and ran to the deck ahead of her so she'd let him in the house. She knocked and went through the door.

"Seamus?"

There was no response. Her heart beat a little faster. "Hello?"

Nothing. She was aware of the television on in his bedroom. She walked down the hall and knocked on the slightly open door. "Seamus?"

He was on the bed staring at the TV.

She almost had to holler. "Seamus." She startled him.

"What?" He started to get up. "Why are you here? Something wrong with the kids?"

She rushed to reassure him "No, heavens, nothing like that." She sat on the chair next to the bed and patted his knee. "They're fine, although they do miss you. Two nights is about their limit."

"I know. I'll pick them up tomorrow after work if that's okay."

"Sure, that's fine."

"Why are you here, Colleen?"

She hesitated and debated about what she should say. She didn't want to scare him off. "Rose called me. She was worried about you."

He sat back on the bed and picked up the remote, clicking through the channels. She waited for him to respond, but he didn't.

"I wanted to make sure you were okay."

"You can see I am."

"Are you?"

"I'm watching television. Is that something to be worried about?"

"Yes," she smiled. "There's too much sex and violence on TV."

He didn't think it was funny so she tried another tack. "Rose told me something else."

He kept channel surfing.

"That Libby left this morning." It was like he didn't hear her. "Seamus?"

"Yes?"

"Did you hear what I said?"

"Yeah."

"How are you feeling? I mean, I can guess how you're feeling but…"

"Fine."

"You don't look fine to me."

"That's your problem."

This was worse than she thought. It was like talking to him through Plexiglas.

"So you don't care that she left?"

"She wanted to go. She's gone. End of story."

"I see."

"You can drop the worried sister routine and let me get on with my life."

This was going nowhere. She didn't want to antagonize him but she didn't want him to take his service revolver and blow his brains out either. She was in limbo. He soon solved that.

"Get out."

She blinked. "Sorry?"

"Get out. You've come to ask if I'm okay and I told you. Now get out."

She stood up. "All right. I guess I'll see you tomorrow then."

"Yep."

"Try and get some sleep."

He didn't answer her. She had no choice but to leave. She walked down the hall. Poor old Dexter practically sat up and begged to be fed. She went into the kitchen and opened a tin of cat food, then washed his dish and put in the whole can. Finally, she changed his water dish. At least one male in the house was happy.

Colleen turned to go and saw it sitting on the kitchen table. A small velvet box. She walked over and picked it up, glancing out into the hall before opening it. A lovely little diamond ring sparkled back at her. It wasn't anything spectacular but she knew he couldn't afford more. He worked hard for his money and would probably have to forego movies and fast food joints to pay for it, and that stupid little bitch left it behind, just as she left Seamus behind.

She wanted to hit something. Since Libby wasn't there, she marched back into the bedroom and hit him.

"Hey!" he said.

"Why, Seamus? Why do you let her do this to you over and over? Are you blind? Are you that stupid you can't see her for what she is?" Colleen held out the ring. "She doesn't want you. She rejected you once and now, ten years later, she's done it again. Wake up and get on with your life, for the sake of your kids."

That did it. Seamus got off the bed and poked her in the shoulder and kept poking as he walked towards her. She had to back up into the wall.

"I'm sick of you. I'm sick of all of you. You think you know her but you don't."

"But she's left you again and I know your heart's broken because I can see it on your face. It kills me to know how hurt you are."

"How hurt I am?" He went over to the bedside table, picked up a glass and threw it at the mirror over his bureau as hard as he could. The mirror shattered and so did the glass. Colleen was petrified. She wanted to call Dave but Seamus came back and yelled in her face.

"I don't know the meaning of the word hurt. I think Libby has that one all wrapped up. Maybe you can ask her how bad it hurt when she was raped by that fucking drama teacher at our school. Or maybe you can ask her how much it hurt when she had to fuck guys to get enough rum to numb the pain, so she could sleep at night. Or maybe you can ask her how it felt to be knocked up and have to go to Halifax for an abortion all by herself, so she wouldn't disappoint me or her family. And ask her how it felt to stay away for ten years, missing her home and her brothers and sisters because she couldn't face me and the hurt she'd put me through."

Colleen was numb. She watched in horror as he turned around and grabbed his own hair in his desperation. "The hurt she put me though! What a laugh. I was a fucking baby. I cried like a baby when she left but I never wondered why she left. I never went after her to find out. I picked up my marbles and went home."

He paced back and forth. "So, you be sorry for me Colleen, because that little bitch ruined my life, didn't she? She's put me through such pain and agony that I didn't have a career or own my own home. I didn't get married and have kids. Yes, I'm a fucking mess. So by all means get on the phone and tell her what a miserable bitch she is for hurting me."

He put his hands over his face. "Oh my god. What have I done to her?" He stumbled back to the bed and sat down, keeping his face in his hands as he bent over his knees.

Colleen walked over to him and rubbed his back as he sat in silence. It was too much. She couldn't take it all in. Surely to God it wasn't true. "I'm sorry, Seamus. I can't tell you how awful I feel for her…for you. It's a tragedy."

He wiped his face and kept his forearms on his thighs. It was as if he didn't have the energy to sit up. "It's more than a tragedy. It's a never-ending nightmare and I can't seem to wake up."

"You obviously only found this out…"

"…Saturday night. She came for supper and she looked beautiful. We had such a nice time and then I go and ruin it by asking her to marry me, when I knew damn well she wasn't ready. She said it often enough, about needing time. She gave me enough clues but I hounded her anyway. She told me she had to go away because she was under contract and I sloughed that off."

"And when she said no?"

"She didn't say no. She said she had to leave and I screamed at her and shook her and demanded she tell me why she wouldn't stay. I forced it out of her and it cost her. It cost her so bad. She was like a limp rag…"

"That's how she was in the bathroom at the wake," Colleen said.

Seamus nodded. "As if the remembering was enough to destroy her."

"What did you do?"

"I tried to comfort her and she finally slept but that wasn't enough for me. In the morning I hounded her again to prove that she loved me, as if I didn't have enough proof already. I tried to make love to her, and even though I knew in my heart she wasn't ready, she let me. Used by one more man in her life."

"That's not true. I know she loves you."

"I pushed her too hard and she got frightened. I forced her out of here again, and how do you think that makes her feel? She only ever worried about me and now she'll feel awful about leaving me again. But she's not the one that needs to feel awful. I do. I caused all this. If I'd let her go away and have some time to think, maybe we could've come together again, slowly. But I wanted what I wanted when I wanted it. And this is the result. She left a day earlier than she planned, and is no doubt missing that last day with her family more than anything."

"God, what a mess," Colleen sighed.

"I don't know what to do."

"I think you should leave her be."

He got up and looked at the mess of glass on the floor. "How did I know that was coming?"

She reached for his hand. "No. You don't understand, I'm not saying to stay away from her. I just think you should give her what she asked for, a little time."

"But she'll think I don't care."

"No, she won't." She kept hold of his hand. "I think maybe your best bet is to write her a letter and explain it exactly the way you've told me. Then she can read it by herself and think about it. Whenever you two are in the same room, there's too much emotion going on. This was a terrible shock for you both, for her to dredge up the past and for you to hear all this horror at once. You never gave yourselves a chance."

He took his hand away and rubbed his forehead. "I'm such an idiot. How in the name of God is she going to forgive me?"

"How are you going to forgive yourself, is my worry."

He gave her a look.

"You're beating yourself up about something you never knew happened. You were away cutting trees to make money for school. It's not like you took off to party with other girls. You came home and she was gone and no one could tell you why. You were a kid. Of course you were upset and angry; you had every right to be. But you had to get on with your life."

He sighed.

"Sweetheart, Libby's gone through something you can't possibly understand because you're a man. An experience like that wounds a woman's soul. She's been hurt so deeply, she may always run away from men. She may never be able to give you what you want, in spite of the fact that she tried."

"I'll never know now."

"You don't know that."

"I do know, because you're right. The kindest thing I can do is leave her alone."

"Maybe. I don't know any more." And then she thought of something. "Obviously her family doesn't know about what happened to her all those years ago."

He shook his head. "Don't say a word, Colleen. If she wanted them to know, she would've told them."

"Maybe she should. Maybe she'd feel better if she didn't carry this burden all alone."

"I don't know. I can't think anymore."

Colleen looked at the floor. "Do you want me to help you clean up this mess?"

"No. This is one mess I have to clean up myself."

CHAPTER TWENTY-ONE

On the way to New York, Ava had two passengers hit on her and three ask for an autograph. To put a stop to it, she wore a sleeping mask and kept it there—she had no appetite anyway. She left the plane as quickly as possible, and ignored the pesky hanger-on who couldn't take a hint.

The studio provided a limo and driver to take her to the Plaza. The manager greeted her and made chit-chat as she hurried through the lobby. He whisked her upstairs to one of their best suites. She nodded and smiled as the bell boy came behind them with the luggage. She placed a tip in his hand and thanked them both. They bid her goodnight and closed the door behind them.

She looked around at the huge, empty suite.

"Welcome home, Ava."

She wandered over to the window. New York City. Home to millions.

"Hello? Anyone out there?"

She unpacked her bags and ordered a vanilla milkshake, then sat on a chair and waited for it to come. When it arrived, she drank it and then looked at her watch. It was still only seven o'clock, so she reached for the TV remote and turned it on. Images of another suicide bombing covered the screen. She turned it off and went over to the window again, noticing for the first time that it was raining. The sky was crying. Her finger traced the raindrops on their zigzag journey down the window pane.

She looked at her watch. It was eight o'clock.

Crossing the room, she passed a mirror and stopped to look at her reflection. "Well, this is fun, isn't it?"

She continued on and sat on the bed, then got up and made herself a rum and Coke. On the way back from the bar, she toasted herself in the mirror again. "Good choice, old dear. Rum and Coke, your specialty." She downed her drink and smacked her lips. "I think I'll have another."

Over to the bar once more to fill her glass and then back to the mirror. "To a long and happy life." The drink was gone in a flash. "Yum. One more, I think."

After her third rum and Coke, she put down the glass and walked into the bathroom, leaning into the mirror over the sink to brush her hair back with her fingers. "I think I deserve a little party. I am a party girl, after all."

She turned away from the mirror and stripped off her clothes. "We all have our talents."

She stepped into the glorious tub and had a leisurely soak in perfumed bubble bath. It didn't smell like Jergen's Hand Lotion at all. Once out of the tub, she wrapped herself in a luxurious towel to dry off, but soon dropped it to the floor to take a look at herself. Not bad, Ava. The few extra pounds she'd gained suited her.

Time to spread lotion all over her body and take her time rubbing it in. Then over to her lingerie bag to remove the sexiest bra and panties she owned. Black lace, naturally. What is it with men and blonde women wearing black lace? No imagination at all, unless it's blondes wearing red lace.

Ava turned on the CD player and swayed to Kenny G as she applied her makeup. Her hair was easy. She bent over and messed it up. Perfect. Now over to the closet to choose the little black dress that cost her a week's wages. She stepped into it and pulled it over her tiny curves. She found her favourite high heels and a small clutch to hold her lipstick and room key. Then she walked back into the bathroom and dabbed perfume behind her ears and on her wrists.

Her image smiled back at her in the mirror. "Beautiful. Have fun."

Ava left the room and pushed the elevator button. The red arrow above the door pinged and the door opened. She always loved this part. The people inside inevitably looked bored and then shocked and then sort of embarrassed when they realized who she was. They either didn't look at her at all or never took their eyes off her. It was an art to learn how to ignore it and pretend they didn't exist.

Tonight there were two men in the elevator who knew each other. They were laughing when the door opened, but as soon as she walked in, they shut right up. She turned around and pushed the button. That's when the frantic hand gestures started behind her back. The door opened and she walked out. As the door closed there was a burst of expletives and yelling.

Too boring.

She walked into the upscale lounge. The lights were dim and the piano music low. All very expensive and chic. She walked over to the bar and sat on a stool, crossing her legs, causing her very short dress to become shorter still.

The bartender came over. "Good evening, Miss Harris. Nice to see you again." He put a cocktail napkin in front of her.

"Good evening, Frank. Nice to see you too."

"What can I get you this evening?"

"A rum and Coke please. On the rocks."

"Certainly."

She looked around. Quite a few men caught her eye. They were an older group, with money and power to burn. Amazing how they all looked at her legs. Poor pathetic things. Wearing three-thousand-dollar suits and still behaving like the boys in gym class.

Her drink was in front of her. She took a sip and then another while counting down from ten in her head. At two, a man—the leader of the pack—approached with a drink in his hand.

"Good evening."

"Good evening." She took another sip.

"Ava Harris, is it not?"

"That's right."

He held out his hand. "Michael Lancaster."

She shook his hand. "Nice to meet you, Michael."

He slid his body onto the bar stool next to her, as she knew he would.

"Are you in town for a movie?"

"Yes."

"How interesting."

"Is it?"

"Well, for someone who knows nothing about the movie industry, it is rather fascinating."

"It's not really." She took a big swallow and then another until the glass was empty.

"May I buy you a drink?"

"Thank you. Rum and Coke."

He flicked his finger at Frank, who instantly produced the new drinks. Ava picked hers up. "Cheers."

"Cheers."

They had a pleasant conversation that lasted two more drinks.

He held out the last one for her. "Would you like another?"

She blinked. "What do I have to do for it?"

"You don't have to do anything."

"That's where you're wrong."

He hesitated.

"I can do most things very, very well, so you have gentlemen's choice tonight."

He handed her the glass. "Well, I'm nothing if not a gentleman."

"How did I know you were going to say that?" She swallowed another mouthful.

He snapped his fingers at the bartender. "Check." The tab was produced and he wrote his name and room number on it.

Michael put his hand under her elbow. "After you."

He steered her out of the bar while Frank cleaned up the glasses and shook his head.

They got on the elevator. "My room or yours?" he asked.

"Yours."

They got off on his floor and walked down the hall. He reached in his pocket and took out the room key. He slid it in and pulled it out. The door opened. And then the door shut.

He was the perfect gentleman. At two in the morning, when he was done with her, he got dressed and escorted her down to her door. He said, "You have to be careful. Even in classy hotels, you never know who you might run into, in the elevator or the hall."

"Or the lounge."

He laughed, thinking she was joking.

She shut the door in his face and stumbled into the bathroom, pulling off her dress. She was naked. She'd forgotten her bra and panties. Didn't matter. He'd either keep them as a trophy or sell them on eBay. She knelt by the toilet and threw up the rum, then washed her face and brushed her teeth. She turned out the bathroom light and teetered to bed, where she picked up the phone and asked for an eight o'clock wake-up call before passing out cold.

Ever the professional, she was up, dressed and ready to go when Trent picked her up at ten.

"God, you look wonderful," he proclaimed as he came through the door. He grabbed her by the shoulders and kissed her cheek. "Vacation's done you a world of good, I see." He looked at her again. "Maybe a little too good. Put on some weight, I see."

"I'll stop eating."

"Good girl." He rushed past her. "Look, we have a busy day and I'm not sure we're going to get it all in, but we'll give it the old college try."

She sat on the edge of the sofa and smiled.

"Where's that pit bull you insist on keeping around?"

"Lola will be here tomorrow."

"Thank God. That's all I would've needed on today of all days." He reached for the phone on the coffee table. "I'll call and tell them we're on our way." He sounded very chummy with whoever it was on the other end of the phone. Good-old-boy kind of chatter, all huff and puff and blow your house down kind of stuff.

Ava gathered her purse and coat and took one last look in the mirror. She mouthed, "Goodbye, Ava," before she was ushered out the door of the room, out of the hotel and into the car. Trent talked the entire time about how wonderful the new director was and how marvelous his new vision would be and that she should be grateful to be working with the next Woody Allen.

"You're overselling it, Trent."

He took offense to that and blustered all the way up to the meeting rooms, and there were plenty of them. A whole day of musical rooms. She sat up and sat down. She was greeted and dismissed. She was ignored and fawned over. She was talked to, talked at, talked about, and talked into. And that was all before the director got there.

When she did finally meet the boy wonder he had on an earpiece and was talking into it. He gestured for them to come in and then turned his back to finish his conversation. There were four other men in the room. It was stuffy and smoky. They stood up in turn and introduced themselves, though she forgot who they were right away.

As she took off her coat, she spied a picked-over meat tray and a pitcher with glasses on a table. She went over and helped herself a glass of water. Trent stopped talking long enough to yell across the room, "Don't you dare eat that cheese, you little dumpling."

The men laughed. She didn't. It was four o'clock and she hadn't eaten. She picked up a fist full of cheese, sat in a corner and ate it. The men never noticed, so busy were they with their creative pissing contest.

A half an hour went by and the new messiah was still on the phone. She ate more cheese. Suddenly the door opened and Hayden walked in. He didn't see her. He greeted the men and there was a commotion of good will. Then he spied her.

"Ava." He sauntered over and gave her a big hug. "Oh baby, baby. I've missed you. Give daddy a kiss."

He kissed her longer then necessary while the men watched, and then let her go.

"You still love an audience, Hayden."

"You know me so well." He reached out and held her chin. "Let me look at you. Exquisite as ever." He paused. "On second thought, you look tired. I hope you weren't up to something last night, you naughty girl. I want you fresh as a daisy tonight."

"What are we doing tonight?"

He grabbed her waist and whispered, "I'm taking you to dinner and then we're having a repeat performance of my Sydney engagement. I've been saving myself all week. How's that for sacrifice."

"Overwhelming."

He laughed and slapped her bottom. "Don't get saucy."

The director finally rushed over, as if she'd just walked in the room. He looked about sixteen years old. "Nice to meet you, Miss Harris. I'm looking forward to working with you. Nigel Barrymore, by the way."

"Hello, Nigel."

Nigel grabbed Hayden's arm and they pulled their forearms back and forth in a hip urban grip. "Hey dawg, how's it goin'?"

"Great, now that my favourite woman is back in town."

More male bonding crap and then they invited her to sit down. She ended up facing them as if she was the defendant and they were the jury. Scripts were handed out. The usual nonsense was spouted and Ava's eyes got heavy.

"As I was saying," Nigel repeated, when he got her attention, "it's a minor adjustment, but I think it's absolutely crucial to the crux of the story. Turn to page fifty-four."

Paper was heard being thumbed through. She looked at it. "Let me guess."

"Excuse me?" said Nigel.

"This is the lover's quarrel between Hayden and me."

"Yes."

"And there's something wrong with it."

"Well, yes."

"It's not graphic enough, not sensational enough."

"True."

"It won't grab the sixteen- to twenty-five-year-olds."

Nigel pointed at her. "Yes! She really is a genius, isn't she Hayden?"

"She picked me, didn't she?"

Ava looked at the director. "So you want me to be either in my underwear, a see-through blouse and panties, a bathing suit, or a thong. Am I right?"

"No."

"What a relief."

"We want you raped."

She stood up. "I'm leaving."

"Sit down, Miss Harris." The sixteen-year-old suddenly became the prosecutor. "I want to explain my vision."

"I know all about your vision. It's about gawking at tits and ass and getting off on seeing a woman powerless and crying for help."

Trent was purple. Hayden wasn't far off. Nigel looked at Trent. "Is she serious?"

"Ava, be reasonable."

Ava walked to the other side of the room and stood by the window. The sky was crying again. Their voices droned on and in the end it sounded like a swarm of bees. She watched tears fall against the window. She wondered if it was crying in Cape Breton too.

Since threats didn't seem to do the trick, they eventually sent Hayden in to butter her up. He took her into another room and sat down beside her.

"Sweets. I know you hate this kind of stuff, and this isn't what you signed up for, but honey, shit happens. They're allowed to make these changes within reason and this doesn't change the outcome of the plot anyway."

"If it doesn't change it, why do it?"

"How the hell should I know? Babe, it's a gig. When your

salary is seven figures, it's not that hard to make it easy on everybody and just do it."

"It's not easy on me."

He put his arm around her shoulder and kissed her ear. "Sweetheart, it's me. It's not like it's going to be some asshole you don't know. I'll be right there. I'll protect you."

"You'll be there and so will thirty crew with bright lights and cameras. And after that, it will be my nieces watching it at the Empire Theatre next fall. Not to mention the millions around the world."

"Jesus, are you an actress or a nun?"

"Pardon?"

"Shit, it's a movie. It's not real. It's make-believe. It's not actually going to happen to you. They'll yell 'Cut' and we'll go get a hamburger."

The only way she was going to get out of that room was to agree, so, in the end, she agreed.

Then they added one tiny thing. She and Hayden would have to have a rehearsal tomorrow because of scheduling problems. But the boy genius thought it would be a great idea to get the good stuff done first. Pump everyone up, as it were.

Released from bondage, Ava went back to the hotel. Hayden was two floors away. They agreed to meet at seven o'clock. She took a shower and ate cashews while she put her face on. She talked to the mirror.

"How did it go today, Ava?"

"The usual. A woman got screwed."

"Happens a lot."

"So I hear."

He tapped on her door and she was ready. They went out for an expensive meal at Elaine's. Hayden talked and Ava listened. He reached out at one point and grabbed her hand. He kissed the back of it.

"I missed you."

"Did you?"

"Didn't you miss me?"

She nodded.

"We've got to decide where this relationship is going." He fiddled with the ring on her finger.

"What do you mean?"

He kissed her fingertips. "While you were away, I realized how much I care about you."

"While you took a different woman to bed every night."

He laughed. "Surprisingly, it helped to clarify the situation."

"You don't say."

"I mean it. I was comparison shopping. And you know what?"

"What?"

"They didn't hold a candle to you." He squeezed her hand and gave it a little shake. "Can we go, before I take you here on the table?"

They got their coats and took a taxi back to the hotel. He kept his arm around her as they walked into the lobby. Michael Lancaster and a woman who looked like his wife walked down the hall towards them. His wife recognized her and poked him in the ribs. He glanced at her and kept going. She did the same.

Hayden barely let her get her coat off before he was all over her. "Give me a second," she pleaded. She shut the bathroom door in his face and turned on the tap. She looked in the mirror.

"Do you even like Hayden?"

She stood there for a few minutes before she shrugged.

"Does it matter?"

She turned the water tap off and went out. Hayden was naked in the bed waiting for her. He patted the sheets beside him.

"Let's rehearse before rehearsal."

CHAPTER TWENTY-TWO

After Colleen left, Seamus cleaned up his bedroom carefully, to protect the tiny feet and paws that ran across the floor many times in the run of a day. He swept, vacuumed, mopped, and dried it with a towel. Only when he was satisfied that not one sliver of glass remained, did he sit out on the deck and look at the beach.

He tried to compose a letter in his head as he sat there, but couldn't get a thought to come out right, so he went into the kitchen and searched for paper. Naturally, he couldn't find any. He took down a drawing of Sarah's from the fridge, found a coloured pencil in the junk drawer, and sat at the kitchen table. His hand stayed poised over the paper for an hour. There was nothing he could say. He finally wrote, "Dearest Libby, I love you. Seamus."

He folded the paper into a tiny square, went into his bedroom and picked up the ring box, putting the note inside. Then he put on a jacket and went out the door. Dexter came with him. He walked to the beach and sat on the log where he sometimes had his morning coffee. It would be dark soon.

Finally he took a flat rock and started to dig. When he thought it was deep enough he took the ring box, kissed it, and put it in the hole. Then he and Dexter filled it with sand. Seamus patted it over. He walked back in the house, lay on his bed and stared at the ceiling all night.

At work the next day, he and Roger only grunted at each

other in passing. One of the clerks who worked at the station asked him if he wanted to go out for a bite. He declined. He later heard her complain about him to another clerk, not realizing he was in the coffee room.

"Is he stuck up or is he gay? I can't figure out which."

"Maybe he's both," the girl laughed.

"What a waste then."

"He was married, though."

"Apparently that means nothing. Lots of gay guys get married. I watched it on Oprah."

"They do?"

"Yeah. They want kids like anyone else."

"Why are all gay men really good looking?"

"Not all of them are."

"Well, a vast majority are. Look at Will on Will and Grace."

"He's not gay in real life."

"He's not?"

Seamus walked out of the coffee room and right past them. "Neither am I."

He went through the day with a pounding headache. The sky looked threatening, a dark, broody twilight in the middle of the afternoon. It made the day seem endless. By the end of his shift, he was anxious to see the kids. He missed them and hoped they'd distract him from his thoughts long enough for him to get a little sleep.

Never far away were thoughts of her. He wondered where she was and what she was doing. Was she thinking of him? He worried about her not eating right. Or not eating at all, which reminded him of food and the fact that he needed some. He did himself a favour and went to the grocery store before picking up the kids. Standing in the vegetable aisle, he remembered the day he ran into her. He passed the mushrooms and stopped. He saw her still, wearing that tea towel around her waist and laughing as she looked in the fridge. He picked up a paper bag and filled it with mushrooms. Look, Libby, here's some for supper. We'll cook them up tonight.

He put the bag back on the display counter and walked out of the store.

All the way out to Colleen's he saw her face. He saw her body. He remembered her perfume. She must be with him. Some essence must have stayed, because it was as if she were right beside him. Or maybe I'm going crazy, he thought.

Seamus pulled into Colleen's and took a deep breath. He had to put Libby away for a while. He needed to love his kids. He mentally kissed her and tucked her into his heart and promised to take her out later, when the kids were asleep.

He walked into the kitchen, a nice normal kitchen, where dishes were still on the counter and pots bubbled away. The TV blared from the family room and Colleen was bent over, looking in her own fridge. "Have you kids eaten all the Dream Whip?" she shouted over her shoulder.

"I didn't. I swear."

She jumped up and turned around. "God. You scared me."

"Sorry."

She came over and gave him a big hug. "I thought of you all day. And all night, for that matter."

"For pity's sake, don't lose sleep on my account. You can't afford it. You look tired out."

"I am a little tired."

He sat at the table. "I'm sorry, Coll. I leave the kids with you too much."

She waved her hand. "I love the kids. It's my pleasure to have them. I told you before; you can pay me and keep them out of that daycare centre."

"I can't do that. I don't want to take advantage of you."

She sat at the table too. "Can I tell you something?"

"Sure."

"Nothing gives me greater pleasure than to see our kids grow up and enjoy each other. We're…"

"…such a little family."

"Don't make fun of me," she sulked.

He reached out and grabbed her hand. "I'm not. Really."

"Well, we are a little family, Seamus. If you and I can make sure these kids love each other as brothers and sisters, think what a lovely time they'll have when they start their own families. That's what it's all about."

"They do love each other, and that's thanks to you."

"Well, I'm lucky I don't have to go to work. I really mean it when I say I'd be happy to take them. If I'm watching them every minute God sends anyway, I might as well get paid for it."

They smiled at each other.

"Well, I would rather them here than with a bunch of kids in daycare. Someone's always sick. They come down with too many colds."

"Then it's settled."

"Thank you, Colleen. I…"

"I know."

Just then Jack and Sarah ran in and cries of "Daddy" filled the air. He spent an hour before dinner playing with the four kids on the family room rug. They told him about their day— well, three of them did. Sarah nodded happily and agreed with everything that was said.

His spirits lifted and even though he knew it was only temporary, he was grateful for the reprieve. Dave came home and they sat down to meatloaf and mashed potatoes. Seamus realized he was starving and had two helpings. Colleen moaned about a goblin eating all the Dream Whip, so they had to eat their butterscotch pudding without benefit of a topping. No one seemed to care.

The kids went off after supper to jump on the beds and the three adults sat around the dining room table with their tea. Seamus knew he should go and let his sister and her hubby have a little time to themselves, but he was lonely, he wanted to stay near someone, if only for a little while.

They saw it at the same time through the dining room window—an unfamiliar pickup truck pulled into the yard. The passenger door opened and their father lurched out and almost fell in the driveway. The truck backed up and took off.

Colleen's face turned white. "Oh no."

"I told you Colleen," Seamus frowned. "You shouldn't get your hopes up."

"Look, guys," Dave sighed, "call if you need anything, but I hate this bullshit. I'll be in the garage." He got up from the table and went out the back door.

"What do we do?"

"What we always do," Seamus said. "Nod and agree with everything he says until he passes out on the couch."

Colleen shoved her chair back as she got up. "I hate this. It's always the same disappointment."

"You go watch TV with the kids in the bedroom. I don't want them to see him like this."

"Do you mind? I don't think I can talk to him right now," Colleen said.

"You go. I know how to deal with drunks."

Seamus walked out into the kitchen and sat at the table. It took his father a while to stagger from the driveway to the porch, from the porch to the door, and then the door into the kitchen. He swayed like the scarecrow in The Wizard of Oz—no bones whatsoever.

He gave an exaggerated salute. "Hello, me son."

"Dad."

"Fine night out there, tonight," he grinned.

"Yep."

"Aren't you goin' to invite me in?"

"Not my house."

"True, true, but our Colleen will let me in. She's a good girl." He reached for the back of the kitchen chair but overestimated its distance. His hand swung down and he nearly fell forward. "Oops." He grabbed the kitchen counter instead.

"Who drove you here?"

"A buddy. Cecil. You know him. Used to work at the coke ovens." He made another attempt to grab the back of the chair. This time he connected. "I gotta sit." He scraped the chair over the kitchen floor and sat on it, leaning forward to wipe his hand down his unshaven face. "What's a guy gotta do to get a drink? I'm parched."

"You don't need another drink."

Kenny pointed at his son. "That's where you're wrong, b'y. You always need another drink." He laughed like a fool at his own joke and then glanced up at Seamus with that look, the one Seamus hated. The one where he starts talking but his eyes don't quite make it to your face until the last syllable.

"Don't be such a hard ass boy. I need a drink and then I'm goin'."

"Where are you going?"

His head bobbed up and down. "Well now, let's see. Might go to the Legion for another beer or might go to the tavern. So much booze, so little time."

"I'll drive you home."

"Don't wanna go home. Nothing there."

"Sure there is. I'll take you home and you can go to bed."

He whined like a baby. "I don't wanna go home. I wanna see my Colleen. Colleen! Where are ya, girl?"

"She's watching the kids, Dad. I don't want them to see you like this."

Kenny's head flew back. "Why not? I'm their Granddad, aren't I? Not that I see the little buggers much." He pointed his finger at his son. "And that's your doin'."

Seamus got out of the chair. "That's right. Let's go and we can talk on the way." He reached out to take his father's arm.

Kenny pushed it away. "Get off. What ya think you are? A cop?" He roared. "A cop. My son, the cop. Ain't that a joke?"

"Let's go, Da."

He pushed Seamus's arm away again. "I'll go when I get my drink, and not before."

"If I give you a drink, you'll come with me?"

"Yes, boy. Yes, indeed."

Seamus went to the cupboard and took out a glass. He knew where Dave kept his liquor. He poured a little amber rum in a glass and added tap water. He passed it to his Dad. "Here."

"Wait. I gotta piss."

"Christ." Seamus took his old man by the arm and dragged him to the bathroom. He pushed him in and shut the door. His father serenaded himself as he peed. Seamus opened the door when he heard him fiddle with the knob, and pulled him back into the living room. He put him in the lazy boy chair, hoping that at some point during this last drink, he'd pass out. Then he'd carry him out to the car and take him away.

Seamus sat on the chair across from him. He watched his father take a gulp of rum.

"Ahh, good, b'y, good." He tried to focus on his son. "Why don't you have a drink? Have one with your old man."

"No, thanks."

"Story of my life." He took another drink. "Where'd you come from? Don't know a man around here whose son doesn't drink with his father. I drank with my old man."

"Was he a drunk?"

His father pointed at him with his glass. "Don't get lippy."

Seamus kept quiet. Kenny nodded his head as if he'd told him off. Very proud he was. He took another drink. Seamus watched the amber rum in his glass. He could see right through it thanks to the fire in the fireplace behind his dad. It glowed, and was something to look at besides his old man. He thought of Libby the night they had a bonfire on the beach with their friends. She stood on the opposite side of it at one point and he watched her through the flames. The firelight lit up her face. She was young and happy and she blew him a kiss when she noticed him staring at her.

His father said something.

"What?"

"Ya gotta face like a dog's dinner. What the hell are you mopin' about now?"

Seamus didn't answer him. He wanted to go home.

"You were always mopin' as a kid. Run to your mother for any little thing. Christ, it was sickening."

"Don't start talking about Mom."

"I'll talk about her if I want. She was my wife. You can't stop me from talkin' about her."

"All right, I'm sorry. Drink up and we'll go."

"You're always tryin' to shut me up."

"It doesn't often work."

His father screwed up his face. "You always did think you were better than me. Why is that?"

This was a really bad time to have to sit and listen to bullshit. Seamus's headache returned and he wanted his kids. He rubbed his forehead.

His father suddenly slapped the arm of the chair. "Jesus Christ. I know what it is. Don't tell me you're still boohooin' about that little bitch."

Seamus looked at his father from under his eyelashes.

"For fuck's sake, get over it. It's embarrassing."

"Don't talk about Libby. Not tonight."

"Here we go again. Telling me what I can and cannot talk about. I can talk about that little bitch as long as I want."

"Dad."

His father took another swig. "Seamus, you have got to be the dumbest guy I ever come across. You couldn't hang onto her ten years ago and apparently she's fucked off on you again."

"How do you know that?"

He circled his glass in the air. "Somebody told me. Who gives a shit?"

"I'm not going to discuss her with you, so drink up and let's go."

"No wonder you don't wanna talk about her. Christ, rejected twice. You're a loser, my son, a big fat loser."

Seamus felt his hands tighten into fists. Stay cool, he told himself.

His father laughed at him. Seamus saw his smirk through the glass. "I think it's pretty easy to figure out why she don't want ya. You're a sooky boy. A girl like her don't wanna sooky boy. She needed a real man to teach her a thing or two. The little slut."

The words shot through Seamus's skull like bullets. Bam! Bam! Bam! Before the thought became a thought, Seamus let out a guttural yell and sprang from his seat. He was on top of his father in an instant, grabbing him by the throat as they fell backwards out of the chair. The glass of rum flew through the air and smashed against the fireplace as they rolled around on the floor.

His father lay under him.

"You fucking bastard. It was you. It was you!"

His hands squeezed his father's throat. Kenny tore at his neck. "No. No!"

"You raped her! You raped her, you fucking bastard."

"No."

Seamus picked his head up by the shirt and brought him to his face. "You tell me, you son of a bitch or I'll kill you."

His father struggled. "No. She's lying."

"Tell me." He squeezed his throat as hard as he could. His father went purple before Seamus let up.

He gasped, "Okay, okay, but she was gaggin' for it, I swear."

Seamus slammed his father's head off the hardwood floor. Again and again he pounded it into the floor.

When Colleen heard the crash, she and the kids became frightened. She didn't want to open the door. She ran to the window, threw it up and screamed for Dave. He ran out of the garage. "What's wrong?"

"He's killing him! He's killing him!"

"Keep the kids in the bedroom," Dave yelled and ran into the house. Seamus had his father by the throat. There was blood on the floor.

Dave grabbed his arms from behind. "Seamus. Get off him."

"I'm going to fucking kill him!"

"He's not worth it, Seamus. He's not worth it."

"I don't care." He struggled against Dave's arms.

Dave yanked him away. "Think of your kids, Seamus. They can't lose their dad!"

It was as if the will suddenly seeped out of him. He got up, stumbling over his father's body, and wiped the blood off his face with his sleeve. He pointed a finger at his old man, who was curled up into a fetal position, moaning.

"If you ever come near me or my kids again, I'll kill you. I'll shoot you right between the eyes, you filthy bastard."

Dave held his arm. "Go. I'll take care of this."

As Seamus stepped over him, his father cringed. Seamus kept going right out the door.

"He's crazy," Kenny whimpered. "He nearly killed me."

"What have you done, you pathetic old man?"

"He's crazy."

Colleen peeked out of the bedroom. "Dave. Dave! You stay with the kids. They're scared. I'll deal with him."

Dave walked towards her. "What the hell happened?"

"I'm not sure. Just take the kids and don't let them see anything."

They traded places. She ran to her father. "Why, Dad? Why did this happen? What did you say to him?"

"Help me, Colleen," he pleaded. "My head—"

She ran to get a cloth and applied it to the back of his head. "How can you do this to us again? Why? It's not fair. You're killing us."

Her father started to cry and rock back and forth. "He tried to kill me."

"Why? Why?"

"I didn't mean to do it. I didn't," he whimpered.

"What Dad? What?"

"Libby."

Colleen put her head down closer to his. "Libby? What about her?"

"I didn't mean it," he blubbered. "He always had everything. Your mother loved him. She loved him more than me. He was the captain of his hockey team. Anything he ever did, he always got what he wanted. And then he got her."

"Libby?"

Her father's face contorted on the floor. "YES! He had her. He always had everything. I just wanted some of it."

Colleen's addled brain suddenly put two and two together. Her skin crawled. She backed up on her knees. "No."

"You gotta forgive me, Colleen."

"No. Tell me you didn't. Tell me you didn't rape her."

"I only wanted a taste. I only wanted what he had. Just a little." He broke down again and cried out. "Forgive me, Colleen. Forgive me."

She tried to get up but found she couldn't stand. She clutched her stomach and then put her hand on the couch to pull herself up. "You're a monster." She didn't know where to turn. She looked at him writhing on the floor. "You only wanted what he had? He never had her! He never did. That was something they were saving, something precious and innocent and you took it from them. You took their gift to each other away. You took it away forever! Do you know how she suffered? Do you have any idea? And all those times Seamus was crying, Where is she? Where is she? You knew. You had to know she left because of you."

"I'm sorry."

"Did you know you got her pregnant? Did you know that? Did you know she had to have an abortion to get rid of your baby?"

"No, no!"

"You disgust me. I never want to see your face again. And I can't believe I'm saying this but I'm glad Mom's dead. This would have killed her, killed her! She loved Libby. She used to tell me that—how happy she was that her son found someone so wonderful."

He curled up into a smaller ball. "Forgive me."

She stood over him. "Ask God to forgive you, Dad, because Seamus and I never will."

Colleen ran out of the room. Where was her brother? Where was poor Seamus? She raced through the kitchen and out the back door. Please God, he didn't drive away.

He was on his hands and knees in the driveway, retching.

She ran down the stairs and knelt beside him. "Oh my God, Seamus. My God."

He couldn't do anything but let the saliva hang out of his mouth. His nose ran and his eyes were closed shut with his tears.

"Help me."

She held his shoulders. "I'm sorry. I'm sorry this happened. How could this have happened?"

"He hurt her. He hurt her so bad and she never told me. All these years, she kept it inside."

"I know, honey, shhh."

"She was alone. Oh my god, I'm going to die, Colleen. I wanna die."

"No, sweetheart."

"I can't bear it." He suddenly sat up on his knees and held his fists to sky. He screamed, "LIBBY!"

Her name echoed over the fir trees and was swept away with the wind, over the churning ocean.

CHAPTER TWENTY-THREE

Hayden left in the morning, saying he'd meet her at the studio.

"Yes."

"Yes? Don't you mean okay, or see ya later or God, you're such a tiger in bed, Hayden?"

"Yes."

He laughed. "Ciao, babe." He walked out the door eating a piece of toast, but before he shut the door he turned back. "Now remember, it's nothing to worry about. You're going to be fine." He waved to her over his shoulder.

She got up from the table with a cup of coffee and looked out the window at the traffic. "Yes, I'll be fine. I'm good at rape." She sighed, took the last swig of coffee and headed for the bathroom. She was showered and dressed by the time Lola, Maurice, and Harold arrived for their grand reunion.

The girls flew into each other's arms. "God, I've missed you," Lola said.

"Oh, me too. You have no idea."

She let Lola go to embrace the boys. When Maurice turned to Ava, he kissed her cheeks four times. "Two are for you and two are for Aunt Vi."

"Oh, just a minute." She ran to the carry-all and took out the baking. "They've been out of the freezer for a couple of days, but they should still be fresh."

"That marvelous woman," Harold trilled, clapping his hands.

They agreed they needed an Aunt Vi fix immediately, so Ava poured more coffee and they sat around the table. She opened the can of blueberry muffins and the fabulous smell hit her like a fist, right between the eyes. She dropped the can, unable to breathe. They jumped up around her.

"What's wrong?" Lola shouted.

"Call 911," Harold screamed.

Maurice gently turned her towards him. "Slow breaths Ava. Look at me. Slow."

She followed his hand up and down. Her breathing eventually returned to normal. "I'm sorry."

"It's okay, honey." Maurice sat her down again and rubbed her shoulders. Lola gave him a look and he held his finger to his lips behind Ava's head and mouthed "Tell you later." He sat next to her. "You okay now, sweetheart?"

Ava brushed her bangs out of her eyes. "Yes, sorry. It just caught me off guard."

"It's only natural," Maurice reassured her.

"Excuse me a moment. I think I'll go splash some water on my face." She left the room in a hurry. Lola and Harold quickly sat down and leaned towards him.

"What on earth was that?" Lola asked.

"A panic attack. She gets them sometimes. You have to tell her to remember to breathe, that's all."

"I've seen her flustered before, but not stop breathing. That's scary."

"It doesn't happen often. I wonder what's been going on."

"She spent the day with stuffed shirts yesterday," Harold sniffed. "Anyone would stop breathing with them in the room."

Lola shook her head. "No. It was as soon as she smelled the baking. It was the reminder of Aunt Vi's kitchen. God love her. She must miss them so. I'm worried about her. She looks pale."

Harold nodded. "She does look rather fragile."

Maurice crossed his arms across his chest. "We'll have to be ever vigilant today, people. Protect her at all costs. Don't let idiots have access to her."

"I guess she better not show up on the set at all," Lola smirked.

By then Ava came back and she looked a little better. "Sorry, guys. Just a couple of late nights."

Maurice wagged his finger at her. "Well, it's in bed early for you tonight."

"I'm in bed all day."

"What's the scene?" Lola asked.

"Originally it was a lover's quarrel, but Nigel, the boy genius director, wants to replace it with a rape scene."

They looked at her. Maurice was the first to speak. "But you hate that stuff."

"I know."

"And they insisted?"

She nodded.

"That's ridiculous," Lola blustered. "It doesn't have anything to do with the story!"

Ava corrected her. "That's where you're wrong. It has everything to do with the young audience they want to attract."

"Rape attracts people? How revolting," Harold grumbled.

"It's exciting, apparently. For the viewers. Some viewers." She tore little bits off her napkin.

"This is going to be a fun day," Lola scowled.

"I suppose it's a bit of a consolation that Hayden is your costar," Maurice said. "It could've been that moron who wanted big boobs." He looked at his watch. "We better get a move on.

Our goodies will have to wait. It can be our reward at the end of this ordeal."

The four friends left the hotel room and headed for the location—an old brownstone on the Upper East Side. They were whisked in past the usual assortment of crew, some of whom they knew from previous productions. It was organized chaos. Ava sat in Maurice's chair and went over the script while listening to Lola prattle on about what she did and who she saw when she was at home. While Maurice tended to her poor damaged locks, Lola wanted to know what Ava had done to occupy herself while she was gone.

She shrugged. "This and that."

"You didn't see…?"

"Who?"

Lola tossed her head back and forth. "You know."

"Don't have a clue who you're talking about. Excuse me. I have to read this."

Maurice and Lola exchanged glances.

Hayden arrived and naturally created a huge fuss. Cock of the walk. The room buzzed with his energy alone. He came over and greeted Ava as if he hadn't seen her in weeks.

"Come on babe. Gotta go over a few things with Nigel. Is that what you're wearing?"

She looked at her jeans and t-shirt. "Yes. This isn't a dress rehearsal."

"I know, but couldn't you wear something more tempting?"

Ava closed her eyes. "I want to go over the scene to find my marks. I don't have to be half naked for that."

"Oh, someone's cranky. Must have gotten up on the wrong side of the bed, but then last night, every side was the right side, wasn't it, babe?" He winked and moseyed away.

"What do you see in him?" Lola asked.

"I have no idea."

Ava went over to Nigel and Hayden. They discussed positions and postures and camera angles. Ava barely participated. She merely watched them from somewhere above her head. Their mouths moved and every so often they looked at her and waited—those were the moments she'd nod her head—and then they'd look at each other and their mouths would start up again.

She saw the camera and the lights and all the equipment that they'd use today or tomorrow or whenever the scene was to be filmed. The equipment that would capture every glorious second of it. She looked at the bed. She'd be spending a week in it. She wanted to tell them it looked all wrong. That beds where some women are raped don't look that nice. They don't have white duvets and fluffy pillows. They have musty mattresses with dead flies on it and mouse shit. They creak when they move. They're damp and smelly and have outlines of old urine and blood stains.

Someone came at her with a see-through blouse and held it in front of her. They nodded and offered it to her. Then Hayden held his hands together in a prayer, pretending to beg. Since she and her body weren't in the room anymore, Ava decided it didn't matter. She pulled her t-shirt over her head, took off her bra and put the shirt on. Hayden and Nigel looked at her breasts. They crossed their arms and held their chins in their hands. They pointed at them every so often and then asked someone else to come in. The lighting director, she guessed, since they looked from her to the lights above their heads and back again.

Then they ignored her for a bit. She glanced over and saw Lola and Maurice with funny looks on their faces. Lola motioned her to come over but she didn't want to. It was hard to be around Lola today, pretending everything was okay. Lola would drag it out of her if she wasn't careful, so she shook her head and wandered over to the bedroom window. It looked out on a small garden, an oasis of green amid all the brick. There was a tree. The leaves were not the usual emerald green of summer, but slightly faded, as if knowing what was ahead of them. The rain helped bring them back to life temporarily, but both she and the leaves knew their lives were short.

Just then a cat came out of nowhere and ran to the tree. He sat under the leaves for protection against the rain. She put her hand on the window pane. "Hi, Dexter."

The cat turned around. It wasn't Dexter, as she knew it couldn't be, but she felt sad all the same.

❀

Colleen was finally able to get Seamus back into the house. He followed her like a child. She quickly took him downstairs and made him lie down on the sofa. She wrapped a blanket around him and told him she'd be back. She knew he wouldn't move, traumatized as he was. She ran upstairs and ignored her father still lying in the living room. He wasn't moving. She hoped he was dead. She went into the bedroom where Dave had all four kids attached to him on the bed. Their tear-stained faces nearly broke her heart.

"Mommy will be right there, but I need to talk to Daddy for a second. I'm right here by the door."

They nodded.

Dave gently removed himself from little arms and legs and walked out of the room. Colleen closed the door slightly so the kids wouldn't hear them.

"What the hell happened?"

"Oh Dave, it's so awful."

"My God, what?"

"You know what I told you about Libby?"

He nodded.

"It was Dad, not the drama teacher."

His face went white. "Your dad? I don't understand. You said it was the drama…"

"The drama teacher did harass her at school, but he wasn't the one who raped her. It was Dad."

"Oh my God."

Colleen tried not to cry. She needed to be strong for the kids. "Seamus is in shock. I put him downstairs for now. You've got to get Dad out of here. If I look at him again, I'm going to be sick."

"I can't believe it."

"Please, Dave. You have to hurry in case Seamus comes upstairs."

"But what do I do with him? He's hurt."

"I don't give a shit. Take him back home and get your sister to check him out. She's a nurse. She'll tell you what you need to do. But please don't tell her why it happened. Seamus would be—"

"Don't worry, I won't say anything. Call her for me and tell her to meet me at your dad's house."

Colleen went into the bedroom with the kids while Dave got his jacket and car keys. His father-in-law lay on the floor and Dave could hardly look at him, let alone touch him, but he knew if Seamus saw him again, he'd kill him, and this time Dave wouldn't stop him.

Kenny was a dead weight. Dave pulled him up and put Kenny's arm around his shoulders, dragging him through the kitchen. Kenny moaned and talked gibberish.

"Shut your mouth."

He had a hell of a time getting him out the door and down

the steps. They made it to the car and Dave opened the door and shoved him into the backseat. He started the car and drove backwards out of the driveway. As he turned to look where he was going, he glanced at Kenny. Kenny tried to focus his eyes. "Tell Colleen…"

"Shut up! I'm not telling her anything. She never wants to see you again. You've done it this time, old man. This is where it ends. You've hurt this family for the last time."

"I'm sorry."

"Shut your mouth or I swear to God I'll kill you myself."

He drove to Kenny's house in New Waterford. Dave's sister Martha was in the driveway waiting for him. They didn't say a word to each other. Between the two of them, they were able to get him inside and on a bed. Only then did she speak.

"What happened?"

"The old man was drunk and went nuts. Seamus and I had to stop him. Just check him over and tell me if he should go to the hospital."

If she thought Kenny's wounds were from anything other than a fight, she kept it to herself. She sat by the side of the bed and looked in his eyes. Then she took his pulse and examined the back of his head. "He's got a bad bump so he may have a concussion, but there's not much you can do about it. It doesn't help that's he's drunk. We should take him to the hospital to be sure."

"No hospital," Kenny shouted. "No hospital. Leave me alone!"

Martha sighed and got up. She went to the doorway where Dave stood. "I'll stay and keep an eye on him. If I think there's any change, we'll take him in."

"Okay. The best thing I can do right now is keep this drunk out of my house and away from my wife and kids."

He phoned Colleen and she said that she could handle things at home. The four kids had fallen asleep on the bed while Dave dragged their grandfather out of their lives. Colleen was grateful for a little peace. She went into the living room and quickly cleaned up the glass and the blood. She righted the chair and put things back to normal.

She checked the kids one more time before running downstairs to her baby brother. He lay where she left him, shivering. She went over and rubbed his limbs.

"It's okay, sweetheart. I'm going to get you something hot to drink."

"No, stay here."

She wiped his brow and took his hands, keeping them between her own to warm them up. He looked at her with his sad brown eyes. Grief etched his face. He looked ten years older at that moment. She couldn't break down now—he needed her. He needed her to tell him what to do. But what could she say? How does one cope with something so despicable? She stayed quiet and let her presence comfort him, to let him know he wasn't alone. Poor Seamus. He spent much of his life alone. He never did anything to deserve this. He loved a girl with his whole heart, that's all. That was his only crime.

As Colleen sat there, that phrase ran through her mind. He loved a girl. He loved a girl. He loved a girl. And she loved him. She loved him. And the only reason they were apart was a giant secret too huge to cross. But they did it; they did most of it on their own. They smashed that wall, but not quite enough. There was one final obstacle and tonight it was removed.

Seamus knew the truth.

As horrible as it was, when Colleen looked at him, she realized he'd been set free. She remembered when he was eighteen and up in his room pacing like a wild animal in a cage, wanting to do something but having no resources to do it. She remembered the agony in his voice yesterday telling her that he should've gone to find her. Why didn't he go and bring her back?

And then she knew how she could help him.

She squeezed his hands. "Seamus."

He looked at her.

"Bring her home."

His eyes widened.

"Bring her home, Seamus. Go and find her. She only ran to protect a secret. But that secret is out. It can't hurt either of you anymore. Go to New York and bring home the girl you love."

The change in his face was instantaneous. Instead of fear, there was sudden determination and hope. When she stood, he pulled the blanket off and stood up too. He looked at her.

"Jack and Sarah will be okay. They're with me. You go."

He reached out and kissed her. "I love you, Sis." He ran up the stairs and out the door.

"And I love you, little brother."

Only then did she allow herself to cry.

CHAPTER TWENTY-FOUR

Seamus got in the car and drove home much too fast. He slammed on the brakes, turned off the ignition and ran up the porch steps into the house. In the living room he stopped and looked around. What was he supposed to do now?

He realized he was on the verge of hyperventilating, so he went into the kitchen and forced himself to sit, taking deep slow breaths.

"Get a grip. Make a plan."

He sat for a while, glanced at the clock, and realized it was too late for any flights to go out tonight, but, he needed to be on one tomorrow morning. He went in search of a phone book, looked up the number for Air Canada, and placed the call. Naturally, he had to wait for the automated voice mail system to wind down with its choices. But he didn't mind; it let him think about what to do next.

He'd call his closest neighbour and arrange to have her come in and feed Dexter. She already had his key. Then he'd pack a few things in a bag—he didn't need a hotel reservation because he didn't intend on staying in New York that long. An agent finally came on and gave him the reservation after he said he'd pay full fare. He read out his Visa Card number over the phone. His ticket would be waiting for him at the airport in the morning. The plane didn't land in New York until the afternoon, but there was no way to get there sooner. He'd have to cool his heels in Halifax first.

Seamus knew he wouldn't call her. He'd call Lola and he prayed to God that Aunt Vi had her number. Libby told him that Lola would be with her in New York and it was the only thing she seemed happy about.

He knew it was too late to call the MacIntoshes, but that couldn't be helped. Aunt Vi answered the phone after four rings. She sounded sleepy.

"Hello?"

"Vi…"

"Who's this? What time is it?"

"It's Seamus. I apologize for calling so late."

He heard a rustling. "Just a minute." She came back on line a few moments later. "Sorry. I had to go to another room. I didn't want to wake Angus. He can usually sleep through a cannon firing, but…"

"Aunt Vi, listen to me."

"Isn't that nice, calling me Aunt Vi. Thank you, dear."

"Please. I need your help."

"What is it, dear?"

"I need to get in touch with—"

"Libby! Of course you do. Oh, I'd be so happy if you two kids could just—"

"Aunt Vi, please. I'm trying to get in touch with Lola."

"Lola? What do you want Lola for? Not that she's not a lovely girl, but I'd always hoped you and Libby would get back together."

"I need Lola's cell phone number. Do you have it?"

"Um, I think I do. I know I had her mother's phone number here somewhere."

"Well, that would be fine too. I can always call them."

"I'll go check."

"Thank you."

He waited. He had to take a breath and stay focused. Remember, he told himself, there was nothing he could do tonight. It was agony waiting anyway. Finally she got back to the phone.

"Here we are, dear. I have both of them, as a matter of fact. You can tell that girl is organized. She has everyone's number down here, even Maurice and Harold."

"Can I have it please?"

"Are you sure you don't want Libby's too?"

He almost shouted, but managed to control himself. "Fine. That would be great. Give me that one too." He wrote down the numbers and thanked her. He was about to hang up when Aunt Vi said, "Seamus, I'm worried about Libby."

"I know. So am I."

"You too? Oh dear. I don't know what to do. It's hard because she doesn't let us help her."

"Don't worry, Aunt Vi, I'm going to help her. I'm going to New York and I'm bringing her home."

"Are you, dear?" She sniffled into the phone. "Oh, I'm glad. I can't tell you how glad I am. I always thought you two were meant for each other."

"We are meant for each other and she'll be home soon."

"Thank you, dear. You're such a lovely boy."

"I have to go."

"Of course. Godspeed. I'll be waiting."

"Goodbye."

He looked at the numbers. Should he call Lola tonight? He wrestled with the pros and cons and decided to wait until he got to New York. He was afraid that she'd say something to Libby, and he didn't want Libby to bolt. The less time between the phone call and his actual appearance, the better. It wouldn't give her the chance to get away as easily.

Seamus packed his bag after he called his neighbour about Dexter. Unfortunately he woke her up too. When he went to get his shaving kit, he looked at himself in the mirror. His father's blood was splattered on his face. It gave him a jolt, as if his father had reached out and touched him again. He threw off his clothes, jumped in the shower, and scrubbed himself until he was red, trying to wash away his father's filth. He started to get emotional again but caught himself in time. He wasn't going to feel sorry for himself or lie down and cower in a corner about what had been done to him and the girl he loved.

His mission was to bring Libby home where she belonged, or die trying.

Seamus set his alarm for six, even though he knew he wouldn't sleep. But his body knew better. He was exhausted from no sleep the night before and now that he had a plan of action, he didn't have to fret about what he'd do. He went out like a light.

At six, he jumped into the shower again to wake himself up. He shaved and got dressed, then grabbed a granola bar and a can of Coke. He put food in Dexter's dish, changed his water and patted his head goodbye. Then he picked up his belongings, locked up the house, and jumped in the car.

Seamus was at the airport by seven. Much too early, but that didn't matter. If he was there, that meant he was going. When he received his tickets, he felt better still, because here was evidence in his hand that his plan was working. He sat in the waiting area and shook his foot, watching people come and go, mostly couples, some with kids, all of them saying hello or goodbye. People looked the same when they said goodbye to a loved one—a helpless sort of moment that you knew they'd rather prolong, but didn't dare to in public in case they cried and embarrassed themselves. People greeting each other were the opposite. They were allowed a show of emotion. There were squeals and sounds of delight, hugs that rocked back and forth. Voices were raised and hand gestures accompanied laughter. He couldn't help but wonder what kind of a greeting Libby would give him.

As he trooped onto the plane with the others, it occurred to him that he'd never flown before. He had a passport because of work, but never used it. He was the only one who listened when the flight attendant mimed the safety card instructions, and he marveled at the people who ignored her, but realized that, unlike him, they probably flew often.

As the plane gathered speed down the runway, he gripped the arms of his seat. The older lady sitting next to him gave him a quick look.

"It's a piece of cake," she whispered.

They flew up in the air and his stomach did a somersault. He was so busy keeping his body stiff against the air currents that buffeted the plane as they ascended that he forgot to look out the window.

"I find if you let yourself go and ride with the bumps, it's not so bad," the lady said. He loosened his grip and forced himself to take a deep breath and relax as he exhaled.

"We're on a train, or an Acadian bus going over the potholes on the number four highway," she winked.

He smiled and closed his eyes. That's just what it felt like. He opened them again. "You're right. Thank you."

They were in Halifax before he knew it. He had a good couple of hours to wait so he grabbed a sandwich and a coffee and took them over to the gate where he'd catch the flight to New York. When he finished eating, he sat back and watched the people gather in the seats around him. His foot shook the entire time.

Finally, they were loaded on board a much larger, very crowded plane. Seamus gave a quick smile to the two businessmen who sat in his row, but they ignored him. This time he was in the aisle seat, and it didn't feel as safe. He was out in the open, somehow. He'd brought nothing to read and realized that was a mistake, as everyone else seemed to have a book or a newspaper in front of them. As if by magic, the attendant walked down the aisle and asked if he'd like to read the *National Post* or the *Globe and Mail*. He asked her if she had the *Cape Breton Post*. She smiled and apologized. He noticed the businessman beside him smirk.

His nerves were frayed on this larger flight because it seemed to him that the plane was too large and too crowded with people to ever get off the ground. But somehow they did, and his hands gripped the arms of his chair pretty much the entire way. They were cramped by the time the plane landed.

It took forever for everyone to gather their things and get off the plane. By the time Seamus left the aircraft he was ready to scream. He tried to find a place where he could call Lola and actually hear her. He took his cell phone out of his pocket and reached into his jacket for the phone numbers. Just before he dialed he realized he didn't have a plan if she didn't answer the phone. He never thought of it.

*

When Ava pulled her t-shirt off without so much as turning her body away from everyone, Lola and Maurice looked at each other.

"I don't like this," Lola said.

"Me either," Maurice said. "She doesn't seem herself, does she?"

Lola bit her lip. "No. You heard her when I asked what she did this summer. She basically ignored me."

"No, I don't like this at all."

They continued to look at her and saw her put on that ridiculous thing they called a shirt.

"She doesn't want to wear that," Lola fumed. "Why are they making her?"

"They're idiots."

They watched her go to the window on the set and look out. She stayed there for a long time. Nigel and Hayden approached her and Hayden took her to the bed. He sat beside her and talked to her. Then she got in the middle of the bed and lay face up. Hayden looked at Nigel and Nigel pointed to the end of the bed. Hayden knelt at the end but got up again. They obviously discussed coming at it from another angle, because they walked to the other side and looked at her from a different point of view. By then two more crew members joined the action. They pointed at her and then at the headboard. All of them nodded.

"This is ridiculous." Lola stormed past the equipment and approached the bed with a sweater in her hand.

"Hey! What are you doing?" Nigel demanded to know.

"She shouldn't have to lay here getting cold while you have a meeting around her. Why isn't her double here?"

"Not that it's any of your business, but she came down with the flu this morning."

"Well, Ava's going to be next if you keep her here much longer."

"Fine. Hurry up."

She got up on the bed with Ava, who was staring at the ceiling.

"Honey, put this on. They're not going to be ready for a while. I don't want you to get a chill."

Ava pointed at the ceiling. "I see a brown stain. Can you?"

"What?" Lola looked up to the ceiling, but could hardly see it for the lights.

"Oh, nothing. I thought I saw something."

"Ava, please put this on." She held the sweater out for her. Ava sat up and let Lola pull it over her head and arms.

"There, that's better. It's freezing in here. Tell them you're not taking it off."

"Okay."

"Ava, are you all right? You don't look good. You're shivering. Maybe you should call it a day."

"I want it over with, Lola. Just leave me alone and let me get this done."

"Okay. If you're sure."

Nigel started to complain. "Look, we've got to get a move on."

Lola got off the bed and went over to him. "I don't think Ava's feeling very well. I think she should go home."

Hayden rushed over to Ava. "Hey, pumpkin. What's wrong?"

"Nothing."

"Lola says you're not feeling well."

"I'm not? I'm okay."

He kissed her forehead. "That's what I thought. Okay, honey. I'll be right back."

Hayden got off the bed and joined the other two. "She says she's fine. What's up, Lola? Don't get territorial on us. I don't want to prolong the agony, either. She doesn't like this stuff, so the sooner she gets this over with, the sooner we can get her out of here."

Nigel shooed her with his hand. Lola looked back at Ava, who only ignored her. She walked away feeling uneasy. That's when her cell phone went off.

Maurice approached her to ask what happened and she pointed to the phone. He nodded and turned back to the makeup chair. Lola walked to a corner of the room that wasn't crawling with people.

"Hello?"

"Lola? Is that you?"

"Yes. Who's this?"

"It's Seamus."

Lola stopped breathing for a moment. She whispered, "Seamus?"

"Yes. You have to help me. Please."

"Okay. What's wrong?"

"Something happened to Libby while you were gone. I can't go into it but she basically ran away again."

"She ran away from you? Then why would I help you?"

"Please Lola, I can't explain it now. Just know that she loves me and I love her and something happened ten years ago that made her run away and now she's done it again, but it doesn't matter. I know what it is now, and I want to help her."

"I'm confused."

"Please, for the love of God, don't tell her I'm here or she'll run."

"Here? What do you mean, here?"

"I'm at the airport. La Guardia."

"But..."

"Lola, I have Aunt Vi's blessing to do this. She gave me your number. I didn't call Libby myself because I knew she'd hide from me again. Please trust me. I need to find her, to tell her I love her and it doesn't matter what happened all those years ago." He paused and took a breath. "Is she well? Does she look well?"

That's when Lola straightened up. "No. No, she doesn't. I'm worried about her, as a matter of fact. She's not herself."

"Where are you?"

"We're on a movie set, and I don't like it one bit. They're making her rehearse a rape scene and I know she doesn't want to do it."

There was silence.

"Seamus?"

"Get her out of there. Right now."

"Well, I'll try but—"

"I'm coming. Give me the address. How long will it take me to get there?"

Lola ran down the stairs to make sure she got the house number correct. She gave it to him before she said, "It depends on the traffic, forty-five minutes maybe."

"Can you keep her safe until then?"

She started to panic. "Safe from what? What do you mean?"

"Please, take my cell number."

Lola repeated it a couple of times to remember it. "You'll be able to spot the house. There are big trucks and trailers parked outside."

"Okay. I'm coming. Stay with her, Lola, whatever you do."

"Okay."

He hung up and Lola bolted back up the stairs, her heart beating out of her chest. She ran up to Maurice. "We've got to get Ava outta here."

"What's wrong?"

"That was Seamus."

"Who?"

Lola flapped her hands around. "You know, the boy…Ava's boy from home."

"Dear heavens."

"He's coming to get her and asked me to keep her safe. He says for her not to do this scene. I don't know why, but he sounds desperate and I believe him."

"Well, let's go."

They ran towards the set again, yelling, "Stop!"

The director and production crew threw their hands in the air in exasperation. Everyone shouted at them to knock it off. Nigel stormed over and screamed, "What is with you people? This is a movie set. You can't disrupt things. It's costing money."

Lola pushed passed him and ran to the bed. Hayden pointed at her. "Lola, this repressed need to be the centre of attention is getting tiresome. If you want to be an actress, go to acting school."

"Shut up, you jerk." She pushed him out of the way and jumped on the bed. "Come on, Ava. Come with me, honey. We have to go back to the hotel."

"We do?"

"Yes, we do. Come on."

Hayden held her back. "Sweetheart, don't listen to her. We need to get this done. You told me yourself, you feel fine."

"I am fine. Please Lola, just leave it. I want to get this over with."

Nigel pointed at Ava. "You see, she's fine. Now get the hell off this set. Security!"

"No, you have to come, Ava." Lola reached out and tried to grab her. Two big guards came towards her and Maurice, who was jumping up and down wringing his hands. "Oh dear. Oh my. Listen to her, Ava."

Harold came back into the room at that moment. He stood dumbfounded as two men grabbed Lola and Maurice and dragged them off. They didn't go willingly. They struggled and shouted as they were pushed down the stairs.

"Leave them alone!" Harold ran after them.

They were unceremoniously dumped outside on the sidewalk.

"You're barred from this set. Don't come back or we'll call the police." One of the security guards went back in, the other stood in front of the door.

Harold ran over to them. He stroked Maurice's arm. "Are you all right, pet?"

Maurice adjusted his jacket. "Yes. I'm okay."

"What was that all about?"

"We need to get Ava out of there," Lola panted, "but they won't let her."

"Then call the police," Harold suggested.

"And tell them what?" Maurice frowned. "They're making a movie and the actress wants to do it but we don't want her to?"

Harold was puzzled. "We don't?"

"Never mind," Lola yelled. "I don't understand it myself. All I know is that Seamus asked me to stay with her and I'm not up there." She looked up and down the street. "I don't know what to do."

"Who's Seamus?" Harold wondered aloud.

"I'll tell you later," Maurice said before turning to Lola. "Maybe you should call him."

"And upset him? He's trying to get here as fast as he can."

"How's he going to get past the guard?"

Lola, her chest still heaving, said, "I don't think that'll be a problem. Not by the sound of his voice."

※

It was Seamus's first view of New York and he didn't see anything, only the cars in front of the taxi as it sped towards the city. He jumped in the first one he saw as he ran out the door of the airport and gave the address to the driver, who nodded his head and turned on his meter.

"I'll give you one hundred bucks if you can get me there as fast as you can."

"No problem." The driver stepped on the gas.

They zoomed around cars and went though yellow lights and Seamus had to hang on to the door as they went around corners. He tried not to think about what he was racing towards. His Libby, at the mercy of movie makers. A rape scene? Who does this kind of shit? And who would even want to watch it? But someone with millions had financed it. Someone knew they'd make a profit. It made him sick.

The only thing that gave him comfort was knowing Lola was with her. She'd protect her till he arrived. He was sure of it, but he couldn't take any chances either. It was imperative that he get to Libby as soon as he could—she needed him. She must be losing her mind, to put herself in that scene and relive the whole ordeal over again. The thought of it made his skin crawl.

The taxi started to slow down.

"Can we hurry, please?"

"Mister, believe me, I want my hundred bucks. If I could get you there faster, I would. But look at the traffic."

Seamus hit his fist on the armrest. "Shit."

❀

The crew finally figured out which way they wanted to approach the scene. Nigel sat on the bed. "You're sure you're okay, Ava?"

She nodded.

"Great. I don't want to be the big bad wolf, here. I'm sorry about your friends, but I'm trying to get this picture made and it's a lot of pressure. You understand?"

"Yes, I understand."

"You're a doll, but you should get a new assistant."

"Can we hurry this along?"

"Okay, in this scene the couple's arguing. They're lovers. It's not a stranger raping you. It's your boyfriend."

"That makes a difference?"

He hesitated. "Well no, of course not. Rape is rape, or sexual assault, whatever you call it."

"I think rape is a better word. More direct."

"Are you sure you're okay?"

"I'm fine. Let's do this."

He consulted his notes. "Okay. Hayden, or should I say Damian, is going to take you, Vanessa, and push you into the bedroom. You stand in front of him, indignant. You can't believe he's being such a bully. You slap his face and when you do, Damian's going to grab you by your wrists and shake you. Then he's going to throw you on the bed." He pointed at the upper right hand corner of the bed. "Now your job is to fall with your head in this corner, on your back. You'll get up on your elbows and ask him what he thinks he's doing. Then Hayden, Damian, will pull you across the bed by your ankles. Hayden may have his own improv moves. I like to give my actors some freedom. Then he's going to say a bunch of stuff and after that he'll jump on you. Have you got that? That's as much as we'll do and we'll see how it looks. Then we can decide which camera angle to use for the actual rape itself. I think about three cameras should do it. We have to cut away, get the close up shots, etcetera. You know the drill."

"Yes. I know the drill."

"Good." He got up and clapped his hands. "Okay, people. Let's do this thing."

❀

Seamus was nearly out of his mind. They weren't moving at all. He checked his watch. It was nearly an hour since he called Lola. And then suddenly his cell phone rang.

"Hello?"

"Seamus, it's Lola. I'm sorry, I don't want to worry you, but I can't wait any more."

"What?"

"I couldn't stay with her. They made me get out."

"What does that mean?"

"They threw us off the set. I tried to get her to come with me, I really tried, but she's inside with them. You have to hurry."

"I'm stuck in traffic!"

"Where are you? If you're not that far, maybe you can run. You'd get here faster."

He asked the cabbie.

"You're about ten blocks away."

"I'm only ten blocks away. I'm coming."

He shut the phone off and put it in his pocket, then took out his wallet and gave it to the taxi driver. "There's about two hundred bucks in there. I'm going to run, so I'm leaving my bag. I want you to drive to the address and stay there until I come out. Do you understand?"

"Okay, man. I'll be there. Go straight down this street. You can't miss it."

Seamus got out of the taxi and dodged the cars surrounding it. A few were moving and he had to jump out of the way. As soon as he hit the sidewalk, he ran. He ran as if his life depended on it. Because it did.

❀

Hayden had his arms wrapped around her as they waited to start the scene. They were behind the door they had to burst out of.

"Okay?"

Ava nodded.

"You're shivering."

"I'm cold."

"I won't rip your sweater off. I don't care what he says. Fuck the Nigels of the world."

She nodded again.

They heard Nigel say, "Okay. When you're ready…and action!"

Hayden opened the door and pushed her into the room. She stumbled and righted herself. "How dare you." She reached out and slapped him. "That's for what you said downstairs in front of all those people." She marched over to the bed.

He followed her. "Well, it's true, isn't it?"

She faced him. "Who do you think you are?"

"I'm the guy who shares your bed, but lately that's been off limits too and I'm sick and tired of it."

"Well, get used to it because that's how it's going to be from now on." She turned away but he grabbed her upper arm and forced her to look at him. It was Seamus's father. He took her by the wrists and shook her and then he threw her on the bed.

"Please. Don't hurt me."

"I'm not going to hurt you. I'm going to love you."

"Seamus! Help me!" she screamed.

He reached across the bed and slapped her face. "I am so fucking sick of hearing about your fucking Seamus!"

He pulled her hair and brought her face close to his. "You little slut. I'm gonna show you how a real man does it." He grabbed the back of her neck and covered her mouth with his own. He kept it there even as he ripped off her skirt and tore off her panties. Then he pushed her back on the bed.

❀

Seamus's heart beat so fast he thought it would burst. He was almost there. He saw the trailers and the people, and then he saw a young woman with black spiky hair gesturing for him to hurry up. Lola. She pointed at the door. Libby was on the other side of that door. He ran up the stairs and pushed aside the man who tried to stop him. He heard her scream, "Leave me alone! Stop it!"

"I'm coming, Libby!"

He ran up the stairs two at a time, blind to the people coming at him. He didn't see the cameras or the lights or the equipment all over the floor. He saw her on the bed, hitting and punching his father as he touched her with his filthy hands.

Seamus yelled and kept yelling. Hands grabbed him. People screamed and ran but he didn't stop. He leapt around things, knocked down light stands and chairs. He reached over and grabbed his father by the back of the shirt. He pulled him off and punched him so hard he landed at the foot of the bed and was still.

He reached down and picked her up. "I'm here, Libby. I'm right here." He felt her arms go around his neck and she held on to him as Sarah did when she was hurt. He wrapped his arms around her and took her off the bed. Then he turned and faced the people who ran up to them.

"Keep away from us!" he screamed. "All of you! Don't you dare touch us. Leave us alone!"

He saw Lola rush towards them. "Please, do as he says. Just let him be with her. Let him talk to her."

That's when Hayden sat up with a bloody nose. "What happened?"

Lola pointed at the two men beside her. "Go get him." Maurice and Harold went over and led Hayden away. "What happened?" he kept saying.

"Everyone, please. Take a break and give them some time to be alone," Lola cried. "This is real life. It's not a movie."

People started to back up and mill about and eventually drift to the farthest corner of the room or downstairs. Lola asked one of the crew to turn off the bright lights. She looked back at Seamus as he stood there with Libby clasped tightly in his arms. "It's okay now, Seamus. I'll keep them away."

"Thank you."

"You're welcome." She started to walk away.

"Lola?"

She turned around.

"It's nice to meet you."

"And you," she cried before running down the stairs.

He finally moved. He wanted to get her away from that bed. There was a couch off to one side of the room so Seamus put his hands under her knees and carried her there. He sat down with her on his lap. Her head stayed on his shoulder. He hugged her closer.

"It's okay, Libby. I've got you now. You're going to be all right. I won't ever let anyone hurt you again. I promise."

She whispered something.

"What, sweetheart?"

He could still hardly hear her.

"Is it really you?"

"Yes, it's really me."

"Seamus?"

"Yes. It's Seamus."

She kept her head down. "You're not a dream?"

"No. I'm real." He kissed her hair. "I'm very real."

"You came after me."

"Yes, finally. Like I should've done ten years ago, and I didn't. I'm sorry."

She lifted her head and looked at him before touching his face. He grabbed her hand and kissed her palm. "I love you, Libby. If only you knew how much."

"I do know. I've always known."

"I know the truth. You don't have to keep it from me anymore. The secret you've been carrying inside."

"You know?"

He choked on his words. "I know it was…my father."

He felt her body go limp as she let out a big sigh and leaned into him. He held her tight. They sat like that for a long time. There was no need for words. They needed time to absorb the truth together. When she finally spoke her voice was stronger. "I know how much that must hurt you."

"Hurt me? It's you he hurt and I want to kill him, the lousy drunk. I almost killed him last night."

"Oh, Seamus."

"I can't believe it."

"I know."

He entwined her hands in his own. She rubbed her thumb over his skin.

"Why didn't you tell me? You could have told me."

She shook her head. "No."

"But you were alone. When I think of it I want to scream. I should've been there for you."

She sat up and touched his face again, as if recording it to memory. She brushed his hair away from his eyes. "No. We'd never have made it."

"We'd have been together."

"No, Seamus. We wouldn't have been together for long."

She looked away. "If I'd told you, you would've killed your father."

"He'd have deserved it."

"But your life would be ruined. You'd have gone to jail and we couldn't be together. Or one of my brothers would have killed him and met the same fate. It would've destroyed your mother and mine. Your sister wouldn't be able to hold her head up in her own community. People would have whispered behind my back."

She looked at him then. "But worst of all, when you'd be with me, you'd be thinking of him and I'd be thinking of him. That would have poisoned our love for each other. We were too young to handle it, Seamus. Much too young."

He didn't say anything.

"You know I'm right."

"You've always been told that you weren't a strong person and look what happened. You were stronger than all of us put together." He hid his eyes with his hand.

She got off his lap and knelt on the floor between his legs, taking his hand away. "Look at me."

He lifted his head. "I'll spend the rest of my life making it up to you."

She reached out and touched his cheek. "No. That's one thing you won't do."

"What do you mean?"

"I refuse to spend one more day of my life in that bed. It happened. It's over. It can't be undone. We've survived it and now it's time to bury it and let it die. I want to live. Now kiss me."

Seamus kissed her and kissed her and kissed her.

Then he put his arms around her. "Come home with me."

Libby nuzzled his ear. "My sweet boy, I am home. You're here."

CHAPTER TWENTY-FIVE

The wedding took place three weeks later on a gorgeous September afternoon.

Seamus wanted her to marry him the next day, but Libby knew in her heart that they needed a little time to get over their trauma. They needed to be with their families and be allowed to rest and have the excitement of anticipation. A wedding wasn't just the wedding day, it was a celebration weeks in the making.

"We've waited this long," she said. "We can wait a little longer."

Seamus and Libby took the cab back to the hotel. Lola, Maurice, and Harold followed behind. When they got to her room, Libby was able to introduce Seamus to her family of friends properly. There were a lot of hugs and thanks exchanged.

Lola called room service and asked for some piping hot tea. When it arrived, the five of them sat around the table and devoured Aunt Vi's blueberry muffins and oat cakes. When Libby opened the tin this time, she took a big sniff. "Mmm, yum."

They laughed.

It was decided that Seamus would fly home on his own and get back to Jack and Sarah as soon as possible. He knew they'd been badly frightened and needed him. Libby and Lola decided to fly to Los Angeles and sort out her affairs there.

LESLEY CREWE

Maurice and Harold promised to be in Cape Breton a week before the festivities to make sure the whole family had makeovers and new do's for the wedding.

Reservations were made and Maurice and Harold said their goodbyes. The other three went to the airport together. Seamus could get back to Toronto that night and leave in the morning for Halifax and be back in Sydney around midday. He said he'd stay at one of the hotels near the airport. Libby and Lola got on a flight leaving almost immediately, so there was a quick goodbye near the security gate.

Lola kissed Seamus goodbye and went through. Libby and Seamus hugged each other and didn't speak. Finally they parted and he clasped his hands around the back of her neck.

"So."

"So."

"I'll see you...?"

"I'll let you know. I'm not sure how long it will take to get things in order, but I have a feeling it will be really quick."

"I'll see you in Cape Breton," he laughed.

"Oh yes, I'll see you in Cape Breton. And once I step on that island, I'm never leaving it again. Ever."

They kissed each other one last time and he let her go. She waved as he turned around and walked away.

"Goodbye, my love," she whispered after him.

She fell into a deep sleep on the plane and didn't wake until they landed.

It was a hectic four days. She put her expensive minimalist cube of a house on the market and used that money to buy her way out of her movie contract with the studio. Trent nearly had a heart attack when he found out she was leaving the business and berated her for being such a miserable client. Libby asked if a half a million dollars would make him feel better. He conceded it would help. Camilla was at least gracious about this change in her circumstance. Luckily she was good at her job and she wasn't unemployed for long. She gave Mercedes a very handsome severance package, glowing recommendations, and sent her on her way. Then she and Lola went through the house and sorted all the things she wanted to keep, mementoes she'd picked up in her travels and pictures of family and friends.

They packed her clothes, putting the clothes and costumes from her movies in a separate pile. These she'd keep for her nieces and sisters.

Libby sold the furniture and contents of her home with the house, and got a moving company to pack what she was taking with her. Then it was off to the bank to straighten out her financial affairs. She made sure the money she had, once everything was settled, was put into a trust fund for her family and a separate account for Jack's and Sarah's education, and hopefully someday, for children of their own.

She had meetings with her accountant and lawyers to go over anything that needed sewing up because she had no intention of coming back. She wanted to make sure she left no stone unturned.

Libby didn't have many friends in Hollywood, but there were a few who she'd been close to. She made sure she saw them before she left. They said they'd keep in touch, but Libby knew they wouldn't and that was fine. She wouldn't either.

Finally it was done and she and Lola parted at the airport. Lola was flying back to Chicago to be with her mom until the wedding.

They hugged each other.

"Thank you for being my sister. I'll never forget what you've done for me," Libby said.

"Thank you for being mine. Although why I'm not as jealous as hell, I don't know. That boy of yours is a hunk."

"He always was."

"Some girls have all the luck."

"We'll find someone for you. In Cape Breton maybe."

"I wish."

"Before you go, I wondered if you'd do me one more favour."

Lola rolled her eyes. "I'm exhausted. Give me a break."

"Will you be my maid of honour and general dogs-body all rolled into one? Please, pretty please?"

Lola's face lit up. "Sure! But you better not make me wear a hooped skirt. I have to draw the line there."

They laughed and said their goodbyes.

It was the longest flight of her life. She was so impatient to get there it felt like fifteen hours. She finally transferred from the big jet that flew into Halifax to the Dash Eight that would fly her home.

Home.

Libby looked out the window the entire time. Every minute was another mile closer to him. It was a clear day. She saw the trees and the water and the rivers that meandered along. She looked over the clouds and thought of her parents. She'd visit them when she got home and tell them about the new life that waited for her.

Finally, they touched down.

She remembered how upset she'd been when she arrived in Sydney in February. A lifetime ago. Now it was pure joy. She got up with the other passengers and slowly made her way to the front. She said goodbye to the flight attendant and walked out of the plane. She looked over at the big window and there he was.

He waved. Jack and Sarah waved too.

Her family. Hers.

As soon as she touched the ground she ran. He disappeared from the window. She stepped through the two open doors and into his arms. They didn't say anything as they hugged each other. Then Libby felt a small tug on her sweater. She looked down and there was Sarah with a bouquet of daisies wrapped in cellophane. She reached for them.

"For me?"

"Yeah."

She bent down and held Sarah's chin in her hand. "Thank you, sweetheart. They're beautiful like you."

Sarah smiled at her. "Yeah."

She looked at Jack, who hung off his father's pant leg. "Hi, Jack."

He hid his face and mumbled, "Hi."

She knew better than to go near him.

They drove to Aunt Vi's and Uncle Angus's house. Everyone was in the yard, waving and jumping up and down. She got out of the car. Aunt Vi ran towards her.

"Oh, Jesus, Mary, and Joseph!" Aunt Viola screamed. "It's herself, in the flesh." She grabbed Libby in a death grip. "Oh girl, we can't believe it. We're so happy to see you. Welcome home, darlin'. Welcome home at last."

Then Aunt Vi ran over and hugged Seamus and ran after Jack and Sarah. Jack hid behind his father's knees again, though Sarah took Aunt Vi's hand and followed her happily.

"Do you like sugar cookies?" Aunt Vi asked her.

"No."

"A girl with a mind of her own. I like that," she nodded. "I bet you like ice cream."

"Yeah."

"Well, Auntie Vi will get you some. Let's go."

Libby walked into the house with Seamus on her arm as Teddy Bear trailed happily behind, but not before waving to Geranium, who had a big "Welcome Home" sign in the window.

The next two weeks were a whirl of planning and cooking. Maurice and Harold arrived as promised and it was one big hair dressing salon at Aunt Vi's. Lola flew in three days before the wedding and she and Libby, along with the sisters and nieces, headed to Jacobson's to buy a dress.

This time it was reversed. Instead of watching, she was the one in front of the mirror as the gang deliberated. And while the gowns were beautiful on her, there seemed to be more dress than her. They had to be taken in to such a degree that it was hard to get a sense of what they might look like. She tried not to show her disappointment but she didn't succeed. It wasn't what she had imagined.

Then Lola snapped her fingers. "My God, Libby, we're idiots."

"What?"

"There are gowns in your trunk. Remember that one you wore when you played Guinevere? It's made to fit and it looked divine on you."

She clapped her hands. "You're right, it's perfect."

She didn't want to leave the poor sales lady without taking something, so she bought some satin high heels. Then it was off the florist to order the flowers and, once again, the gang finished off their day with a great lunch.

The day of the wedding, everyone was up at the crack of dawn. There were a million things to do and it was Grand Central Station for a while. They were to be married in the small United Church in Albert Bridge, which overlooked the Mira River, with a potluck supper at the Albert Bridge Fire Hall afterwards.

The food was taken over by the carloads throughout the day by husbands and brothers. Most of the MacKinnon women hadn't seen the fire hall. Colleen called Aunt Vi and asked if she and her friends could decorate it, to help them out. Aunt Vi whispered to Libby, "God love her. It makes her feel included."

Maurice chased Aunt Vi around the house until she finally agreed to sit for him and have her hair done. He patted her head. "Aunt Vi, what am I going to do with you? This cast-iron hair has to go."

"Go where?"

"Anywhere! Just not on your head."

When he was done, she said, "Hand me a mirror." He did. She looked at herself and didn't say a word. Then she looked at her relatives. "What do you think?"

No one said anything. Finally Libby blurted, "Sorry, Maurice. It's lovely, but it's not Aunt Vi."

Aunt Vi handed Maurice the mirror. "Just as I thought. If anyone wants me, I'll be in the shower." With that, she limped upstairs.

Maurice and Harold looked heartbroken. Rose walked over to them. "Cheer up, girls. One out of ten ain't bad."

Because Uncle Angus was giving her away, Libby's oldest brother Johnnie was driving her to the church.

Everyone waited for her downstairs. Libby looked at herself in the bedroom mirror.

"Goodbye, Ava. Thank you for taking care of me when I needed you, but I don't need you anymore. Wish me luck." She smiled and blew a kiss at her reflection. She walked down the stairs and into the kitchen. There was a collective intake of breath.

Aunt Vi started to cry. "Oh, I wish your Ma could see you. What a pretty picture."

Her dress was simple—a creamy colour with a small gold embroidered trim. It had a straight bodice across the top and flowing bell sleeves. It was tight to her body with a 'V' seam that started below her waist. The skirt fell full to the floor. She wore her hair down but the front was caught up and entwined with a coronet of white flowers. She carried a small bouquet of white and cream roses, tied up with ribbon.

"I'm ready."

"Then let's go," Uncle Angus shouted. "I'm starvin'."

There was a mass exodus of the clan down the back stairs. Geranium wasn't in the window. She ran out of the house and joined the other guests. Johnnie stood by his pickup truck in a suit that he might have bought when he was eighteen. He looked about as comfortable as a boy on his first date. His white socks didn't help.

He came forward and escorted her to the truck. "You look pretty. I washed the truck for you."

"I see that. Thank you."

"Couldn't get the fishy smell out of it though."

"It smells like you. Suits me fine."

They drove in a convoy but Libby asked Johnnie to take her into the cemetery so she could show her mother the dress. The others continued on. He stopped the truck and helped her out. The marker was very close to the road so she stepped on the edge of the grass and looked down at her mother's name written in granite.

"Ma, it's my wedding day. Seamus and I are finally to-gether and I know you'll be with me in church. Thank you for bringing me home. I love you." She knelt down and touched her mother's name, then turned around and smiled. "Let's go, Johnnie, I'm starving too."

When they pulled up to the church, Uncle Angus was there

waiting with Lola and Colleen, who held Sarah's hand. Sarah was the flower girl. She had on a sweet little white dress and a coronet of flowers in her hair too. She carried a basket of white rose petals.

Johnnie helped his sister out of the truck, kissed her and went inside the church. Colleen came over and hugged her. "You look beautiful."

"Thank you."

Colleen held her arms. "He's so happy today. You should have seen him. And best of all, his in-laws are here, said they wouldn't miss it for the world."

"That's wonderful."

"Okay, I'll see you in there." She knelt down by Sarah. "You do what Lola says, sweetie. When she says go, you walk up the aisle towards Daddy and scatter your petals, okay?"

"Yeah." Sarah turned to Libby and held out her foot. "New shoes."

Libby held out hers. "Me too."

They went up the stairs and Colleen disappeared inside. Lola put Sarah in front of her, then turned around and looked at Libby. "This is the role you've waited for your whole life. Enjoy every moment."

Libby shook her hand at her. "You're going to make me cry. Stop it."

"Don't you dare look at me up there," Lola said. "This isn't waterproof mascara." She turned around.

Uncle Angus took her arm and gave it a pat. "This is it. Are you ready?"

She hugged his arm. "I've never been more ready for anything in my life."

The organ started to play the wedding march. Lola said, "Go, Sarah."

Sarah walked ahead like a little pro. Everyone smiled and whispered at how sweet she was. She scattered her petals and only stopped three times to show people her new shoes.

Lola followed in a simple cream, knee-length dress with a wide gold satin ribbon around the waist. She carried a small bouquet of white rosebuds.

Then it was Libby's turn. As she started up the aisle, she couldn't believe all the people there. They'd only invited family and the place was packed. It took a moment to realize all these people were her family. How incredibly lucky she was.

And then she saw him.

Seamus stood there in his new dark suit with a blue satin tie. His best man, Jack, stood beside him wearing the same thing. He saw her and he smiled that smile of his and he never looked away from her. She realized she wasn't going to cry and neither was he. There had been enough tears shed in their lifetimes. This was a happy day. Such a very happy day.

Besides, there were enough tears among the guests. She heard Aunt Vi wailing in the background, with Maurice and Harold a close second.

She was suddenly beside him and Uncle Angus kissed her. He placed her hand in Seamus's hand and answered "I do" when the minister asked, "Who giveth away this woman to this man?"

She didn't remember a word of it. She saw his smile and felt his hand in hers. But she did remember saying, "I, Elizabeth Ruby MacKinnon, take you, Seamus Duncan O'Reilly, to be my lawfully wedded husband." And she heard him say loud and clear, "And I, Seamus Duncan O'Reilly, take you, Elizabeth Ruby MacKinnon, to be my lawfully wedded wife. Forever and ever and ever."

Everyone laughed.

It was time for the ring. Jack searched in his left pocket and got a panicked look on his face. His father pointed to the right one. He produced it and shouted, "I found it!"

Seamus placed a wedding band on her finger and she placed one on his and they held each other's hands as the minister said, "What God has joined together, let no man put asunder. You may kiss your bride."

And when he kissed her, the whole church erupted with applause and joyous shouts. They parted laughing. She turned around and kissed Lola, who looked like a raccoon thanks to her awful mascara, and then she grabbed Sarah's hand and Seamus grabbed Jack's and cried, "Come on, everybody. Let's eat."

They ran down the aisle as a family.

It was one heck of a party.

Libby and Seamus had a small glass of champagne and toasted themselves, but that was all. They were too excited to eat or drink. After a few happy hours with their loved ones, Seamus reached for her hand and they quietly slipped away as the celebration went on without them.

They weren't going on a honeymoon. Libby's refusal to leave the island was one problem and Seamus said since the rest of their lives were going to be one big honeymoon anyway, why bother?

They knew where they were going. They drove into his yard and left the car. It was a warm night so they walked down to the beach.

"Help," she laughed. "I'm getting stuck. I'm punching holes in the grass."

"Already, she's a pain." He went over, lifted her up on his back and piggy-backed her down to the beach. She let her heels fall into the grass. They sat on the log for a while, looking up at the full moon that shone on the water.

"I have something to give you," Seamus said.

"Silly, I told you not to buy me anything."

"I had it already."

He dug in the sand.

"What are you doing?"

"Getting your present."

"Yippee, a clam!" she laughed.

"Yeah, you wait," he smirked.

He finally unearthed the small velvet box and handed it to her. She smiled and opened it but the paper fell out first. She unfolded it and looked at the picture. "Thank you. Did Sarah do this?"

"Yes, but look on the back."

She turned it over. "Dearest Libby, I love you. Seamus. And in coloured pencil no less." She smiled. "You're sweet." She leaned over to kiss him but he grabbed the box. "Hey, wait a minute." He took the ring out of the box and knelt in front of her. "Mrs. Seamus Duncan O'Reilly, will you marry me?"

"Why, Mr. O'Reilly, I believe I already did."

"I think you're right." He placed the diamond on her finger and she held it out for him to see. "It's perfect."

They looked at each other. She stood up, smiled, and then took off down the beach. He ran after her, but she was quick. She ran through the surf in her bare feet, holding up her gown. As she ran, he knew he'd seen this before. The night he saw her from his balcony. This was it, as if somewhere in time this moment had been foreseen and he'd been given a little glimpse, a small lifeline to hang onto.

He watched her in slow motion. She turned around, laughing at him, her beautiful blonde hair cascading down her back.

That beautiful laugh he waited a whole lifetime for. She was like a dream and then suddenly she was very real.

"You can't catch me."

Of course he did, and she knew he would. He carried her up to the dunes and lay her down on the edge of the field. He got down beside her. She reached up and put her hands through his hair.

"I remember the scent of wild strawberries the night of our prom. Do you?"

He nodded.

"I love wild strawberries," she whispered. "Almost as much as I love you."

He kissed her then, and all he could remember afterwards was how soft her skin was, how sweet her mouth was, how stars and strawberries and the saltwater breeze made him drunk with desire. His breathing became ragged and he groaned with the wanting of her, and just before he fell over into that heavenly darkness, she said, "Don't stop. Don't ever, ever stop."

Lesley Crewe

1. **So far, you've written a mix of serious, more dramatic novels and lighter, more comic novels. Have you tried to follow each serious novel with a funnier one, or is it by chance that a certain idea grabs you at a certain time?**

I wrote my books in the following order: *Relative Happiness*, *Shoot Me*, *Hit & Mrs.*, *Ava Comes Home*, and *Her Mother's Daughter*. I didn't want to publish Hit & Mrs. until I'd been to New York myself, to add details that rang true. But it's also true that if I spend time writing about something emotionally draining, it's a fun break to be silly with the next set of characters.

2. **Your protagonist in this novel is known by two names: to the people she grew up with, she's Libby MacKinnon, and to everyone else, she's Ava Harris. How did you decide what her real name and her stage name would be?**

Around the time I was trying to decide what to call my character, my friend had a baby girl who she named Ava, and I thought it was a pretty name. It was as simple as that. And obviously, if you're writing about Cape Breton a last name starting with a "Mac" or "Mc" is a given. For other characters,

I often open the phone book, blindly stab at a page, and use the first name I point to. It's an odd process. I also tend to use names that come up in my everyday life—friends, neighbours, and relatives. They sound more natural that way.

3. **At one point, Aunt Vi and Ava give Lola a crash course in how their neighbours end up with nicknames like Geranium and Archie Itchy Arse. Are those kinds of nicknames a real-life Cape Breton phenomenon?**

Yes, it's one of the fabulous traditions we have here. Both of the above names are, in fact, real. My husband's uncle Art was nicknamed Swamp. One time he actually received a letter addressed simply "Swamp, Cape Breton." How perfect is that? (And I believe he had a relative whose name was Alec the Pond.) Last year I met a wonderful elderly gentleman whose nickname was Diddy. I asked him how he got it. He told me, "My parents always said, 'Did he do this or did he do that?'—hence, Diddy."

4. **The more we hear about Ava's experience with life in Hollywood, the less glamorous it sounds, especially when she's talking to her nieces. Have you visited Hollywood yourself, and do you think you could ever live there?**

No, I haven't. I am the antithesis of Hollywood—the wrong look, hair, age, weight, social status, and connections. I would shrivel and die on Rodeo Drive! In Cape Breton, we live a very authentic kind of life. You are who you are, and everyone knows it. I wanted Ava to be living a false life, and there was no better place to put her than in a city hooked on make-believe.

5. **Hayden is a surprisingly sympathetic character—he can be incredibly selfish and shallow, then turn around and be just as romantic and generous. How did you feel about him as you were writing him? Do you think he really means it when he tells Ava he loves her?**

He drove me up the wall. Most of the time I wanted to slap him, but I did have a soft spot for him too. I always imagined him to be rather insecure underneath all his bravado. Hayden is never sure if women like him for himself or the fact that he's a movie star. I believe he does mean it when he tells Ava he loves her. I feel sorry for him in a way.

6. **The prom is an important event in both *Ava Comes Home* and *Her Mother's Daughter*. What was your prom like? Was it as magical as the prom nights you write for the girls in your books?**

I hate to burst your magical bubble, but the guy who took me to my prom left me for someone else at the end of the evening. I can't remember how I got home. I do, however, remember his checkered jacket and pants. They were horrible, but that's what all the guys wore in the early seventies. I don't think I was much of a prize either, in my homemade white gown that cost about twenty bucks. That's part of the fun of being a writer. You can make stuff up.

7. **Ava having been raped is the awful secret at the centre of the novel, and a terrible reality for all too many women. How difficult was it to write about Ava reliving the trauma of what Kenny did to her?**

I knew I didn't want to linger on it. It's upsetting to try to convey something so terrible. Being powerless in that situation is a real fear for most women. The worst part for me was when Ava watched the little dog walking freely by the side of the road. I think she knew then that something was going to happen to her, but she had no recourse to get out of the situation. She was a child and he was an adult. He was driving and she was being driven. She was alone. That part made me cry.

8. **Aunt Vi's cooking skills are legendary— not even Ava's figure-conscious Hollywood friends can resist her baking. Is her prowess in the kitchen based on anyone you know?**

My grandmother Abbey was a fantastic baker. My childhood is filled with memories of Grammie's pies, cakes, cookies, and bread. Her mince tarts (pork pies), shortbreads, and fruitcake at Christmas were a tradition, and I can still smell her roast chicken dinner with mashed potatoes, carrots, turnips, and gravy. I miss her.

9. **At the end of the novel, Libby is gloriously happy about her marriage to Seamus, and declares that she will never leave Cape Breton Island again. Do you think she sticks to that pledge as the years go by?**

I think Libby and Colleen will fly to New York once a year to meet Lola and have a girlie weekend shopping trip, taking in as many Broadway shows as possible and eating out at great restaurants. Every wife and mother deserves that kind of break! But for the most part, Libby will stay close to home. She's seen enough of the world out there.

10. **Finally, if you were casting a movie version of *Ava Comes Home*, who would you want to play Ava and Seamus? Are there any other characters you think a certain actor or actress would be perfect for?**

This was very difficult to answer. I had to consult with my daughter, and we threw lots of names around, but none of them were quite right. Sometimes it's not so much a character's face but their manner you're trying to capture—someone delicate for Ava, and someone rather stoic for Seamus.

The best we could come up with is the American actress January Jones for Ava/Libby and the British actor Henry Cavill for Seamus. You can Google their names if you'd like to see what they look like. I also think the actor Simon Baker would be good for Hayden. But now that I've said that, eighty percent of the people who read this will disagree with me! We all have our own images of these characters, and what's right for me might be a disaster for someone else. That's what is so great about reading books. They're personal.

Reader's Guide

to

Ava Comes Home

1. From the outside, Ava Harris has the perfect life: she's famous, talented, beautiful, and a successful, critically acclaimed actress. It soon becomes clear, however, that she's not a very happy person. Have you read other books where a character's life seems perfect, but doesn't actually make them happy? How often do you think that holds true for real celebrities?

2. After Libby left, Seamus married Sally Hooper and built a life with her. Although he loved her very much, he never stopped loving Libby too. Do you think it's possible to be equally in love with two people at the same time?

3. Colleen and Seamus care about each other very much, but there are times when Seamus resents Colleen's overprotectiveness, especially when she interferes in his relationship with Libby. How is Libby's relationship with her older sister Rose similar to Seamus's relationship with Colleen? Do you think Colleen and Rose will get along better now that Seamus and Libby are married?

4. When Kenny raped Libby, Libby was left incredibly traumatized, and the experience changed the course of her entire life. It was her secret reason for leaving home, and she continued to keep that secret for many years before finally telling Seamus what happened. Do you think keeping the rape a secret for so long it made it harder for Libby to work through her trauma? How do you think things might have gone differently if she had told someone what happened right away?

5. Ava knows many people in Hollywood, but Lola, Maurice, and Harold are the only ones who can truly be called her friends. What qualities do those three share with the people Ava cares about in Cape Breton? Do they also have things in common with less pleasant Hollywood people like Hayden, Trent, and Camilla? Are there any Cape Breton characters who remind you more of Hayden, Trent, and Camilla?

6. Gossip is a theme that recurs a number of times in the novel. Can life in a small town can be just as gossipy as life in Hollywood? If Ava wasn't a movie star, do you think the people of Glace Bay would still gossip about her as much as they do now?

7. In many ways, Hayden and Seamus are extremely different men. Hayden can be very self-involved, but he's also laid back and a lot of fun. Seamus is not as carefree, but he's steady and reliable, and passionate

when he falls in love. Do you think Ava is attracted to Hayden because he's so different from Seamus? Or do Hayden and Seamus share some personality traits too?

8. Not long after Ava's mother dies, Lola finds out her mother has breast cancer. Do you think being around Ava and her family affects Lola's decision to go home and spend time with her mother? If Lola and Ava had still been living in Hollywood when Lola found out her mother was sick, do you think she would have made the same choice?

9. If you were casting the movie adaptation of *Ava Comes Home*, who would you pick to play the major characters?

10. Aunt Vi, Uncle Angus, and Ava's siblings are traditional in many ways, but they're very welcoming of Lola, Maurice, and Harold when they come to visit. Do you think the fact that they open their arms to her friends helps Ava reconnect with her family? If her friends and family had not gotten along, do you think Ava would still have decided to stay in Cape Breton for the summer?

Nicola Davison

LESLEY CREWE is the author of ten novels, including *Beholden*, *Mary, Mary*, *Amazing Grace*, *Chloe Sparrow*, *Kin*, and *Relative Happiness*, which has been adapted into a feature film. A freelance writer and screenwriter, her column "Are You Kidding Me?" appears weekly in the *Chronicle Herald*'s community newspapers. Lesley lives in Homeville, Nova Scotia. Visit her at lesleycrewe.com.